THREADED

TAY ROSE

Copyright © 2023 by Tay Rose.

Cover Art by Maria Spada.

Chapter Header Art by Momo: @momosbookss (Instagram)

Editing by Brittney Corley of This Bitch Reads Media.

Proofreading by Taylor Robinson of Taylored Text, LLC.

All rights reserved.

This is a work of fiction. Any relation to any person or place is entirely coincidental.

No part of this book may be reproduced in any form or by any electronic or mechanical means, including information storage and retrieval systems, without written permission from the author, except for the use of brief quotations in a book review. Please direct inquiries to tayrosebooks@gmail.com.

Paperback ISBN: 979-8-9876709-1-0

E-Book ISBN: 979-8-9876709-0-3

For those whose life took a path they did not anticipate, but have learned to find beauty in the unknown.

AUTHOR'S NOTE

Threaded is an adult fantasy romance containing content which may not be suitable or appropriate for all readers, including sexual content, adult language, violence, depictions of childhood trauma, and mentions of sexual abuse. Reader discretion is advised.

This is book one in a series and ends on a cliffhanger.

PROLOGUE

Two sisters stood together in an ethereal plane, in a world that existed beyond the comprehension of mortal minds.

One was older, but only just. Long ago, her younger sister was taken from her, hidden away in the darkest of the realms by one who believed possession and control could remedy a broken heart.

The elder didn't know how much time had passed since she'd last seen her sister. That concept—*time*—did not exist to her. All she knew was her balance, her scale, the other side of her same coin, had been gone.

But now she was back.

The sisters embraced once more, both feeling complete to be reunited again. As if all was set right.

If only that were true.

The younger sister released the elder, stepping out from her embrace.

He will come for me. You know he will. She spoke with the whispers of the night wind through the stars.

Her older sister frowned. *I would like to see him try to take you from me again.* Her words burned through the infinite expanse like a spark of warmth in a mortal's chest.

The younger smiled sadly. *You are strong, lifted up by many who hold your presence in their hearts and minds. It seems that with my time ... away ... I have not been so lucky.*

You are not weak—

I am, my sister. At least, I am right now. Wildfire flashed in the younger sister's eyes. *Yes. Only for now.*

Then we have time. For you to grow your strength. The elder's voice was strong and sure.

You know we do not. Once he discovers I am gone—which he likely already has—he will come for me. He will not waste time. I spent five thousand years with him, sister. He will come, and he will draw me away from you by taking this fight somewhere you can not go.

The elder's strong expression faltered, just slightly. *I made the decision to save that world. Have I doomed it?*

The younger grabbed her sister's hand. *No. I will not let him take that world from you—from us. That world is ours, and its people are our children.*

The elder regarded her sister. *You have a proposal. Tell me.*

The younger pulled all her immortal grace to her before meeting the elder's gaze. *If we join, then together, our power in that world might be enough to stop him.*

The elder blinked, and then scoffed. *Impossible. If we join, in these forms, then we would doom not just that world but all the realms.*

I don't mean in these forms, nor in any form on this plane, my sister.

The elder snapped her gaze back to her sister. Comprehension spread across her face. She thought for a moment; the possibilities playing through her mind on an endless, eternal loop.

This ... this could work.

We would have one chance. I have no more grace to give, and you can only give yours once. And even then ... we would not survive it. Not as we are now.

I know. It is the only way. The younger's voice was stoic and assured. She'd thought about this for five millennia while trapped in that endless darkness devoid of starlight. She knew this was their only hope.

The elder looked away from her, gazing out across the violet expanse of their endless realm. She had long ago doomed herself to spend the remainder of eternity there, unable to visit the beautiful world with stars and seas and life she'd helped to create. She had no desire for her sister to do the same.

But there was one thing she loved more than her sister. One thing she loved more than the single, sparkling north star that grounded her in ways her sister could not. She would gladly give away her entire, immortal being to save that world.

She looked back to her younger sister.

Who?

Just as the word spilled into the void between them, the two sisters felt a soul flash into existence. A soul that ached for freedom, that longed to be filled with the power and might of not just the world she'd been born into, but all the realms stretching across the eternal time and space separating her from those two sisters, so far away but also so very close.

Her, the younger sister breathed.

Yes, agreed the elder. *Her.*

Far across those same realms, in a golden palace nestled between ancient mountains and a glimmering ocean, a queen shot awake in her bed.

Her heart pounded. The pools of her magic deep in her gut rolled like a maelstrom through the seas. The taste of ash lingered on her tongue.

And she knew.

Her consort grumbled sleepily beside her as she wrapped a silk robe around her body. She strode from her bedchambers, into her living quarters, and out onto an expansive balcony facing the mountains. The night was clear, the stars twinkling, and above her the twin moons glowed as matching crescents in the sky—one gold, one silver. As the queen watched, the gold moon began to pulse, like a heartbeat, its rhythm matching the beat of her own in her chest.

Lifting a shaky hand, she watched a single droplet of liquid gold push its way through her skin and onto the pad of her finger. It lingered there for a moment, as if saying farewell, before shooting into the sky like a soul ascending to the realm of the gods. The droplet arched through the sky, and the queen watched its path until it winked out of her sight.

My time is over, she thought.

Thus begins our twenty-one-year wait.

CHAPTER 1

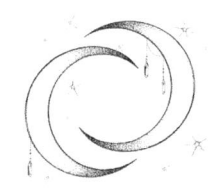

Mariah Salis had always found it easier to tumble head-first into chaos than to sit comfortably still in peace.

Chaos didn't fit in a quiet, antiquated place like Andburgh. Wildness didn't belong in a woman; not when everyone around her stared her down like she was a beast in need of taming.

For that was all she was. A cornered animal, snapping at her chains, itching for the day when she could finally be set free.

"Focus, Mariah. Again."

Her father's deep voice cut through the darkness of her thoughts. She grunted a response before hauling herself up from where she'd landed in the dirt. Dusting herself off, Mariah picked up the worn handle of the training sword, the dulled blade rusted and cracked along its edges. She turned and mounted the fallen birch tree again, the trunk just thick enough to stand on with one foot in front of the other, and just smooth enough that one wrong step could send her careening off into the hard, packed earth below.

Of course, on the day when Mariah had wanted nothing

more than to embrace the chaos lurking beneath her skin, her father had chosen to give a lesson on *balance*.

But Mariah had no interest in feeling balanced. Especially not today, not when her birthday loomed in the distance, both a beacon of hope and an omen of unwanted servitude. She wouldn't let the latter come to fruition, however—no, she would be sure to hide herself far beyond the distant shores of the Mirrored Sea before she let that happen.

Birthdays weren't good for much, but at least this one, her twenty-first, she would finally have the excuse she'd waited for to leave this place.

After all, it wasn't unusual for a woman to disappear from Andburgh shortly after turning twenty-one. In fact, it was pretty common.

Mariah just had to figure out how.

"Take a breath. Gather your balance. Then start again." Her father folded his arms across his chest, his gold-hazel stare shining with encouragement. Wex Salis was the sort of man who got along with everyone, his easy-going nature allowing the other shrew-nosed residents of their town to forgive the peculiarity in which he raised his daughter.

Mariah loved him for that glowing positivity.

Right now, however, it annoyed her.

She inhaled a steadying breath before refocusing her gaze on the log beneath her, on the sword in her hands, on the emerald of the leaves of the Ivory Forest around her. She grounded herself on the otherwise unsteady surface under her feet and then began again. Her steps moved across the log, her body turning with each step, her arms lifting that dulled blade and swinging it in a smooth progression: left slice, high parry, right slice, low parry, right jab. She felt herself flowing across the log, imagining herself like a dancing leaf caught on a breeze, ready to carry her far, far away.

She loved these lessons with her father, and not just because they gave her the skills necessary to wield sword and dagger and arrow. Mariah loved them because they gave her the tools to one day float away from Andburgh, just like that leaf on the wind. Her family was her world, but she'd grown tired of the small scope of what surrounded her. She craved adventure and passion and all the things she could never find here in this town on the crossroads.

She *especially* thirsted for a chance to swing her sword and have it be met with the clash of real steel.

It was that last thought that had her next step coming down too forcefully, had her arms hauling her blade through the air too quickly. The slight loss of control sent her balance tipping, the soles of her boots slipping down the smooth bark of the trunk. Her hands released the smooth leather pommel of the training sword as she fell, crashing into the packed earth below.

Again.

Her breath whooshed from her lungs, her ears ringing from the impact. Distantly, Mariah could hear the sound of soft snickering, followed by a *thump* and a grumble. She clenched her teeth and forced her eyes open, turning her head to cast a dark glare at her brother. He lingered against a solid oak tree, his face twisted into a pout as he rubbed his upper arm. Her father stood beside him, smiling patiently down at Mariah.

"You lost your focus again."

She pushed herself up until she knelt on the hard dirt, wiping dust from her sweaty brow. "No shit," she grumbled, before tilting her head up to meet his gaze. "Can we just say this lesson was a raging success and never speak of this day again?"

Wex chuckled. "I'm not sure about the 'raging success'

part, but if you're asking if we can be done for the day, then yes." He shot a glance at the clear sky above, the crisp air of early autumn still warm on their skin. "Why don't you head inside and clean up. Your mother should be finishing up her shift at the clinic soon. Bring her lunch and ride with her home."

Mariah blanched as she met her father's hazel gold stare. "But—"

"Just do this for her, Mariah. One last time." Wex's voice was calm even as he interrupted her. "And then tomorrow, you can disappear off to wherever you want to go. But give your mother this one final day."

That silenced Mariah quickly. Her family knew her plans, knew what she wanted. She wasn't sure how she would make it happen, not yet. All she knew was once she was twenty-one, once this society of theirs considered her a full adult, she would leave this place and never come back.

She knew it would break her family's—her *mother's*—hearts. But she didn't care.

She didn't belong here, and they all knew it.

Caged beast. Chains. She needed freedom as much as she needed the air she breathed.

"Fine," she said finally, her voice tight. "I'll go." She pushed up to her feet with a soft grunt, wiping even more dirt from her black leggings.

Gods, she really was disgusting.

"I'm going to take a shower first." She glanced over at her brother, noticing he'd now inched his way closer to the racks of bows and arrows at the edge of the training clearing. Mariah favored the short sword—something nimble that allowed her to draw her sparring partner in close before she struck with a wicked grin on her face.

Ellan, however, preferred the bow. Soft hearts called to softer weapons, it seemed.

"I'm sure Father would appreciate the help in moving this log out of the clearing, Ellan. Why don't you help him?" Mariah's voice dripped with sugared sweetness as her brother whipped his head back to her, his dark hair brushing around the face that looked so much like her own. The two of them could've been twins, truthfully. Mariah was two years older, but the differences between them were small. They both had the same full lips, the same high cheekbones, the same almond-shaped eyes. But where Ellan's hair was a dark auburn, Mariah's was near-black, and where Ellan's eyes were soft green-gold, Mariah's were sharp forest green.

And where Mariah was all wild, untamed mountain lion, Ellan was a gentle, sensitive fawn.

But that certainly didn't stop him from glowering back at her as their father smiled brilliantly at Mariah's words.

"What a wonderful idea, Mariah! Come, Ellan—while your sister is showering, you can help me hitch up my horse and move this log out of the clearing. We could even chop it up and use it for a bonfire tonight!"

A grin spread across Mariah's face at her brother's dejected expression. She quickly turned away, sprinting towards their small cottage nestled in the woods before she, too, could be pulled into chopping firewood.

Heading into town might be a terrible prospect, but at least it was better than *that*.

Mariah washed down the bite of her roast turkey sandwich with a swig of water, the liquid cool on her tongue under the warm autumn sun.

She'd met her mother just as Lisabel Salis was leaving the clinic, her mother's eyes tired as she led her gray mare into the quiet side street. Together, they'd ridden back into the main square of Andburgh, tying their horses at a post before finding seats at one of the many picnic tables in the bustling town circle. It was really just a ring of buildings with faded wooden facades surrounding an open expanse of cobblestone, but for some reason Mariah couldn't fathom, it was considered the most desirable place to spend time in their crossroad city.

It smelled like horseshit.

Mariah's gaze continued to wander as she took another bite from her sandwich, the flavors exploding in her mouth. Gods, she would miss her father's cooking when she left. That was a guarantee.

In her idle staring, she took in the various shops and boutiques that made up the square. Nothing of particular note; clothes could be fun, sure, but to Mariah it was such a waste to spend so much on something it would only be acceptable for her to wear once. But nestled between those bright shops filled with prints of floral and lace were the taverns, their dark-tinted windows hiding what she knew were rooms dimly lit by weak *allume* lamps and occupied by patrons who'd helped her find a little bit of the escape she'd always so desperately craved.

Yes, she hadn't been a fan of those boutiques, but she loved those taverns. Losing herself in the bottom of a glass was a favored past-time.

Thank the Goddess there were guaranteed to be taverns in wherever her journeys might take her. People always needed a place to get drunk.

There was one particularly seedy establishment where she felt her attention linger. Its door was painted black, its windows tightly shuttered, but Mariah knew what it looked like. Red leather booths. A black, stained bar. Dark floors sticky under her boots. The smell of sweat and beer and hazy memories, the feeling of hot skin against hers, the sound of ragged breathing in her ears.

She'd spent the Summer Solstice there. And besides her arrival and eventual meandering to its rooftop ... she didn't remember much else from that night.

Or, at the very least, she'd chosen to forget.

"Mariah." A gentle voice pulled her from the dark pit of her memories, wrenching her gaze back to meet those of soft golden brown.

"Sorry." She winced, glancing back down to her sandwich and taking another bite. "You know how much I don't like coming into town."

Her mother scoffed. "Don't like coming into town when the sun is up, you mean." Mariah shot her eyes back up to find her mother's gaze glinting with humor. "And don't talk with your mouth full; you might love that horse of yours more than most people, but I did not raise you in his barn."

Mariah smiled, chuckling softly before swallowing her bite. "Sorry," she repeated.

Lisabel rolled her eyes. "Stop apologizing and just start acting like the adult you so desperately want to be." Her words were harsh, but Mariah could hear the lightness behind them.

Her mother wanted nothing more than to see all of her daughter's wildest dreams come true. Even if Mariah didn't quite know what those dreams were yet. All she knew—all any of them knew—was she would never be able to chase them in that slow, tiny town. It might be a place of crossroads, but the people here weren't the sort to embrace any type of change.

It all started with its lord. Pompous, elitist Lord Donnet. His only qualification to rule Andburgh came from his name, and even that was washed up and scoffed at by the rest of the

Onitan ruling class. He traveled far too often to other cities, feasting and drinking with other lords who had more to their names than he ever would.

Of course, he spent just enough time in his own city to collect his taxes. Mariah could still remember the night over eleven years ago when Lord Donnet and his cronies had nearly burst down the door to her family's cottage at midnight, demanding their due. Mariah's mother and father, while hardworking and able to offer valuable skills to the people of the city, didn't have much to their names. When they'd been unable to scrounge sufficient coin to pay the Lord's demands, payment had to be made in other ways. Wex had handed over his antique collection of swords and armor from his days with the Royal Infantry, and Lisabel, with anger burning in her golden eyes, had given them a small chest containing a delicate, silver dagger etched with a hundred pairs of wings, including the wings of a great dragon on its hilt.

"That dagger belonged to my father," she'd nearly spat at the Lord. "It is the only of its kind, and the only piece of him I have left. I hope you are satisfied."

Lord Donnet had only regarded the dark steel with mild disinterest before tossing it to his escort. "It hardly seems enough to pay your debts to the crown, Mrs. Salis, but I am feeling rather benevolent today. Therefore, yes, I am satisfied." The Lord had turned, glancing to where Mariah stood in the small living room, her sharp eyes watching the entire exchange. Donnet had perused her, his slimy gaze sliding up and down her body, leaving her skin feeling oily and prickly. He'd opened his mouth again, as if to speak one more time, before her father had beat him to it.

"If that is all, My Lord, then we should like to return to bed. It is late, and my children have schooling in the morning."

Donnet hadn't looked away from Mariah; he only closed

his mouth and smiled. "Of course," he said, finally turning back to Wex. "I only wanted to let you know that your daughter is quite a beauty. It is too bad she was not born to ... better circumstances." And with that, the lord pushed his way out the front door to the Salis home, his lackeys following at his heels.

Mariah decided that night she hated that man.

That was also the night she'd realized even though her parents did their best, she wouldn't let this rotten town trap her in its grip like it had done to them. So she'd decided to do what no other girl she knew had done.

She decided that when she was twenty-one, she would leave.

"Your mind is wandering again, Mariah." Lisabel's voice once again snapped Mariah back to the present. She looked to her mother and smiled weakly.

"How can you tell?"

"I can always tell. Mother's intuition." Lisabel paused. "Plus, your eyes get all hazy and unfocused. And your mouth hangs open. That one is quite the tell."

Mariah's smile turned into a wide grin. "My mouth does not—"

"Mariah! Is that you?"

A shrill, sing-song voice cut through Mariah's familiar banter with her mother. She instantly grimaced, her jaw snapping closed and clenching. She held her mother's stare, whose golden gaze had softened into one of sympathy before breaking from Mariah and moving to the source of that voice over Mariah's shoulder.

"How lovely to see you, Annabelle." Lisabel's voice was as warm as honey, dripping with all the practiced calm of one who'd spent a lifetime healing those unable to mend themselves.

Mariah, meanwhile, couldn't even hide her grimace as the girl behind her—Annabelle—spoke again, her unnaturally high voice grating against her ears.

"Oh, I am so well, Mrs. Salis! It is such a wonderful surprise to see you out and away from the clinic on such a beautiful day!" The voice moved around Mariah's back, and now a figure stood beside their table, carrying with her the overly sweet scent of too much peony and rose perfume. Mariah finally lifted her gaze to meet Annabelle's brown doe eyes, her golden hair curled into perfect ringlets and piled atop her hair, her ridiculous fuschia gown full of bustled skirts and too much lace.

"And you too, Mariah! It is so rare that I get to see you now that we are no longer in schooling." Annabelle twisted her delicate, powdered features into a mockery of a frown. "Tomorrow is your twenty-first birthday, is it not? I have not heard anything about your planned *debutante*!"

Annabelle Tanne, daughter of one of the wealthier merchants in Andburgh, had always been far too interested in Mariah's participation—or lack thereof—in society.

It made Mariah want to punch something. Specifically, Annabelle.

"That's because I'm not having one."

The gleam in Annabelle's eye faltered. "You're ... not having a *debutante*?" She seemed to be scrounging for the words. "... Why not? Are you ... are you unwell?"

Mariah's gaze hardened; the harshness of the forest in her eyes swallowed the doe that lived in Annabelle's. "Why would I possibly wish to plan a debut if I'm leaving Andburgh?"

That got the other girl's attention.

"You are leaving?" Annabelle gasped. Mariah fought back an eye-roll; again, leaving the city wasn't uncommon for women in this part of Onita.

What was uncommon was a woman leaving of her own accord, and not tied to some man with a noose around her ring finger.

"Yes. Leaving. Something I've waited far too long to do, anyway."

Annabelle turned her stunned expression to Lisabel. "And you, Mrs. Salis ... did you know of this?"

Mariah's mother, as calm and stoic as ever, kept her reply soft and even. "Of course."

Annabelle was clearly floundering. "But ... but ..." She glanced between Mariah and her mother. "Don't you wish to ... to enter courtships? To find love? To marry?"

Not even if the stars winked out and the moons fell from the sky.

"Why would I need a courtship if I could get whatever I wanted from a man by just walking into any tavern in Onita?" Mariah shrugged, reveling in the horrified look that flashed across Annabelle's delicate face. "Besides, love is just like everything else in this town: pathetic and weak. I'm ready to see what else the world has to offer." With that, Mariah stood from the bench, her appetite suddenly gone. She wrapped up what remained of her turkey sandwich, stuffing it back into the leather bag she'd brought with her into town.

"I'll ready the horses," she said to her mother without meeting her gaze. Annabelle had already taken a few steps back, still too stunned by Mariah's confessions to speak. "Always a pleasure, Annabelle."

Mariah strode back to where their horses were tied, her mind twisting and catching on the words that had woven their way from her mouth. They mirrored the phrase that chased her from dreams and nightmares her entire life, said in a voice that whispered of shadows and starlight.

Love is a weakness.

CHAPTER 2

"Ellan, I think that's enough. You're going to singe your beard."

Mariah swallowed down her swig of whiskey, using it to force back the snort bubbling in her chest at her mother's words. The second the burn from the liquor faded, she turned her head to look at where her mother and brother sat across from her, the monstrous bonfire between them flickering in the dusk light.

"I'm sorry, but … what beard?" Mariah's voice cracked with laughter.

Ellan puffed out his chest, sitting straighter on the log bench. "Don't tell me you haven't noticed it. Mom obviously did." He stroked his chin, which was notably absent of any facial hair.

Mariah turned a baffled look to her mother. Lisabel only stared at her son, a smile on her face and amusement dancing in her eyes. When she looked back to her daughter, that was all it took.

Mariah burst out into whooping, cackling laughter.

Ellan grumbled to himself under his breath, his words lost to Mariah over the crackling and popping of the great bonfire between them. Her brother looked down at his hands, and in his palms a small kernel of flame began to grow, a shimmering ball of red and gold and blue. Once it was about the size of an egg, he tossed it idly into the already monstrous fire, the flames sputtering up briefly before swallowing it whole.

"Ellan." This time, Lisabel's voice was stern. "I told you that was enough. This thing is already close to being out of control."

"It's not out of control, Mom. I've got it." His voice was still a mutter.

Mariah glanced away from her mother and brother and stared deep into the flames. Her mother was right; it was a ridiculous blaze. But she also trusted her brother in that instance.

Ellan was, after all, a wielder of fire magic.

And Onita was a kingdom rich in magic.

Allume, the raw magic native to the realm of the gods, collected and transported all throughout the kingdom through a complex system of piping and panels made of *lunestair*, or moonstone, provided warmth and light and energy to every building and structure in Onita. It even powered the small rechargeable lamp sitting beside Mariah on the log bench, the soft golden light dim against the roaring of the fire. *Allume*, and the ability of Onitans to harvest it twice a year on the Solstice and contain it with *lunestair*, had long ago set Onita apart as being a nation of technological advancement and comforts far outpacing those of the neighboring kingdoms.

Then, of course, there was the magic existing in the veins of Onitan people, power said to have been gifted by Qhohena, the Goddess of the Golden Moon, herself. Not in the same way the

Queen of Onita had been gifted magic, but a privilege, all the same.

A privilege Mariah was fucking thankful she didn't have.

It had been unlikely, but it nevertheless used to be a fear of hers.

After all, it was rare for a woman to have magic. Most gifts, elemental in nature and almost always specific to fire or air, manifested in men around the time of puberty. Not every Onitan male had magic—her father, for example, bore no gifts—but there were more with magic than without. In fact, Mariah couldn't remember a single male during her schooling years who didn't end up exhibiting a gift of either fire or air.

There were even two girls who'd been … gifted. Except unlike their male counterparts, who had received great celebrations and pride from their families, they had quietly disappeared from town, shipped away to temples to Qhohena placed all around Onita, forced to give up their past lives and enter a new role as servants of the Goddess.

Mariah wanted out of that town more than anything. Wanted to run as far away from its disgusting lord as she could. But to have to leave like that, entrapped into a role she hadn't chosen for herself, a role that would last a lifetime … that would've been far, far worse than having to stay in Andburgh forever. So, when she began to mature, when her cycles began and her body started to change and there wasn't a single hint of anything supernatural in her veins, she couldn't have been happier.

Sure, she was always afraid that perhaps she was a late bloomer. That one day she would wake up and suddenly be like her brother, able to manipulate flames to her will. But that day never came, and now, finally, she was mere hours away from being considered an adult, from turning an age at which the shackles of her society would fall from her wrists.

"Oi!" This time, it was Mariah's father who cut through the haze of her thoughts, his deep voice calling out from where he stood a bit away beside their small, quaint cottage. "Ellan, why don't you come help me finish prepping the elk steaks? And also help with the potatoes, they should be nearly boiled—"

Ellan sighed and tossed the stick he'd been fiddling with into the fire, much like how he'd tossed his little fireball a few moments earlier. "Coming," he said glumly, rising to his feet and sauntering off towards their father as only a nineteen-year-old boy could. Mariah watched him go, amused at the way he was still clearly upset about the comments made about his beard—or rather, the lack thereof—until her mother's voice pulled her back to that raging fire.

"Mariah, why don't you come sit closer to me. And bring that bottle of whiskey with you; I could use a refill."

Grinning, Mariah snatched up the glass decanter leaning against her left foot, still holding her own glass in her right hand, before rising and moving to sit beside her mother. She set her whiskey glass down on the bench beside her as she uncorked the decanter and poured two fingers of the rich, golden liquid into her mother's glass. She topped her own glass off and put the cap back on the decanter, setting it back on the ground beside her feet. Twisting to face her mother, she lifted her glass up, clinking it softly against Lisabel's. "Cheers," she said, her voice warm from the liquor already beginning to settle in her belly.

It wasn't often she was cheerful, but it was quite difficult for her to be upset with a glass of smooth whiskey in her hand.

Her mother smiled lightly, but it didn't meet her eyes. Those same eyes also didn't lift to look at Mariah, remaining fixed instead on the flickering of the red-gold flames.

A wave of nervousness at her mother's expression had

Mariah's stomach lurching. She took a generous sip from her glass, the burn washing through her, preparing herself for Lisabel's next words.

"We need to talk about your plans to leave—"

"I'm still planning to leave after tomorrow—"

Lisabel and Mariah spoke at once, and Mariah couldn't help the half-drunk giggle that spilled from her lips. She looked again at her mother.

"I'm sorry. What did you say?"

Lisabel finally pulled her gaze from the fire, that same light smile on her lips. Her golden-brown eyes danced with a mother's amusement and something else Mariah couldn't quite place. Something guarded, and wary, and uneasy.

"I said, we need to talk about your plans to leave. Whenever that exact date might be."

Mariah's mouth popped open. She'd half-expected her mother to make at least one attempt tonight to ask that she stay, just for one more year, just until Ellan turned twenty-one, just until he found a wife and married, just until he had his first child. But Mariah knew there would always be one more milestone, one more event she would be asked to stay for, and if she said yes now, she would keep saying yes, and before she knew it her life would be wasted in this sorry, miserable place beneath the thumb of a sorry, miserable man.

Lisabel quietly took a sip from her glass of whiskey before setting the glass down and reaching into her coat. Mariah watched as her mother withdrew a dark, rectangular object, her eyes unable to identify what exactly it was in the flickering light of the fire, her *allume* lamp left forgotten on the bench on the other side of the blaze. Her mother turned back to Mariah, shifting further into the light, finally allowing Mariah to get her first good glance at what was clutched between Lisabel's delicate, healer hands.

It was a book.

In the firelight, Mariah could only tell the binding was dark, either black or a dark blue. The light flickered and reflected off of delicate, curling inscriptions, a beautiful design that looked like nothing at all ... and yet, so incredibly familiar. When Mariah finally lifted her attention from the book back to her mother, she found Lisabel's eyes glistening in the red-gold light, tears barely clinging to her lashes. With a blink, the first one fell, and Mariah watched with soft fascination as it tracked a line down her mother's cheek.

"I am sure you thought I would use tonight to try to get you to stay. But, Mariah, I want you to understand—that could not be farther from the truth." Another tear fell, but Lisabel's voice didn't waiver. "I want you to leave. This place ... it is not for you. It has never been for you. The moment you came into this world, I knew you were destined for something so much more. I want you to see the world, to experience everything your soul craves. But I can't have you losing yourself in your search for freedom."

Mariah's skin prickled as Lisabel dropped her gaze to the book she held in her hands. Gently, she reached out, handing the book to her daughter. Mariah took it, setting her own glass of whiskey down so she could run her fingers over the soft leather binding. It felt so delicate, so worn, as if a thousand hands had touched it before hers, but the pages were still a crisp cream, not showing a single sign of aging as she fanned them through the air. Mariah flipped the book over, and noticed a single, delicate word inscribed on the back:

Ginnelevé. It was an unfamiliar word; clearly Onitan, but not one she recognized.

"This ... this book," Lisabel started, tripping slightly over her words for the first time that night. "It holds much wisdom between its pages. Wisdom that has been accumulated over many generations, and has served me well at many times during my life. If—*when*—you ever feel lost, truly lost, when you need a reminder of who you are and what you are capable of...that book will tell you everything you need to know."

The ice flooding Mariah's veins chased away any remaining warmth from both the whiskey and the fire. She stared at the book, and then at her mother, her world tilting slightly off-kilter as something that could only be dread twisted through her gut.

"I don't ... I don't understand ..." Mariah's words trailed off as she floundered, fully unsettled as she gripped that soft leather binding between her fingers. Her mother reached out, placing a gentle hand on her daughter's arm.

"I know. It is okay. You do not have to understand. But one day, you will. And I believe that on that day, when you realize everything you were ever meant to be, you will change the world." Another sad smile on Lisabel's lips. Another tear falling silently down her cheek. Another soft squeeze on Mariah's forearm.

They sat like that for a long moment, Mariah feeling the pressure of her mother's touch bring her slowly back to the earth. Finally, she twisted away, picked up her glass of whiskey, and drank the rest of its contents in a single, deep swallow. Mariah set the book down on her lap, picked up the decanter, and refilled her glass before settling herself back onto the log bench. She took a sip, staring at the flames, when her mother spoke again.

"There's something else. Something I need you to do before you go." Lisabel's voice was harder than it had been, thick emotion replaced with an unrecognizable coldness. Mariah whipped her attention back to her mother, surprised.

"What is it?"

Her mother stared into those flames, her face a cool mask that looked so out of place on her soft features.

"Do you remember that night, when you were nine? When Donnet and his deputies showed up demanding payment for taxes he claimed your father and I owed?"

This time, it was not ice, but fiery rage that razed through Mariah. "Yes." She would never, never forget that night.

Lisabel didn't move a muscle as she continued. "I did not want you to see that, but now, I am glad you did. Because you saw what he took, and I don't need to explain to you what it was."

Mariah knew instantly what her mother referred to. The chest belonging to Lisabel's father—Mariah's grandfather. The dagger it contained, the fine blade adorned with a hundred sets of wings, dragon wings flaring across the cross-guard of its hilt.

"Your father has been training you your entire life. He only ever wanted you to be able to protect yourself, but ... you are *good*, Mariah. Better than most who serve in the Royal Infantry, that's for sure. And that dagger ... it means everything to me, to this family. You must get it back. Before you leave this place forever, you must get it back." Finally, Lisabel turned to look at her daughter, the same fire that burned in her son's veins dancing in her eyes. "Do you understand what I am telling you?"

Mariah only stared open-mouthed at her mother before nodding once.

Because ... *fucking Enfara*. Her mother wanted her to steal her grandfather's dagger back from Lord Donnet. Her sweet, kind, peaceable mother wanted her to commit a crime punishable by death.

If she were caught.

Not that she would be caught, of course. She knew, without a doubt, she could get that dagger back.

That didn't lessen her shock, however.

Just then, her father and brother reappeared from the cottage, walking out with plates laden with mashed potatoes, heads of broccoli, and tender elk steaks. Their voices carried over the crackling flames, Ellan laughing at something their father must've said. The sound was all it took for Lisabel to morph back into the gentle woman Mariah knew. She gave her mother one last bewildered expression before turning to her approaching father and brother, the smells of the food finally reaching her nose. Her mouth instantly watered and her stomach rumbled, empty but for the whiskey she'd definitely been downing too quickly.

Her father strode to them, his keen hazel eyes darting between Mariah and her mother.

"Enjoying our night by the fire?" There was an unasked question in his voice, one that had Mariah wondering just how much he knew about what her mother had planned to talk to her about that night.

"Yes, it is such a lovely night," Lisabel answered, leaning back to accept a kiss on the forehead from her husband. "And that food you boys have put together looks absolutely delicious."

"It better be," Ellan answered from across the fire. He'd settled himself where Mariah was earlier, already cutting into his elk steak. "Not only did I freeze my ass off hunting this beast the other day, but those potatoes were a bitch to mash."

"Oh, quit whining, Ellan. Make yourself useful and add some more flame to our fire."

Ellan shot his sister a withering look before lobbing a fireball into the flames, the force sending embers flying into the air towards Mariah. She chucked an acorn she found on the log beside her at him in return, the *thump* that sounded as it hit him squarely in the forehead bringing a grin to her face. Ellan looked ready to send another ball of fire her way before their father intervened.

"Enough," Wex commanded. "Before Ellan burns the entire city down."

The family ate the rest of their meal over the crackling of the fire, their boisterous banter blending into the sound of the forest around them. They stayed there until the roaring fire died down to flickering embers, all four hesitant to put the day to rest. Sometime, well past midnight, when Ellan had slumped against the log bench, passed out from too much whiskey, a soft breeze began to stir from the east, swirling Mariah's long, dark hair around her face and gilding it in metallic moonlight. As if in answer to the breeze, a deep, dark place within her stirred to life, like a beast cracking open a heavy-lidded eye. A chill swept over Mariah's skin, a chill she chased away with another long pull of whiskey straight from the decanter as the early autumn breeze continued to tickle her ears and whisper words she couldn't understand, eventually chasing her to bed just as the moons began to inch their way back towards the horizon.

CHAPTER 3

A dagger of sunlight streamed into Mariah's room, burning her eyes with a vengeance.

Groaning, Mariah turned her head, burying her face into her pillow. Her bed creaked as she shifted and rolled on the small feather mattress, desperate to escape the light but knowing it would be fruitless; the lack of blinds on her tiny bedroom window meant the sun would never cease its beating against her closed eyelids. Huffing a sigh, she sat up in her bed, stretching her long, well-muscled arms above her head.

And ... there. Just as she finished her stretch, all the blood in her body rushed to her skull, the pressure like a hammer against her brain. She dropped her arms back onto the down comforter, her head slumping into her palms as she moaned again.

Goddess, she hated hangovers. Especially when she was home, where she knew her mother would frown deeply at her if she tried to begin her morning with another dash of whiskey in her coffee. Just the thought of that, though, had her headache receding slightly, enough for her to lift her head from her hands. Glancing to her nightstand, she spotted the glass of water she must've filled the night before, the ice long melted, condensation soaking into the wood. She reached out and downed the glass in seven long, greedy gulps.

As she set the glass back down, the haze around the corners of her vision lessened just slightly, all the words exchanged over that fire came rushing back to her.

And just like that, she was dizzy again.

The book, now tucked away under her mattress. The memories of Donnet, and what he'd taken that night so many years ago. Her mother's words, her insistent charge to get that dagger *back*.

Her twenty-first birthday. The freedom she'd craved for so long, ever since she'd decided being held captive in this town wouldn't be her future.

Icy anticipation flooded her veins at everything this day, this birthday, promised. Mariah peeled herself out of bed, shivering in the chill autumn morning air seeping in through the cracks in her window, and padded to her closet. She stripped off the cotton tunic she'd worn to bed and pulled on a pair of soft fleece leggings and a gray sweater, the material warm against her slightly pallid skin. Swallowing back a bizarre urge to either kick out her window and run away *now* or sprint to the bathroom and vomit, Mariah opened her bedroom door and walked down the hallway to the open family room, following the faint smell of smoke lingering in the air from the night before.

"What's for break ... fast ..." Mariah's forced, cheerful greeting died off quickly as she took note of her family, all seated at the dining table together, faces fixed in neutral expressions. Even Ellan was up and seated at the table—*Ellan*, who never got out of bed this early unless it was to sneak a girl out of the house before their mother noticed.

Wex and Lisabel were also seated at the table: Wex at the head, Lisabel to his right, Ellan to his left. Their gazes, filled with a strange combination of curiosity and fear, weren't focused on Mariah; instead, all three of them stared at the wax-sealed, cream-colored letter Lisabel held in her hand, her head cocked slightly to the side.

Mariah stood in the entryway to the family room for several moments, analyzing what in the Goddess's name was happening, trying desperately to pick apart the look on her mother's face. But her brain was still hazy with sleep and the remnants of liquor, and she couldn't do much more than watch her family all continue to sit together in eerie silence. After what felt like an eternity, her mother finally pulled her attention from the letter and turned her golden-brown gaze to Mariah. She twisted in her chair, extending the letter towards Mariah, and spoke.

"This is for you. A messenger arrived no more than a few minutes ago."

Confusion burst through Mariah, followed quickly by a wave of panic. No one should be contacting her. No one *ever* contacted her. She kept no friends in Andburgh—at least, not the kind who would send friendly birthday notes to her family's home.

Suddenly, memories of her conversation with Annabelle flashed through her mind. The confession she'd made to the golden-haired princess of Andburgh society: that as soon as she turned twenty-one, she would be leaving this place.

And there was one individual in town who Mariah knew wouldn't take kindly to her rejection of this miserable little place.

"Annabelle. That *bitch*. She fucking sold me out, didn't she? She told Donnet or his cronies that I'm planning on leaving. I'm going to *kill* her—"

"It has nothing to do with Annabelle," Lisabel sternly interrupted. "Or Donnet. Just ... open it."

Mariah's red-hot anger bubbled into icy fear, like a hot metal dipped into cold water. The look on her mother's face held her tongue, biting down on the barbed remark trying to escape. Her eyes flashed to the sealed letter, noting the fine cream parchment and the sheen of the gold seal on the back. Slowly, she forced her legs to move towards the dining table, her limbs suddenly leaden with the strange, heavy feeling of dread.

She reached the table and took the letter from her mother's outstretched hand, glancing into those golden-brown eyes that had always been the rock grounding her swirling chaos, had always been so strong even when faced with so much. A soft, knowing smile spread across her mother's face, a clear attempt to soothe whatever whirlwind was threatening to spin through Mariah at that moment. Mariah lifted an eyebrow at her mother, but Lisabel only dropped her gaze to again stare at the parchment now clasped firmly in Mariah's hand.

Mariah watched her mother for a few more heartbeats, running her thumb across the smooth parchment. It felt incredibly fine, soft as silk beneath the pads of her calloused fingers. Pulling every scrap of resolve she had to her, she lowered her gaze to the paper, and read the words written in delicate, feminine calligraphy on its front:

Ms. Mariah Salis.

Mariah swallowed loudly, unsure if the sudden dryness in her mouth was caused by that still-present hangover or by the letter. She flipped the parchment over, eyeing the gold wax seal up close, and her heart dropped out of her chest to the worn, wooden floor.

Now she was *sure* she needed to throw up.

She knew that seal; it had been drilled into her from her very first days of schooling. The personal seal of the Queen of Onita, sent from the great palace at Verith, the glimmering coastal capital of their kingdom. With shaking hands, Mariah slid a finger under the seal, breaking it. She carefully opened the letter, a bolt of pure, unadulterated excitement tinged with the sharp sting of terror lancing through her as she began to read.

Ms. Mariah Salis:

From the desk of Her Majesty, Queen Ryenne the Fair, of House Shawth.

Over twenty-one years ago, our beloved Golden Goddess, Qhohena, the light of the Golden Moon, made it known my time as your queen was nearing its end. An abdication occurred, and that night, a single drop of my magic was sent forth into Onita, seeking out the one who is Goddess-blessed and worthy of ascension onto the Golden Throne of Onita.

Since then, I have held onto what remains of my magic the best I could to protect our future queen from harm; however, my magic, the blessed magic of Qhohena gifted only to the Queen of Onita, now calls to its new lady, and it is time for the Choosing.

As a recipient of this letter, you, dear child, are an Onitan woman who has not yet exhibited any Goddess-blessed magic of your own and who may have received that drop of the Queen's power upon the completion of the Abdication all those years ago. While I cannot compel your attendance, your presence is hereby requested at the Queen's Palace at Verith within seven days' time. There, you will present yourself before me for the Choosing, at which time my magic will finally identify who it selected to be the next Queen of Onita.

I, and all of Onita, await you.

In Qhohena's Name,

Queen Ryenne Shawth

Mariah read the letter again to herself, unable to form a cohesive thought. *Abdication ... Queen ... Choosing.* Words and thoughts continued to form and dissipate in rapid succession.

Ellan, of course, was the one to break the tense silence. "Well, M, what does it say?"

Mariah, without glancing at her brother and keeping her voice soft and controlled, read the letter aloud to her sitting family. A heavy pause settled upon the house, the air growing stifling and thick.

"Today is my twenty-first birthday." Mariah's words were still quiet, her voice revealing nothing beyond cold detachment. "And I thought I might actually, finally, be able to be free. That the worst that might happen is our dumbass lord discovering my intentions to leave and trying to stop me."

No one spoke a word as something shifted within Mariah, that frozen tundra melting to something hot, burning, consuming.

This was worse than Donnet intervening in her life. It was

so much worse. While she was sure she could've handled the lord, could've slipped through his grasp no matter what, this was something else entirely.

She could not evade the *queen*.

"Be careful what you wish for, I suppose." Her voice dripped with ravenous anger.

Mariah let whatever it was bubbling up deep inside wash over her, pushing her to her feet and out of the house to the field and training pitch beyond.

Lisabel Salis watched as her daughter hacked away at the oak training dummy with the ferocity to rival a wild Kreah desert sphinx. Such raw emotion and desperation existed within Mariah, though she hardly ever let it show. Ever since her daughter's birth, Lisabel had known something untamed and inherently *free* existed in her daughter's soul, something that would always call her away to a life bigger than their simple existence at a crossroad city in the center of the kingdom.

She'd told her daughter as much the night before. Had needed to speak those words to Mariah before she left, finally free to chase what she'd always sought.

She knew what Mariah feared most wasn't just being stuck in Andburgh; it was being caged. *Anywhere.* To be told what to do by someone who wasn't her, told who to be and how to act and to have her free will drained from her body until she was nothing more than a husk of herself.

Her daughter was still so young. She feared so much.

There was so much she didn't yet understand. So much Lisabel ached to tell her, but could not. Not without risking Mariah's life, the life of her family, everything on this continent she held dear.

But, what Lisabel did know, and what she could do, was get Mariah to listen. To trust and have faith and realize the gift that had just fallen into her lap.

Far easier said than done. Her daughter wasn't known for being easy to reason with.

A soft sigh pushed past Lisabel's lips as she finally raised her voice. "Mariah. That's enough."

Her daughter froze at the sound, the muscles in her back and arms tense beneath her gray sweater. She still gripped her sword, poised over her head, the blade frozen at what would have been another strike against the well-beaten oak dummy. Slowly, Mariah let her arms and her sword drop until both hung limply by her sides.

"Look at me." Lisabel's voice was soft yet commanding. She held herself as tall as she could, gathering the poise of her years to her as she prepared to face her daughter at her most unsteady.

Her daughter slowly turned to face her, her sword still dangling from her fingertips, her posture tense like that of a caged animal backed into a corner, ready to either fight or flee. As those forest-green irises flashed up to meet her stare, Lisabel swore she saw something *silver* and other glint in the gray lining the rich green.

A chill raced up her spine, and it was only her years as a healer that kept the hair on her arms from standing on edge.

Not now, she thought. *Get her out of Andburgh. By any means necessary. That is all that matters now.*

"You have to go to Verith, Mariah."

Those forest eyes flashed silver again.

"Why."

The voice that came from her daughter's mouth was harsh and unforgiving, matching the tenseness in her shoulders. Mariah continued to hold herself utterly, eerily still, her only movement the gentle morning wind lifting the near-black strands of her hair around her face.

Lisabel drew in a steadying breath. "Do you remember our conversation from last night?"

A nod.

"*That* is why." Lisabel took a small step forward. "I told you; I want you to leave. That this place has never been for you. And I meant it." Another step forward. "I also think you know that the biggest hurdle to your departure was always going to be the *why*. The excuse. The reason that would allow you to vanish from this place without the others in town wondering where you had gone, to keep them from coming after you and trying to bring you back."

Mariah blinked, and her shoulders dropped almost imperceptibly. Lisabel could almost see her mind working, piecing together what her mother was telling her as the eddies of her emotions slowed and slowed.

Lisabel used that as her chance to stride the rest of the way down the stone walkway until she stood face to face with Mariah in the center of the training pitch. Her daughter was taller than she was, and she now had to tilt her head up just slightly to take in her face, skin tanned burnished gold after the summer spent training outdoors, eyes a deep, rich green rimmed in gray like a dense fog guarding the entrance of an ancient forest. She reached her hands out and tucked the dark strands of her daughter's hair back behind her ears before cupping Mariah's cheeks in her palms.

"You have to go to Verith," she repeated, softer this time. "Don't you see? That letter may not be what you wanted, but it is your way out. Do not miss that chance ... because you might not have another. Especially not one so simple. Go to Verith, attend this Choosing, and then you will be free and in the capital. You can board a ship and go anywhere in the world. It is everything you have ever wanted, my light."

Mariah closed her eyes, inhaling once, before releasing a great, shuddering breath. Lisabel could feel the otherworldly wildness that had consumed her daughter mere moments before retreating, not away, but *into* Mariah, settling itself with her daughter's very essence before vanishing from Lisabel's senses. Mariah reopened her eyes, and when she looked again at her mother, her gaze was no longer filled with rage and fear, but with understanding and resolution.

"I understand," Mariah whispered, and Lisabel smiled. She dropped her hands from her daughter's face and took a step back, aware of her husband and son watching the exchange from the entrance to the training clearing. She held her daughter's gaze, watched those forest green depths fill with resolve as her eldest child, the girl who'd always belonged to the dark and wild corners of the world, decided her own fate.

Mariah lifted her chin, her expression filled with steely determination.

"I will go to Verith."

CHAPTER 4

Mariah's fingers gripped the grooves in the stone, muscles straining as she scaled up the manor wall.

"*Manor*" was a generous term for Lord Donnet's residence. It was multiple stories, sure, but it was unimpressive, long past its best days. Much like the rest of Andburgh.

Mariah couldn't be more thrilled she was finally down to her final moments in this miserable town. Just this one last, teensy task, and she would be on her way to the capital.

From the capital, only the Goddess knew where her path would take her. She didn't particularly care about her ultimate destination, as long as it was far, far away from here.

After the letter had arrived that morning, after she'd had her moment to allow herself to break, after her mother had shown her the blessing this letter truly was, she'd moved quickly with her father to pack everything she might need for her travels. It wasn't much—she preferred to live light and pack even lighter—but soon, saddlebags stuffed to the brim with essentials were stacked beside the door to their cottage. The only thing Mariah didn't have was a dress suitable to wear to this Choosing at the great palace in Verith, but she didn't let that fact slow her frantic packing; they would have time once they arrived in the capital to find something suitable to wear.

They, because it was decided her father would travel with her. Not only would it be more convincing—no one would ask questions about a father traveling with his daughter to the capital on a summons from the queen—but it would give her some breathing room in her escape.

She could take her time, knowing the way out was being watched by friendly eyes.

Once the bags were packed and the horses readied, Mariah had said her tearful goodbyes to her brother and mother. The latter had gathered her up in a tight embrace, whispering the familiar words of endearment that had accompanied Mariah her whole life.

"I love you more than the stars in the sky, my light. Never forget that."

Mariah could only answer with a choking sob. She squeezed her mother tightly, one more time, before she and her father had set off down the forest path, heading towards Xara's Road, one of the Onita's main thoroughfares.

That was when Mariah had told her father of their ... detour, and what her mother had told her to do. Wex was less than thrilled; in fact, he'd turned grave and serious, gathering the reins of his warhorse in his hands, obviously ready to turn them around and head back home. But then he'd looked at his daughter, at the staunch look on her face, had seen the determination shining in her forest green eyes.

"I need to do this," she'd said. "Mom needs me to do this. She cannot go another day knowing the last remnant of her father is rotting away in that place. We won't ever get a chance like this again."

Eventually, after a long stand-off, he'd conceded. Not

happily, but he also wasn't about to let his daughter attempt something like this on her own.

And so, now there Mariah was, easily scaling up the side of Lord Donnet's manor, her father stationed in the trees just off the road, waiting to help her make a quick getaway once she had her loot in hand.

She would get that Goddess-damned dagger back. Would go into the depths of Enfara itself to get it back for her mother.

Not that this lord's manor was anything close to the cursed pit of the gods.

She reached a window on the sixth floor, and with a soft nudge of her palm, it swung open on hinges, their whine high and soft. She hoisted herself up, throwing her feet over the ledge, and dropped as silent as a cat onto the polished tile floors.

It was no secret Lord Donnet kept his trove here on the sixth floor of his manor. He bragged about it often enough whenever he was in town, too sure of his status and hold over the town to be cautious. It never occurred to him that anyone would ever be so bold as to *steal* from him.

It was that same logic that led Mariah to believe his trove would only be secured by a simple lock and otherwise left unguarded.

Honestly, it was almost *too* easy.

Mariah glanced around the empty hallway, listening intently for any hint of sound. When she heard nothing, she began to silently inch across the floor, the hallway lit only by the light of the moons outside. She could just barely make out the outline of an old, oak door, adorned with a brass handle that was—she *knew* it—outfitted with only a single keyhole.

Suddenly, male voices filled the corridor, and the faint gold light of an *allume* lamp grew at the far end of the hallway. With a soft curse, Mariah flung her body behind a great marble statue that squatted in the hallway, pressing herself as close to the wall as she could. She wore all black, even her face obscured behind a piece of black cloth, and was confident enough she wouldn't be spotted that she allowed herself to peek through a hole in the statue to glimpse the newest arrivals.

The light grew brighter and, of course, Lord Donnet himself strode into view, flanked by two of his deputies. His throaty voice was loud, echoing harshly off the hallway walls.

"Well, it won't be a girl from Andburgh. I can promise you that much." Donnet's words were tinged with unmistakable bitterness. "We have no Royals here. A new queen always comes from one of the Royals. But, regardless, it's such a waste of time. To summon every unmarried, non-magic girl in the kingdom to attend a pointless ceremony? As if the queen even does anything beyond running the Solstice, anyway. She's just as useless as her magic is, that's for sure."

Mariah's ears pricked at the words, curiosity twisting in her gut. That was *nothing* she'd ever heard before. In schooling, it was drilled into them that the Queen of Onita was sovereign and supreme in her rule, the magic she bore a piece of the Golden Goddess herself.

Not that Mariah really bought into all that bullshit. But still, it was curious that Donnet seemed to have such a different view of the monarchy from what she knew.

Mariah watched Donnet as he slipped a thin key out from a pocket, inserted it into the door to the trove room, and stepped inside. That was also when she noticed his two deputies carrying a crate between, obviously leaden with the weight of gold and valuables stolen in the name of taxes. Mariah narrowed her eyes as the three men walked into the room, the door clicking softly shut behind them.

She didn't fail to note the hinges on that door made no

noise. It was almost as if Donnet *wanted* someone to steal from him.

The men were in the room for a few minutes, and Mariah settled herself in her hiding place behind the statue. She was in no hurry. She still had plenty of time before her father began to worry, and this was one of the first lessons he'd ever taught her.

"Do not act with brashness when secrecy is your goal. Move quickly, but always with intention, and sometimes that intention will be to wait."

So, wait is what she did.

It wasn't long before footsteps creaked just beyond the door, and Mariah tensed as she watched Donnet and his two deputies step from the room. Behind them, she saw the flash of gold, *allume* lamps still lit on the walls.

Perfect.

Donnet locked the door with half his attention, still speaking to one of his deputies. Then, as quickly as they'd arrived, the three men disappeared back down the hallway, the lamp light and their voices fading along with them.

Mariah moved.

With the same silent steps she'd practiced for over a decade, she slipped out from behind the statue and sidled up to the door. She pulled two metal pins from her hair, dropped to a knee, and immediately set to work picking the simple lock. Within seconds, she heard the bolt slide back with a quiet *snick*. She reached a hand up to twist the bronze knob, pushing the door open. She smiled to herself before pushing the pins back into her braided hair.

After all, picking a simple lock just like that one was one of the first lessons her father had taught her. By age ten, she'd mastered it.

She rose to her feet and stepped into Donnet's trove, immediately hit with a wave of raw, unbridled *rage*.

Every inch of the room was covered with the glint of gold, silver, and bronze, with hammered and forged steel, with alabaster statues and marble decor. Everything that remained of the wealth of the people of Andburgh—at least, those who didn't have the benefit of being a friend of Donnet—was held in this room, hoarded here like a dragon with his treasure.

That last thought shook Mariah slightly from the haze of her anger. No, the dragons of old, the ancient protectors of the continent, were vicious, but they never would've been this cruel.

Pushing her rage to the back of her mind, Mariah moved deeper into the room, her eyes searching desperately for a small, cherry wood chest, its make simple yet beautiful. The seconds ticked, and Mariah's heart began to beat faster in her chest.

What if it isn't here?

The thought tickled the back of her mind as she worked her way into the darker corners of the space, fingers reaching under tables and into shelves on the wall. A single bead of sweat trickled down the back of her neck as her hands came up empty, again and again, until—

There. She'd just turned from the wall to face another one of the many tables brought into the room to hold the expansive collection when she saw it. It was partially hidden beneath a fine, velvet cloak, only half of the cherry wood visible to her eye. But she knew it was her quarry. That chest had floated through her thoughts every day for the past eleven years.

Mariah leaped to the table, throwing the cloak off the chest and onto the floor. She flipped the silver latch holding the lid closed and gently opened the small chest. Within it, lying on a piece of soft, worn cotton cloth, was her grandfather's dagger, sheathed in a cracked leather scabbard. Carefully, Mariah lifted the dagger, the buckles on the scabbard belt tinkling softly in the silent room. Glancing once back at the door, she strapped the dagger to her waist, cinching the straps until it was secure.

Once the dagger was firmly on her person, Mariah paused. She looked around the room, one last time, at all of this stolen wealth that served to trap the people of Andburgh here, forever unable to escape and experience more of this world.

And Mariah made an impulse decision.

Scooping up an empty canvas sack on the ground near her, an obvious remnant of a recent dumping of more "tax" collections, Mariah rushed to the nearest stack of coin, the gold and silver and bronze glinting in the soft *allume* light from the chandeliers overhead.

And she began to fist as many of those coins into her sack as she could.

The tinkling of the coins as she scooped them in greedy handfuls was loud — far louder than she wanted to be—but she had no more time to waste. Mariah'd been here long enough and knew her father was likely beginning to grow anxious. She wouldn't put it past him to come storming up to the manor in search of her, blowing her cover but, in his mind, saving her life.

Mariah vowed to be long gone before he got that desperate.

Once the current stack disappeared into the depths of her sack, she moved to the next table, to the stack gathered there, and did the same thing. Soon, after raiding the coin stacked on four of those tables, her canvas bag felt sufficiently heavy. Not enough to impede her ability to scale down the manor, but enough to ensure she could pay to go anywhere she wanted to go.

She hoped, prayed, that if the people of Andburgh ever learned of her heist, they would be glad that at least their hard-earned funds were no longer here, collecting dust, but had helped one of their own forge a new path for herself.

Mariah almost snorted aloud at that thought. One of their own. It was a nice thought, but she knew they saw her as nothing more than a strange, angry girl. Knew they would be glad once they learned of her permanent absence.

Pulling out the small length of rope she'd wrapped into her belt, she secured the canvas sack to her back before slipping back out of the trove room. Closing the door softly behind her, she locked it quickly with the picks she hid in her hair, before pausing just a moment in the hallway, listening intently.

Just as she'd expected. Nothing.

Idiots.

She hurtled silently towards the still-open window—the window Donnet and his men were too obtuse to notice was open to the chill breeze—and threw her body over the ledge, her feet and hands instantly finding their purchase. She scaled expertly down the side of the old manor, the thick stones making her task far easier than the slick walls and trees her father had forced her to climb as part of their training. Eventually, she made it back to the solid ground, dropping to the packed earth below and racing lightly through the shadows to the wrought iron fence surrounding Donnet's manor. She threw her body over the low barrier easily and disappeared into the night like a ghost, carrying the wealth of a city on her back and the heart of her family across her hip.

"You took too long." Wex's voice was a low growl, rumbling out the second Mariah darted within twenty feet of where he stood in the shadows with their horses.

"Oh, please," Mariah said, sauntering out from the trees. "My timing was perfect. They never even knew I was there."

Her father only eyed her, obviously searching for any sign of a struggle or difficulty. "Still. Too long. You pushed it."

Mariah grinned. "Yeah, but ... it was worth it." She shrugged off the canvas sack from her back, the coins within clinking as they hit the ground. Her father's eyes widened.

"Mariah," he said, his voice tinged with panic. "That was *not* what you went there to do. Did you even get the dagger, or did you get too distracted by the coin you found?"

She hardened her stare. "That coin was not his. I will put it to much better use than he ever would, letting it gather dust in that old, miserable manor." She shifted slightly, letting her cloak blow open just enough to reveal the black leather belt, the worn scabbard it carried, the silver dragon wings on the hilt of that dagger. Her father's eyes relaxed in the light of the *allume* lamp he held. "And, of course, I got the dagger. I told Mother I would." Her tone was matter-of-fact.

Because it was a fact. She'd told her mother she would get the dagger.

So she had.

Wex regarded her for a moment longer before turning silently back to his horse. Without another word, father and daughter rode through the dark woods until they found Xara's Road, Mariah shedding the uniform of the thief as they traveled. The next day, when the sun rose, they appeared to be no more than two simple travelers on the road, a father escorting his daughter to the capital upon the directive of the queen.

And every time Mariah felt the worn scabbard of her grandfather's dagger dig into her thigh, every time she heard the tinkling of coin from her saddlebags, she smiled.

CHAPTER 5

Their travels over the next four days were uneventful as they journeyed east toward the capital, the smell of horse manure and falling leaves burning into Mariah's nose until she feared it would be all she would smell until the day she died. Each night, as they inched their way to Verith, the inns frequently found along the road grew packed with other young women who must've also received the queen's summons, accompanied by their fathers or mothers or brothers. Most of those women wore looks of excitement, hope dancing in their eyes, and while Mariah appreciated the sentiment, she had a feeling she was feeling the same for *very* different reasons.

To avoid the increasing crowds, Mariah and her father found themselves resorting to the quieter, more quaint inns, opting for a simple, slightly under-seasoned meal and a lumpy mattress over braving the rowdy crowds at some of the more high-end lodges.

Comfort could be bought, but peace was priceless.

Especially when she carried the stolen wealth of a town in her saddlebags.

Around noon on the fifth day, with the sun gleaming high in the sky and Xara's Road teeming with life, the great golden city walls of Verith roared into view.

The capital of Onita sat upon the glittering Bay of Nria, jade blue waters stretching off well beyond eyesight toward the Mirrored Sea, sprawling in its vastness until it met the base of the coastal Attlehon Mountains rising almost suddenly from the flat land along the bay. The road was now thoroughly packed with travelers of all kinds and origins, all making their way into the shining jewel of the kingdom. Mariah sat upon her buckskin gelding, Kodie, and gazed with uninhibited awe upon the great splendor of the outer city walls. They were utterly impenetrable, a display of the absolute strength and prosperity that had developed since the kingdom was founded nearly five thousand years ago.

It took Mariah and her father close to an hour to weave through the stifling traffic, slowly pushing their way to the massive open gates. Eagle-eyed guards, garbed in black leather armor and cloaks of gold cloth, scanned the crowd from atop the tall battlements. Their surveying looks had Mariah's heart pounding in her chest, her fingers fidgeting on Kodie's reins as the feeling of her grandfather's dagger burned against her leg. Those guards barely tossed them more than a cursory glance, and with a giant sigh of relief, Mariah passed unimpeded through the solid iron gates and into the ancient city of Verith, her father close behind.

Mariah and her father traveled down the winding, packed city streets, their horses' hooves clicking against the worn, golden pavers below. As Mariah's gaze wandered, she noticed most of the doors to the residences and businesses lining the streets were adorned with flags or tapestries bearing Queen Ryenne's sigil: two black crescent moons crossed over each other on a field of gold. It was obvious word of the Choosing had spread fast throughout both the city and the kingdom, and its people wished to celebrate the reign of their beloved queen one last time.

They continued traveling deeper into the sprawling city, the sun beginning to inch back toward the horizon. Verith was divided into two distinct sections: one side, where the markets and rich trade of Onita flourished and fed the people of the kingdom, was nestled on the Bay of Nria, its busy port full of ships from all across the continent, the sails and hulls reflecting the blending of cultures there on the shimmering water. Most of the residents of Verith resided in that bustling market district, its people taking advantage of the widely available work and opportunity brought by the healthy economy.

The other side of the city, the side backing up directly to the Attlehon Mountains, stood in stark contrast to the markets along the bay. The foothills of the mountains caused the streets to rise and fall underfoot, yet it was much quieter on this hilly side of the city. The mountain district, as the Verithians called it, was where various military forces of Onita resided and trained, using the relative quiet as a reprieve from the usual hustle and bustle of the capital. It was also where those of the upper echelon of Onita kept residences—lords, generals, ambassadors, along with the wealthier merchants and businessmen. From the voices of those Mariah passed on the streets, she could see it wasn't that those who resided in the market district were prohibited entry or residence to the mountain district; it seemed to be a more conscious choice, a willing separation from the people and those who governed them.

It was into the mountain district that she and her father

now headed. Cresting the rise of a hilled street, a glint of blinding gold caught Mariah's eye, and her breath caught in her throat as the full sight before her came into view.

In front of her, rising up high and glowing like flames in the setting sun, was the golden palace of Verith, its spires built into the side of the mountains looming behind it. The structure was massive, imposing, a display of power for the ancient and mighty kingdom, yet was still delicate, almost feminine. The palace consisted of a rectangular building at its center, lower than the others but still daunting, the rear of that main building molding into the mountainside. On either side stood tall, twin towers, and built into the mountains itself were more structures—even in the warm evening light, Mariah could still spot the tinkling of *allume* lights that appeared to come from the Attlehons themselves, but she knew were still only part of the palace.

The fact that she would get to see that incredible palace up close and personal, perhaps even set foot within its gilded doors, brought a chill to Mariah's skin. Her mother was right; what a start to the adventure she'd craved for so long.

Moving further into Verith's mountain district, Mariah continued to stare up at the golden palace, watching the spires turn from the brightest gold to burnt amber as the sun set below the bay and fall twilight settled over the city. Beside her, her father nudged his horse closer to Kodie and Mariah, his presence drawing her attention away from the palace and back to the now-quiet streets around her. She turned her head to meet her father's gaze.

He smiled at her warmly. "We should probably find a nice place to stay for the night. I'd say we are far enough into the mountain district that it shouldn't be too hard to find something suitable. I've actually got just the place to try."

Mariah nodded and softly voiced her agreement, following

after her father as he urged his warhorse down streets now lit by *allume* lamps in the early dimness of dusk.

They rode for another fifteen minutes, their only company soldiers and city guards either coming or going from their posts throughout the city. Mariah remembered with a jolt that her father had once been one of those soldiers, dressed in the black and gold garb of the queen, spending his days either training or keeping the people of the kingdom and this city safe. She glanced over at him, noticing the ease and confidence with which he guided his black stallion down the streets. *I bet he once roamed these streets to the point where they were all but memorized to him*, she thought.

Eventually, her father pulled his horse to a halt in front of a quaint, quiet little inn located on a side street just off the main road, its freshly lacquered sign hanging over a solid oak door. *The Silver Moon*, it read. *Odd*, Mariah thought. Everything in this kingdom was *Golden* this or *Gilded Moon* that. Their world had two moons that hung in the night sky, but it was only ever the gold one that received notice.

Onitans, for some reason, chose to pretend that the second moon, the silver light beside the gold, didn't exist. Mariah had always been slightly baffled by it, but had never cared enough to learn more as to why.

Much as they had every other night on the road, Mariah and her father left their horses in the care of a stable hand and carried their saddlebags into the inn, Mariah clutching tightly to the canvas sack she refused to let out of view. She adjusted her grandfather's dagger on her thigh, shifting it around so it was fully hidden by her dark cloak, just as they were greeted by a short, full-bodied woman with gray hair standing behind a well-polished bar. She called out her greeting while hand-drying a mug, but it wasn't until she turned her gaze up to take them in that her eyes went wide.

"*Wex Salis?!*"

An answering, brilliant grin spread across Wex's face. "It's been a few years, hasn't it, Beva?"

The woman's face broke into her own beaming smile. She set her mug down carefully on the bar top, her rag tossed carelessly beside it, before wiping her hands across her apron and walking out from behind the bar. At the same time, Mariah's father moved forward, and within seconds enveloped the woman in a great embrace.

A joyous laugh burst from the woman's—Beva's—lips. "It has been so many years, my boy!" She pushed back from Wex's hold to look him in the eye. "What are you doing here? How is Lisabel? Beautiful as ever, I am sure. Is she here in Verith with you?"

Wex chuckled and smiled at Beva. "Lisabel is wonderful. She remained at home for this journey, but I'm sure she sends her regards." He paused a moment before continuing, "I am actually here with my daughter." He turned from Beva to look behind him at Mariah, who still stood in the entryway to the inn. "Beva, I would like to introduce you to Mariah."

Beva's attention snapped to Mariah, her gaze warm yet shrewd and intelligent. She took in Mariah for a few moments, eyes seeing far more than Mariah was willing to show, before shoving Wex out of the way unceremoniously and bustling towards Mariah. Before Mariah could speak her greetings, Beva wrapped her up in a giant hug, the shorter woman somehow managing to grip Mariah tight, the smell of apple cinnamon and warm bread wafting over her.

"It is so wonderful to meet you, my dear." The woman pulled back from Mariah, tears lining her eyes. "The last I knew of you, you were but a small thrumming heartbeat in your mother's belly." Her stare turned intent then, taking in Mariah's complete appearance before her eyes widened slightly.

"Wex, are you sure this is your daughter?"

Mariah's father, slightly puzzled, answered slowly, "...yes? Why?"

Beva's smile turned light hearted again. "Because she is far too beautiful to hail from your line. Takes much more after her mother, I reckon."

Wex's face twisted back into a grin. "Now, I couldn't agree with you more on that."

Mariah could only smile lightly as she watched her father settle into light banter with his old friend. It was fascinating to see her father like this—he seemed younger, in an element that had been lost to him during their life in Andburgh.

She wondered absently if he missed it—the bustle of the city, the demands of the life of a soldier, the vibrancy of living in the beating heart of their continent. Whether he craved the same escape she was no more than a few hours from finally reaching, but his love for his wife and his family kept him rooted firmly in place.

Beva turned back to Mariah, pulling her from her thoughts. Her face grew serious, her gray eyes darting from Mariah to Wex and back to Mariah again.

"You are here for the Choosing." It was not a question.

Mariah answered anyway. "Yes. I am."

Beva nodded once, accepting the simplicity of that answer, not asking for all the words unsaid in the air around them. "Good. Now, Mariah, I am going to put you up in one of my best rooms. Your father can have the room across the hall." Wex looked ready to protest, but Beva shut him down with a hard glare. "It is my honor. After everything your father has done for me, it is the least I can do."

Wex only grumbled a response. Mariah, on the other hand, spoke without thinking.

"That is very kind of you. We can pay, of course—" She was cut off by a sharp look from her father, a clear warning for her to shut her mouth.

Interesting. So, while Beva was a friend, her father didn't want her flashing her stolen gold, even here.

Beva scoffed. "Nonsense. It is only one night, and I owe your father much more than a couple rooms and a hot meal. It is nothing. Now, I'm sure you've had your horses tended to out front. Sit down, and I'll get some food and ale out to the both of you. And don't you dare argue with me, Wex."

So Mariah and her father sat. As her gaze wandered absently around the inn, she noticed they were some of the only patrons in the quaint main hall. Taking in the well-lacquered tables and bars, the roaring hearth, and the comfortable seating, Mariah knew it must get more business than just this, but with all the newcomers to the city, it was a shock to see it so empty.

Her father, noticing her gaze and furrowed brow, answered her silent question. "It is a few hours before shift change."

Mariah looked back at him, still utterly confused.

He sighed. "Beva has long been a friend of the Royal Infantry. When stationed here, this is the soldiers' first bar of choice—close enough to the barracks, yet far enough from the watchful gazes of their captains. And when they filter through here, many of those young soldiers haven't had a hot meal in weeks. You'd be surprised how much you'd pay from that freshly cashed soldier's salary for a well-cooked meal and cold ale away from all the orders and rigid structure. And everyone knows that Beva's is the best place in the city for both."

Mariah glanced around again, the new knowledge like a fresh film over her eyes. Sure enough, there *were* other patrons in the inn: a young man, still dressed in his black and gold soldier livery, quietly sipping his ale by a window, and a grizzled man with his daughter, almost mirrors of Wex and Mariah.

Minus the stolen dagger and misappropriated coin, of course.

Beva reappeared then, carrying a tray laden with ale and steaming beef pot pies. She set the food and drink in front of Mariah, once again wiping her hands on her apron before glancing down at the floor around them. Mariah leaned forward, inhaling the rich scents of the meat—and was that tarragon?—wafting from the plate.

"These your bags? Let me take them up to your rooms while you eat."

Mariah started, "No, that's alright, we ca—"

Her father interrupted her with a gentle kick under the table. "That would be lovely, Beva. Thank you." He smiled warmly up at her, a smile she returned to him before picking up the saddlebags from the floor, along with a carefully wrapped parcel Mariah somehow hadn't noticed when they were untacking their horses. Mariah's gaze tracked the woman as she strode from the room and up the stairs, her heart fluttering at the sight of the canvas sack she could see just barely sticking out from one of her saddlebags.

"If you had said no, she would've just sat there and stared at me from the corner until I let her take the bags up. Just easier to go ahead and let her be the host she is." He paused, chewing his food. "She wouldn't poke her nose into things that aren't her business. It's just ... it's better to not flash too much coin around, even here in the mountain district. Better to take the hospitality for what it is and save what you can for when you need it."

Mariah nodded to her father, jaw tight, eyes still fixed on

the innkeeper. When Beva disappeared from her sight, she whipped her head to him.

"What was in that parcel she took up with the bags?"

Wex started, eyes going wide, then relaxed and shook his head wistfully. "Sometimes, I forget how observant you are. I guess I should pat myself on the back for that. Goddess knows why I was ever worried about you the other night."

Mariah didn't respond, opting instead to take a bite of her pot pie and a sip of ale, her expectant gaze never leaving her father.

Wex sighed, leaning back and taking a sip from his own pint. "Fine. Consider it a ... birthday present. Another one. From myself and your mother." He paused. "Well, alright. Mainly from your mother. She picked it out some time ago, actually. Saved up then had a seamstress in town make it custom. She somehow always knew you'd one day need to wear something other than boots and leggings."

It was Mariah's turn to look stunned, her jaw slackening, freezing with a bite of food halfway to her mouth. "You and mom saved up and bought me a *dress?*" Pure shock—and a little bit of anger—coursed through her veins. Her parents were robbed by their lord because they'd been unable to pay taxes. She knew how hard her parents worked for *everything*, how many years her father had spent in service to the crown, how many long hours her mother still spent at the clinic, just to ensure she and Ellan had a warm meal three times a day. Not that Mariah didn't have a secret taste for the finer things in life —that canvas sack certainly was proof of that—but for them to splurge on something as ludicrous as a gown for her, without even knowing if she would ever actually *wear* it ...

It was decided. She would make a trip back to Andburgh one day, just to scold her mother for attempting to gift her with this *nonsense* while simultaneously charging her to recover a dagger that'd been lost when they were unable to pay what their lord demanded.

Seeing the rising anger in his daughter's face, Wex backtracked quickly. "Mariah, calm down. It didn't set us back much at all, I promise. Your mother was adamant we do this for you, and you know I can never say no to her. Just ... take a look at it first. Then you can decide what to do with it. But I know your mother would be beyond thrilled if you wore it tomorrow."

Mariah closed her eyes and inhaled deeply through her nose. She counted to five silently to herself, her roiling emotions slowly returning to their normal contained cacophony, before opening her eyes and meeting her father's gaze.

"Just ... please tell me it's not some awful monstrosity exploding with tulle and lace."

Wex, relieved, roared with laughter.

"Do you think we don't know you at all? Of course it is."

As it turned out, there wasn't a scrap of tulle or lace on the gown her mother had designed for her.

Beva, with all her cunning intuition and innate kindness, had somehow known exactly what that package contained. When Mariah trudged up the stairs, exhausted from their five, hard days of riding to reach the capital in time for the Choosing, she'd found its contents gently unwrapped, hanging up beside the full-length mirror adoring a corner of the cozy room so it could unfold and breathe.

Mariah sat on the soft feather bed, legs crossed beneath her, and leaned back on her hands as she stared at the dress. Upon reflection, she wasn't at all surprised her mother had commissioned something so deliciously perfect, even if anger at its very existence and the expense of it still bubbled under her skin. Lisabel had always known exactly who her daughter was since the earliest of Mariah's memories and had never asked Mariah to hide or change a single morsel of it.

Mariah smiled softly to herself, thinking about what tomorrow might bring. This dress would cause quite a stir at the palace, she was sure of it; it was so different from the styles usually favored by Onitan women, yet Mariah wouldn't have it any other way. For a fleeting moment, she let herself dream about what may happen when the moons set and the sun rose in the sky, when she donned that dress and made her way to the palace, of the stunned silence that'd follow when she walked up those stairs, a smug smile on her lips. She would stand in the back of whatever room they lined her up in, watch the new queen be Chosen, and then would slip back out the way she came. But instead of returning to this inn, she would make her way down to the market district, her bag of gold and silver and bronze coin in hand. Maybe she would board one of those ships and pay for passage to the Kizar Islands; she'd always dreamed of cavorting with the pirates who called the archipelago home. This was what she'd spent her whole life, ever since that night when she was nine years old, dreaming about. The reason she'd let her father train her so relentlessly, why she'd risked everything to scale the walls of a lord's manor just to retrieve an old dagger and a sack full of coin.

So that one day, she could step foot into the world alone and never look back.

CHAPTER 6

The slight rocking of the carriage for hire was enough to bring on a wave of queasiness. Mariah leaned her head back against the cool lacquered wood and shut her eyes, inhaling deeply.

She refused to admit she was nervous. Her hands might've been shaking, a thin layer of sweat may have clung to her skin beneath her gray cloak, but it was absolutely not from nerves. She told herself she was ready to face whatever that day might bring.

Not nervous, not nervous, not nervous ...

The words were a mantra, but each time she repeated them, she only felt more nauseous.

Glancing up at the roof of the carriage, she again wondered where her father had managed to secure the cabbie. With the amount of people who must now be in the city for the Choosing, she'd fully expected to get herself to the palace that morning on her own. She'd gotten dressed quickly, slipping into the gown before styling her hair and applying simple makeup to her face—a sweep of gold shimmer across her eyelids, a line of kohl along her upper lash-line. It'd been just enough to make the deep, glowing green of her eyes pop against her tan skin. Just as she'd stepped out of her room, wrapped in her cloak and prepared to head down to the stables to saddle Kodie, Wex had emerged from his own room to stop her. He'd taken her hand and squeezed it gently before dropping it and telling her to follow him. They'd walked out the front door of the inn and, sure enough, the cabbie was there patiently waiting, her father telling her the driver was hers for the day.

Mariah could only turn and gape at her father in bewilderment, wondering if he'd finally softened up to the idea of actually using her spoils from Lord Donnet. He'd chuckled at her softly, gathering her up into a great bear hug and placing a kiss on her forehead, before shooing her gently into the cabbie and directing the driver to take her to the palace.

She inhaled deeply through her nose, holding the air in her lungs for several heartbeats before expelling it through her mouth. Her gaze drifted to the open window of the cabbie. The winding streets continued steadily uphill, taking them right up to the base of where the Attlehon Mountains roared into the sky, the golden palace gleaming at their feet.

People began to fill the streets, and her carriage wasn't the only one. They'd joined a procession: a march of young women, all headed to the palace to learn which one of their lives was about to alter forever. For some, Mariah imagined it felt like a parade of hope, towards some new beginning or unfulfilled destiny.

For her, it only felt like a funeral procession.

That great, eerie pit deep in her stomach stirred suddenly, like a big cat opening an eye before stretching out its claws, curious about the gathering energy in the air.

Mariah drew another deep breath, shutting down as hard

as she could on whatever *that* was. Nothing would get in the way of her impending freedom.

Nothing.

Soon, far too soon, the great gates of the palace rose up in front of them, gilded and gleaming, a bastion of the strength of the ancient kingdom. The walls surrounding the palace were even more impenetrable than the city gates, made of thick blocks of mortared white stone. However, the gates themselves were open, and the guards simply glanced at the queen's letter Mariah handed to them before waving her cabbie through.

Inside the gates was a massive courtyard, the road arcing in a great circle around its entire perimeter. At the center of the courtyard was a fountain, a towering statue in its center in the shape of a woman, her skin made of white stone, her flowing hair and robes gilded, the golden bucket she held pouring water down into the pool beneath her feet.

Qhohena, the Golden Goddess, the giver of life and the mother of their world. The great patroness of Onita, her favored people, and the benefactor of the queen and her magic.

Mariah allowed herself a single, fleeting moment to marvel at the statue before she pulled her attention back to the buzzing courtyard around her. The carriage was still moving, gliding smoothly over the road beneath, until it came to a stop beside a row of other carriages and cabbies. Glancing behind her, Mariah noticed they were now to the left of the statue and the grand staircase leading to the true palace entrance; they must've passed by the steps while she'd been enraptured by the statue of Qhohena.

Okay … maybe she'd stared for more than a fleeting moment.

Mariah felt the cabbie tip slightly to the right as the driver stepped down from his perch. A soft knock sounded on her door a few seconds later.

"My lady? We have arrived. Do you require assistance?"

Mariah couldn't help but choke down a laugh; never in her life had she resembled anything close to a "lady." She certainly had never been called one.

However, the driver saved her from worrying about ruining her incredible ensemble, so she swallowed her retort and instead pushed the door open, meeting the middle-aged cabbie's brown gaze as she smiled at him.

"No, thank you. I can get down on my own." He gave her a warm smile and nodded once before stepping back, moving away from the carriage to the horse who pulled it.

Mariah felt her own smile grow further, touching her eyes, when she heard his soft, crooning words to the beast filter back over the din of the crowd.

With a deep, steely breath, Mariah shrugged out of her gray cloak, folding it on the leather bench of the cabbie, running her hands quickly through her long, dark tresses one last time.

This is nothing, she instructed herself. *Plus, you look fucking fabulous.*

Her grin turned savage as she swung her body out of the carriage, her feet gracefully hitting the ground as she stepped from the cabbie and closed the door behind her with a soft *click.* She inhaled deeply, tossing her hair over her shoulder, and began to turn to face the crowd at her back when a voice froze her in place.

"Holy *shit*, you look incredible."

The voice was bright, bubbly, and feminine, like tinkling coins. Mariah whirled and found herself facing a young woman who could only be described as gold: golden hair, golden-tanned skin, even her eyes were the color of warm amber. She wore a heavy lavender gown, the skirts full of tulle and the corset bodice detailed with lace, and her face carried an expression of both envy and awe. Mariah allowed herself a quick glance down at herself because, well, the girl had a point.

She *did* look incredible.

The gown her mother had designed for her was unlike anything worn by the other women swarming the palace courtyard, and she could already feel more gazes being drawn to her the longer she stood there. It appeared to be made of molten, liquid gold, poured over her form and hugging her athletic curves like it was painted on. The straps over her shoulders were thin and delicate, and the neckline plunged to the center of her chest, highlighting her collarbones and the swell of her breasts. The back rose to just below her shoulder blades, the tanned skin and toned muscles of her back highlighted and accentuated.

Her skirts dripped down around her legs like melted sunlight, pooling in a short train around her feet. Two high slits were cut up both sides of the dress, the lean expanse of her legs on full display. On her feet she wore simple, strappy heels; it had been quite some time since she'd worn something other than boots, but Mariah had learned a long time ago that clothes were just as much a weapon as her grandfather's dagger she'd strapped high on her thigh, hidden from view.

And thankfully, she'd learned how to use both.

"Thank you. I was worried it might be unseasonably warm today. Didn't want to get bogged down by so many layers." Mariah's eyes glimmered with humor as she leveled a pointed look at the full, heavy skirts of the girl's gown.

The girl's eyes widened slightly before her face twisted into a friendly smirk. "You *bitch*. I knew I'd like you the second I saw you." She lifted the heavy tulle of her skirt, huffing a laugh. "I'm already sweating my fucking face off in this Goddess-damned monstrosity."

Mariah twisted her gaze into one of mock scrutiny. "I

mean, it's not terrible. If you're not Chosen and want to find a new role in the palace, I'm sure they'll be able to put you to work as a cake-topper."

The girl was silent for two heartbeats, and Mariah felt her face fall, worried she might've gone too far.

It wasn't as if she'd had much practice at making—and *keeping*—friends back in Andburgh.

Until the girl burst out laughing, a laugh like chiming bells, the sound bringing a chuckle to Mariah's own lips.

Once the girl had regained control, carefully wiping tears from her face, she stepped closer to Mariah, sticking out her hand in greeting. "I'm Ciana. We're going to be friends—sorry, you don't get a say in that. Either accept it or ... well, accept it."

Mariah was laughing again as she clasped Ciana's hand in her own. "I think I'll accept it. I'm Mariah." She paused, releasing Ciana's grip but still smiling as she gestured toward the palace steps. "Do you want to try to walk up those gods-awful stairs with me and make fun of all the other bitches here who think they look good?"

"Abso-fucking-lutely."

Ciana stepped forward, reaching to loop her arm through Mariah's as if they were childhood best friends, but then suddenly froze, her gaze darting over Mariah's shoulder, back towards the lines of carriages and the stables just behind them. At that same moment, Mariah felt a wave of awareness wash over her, like she was being prodded with thousands of tiny needles, the hairs on her arms and back of her neck rising.

"Holy shit," Ciana whispered, her voice suddenly breathless. "If they work in the palace, then I'm never leaving. Will gladly take that job opening as a cake-topper."

Mariah slowly turned, unsure at all what to expect, her senses still erratic.

She wasn't prepared for what she saw.

A carriage had just pulled out, leaving a gap that opened to a direct view of the palace stables. It was there, no more than two dozen feet away under the awning over the stable walls, where a group of about twenty men lounged, all appearing to be somewhere in their late twenties to thirties. Even at the distance, Mariah could tell by the way they all either sat or stood with too-casual grace that they were some form of soldier or guard in service to the palace. The weapons adorning them only further convinced her. But none of those things were why her throat suddenly went dry and her heart leaped into her throat.

Every single one of them was *ridiculously* attractive.

And all of their eyes were trained on her.

The men were vastly varied in appearance: all ranges of hair color, skin color, and eye color. Despite the pounding of her heart, Mariah met the stare of each one, holding it for a second before moving on.

One of them was making her skin crawl, and she had to know who.

She made her way down the line, reaching the end, growing increasingly more frustrated when that twinge in her gut refused to relent, until—*oh*.

Her eyes finally landed on a tall form hidden almost completely in the shadows of the stable entrance, melding into the darkness as if he belonged there more than he did in the bright autumn daylight. It was like he wanted to avoid being seen at all costs, but the way he was staring at her ... it was with such burning intensity she thought she might leap out of her own skin.

Even hidden from the light, Mariah could tell that his hair was black, a light-consuming onyx, as was his clothing. His shoulders were broad, the muscles in his crossed arms flexed, and just like the others gathered with him, he oozed the preternatural grace of one trained for war from birth.

But what really caught Mariah's attention were his eyes.

They were a bright, glowing, gemstone blue, but not quite sapphire—they were deeper, clearer somehow. Then she remembered a stone her father had once shown her, a stone only mined from deep in the northern Everheim Mountains, a stone of the exact same shade of rich and wild blue.

His eyes were the color of tanzanite.

That feeling of awareness intensified, her ears beginning to ring, the world starting to shake and crumble around her—

Until it all suddenly stopped.

The supernatural feeling that had threatened to overwhelm her vanished in an instant, and the world came to a stand-still. The ringing in her ears was replaced by the din of the crowd around her.

Mariah blinked, flitting her gaze back to the man in the shadows. There was a moment, before he regained control of his expression, when she saw a look mirroring the confusion and nausea still roiling through her own gut. He met her stare again and a cold mask slid instantly over his attractive features, his tanzanite gaze turning to daggers.

The only thing Mariah could think to do in that moment was smirk and *shove* down the turmoil still tangled in her mind before dragging her gaze from him. Still feeling the weight of the other men's stares, she tossed her hair over her shoulder one more time before turning back to Ciana. Mariah grabbed the other girl's arm and drug her away, heading across the courtyard towards the palace steps.

As strange as that encounter was, she refused to let it distract her.

Today was the day Mariah would finally get free.

CHAPTER 7

On any other occasion, Mariah would've been enthralled with the gilded, sweeping architecture of the throne room of the palace.

However, today, right now, she was far too distracted by the pounding of her heart and the ringing in her ears to appreciate the wondrous beauty around her. All she could focus on was the feel of the smooth, cold wooden bench below her.

She could also notice the throne room was massive, cavernous in scope, its ceiling tall enough to make the structure of the room feel impossible. At the front of the room, situated upon a raised dais, sat a beautiful golden throne, the intricacies depicting the best of Onita's history—rich harvests, golden skies, tall mountains, curving rivers, and membranous wings—carved into its surface visible even from the very back of the room. On either side of that golden throne were two towering pillars made of a shimmering, opaque stone—*lunestair*, if she had to guess. Those pillars were glowing softly, golden light pulsing ever so gently within their cloudy depths.

Long, wooden pews were arranged in neat rows down the entire length of the room to accommodate all the women in attendance, and it was upon one of those pews on which Mariah sat. Despite the hardness and the slight chill, the wood felt solid and *real* and was the only thing keeping Mariah grounded as she forced herself to take deep inhales and long exhales. Ciana sat beside her, fanning herself incessantly, lacking all of Mariah's nerves but also looking like she would give anything in that moment to be free from her full skirts and tight corset.

Mariah didn't know her new friend well, but something told her that if Ciana could've stood and stripped down to her undergarments right there in the middle of the throne room of Onita, she would have.

Upon entering the great palace gates, they—along with every other woman there—were funneled and ushered into the throne room, reluctantly finding nondescript seats somewhere in the center of the room. Mariah had wanted nothing more than to hide, to blend in with the crowd until this ritual was over and she could get out.

The stream of women was nearly endless, until eventually it slowed to a trickle, and movement through the doors to the throne room stopped. Everyone found a seat, and nervous whispers and the brushing of fidgeting skirts filled the cavernous room, scratching against Mariah's skin like mosquitos in the summer. The great wooden doors of the throne room shut behind the last of them, a boom echoing throughout the vast space. A hush swept over the amassed women, and even Ciana dropped her arms to her side as her eyes widened, the anxiety of the moment written clearly across her bright features.

And of course, because Mariah needed one more issue to

concern herself with in that moment, the strangeness deep within her she'd shoved down in the cabbie on the way to the palace stirred again, unspooling itself through her gut like a ball of yarn and stretching tendrils out into her limbs.

Mariah forced a breath out through her nose and closed her eyes, diving inside herself, desperately trying to halt whatever it was weaving its way through her. She pushed and pushed and *pushed*, but it wouldn't retreat, seemingly content to drift idly through her veins.

She had no idea what was happening and had never felt less in control.

She *hated* it.

"Mariah? You okay?"

Ciana's light, gentle voice had Mariah's eyes snapping back open. She forced herself to swallow, the strange crawling sensation in her veins still there, as she turned her head to the other girl and smiled wanly.

"Yeah, I'm fine. The anticipation is just killing me." The lie burned as it was pushed through gritted teeth.

Ciana looked unconvinced, but before she could respond, the doors behind the grand golden throne opened on slow, silent hinges. Everyone in the throne room rose to their feet in a single wave, Mariah and Ciana being drawn up with the tide.

Out of those doors walked a beautiful woman, appearing to be just a few years older than Mariah, garbed in a stunning crimson velvet gown that trailed behind her in a long train. Her hair was long, blonde, and wavy, falling nearly to her waist, and atop her head rested a golden crown. Even from the distance at which Mariah sat, she could still make out the shape of delicate snowdrop blossoms in the golden metal, the flower that grew deep in the steppes of the Attlehon Mountains, the ancient symbol of the Queen of Onita.

Mariah could feel herself holding her breath as Queen Ryenne Shawth, Lady of Verith and Qhohena's Chosen, walked slowly, gracefully, to stand before her golden throne. Out from those same doors behind her followed six other women—her Ladies, her closest confidants and advisors sworn to serve the queen for the entirety of their lives. As the Ladies took their place in the seats on either side of the *lunestair* pillars, seven men melted out of the shadows behind the raised dais. Mariah's blood pulsed in her veins as she beheld Queen Ryenne's Armature, her blood-bonded knights, themselves each chosen and blessed by the Goddess and the Consort God, their lives linked to their queen for the entire long length of her life.

One of those knights stepped closer to the throne than the others, standing by the right arm of that golden chair. "That must be Kalen," Ciana whispered to Mariah. "The Queen's Consort." Mariah nodded slightly, taking in the male, his light brown hair slightly tousled and roguish, his sharp eyes missing nothing in the cavernous room.

Standing before her throne, Queen Ryenne glanced to her left, to where a middle-aged woman with hair that must've once been golden blonde but was now streaked through with soft gray stood. The woman was dressed in pale golden robes, and stepped up onto the dais to stand beside her queen. Mariah didn't miss how Kalen's eyes narrowed, the tightening in his face clear even from a distance, as he watched the woman move forward.

The two women stood in silence together for a few heartbeats, their intense gazes staring out at the masses of women gathered before them. Mariah began to feel her own skin crawl under the heavy weight of those eyes.

It was the middle-aged woman who spoke first, breaking the expectant silence.

"Warm greetings to you all. I am Ksee, High Priestess of Qhohena, Beloved of our Golden Goddess. It is my honor to introduce Her Royal Majesty, Queen Ryenne of House Shawth, Chosen of Qhohena, Protector of Onita and Lady of Verith. You may kneel in her presence."

The power in Ksee's voice washed over the throne room, and on instinct the gathered women, Mariah included, dropped to their knees, their heads bowing to the queen, who stood, as regal as a goddess, before her golden throne.

Ryenne herself spoke next.

"Rise."

Her voice was soft, yet carried a power that couldn't be ignored. It slid over Mariah's skin like a cat, pulling her up from her knees, her head and gaze lifting ...

... to directly meet the ocean-blue stare of the queen.

No, that can't be right, Mariah thought. The throne room was massive, and there were thousands of women packed into its space. Out of everyone there, it was impossible for the queen to suddenly be noticing *her*.

Mariah continued her defiant inner monologue but couldn't shake the way the air kept poking at her skin.

The queen's gaze snapped away, continuing her survey of the throne room.

"I would like to begin by thanking you—each and every one of you—for traveling however far your journey was to join me. Whether you hail from the market district here in Verith or from Tolona at the southern border, I welcome you to my home and to the birthplace of our grand and blessed kingdom." Ryenne paused, drawing a breath, before continuing.

"I have been blessed beyond measure to have spent the last three hundred and fifty years of my long life in service to Onita. Qhohena chose me long ago to lead this kingdom, and just like the nine queens who preceded me, I serve this kingdom at her whim and her mercy.

"While it is true that some queens have sat their thrones for far longer than I, their reigns sometimes stretching beyond five hundred years, the Goddess has decided for my fate and reign to be different. A little over twenty-one years ago, early in the morning on the day of the autumnal equinox, my magic slipped from my grasp. It was a sign from Qhohena, an abdication of her power. I will never abandon my people, but the will of the Goddess is law."

Ryenne paused again in her speech, her words settling over the amassed crowd. Mariah's mind moved too slowly, as if trudging through thick mud, as she processed the queen's words.

Did she say the morning of the Autumnal Equinox? Twenty-one years ago?

Mariah had been born that very same evening. But she knew her mother began her labor early that morning, struggling all day to bring her stubborn daughter into the world.

A mere coincidence. Mariah would not—*could* not—consider anything else.

Survive this Choosing. Board a ship. Finally leave.

The mantra again spun through Mariah's mind like thread on a loom.

Ryenne's soft, strong voice pulled her back.

"Now, today, we complete the process that began not so long ago, on a warm autumn night. The drop of my magic that slipped from me now resides in one of you. Today, I will let the rest of my magic seek out and find its missing piece, that single morsel guided by Qhohena herself to find her next Chosen. Have no fear; the magic is harmless. It belongs to the Goddess, and to her people offers only life and light.

Open your hearts, your souls, and let her power wash over you."

It might be considered by some to be blasphemous, but opening her heart and soul to this was the absolute *last* thing Mariah wanted to do at that moment.

Ryenne lifted her arms just as her words finished ringing out through the throne room, and droplets of golden light began to pour from her fingertips, dropping to the dais floor before coiling, twisting in the air, beautiful as it danced in the sunlight of the throne room, a shimmering stream of gold. Mariah gazed at the golden light in a daze, and for a moment everything slipped from her mind. It was enchanting, intoxicating in the way it moved through the air. She forgot where she was, too enraptured by Ryenne's—*Qhohena's*—magic to notice that *thing* stirring in her gut once again.

Not until she felt a firm hand grip her arm.

Ciana's tight grasp snapped her back to the earth, her hiss in Mariah's ear making her blood run cold.

"*Mariah,*" Ciana whispered, "how are you *glowing?*"

Mariah's blood pounded in her ears as she spared a glance down at her body, her own hiss of surprise slipping through her teeth as she saw that Ciana's words were true—she *was* glowing. Faintly, subtly, but it was there: a subtle glow coated her entire body, the light refracting off of the gold material of her dress.

"*Fuck,*" she hissed frantically through her teeth. She clenched her jaw and shut her eyes, forcing her attention back inside herself where that *thing* continued to wind and twist around her gut. A *thing* very quickly beginning to cause her blood to boil into her anger, a *thing* far too close from ruining every plan she'd dreamed of for herself.

Deep breaths, M. Mariah inhaled once and let it out again, slowly. On instinct alone, she reached invisible hands within herself and slowly, too slow, grabbed hold of that mass, noting for a distracted moment how it all looked so distinctly silver. With a desperate push, she wrapped her consciousness around that mass of silver, forcing it back into the great pit in her soul where it had crawled out from. She struggled for a moment, a battle of wills taking place on some other plane of existence, but soon felt the foreign tickling in her veins begin to subside, felt Ciana's tight grip on her arm began to relax. She cracked an eye open, and relief washed over her as she saw she was no longer glowing; the only light coming from her was the sunlight above reflecting off her shimmering dress. Her hands shook slightly as she released them from where they were clenched into fists at her side.

What in the name of the Goddess was that?

Ciana's sharp intake of breath beside Mariah ripped her thoughts away from her inner turmoil, wishing with raw desperation that this could all be over and she could leave this damned throne room. She was so close, *so close* to getting what she wanted, from putting as many leagues as she could from herself and the town that had broken her. Slowly, she widened her eyes, lifting her head up to take in her surroundings.

What she saw made her heart freeze into a block of ice.

The golden stream of magic from the queen had been winding its way through the amassed women, dipping in and out of rows, playfully grazing cheeks before moving on. Searching for its missing drop, the single piece it had waited so long to see again.

It was now only five rows in front of where Ciana and Mariah stood.

Mariah stood as still as a statue, her heart thawing and pounding incessantly in her ears, her hands shaking.

Calm yourself, Mariah. There is no way it's you. Just stay still, and let it move on, and then you can leave.

That golden stream kept coming, twisting and turning gracefully in the air above them. Mariah held both her breath and her body completely still as it passed directly overhead, not seeming at all to recognize her presence. The second it passed, Mariah let out a shuddering exhale, her shoulders sagging at least six inches in relief. She felt a grin twist at her lips, and she turned to Ciana, ready to whisper her relief to her new friend.

But then. It stirred. Not that silver mass she'd fought since the morning of her twenty-first birthday, the power that had lit up her skin no more than a few moments earlier, but something ... *else*. Something warmer, softer, gentler. A delicate golden flower hidden amongst a mass of silver vines all knotted together in the core of Mariah's being.

Before Mariah could realize what was happening, shock slowing her reaction, that delicate golden thread snuck out of the tightly wound ball it was concealed within, rising into her veins and filling her with a warming, soothing power.

As if lightning bolted into the throne room, the shimmering golden magic above whipped itself back, retreating from the rows behind Mariah with a *snap* that sounded like a pebble being tossed into water. It jolted itself back to Mariah, growing taunt before drawing up and staring at her from above like a Vathan viper poised to strike. Mariah felt the threat, her instincts screaming as she let the challenge rise in her blood.

But that calming, golden thread within her again appeared, melting into Mariah's emotions, wrapping her soul up in a gentle, soothing embrace. The sudden tenderness caught Mariah so off guard she felt her wariness drop, her walls fall, her guarded nature broken.

And then suddenly, her body was no longer her own.

She saw her hand outstretched above her, but never remembered lifting it.

She took a step forward, but never remembered moving her feet.

The stream of light above her head danced, winding in joyous celebration. It slowly drifted down towards Mariah's outstretched and open palm, coyly winding closer to where she stood.

The second it met the tips of Mariah's fingers, the world ignited.

CHAPTER 8

Queen Ryenne of House Shawth, tenth Queen of Onita, could only watch as her magic poured out of her and into that beautiful, dark-haired young woman in the center of the throne room, golden power exploding in the air around them.

Even at her own Choosing, the magic hadn't reacted so enthusiastically. Now, it was as if the floodgates were opened, those golden drops of liquid magic draining out of her faster than she could've ever prepared for. She knew there would be pain—the magic was so closely tied to her very essence, wound tightly with her life-force, it felt as if a part of her soul were being wrenched away—but hadn't expected anything such as *this*. Distantly, she felt a nudge from her thoughts, reminding her that she had to hold tight to just enough to hold her throne, to keep her Armature by her side, to see the ascension of this new queen.

But ... she could not stop that magic from pouring out. The river in her soul felt so thrilled, so free, so full of new life and raw exuberance as it streamed across the throne room. And that young woman to whom it fled ... Ryenne had spotted her the moment she'd walked into the room. Not only was she dressed in a gown of liquid gold, so different from every other woman here, but the way she'd carried herself ...

Goddess bless them all.

With every passing heartbeat, she felt the pool of magic within her draining. Experience alone told her where it must stop, exactly where the bottom of that well lay. The moment she felt it begin to bottom out, mere dregs compared to what had lived in her mere seconds before, Ryenne clamped down *hard* on the magic pouring from her, barricading it like a dam. The few drops of magic that remained shuddered, disappointed at being held back, but Ryenne's block held firm.

The light igniting the throne room in an ethereal glow had ceased, the early autumn sunlight streaming in from the glass ceiling above a cold shadow in comparison. The dark-haired woman had dropped to her knees, panting heavily. A blonde-haired woman next to her had dropped as well, gripping her shoulders and whispering frantically into her ear. Ryenne steeled herself with a breath and pulled the scraps of her magic close, the only remaining comfort from her Goddess.

She had waited over twenty-one years for this.

It was time to meet her successor.

Ryenne gathered her heavy velvet skirts in her hands and descended the dais. The crowd parted before her, and with a grace taught by centuries of practice, she strode through the throne room to where the dark-haired girl knelt, her golden gown pooling around her knees, her companion still holding her tight. Ryenne halted directly before them, and the golden-haired girl looked up, meeting the queen's stare with a fierce amber gaze. Ryenne held that stare for three heartbeats before tilting her head, an indication to the girl that she meant no harm, to step back so she could approach. The girl still hesitated, appearing torn, before conceding, standing to her feet and stepping back into the gathered crowd with a final, worried glance back at her dark-haired friend.

Curious, Ryenne thought, *for someone to inspire the kind of loyalty to consider defying a queen for.*

Turning her attention back to the dark-haired woman, she gathered her skirts up in her hands once more and, with a fluid movement, dropped to her knees. She heard a few soft gasps at her back but paid them no mind; this young woman with an air of wildness about her was now an equal, soon to be a Queen of Onita, Chosen by the Goddess herself.

For her, Ryenne would kneel without hesitation.

She placed her right hand on the woman's golden-tanned arm, the skin beneath her fingers warm and feverish. The woman lifted her head, and eyes of brilliant forest green met her own, eyes shimmering with all the ancient power of Onita itself. Something in them instilled both awe and fear in Ryenne, enough to make her blood run cold, even as her skin prickled with warmth.

This woman would walk a path none had gone before.

And … that frightened her.

Ryenne held that forest-green gaze as she spoke to the woman softly, gently. "What is your name?"

Those glowing eyes blinked, the magic roaring in their depths burning brighter. "Mariah Salis."

Only the centuries of court politicking kept Ryenne's shudder from escaping her lips. *Salis* was not a name she knew. *She's common born. Not Royal.* Her fear settled deeper, growing claws and turning her veins to stone. She kept her features schooled into neutrality, however; no matter who this woman was—or wasn't—the magic of the Goddess had claimed her.

And Ryenne, if nothing else, had to trust in that.

"Will you stand with me, Mariah?"

The woman blinked again before nodding slowly, the long strands of her near-black hair shifting over her shoulders. Ryenne reached out her left hand, her right still resting on Mariah's forearm, and pulled the girl to her feet. They rose together, unified for just a moment by the magic that dwelled in their veins. Mariah let Ryenne lead her back through the still-parted crowds to the front of the throne room, up the dais steps, until they stood between the shimmering *lunestair* pillars, the golden throne at their backs. Ryenne's skin scratched with the familiar weight of thousands of gazes. Beside her, the air seemed to vibrate around Mariah, and she noticed the girl's hands were clenched into fists at her sides, desperate to hide the tremor coursing through her. Despite the clear panic surrounding her like a shadow, Mariah kept her face still, a mask of cold, calm indifference.

All of it filled Ryenne with an interesting combination of worry and fascination.

Ryenne gently released her grip on Mariah, gathering her skirts in her hands before turning to face the crowd at her back. Without being prompted, the young woman beside her followed her lead, her chin held high in a look of pure, wild defiance.

Despite herself, despite the intensity of the moment, Ryenne found herself barely able to suppress a grin. She saw so much of her younger self in this woman.

So much of herself and yet ... so little, all at the same time.

Ryenne returned her attention to the throne room and the masses gathered before them. The air was heavy and viscous as the crowd stood frozen, their expectant gazes written with shock as they beheld the two women on the dais. The queen flashed a brilliant smile, her own presence slogging through the weight of the room.

She suddenly felt so weighted, so tired. She forced it away, forced herself to be their queen, pushed every scrap of royal exuberance she had left out into that cavernous room.

"And so it is done. Qhohena, in her brilliant wisdom, has made her choice known."

She turned her gaze and her smile to the woman beside her. Mariah's face was still a mask of pure indifference, but there was something else there, hidden deep in her green eyes.

It looked a lot like shock and a little like fear.

With a sudden, wild desperation, Ryenne shot a brief, pleading prayer to her goddess.

Guide her, Qhohena. She will need it.

Looking back out at the throne room, Ryenne finished her address.

"I present to you all, for the very first time, the new Queen Apparent of Onita: Mariah Salis."

CHAPTER 9

Mariah sat at a great, wooden counsel table, its surface polished and gleaming, the sound of a great fire crackling and popping in the magnificent hearth, and had no idea how she'd gotten there.

She remembered Queen Ryenne's words: "*I present to you all, for the very first time, the new Queen Apparent of Onita: Mariah Salis.*" After that, nothing. She must've moved, gone through the motions to lead her to where she now sat, but she remembered none of it. Her mind was swarmed by the sound of buzzing bees, all threatening to burst out of her and drown out the room in a tidal wave of confusion and fear and *anger*.

So much anger.

This wasn't supposed to happen.

Slowly, she became aware of the weight of eyes on her. She turned her head slightly and found the blonde-haired queen seated to her right, staring at her, a guarded expression on her ageless face. Around the rest of the room—which was a sort of office—lounged Queen Ryenne's Armature, the warriors intimidating yet graceful as they, too, watched her closely. The high priestess, Ksee, was also there, hanging back against a far wall, her posture poised and practiced.

"Leave us." The queen's command was quiet yet full of authority. Mariah couldn't help but sit up straighter.

Even that small movement sent a wave of nausea rolling through her gut.

Ryenne's Armature rose at once, quietly filing out of the oak office doors without hesitation. Ksee lingered momentarily, her piercing gaze darting between Ryenne and Mariah. Ryenne leveled a pointed look at the priestess, a look that had Ksee pursing her lips slightly, casting a final, veiled look at Mariah, and stepping quietly from the room.

It only took a few heartbeats for the room to empty, leaving only Mariah, Ryenne, and a third figure: Kalen, Ryenne's Consort. Curiosity pushed just barely through the haze of her anger and confusion, taking note of his light brown, slightly unkempt hair, his warm brown eyes flicking between his queen and Mariah, the gentle and reassuring smile touching his lips. She watched him place a hand on Ryenne's shoulder, tilting her head just slightly as she watched the Queen and her Consort share a moment.

That sort of love ... it was curious to her. She'd only seen the love her parents shared, but they had the lives of mortals, such fleeting existences compared to the two people who now stood before her.

Kalen and Ryenne had been together for over three *centuries*. That length of time, that sort of commitment, was unfathomable to Mariah. The thought of sharing so much life with anyone sent a shiver crawling up her spine, slimy disgust resting in her chest.

That sort of love could only be a weakness.

"I'll be outside," Kalen said, his soft voice tugging Mariah from her distaste and curiosity and back into her resting state of confused, panicked rage. Her pulse again began to race in her ears as she watched Ryenne nod once, her ocean-blue stare never leaving Mariah. With a soft smile directed at Mariah, a smile that she aptly ignored, Kalen walked out through the same office doors the rest had stepped through, clicking them closed behind him.

The two women sat in silence for several moments that felt like a lifetime. Mariah was swirling, spiraling, her racing heart only picking up speed the longer she held the queen's stare. The walls of the room felt like they were beginning to close in, pushing and pushing until they were squeezing the air from her lungs and crushing the bones of her body and—

"So. Mariah Salis. Where are you from?"

The queen's question was a jolt, a gentle slap that snapped Mariah back to reality. Her panic and rage suddenly withdrew to rest just below her skin, coiled in her veins, but for the moment contained.

"Andburgh." She didn't even know she was answering until the word left her lips. Her voice sounded strange in her ears, as if she were trapped underwater, clawing desperately for the surface.

Ryenne tensed slightly, and Mariah zeroed her attention on the movement. That curiosity twisted again, and she latched onto it like a lifeline; anything was better than these foreign, suffocating feelings holding her captive. "Andburgh," the queen said. "Interesting. The Crossroad City."

Mariah nodded, watching Ryenne warily and holding back her instinctive scoff that begged to be released. Andburgh was hardly a city; more like a useless, tired piece of dirt that happened to sit where two main roads collided.

Ryenne continued, "And your parents? What do they do?"

Mariah's voice again came out icy and flat, but at least the questions looping through her brain about the queen, about what she was thinking, kept her grounded enough to push the words from her mouth. "My mother is one of the town healers. My father used to be a member of the Royal Infantry, but retired after the last war in the Everheim Mountains."

Ryenne was still tense as she watched Mariah, her guarded expression holding her thoughts close. "So ... you're a commoner then, right? You're not Royal?"

That question finally snapped something in Mariah, her intrigue with the queen breaking back down into her instinctive, coiled rage.

She was a cornered animal, after all. Forced into a situation she'd thought impossible, still refusing to believe it to be real. Still convinced she could fight her way out.

Just then, she felt something stir deep in her gut. A ball of silver, beginning to unknot and unwind through her veins. An orb of gold, unspooling and wrapping around her heart, her soul. She sat up straighter, and knew, somehow, that her eyes were blazing with more than just her fear and anger.

She gave herself no opportunity to think before she levied that glowing gaze at the queen. "Of course I'm not Royal. There are no Royals in Andburgh. And thank the gods for that."

Just the thought of the group of near-nobility who held most of the wealth and nearly as much power in Onita had Mariah fighting back a snarl from her face. The Royals were families which, at some point, had a daughter who'd been Chosen as a Queen of Onita. Of the ten previous queens, Ryenne included, all but the first had come from one of the seven Royal families. Ryenne's own family, House Shawth, was the most prevalent and powerful of the Royals: three queens were from House Shawth, and the family enjoyed considerable power from its seat in Khento, just north of Andburgh. The power of Royal blood was so revered in Onita that most believed it simply impossible for a queen to be Chosen outside of those who held the power.

Mariah nearly gagged on the thought. She'd known her escape was too easy. Of course, she should've known she would end up being a walking, breathing impossibility.

Her statement continued to echo through the office, and a look of shock—or maybe fear?—passed over Ryenne's features. It vanished, though, and the mask of the most powerful woman in the kingdom once again took its place. Ryenne glanced quickly around her, scanning the office once before her eyes darted to the door. A light knock rapped against the heavy wood, and Mariah couldn't suppress her flinch of surprise, the new feeling cooling the rage in her blood, just enough to inhale a shaky, whispery breath.

Ryenne glanced back at Mariah. "It's just Kalen. The room is secure," she said. Mariah furrowed her brow at the Queen.

Secure ... from what?

A smile ghosted across the queen's full lips, as if she read the words Mariah left unspoken.

"We have quite a bit to discuss, you and I."

"To begin," Ryenne said, "what do you know about an Onitan Queen's Armature?"

Mariah cocked her head warily. "Only what we're all taught in schooling: that they are warriors bonded to the queen."

Just as she said those words, she felt a new feeling wash over her, melding with and chilling her anger, just a bit more. Something stronger than curiosity.

She was suddenly *intrigued* by the queen's intent to discuss the Armature. With everything that happened in the past few minutes, of all the upheaval that caused her world to spin, she hadn't had a chance to think about everything this new situation could entail.

Ryenne nodded. "Yes, that is the basic premise of it. They receive a piece of their queen's magic, an act which creates a permanent bridge between their souls. He is then granted the same near-immortal life of his queen, as well as the benefits of a mental connection to her. I can speak to them, in a way, mind to mind; not with words, but with emotions, with feelings."

Ah. So that explained the soft knock on the door. The assurance Ryenne was able to give that it was only Kalen. More fascination prickled in Mariah's mind, her anger receding back just an inch more.

"The bond of an Armature serves to strengthen a queen," Ryenne continued. "Not until a Queen has bonded to all seven of her Armature may she ascend the throne and proceed with her coronation. Their strength becomes hers, and their unquestionable loyalty and protection guards her back better than any normal soldier ever could."

Mariah could only stare at the queen as she spoke, her curiosity slipping and her anger rising once again. This ... this wasn't her life. This wasn't what she wanted, what she'd risked *everything* for. She was meant to have walked back out of this palace today, to grab the sack of coin she'd left with her father at Beva's inn and board a ship, to sail across the Mirrored Sea to the Kizar Islands. To whatever land lay beyond.

It was an impossibility that she'd been meant to be here. Sitting alone with the Queen of Onita, discussing bonds and Armatures and thrones and coronations.

"Mariah."

The queen's voice was sharp, as if she'd watched Mariah drift away and into herself, much the way Mariah's mother often caught her doing. It cut through Mariah's dark haze like a knife, yanking her back to Ryenne's sharp stare of ocean blue. The Queen didn't appear shocked by whatever she saw reflected back at her in Mariah's own eyes, her expression instead softening with quiet understanding. Ryenne heaved a deep breath, even as Mariah remained tense, gripping the arms of her chair.

"I am sorry. I know this is likely unfathomable to you. I doubt it even feels real. I was raised from birth in anticipation of being Chosen as queen, and even still I remember the shock I felt at my Choosing like it was yesterday." A shadow danced in her eyes, vanishing as quickly as it appeared. Mariah didn't respond, sitting frozen as the queen continued.

"But, Mariah, listen to me. This *is* real. Whether you want to believe it yet or not." Ryenne's voice sharpened, deepened, and goosebumps rose on Mariah's skin. *This* was the 300-year-old ruler of an ancient and powerful kingdom. "I have only known you for a few minutes, but I know my Goddess. Therefore, I know you. Who you are, on the inside. You are *strong*. You will be exactly what this kingdom needs, or else you would not have been Chosen. And believe me, this kingdom *needs* a strong queen. One that Qhohena knows I could never be."

Mariah blinked, those words again ripping through her silence. "What do you mean? Onita has been at peace for the entirety of your reign. 300 years is young for an Onitan queen. This never should have happened; not in my lifetime. So, why now? And, just ... why *me*?" Mariah recoiled as her voice broke on that last word, fear raising its twisted head and, for once, wrestling control from her anger.

Ryenne's gaze softened again, her expression turning almost sad, something that could've been regret shining behind her eyes. "Onita has been at peace and I have succeeded as its queen because of my family, not because of me or anything I have done. And trust me, I am smart enough to recognize that as the weakness it is." She paused, taking a deep breath. "Which brings me back to you. A commoner from the Crossroads. Not a Royal with a wealthy, powerful family behind you."

Mariah's gaze hardened. "Yeah, we discussed that already. And I'm not entirely sure why it matters." *Especially since I'm not supposed to be here.*

Ryenne suddenly leaned forward, grabbed Mariah's hands in her own, and pulled her close. "Mariah," she began, her blue eyes urgent and insistent. "Listen to me. If you take nothing else from me, take this. Your ascension to the throne will not be easy. Much of what is in this kingdom is not as it seems. You must select and bond with your Armature—*all* of your Armature—as quickly as possible to protect yourself and Qhohena's magic. I can do nothing to stop the politics of this kingdom from seeking its own agendas. You must rely upon those Qhohena gifts you with to protect yourself."

Mariah blinked, her blood rushing cold at the urgency in the queen's voice. "What ... I'm confused. I don't understand. I don't *want* this. It can't be—"

At that moment, a sharp rap sounded on the study doors. Ryenne released Mariah's hands and sat back, the cool mask of the powerful queen slipping back into place over her features. Kalen reentered the room first, his eyes immediately glancing between his queen and Mariah. There was something shadowed glinting in their warm brown, a shadow so like what had passed through Ryenne's eyes just a few moments earlier. Behind him, the High Priestess strode into the room, an imperious look on her face. Her tarnished gold gaze also darted between Mariah and Ryenne, but ultimately rested on Mariah with a look of bland, subtle interest.

"I apologize for the interruption, Your Majesty, but we must discuss the plan for our new ... guest." Mariah bristled at the pause in Ksee's words, as if the priestess couldn't settle on what to call her.

She might not want to be there, but after what had happened, she knew she was more than just some *guest*. She opened her mouth to speak, but Ryenne responded first.

"It's quite alright, Ksee." The queen's voice sounded different as she spoke to the Priestess, her tone older, firmer. "Mariah and I were just finishing up. We needed a few moments alone, just queen to queen apparent."

Ksee turned her attention back to Mariah, a sneering smile twisting her face. "It is indeed such a special day. The tenth queen apparent to our great kingdom, and soon to be the eleventh queen. Your family must be so proud."

Something hidden in Ksee's words made Mariah's skin crawl, and her tongue again loosened before she could clamp down on her self-control. "Yes, my healer mother and soldier father will be so thrilled to learn of our new *blessing*."

More like a curse.

Ksee went eerily still, her gaze boring into Mariah with such unequivocal intensity before shooting to Ryenne. "She is not Royal?" Ksee paused, taking in Ryenne's stony expression. "You already knew."

Ryenne looked at Mariah with thinly controlled frustration. "Yes, Mariah and I were just discussing her family when you came in. They hail from Andburgh, the Crossroad City."

Ksee's glittering, cold mask didn't falter as she nodded, only once, those piercing eyes still watching Mariah. She looked ready to speak on the subject further, but ultimately decided to hold her tongue. Ignoring Ksee and her cold, curious response, Ryenne spoke again.

"And we were also discussing Mariah's Armature selection. It is one of the most important steps a new queen apparent must take. The sooner we can arrange it, the better." Pausing again, Ryenne turned her gaze from Mariah to Ksee. "As long as our training goes smoothly tomorrow, I would like to see if it can take place tomorrow evening. Can you ensure it is so?"

Ksee blanched slightly, but merely bowed her head. "That is a rather quick timeline, Your Majesty, but her Marked have trained years for this. I am sure we can have what we need ready in time."

Ryenne nodded once. "See that it is." Ksee bowed her head to the queen, then turned on her heel and slipped back out of the office, all but ignoring Mariah as she left. Once the priestess departed, the queen returned her attention to Mariah, the mask of the Queen slipped slightly as she beheld the dark-haired young woman. Mariah met her stare, unflinching, wondering what more could possibly be thrown at her today.

"There is one more thing, Mariah, that we must discuss."

Unsurprised, Mariah sat still, waiting, trying to hide the heavy beat of her heart.

Unexpectedly, Ryenne's face broke into a smile. "Every queen, and queen apparent, is permitted to appoint up to six Ladies to serve in her court. I would like to see you make that first appointment now, if possible. Is there anyone who you would like to be the first to join your new court?"

There was not a single moment of hesitation for Mariah. She'd only known the girl for a few hours, but there was no one else she wanted by her side.

If she would be stuck in an impossible situation, then at least she could bring the first female friend she'd ever had along with her.

Plus, this would be much better than serving as a life-sized cake-topper.

"There was a blonde girl who stood next to me at the Choosing. Gold hair, amber eyes, lilac gown. Her name is Ciana. I appoint her."

CHAPTER 10

Somehow, Ryenne's staff managed to locate Ciana. Whether she hadn't yet left the palace, or if they knew where to look for her in the city, no one said, and Mariah didn't ask when the blonde-haired woman, still dressed in that massive, lilac gown, finally rushed into Ryenne's study and swept Mariah up into a hug.

Mariah clenched the other girl tight, Ciana's embrace grounding her, a reminder that there was still some sense of *normal* to be found in her new prison. There was something about Ciana, so full of bubbling and sparkling personality that allowed Mariah to momentarily forget about what had happened and what was coming and just *be*.

With a final squeeze, Ciana pulled away slowly from Mariah. She met her friend's stare, scrutinizing Mariah as if she were an ant under a magnifying glass. Her gaze was sharp when she finally spoke.

"I always expected to be more impressed when meeting a queen."

Mariah froze, for just a heartbeat, before a slow grin spread across her face.

"Good thing I'm most definitely not a queen. Still plenty of time for you to become impressed." Just as Mariah said those words, Ryenne, who'd stepped into the room shortly after Ciana, softly cleared her throat. Ciana went rigid, and Mariah huffed a soft laugh as her friend hastily twisted herself to face the queen. The golden-haired girl immediately bowed her head, gathering her lilac skirts as she curtsied low to Ryenne.

"Your Majesty, my apologies. I didn't hear you arrive. You are every bit as regal and powerful as I expected." Ciana paused, rising from her curtsy, lifting her head just enough to look back at Mariah. "Truly, it's this one who could use some work."

Ryenne smiled broadly, flashing white teeth as she laughed quietly. "I beg to differ. She's already far more impressive than I was after my own Choosing." Both Ciana and Mariah snapped their attention to the queen, who only regarded them both with that same soft amusement. She stepped closer to Mariah's friend, regarding her sharply.

"Ciana, is it?"

Mariah moved to stand beside Ciana, noticing her eyes had gone wide. "Yes, Your Majesty."

Ryenne tilted her head to the side, her pale blonde hair shifting across the red velvet of her gown. After a moment, she moved her stare to Mariah, something like approval shimmering in her ocean-blue gaze.

"Good choice."

Shock poked at Mariah's skin before fizzling out into something close to ... pride?

It felt good, she suddenly realized, to be praised by the queen. To know she'd done something right, passed this first test she hadn't known she'd been taking.

She was still furious, still so angry and full of fear and confusion, but ... maybe, just maybe, this would be okay. She was out of Andburgh, after all. She had a new friend who she could trust, someone to joke with and speak to. It also wasn't lost on her that here, in this palace, she could have *power*.

And power ... power could bring anything. Even freedom.

Suddenly, a loud grumble ripped from Mariah's stomach into the dead silence of the room, wrenching Mariah from her musings. Her smile instantly fell as she grimaced, a hand touching her stomach lightly. Her mind raced, and she realized that it was now likely near noon, and she hadn't eaten anything since her dinner at Beva's the night before.

The silence now shattered, Ciana burst out laughing, nearly doubling over in her hysterics, the sound like tinkling bells ringing through the room. Ryenne chuckled again and took a step forward, gesturing toward the table in the room.

"Come, let's enjoy lunch," said the queen. "I'll have food brought up and we can eat here. Then we can focus on getting you—*both* of you—settled into your new rooms."

"This is ... this is *mine*?"

Beside her, Ciana brusquely hit Mariah's shoulder with her own. "Don't question it, you idiot," Ciana hissed. "If you don't want to move in here, I'll gladly take it instead."

A chuckle came from behind them as Ryenne glided around the two young women. "Yes, Mariah, this is yours." She paused, looking around the grand foyer. "These are the traditional quarters for the queen. Every queen since Xara has resided here."

Mariah's attention snapped to Ryenne. "If these are the queen's quarters, then where are you living at the moment?"

"Don't worry about me." While the queen's voice was commanding in a manner that didn't invite further questions, she elaborated with a gentle glance back at Mariah. "There are dozens of expansive guest quarters in the palace for visiting lords, ambassadors, and other high-ranking members of the ruling class. My Armature and I will be residing there until your coronation."

Mariah narrowed her gaze at Ryenne. "And what about *after* my coronation? What will happen to you all then?"

True sadness crept into Ryenne's expression. "Don't trouble yourself with that, Mariah. My Armature and I will be fine, and that is all you need to know."

"Queen Ryenne ... I can't move in here knowing these were your quarters. I have no interest in kicking you all out of your home." *I have no interest in being here at all.*

The words were there, on the tip of her tongue, ready to be spoken. But for some reason, Mariah held back. Swallowed them down. Pushed them away.

"Do not argue with me on this, Mariah." Ryenne's voice was firm. "These plans were made long before you arrived here today. These quarters will be yours, and your Armature, once selected, will take up residence in the seven other quarters in this hallway. That is final."

Mariah stared into Ryenne's hard, ocean eyes for a long moment before conceding, dipping her head to the queen. "Yes, Your Majesty." Her gaze then wandered around the resplendent foyer, finally allowing herself to soak in the space she was now to call *home*. "I *suppose* I can tolerate living here," she said, a smile ghosting her lips. Beside her, Ciana squealed in delight before taking off into the suite, a blur of lilac and gold.

They'd walked through a set of beautiful white double doors, gold detailing depicting a map of Onita, into a grand foyer of more white and gold. The left wall of the foyer ran straight into the open living space beyond, but to the right, behind a set of glass paneled doors, was what appeared to be a comfortable sitting room, filled with plush couches, chairs, and white fur rugs. A gilded fireplace was built into the far wall, and just to its right was a bar, stocked full of decanters of various shapes and sizes and colors.

"Oh, my *Goddess*, Mariah." Ciana's near-groan from the room beyond the foyer pulled Mariah's attention away from the sitting room. She made a mental note to inspect those decanters and their contents later that evening.

No matter what else happened that day, she already knew she would need a drink.

She stepped forward, Ryenne by her side, until she passed through the great archway at the other end of the foyer hallway and sucked in her breath.

The room was magnificent and unlike anything she'd ever seen. Cavernous in size, the open living area perfectly combined regal luxury with livable comfort. The far wall consisted entirely of windows, the Attlehons beyond ancient and glorious. There were glass doors placed throughout the far wall leading out to what Mariah could see was a massive outdoor space, a patio with outdoor seating offering an even closer vantage of the magnificent view.

As her gaze focused back on the interior of the space, Mariah's attention snagged on a collection of giant, plush couches, obviously designed to host more than just herself. Closer to the foyer was a great dining table, the dark gray of the wood perfectly complementing the white and gold of the marble floors and, of course, the kitchen.

The *kitchen*. That was where Mariah's stare eventually rested, what caused her jaw to hang open. It consisted of smooth, white marble countertops that wrapped around the entire left corner of the living space, an island also topped with that same white marble in its center. The cabinetry was painted a gray so dark it was almost black, the hardware a gleaming gold. A massive *allume*-powered stove and oven were set into the countertops, a great porcelain basin sink in the island.

Mariah didn't consider herself a chef by any means, but as she stared at that kitchen and the plush, gray barstools at the island, she couldn't help but daydream about slow mornings, eating breakfast at the island bar as she watched the sunrise reflect off the Attlehons beyond the windows.

It was suddenly difficult for her to remember why the events of that day were so bad. Why she'd felt so much fear and anger.

If she hadn't been Chosen, she would be on some rickety old merchant's vessel, breathing in the smell of fish and brine. She wouldn't be calling this stunning space *hers*.

"This is ... incredible." Mariah was breathless as she turned to look at Ryenne. The Queen had moved through the room to stand beside another set of double doors across from the kitchen area. Twisting back at Mariah's words, a smile on her lips, Ryenne inclined her head towards the doors. Mariah padded over to her, Ciana scampering through the balcony doors from where she'd been marveling at the patio space outside. Once Mariah and Ciana joined her, Ryenne turned, pushing open those double doors on silent, well-oiled hinges.

Somehow, impossibly, the room beyond those doors managed to put the living area to shame. It was a bedroom, but Mariah's head spun at the simple decadence. A massive, four-poster bed sat against the far wall, the frame made of the same dark gray wood as the dining table and chairs. The floors beneath their feet were covered in soft, white rugs, and the bed was draped with a pale gray down comforter and several gray and gold throw blankets, white silk sheets just visible beneath piles of fabric. To the left of the bed was another window, this one not opening to the patio beyond but instead equipped with a seat beneath, a reading nook made cozy with cushions and more gilded cashmere blankets.

To the right was yet another door, this one sitting on a rolling track like a barn door rather than traditional hinges. Of their own volition, Mariah's feet carried her to that door, pushing it open to reveal a space that felt wrong to just call a *bathroom*.

"And this," Ryenne said, stepping up beside Mariah, "is my favorite room in the entire palace." Mariah could only nod weakly, her mouth hanging open in an undignified expression.

The floor was again that same white marble veined with gold, and the right wall was made entirely of mirrors with an expansive vanity constructed beneath the reflective surfaces. Mariah met her reflection once in those mirrors, unadulterated shock written across her face, before ripping her gaze away to take in the rest of the room. In the back left corner sat a massive shower walled in by glass, the tiled interior along with the three shower heads screaming of opulence and royalty. But it was the final fixture in the room that had the world beneath Mariah's feet tilting on its axis.

She supposed, in some way, she could call it a bathtub. Lined with *allume*-powered jets, ledges, and seats, it could easily fit at least three people. It was decadent, outrageous, and somehow … *sinful*. Mariah couldn't deny how her body heated with curiosity at that last thought, at the idea that maybe, just maybe, she would be able to hold on to all the wild little pieces that made up her soul.

Before she could spiral too far down that train of thought, Ciana's bright voice chimed out behind her, her question making Mariah smile.

"So … where's the closet?"

The closet, as it turned out, was hidden within the bathroom, its entrance disguised as a nook between the end of the massive vanity and the extravagant shower. After Ciana had her chance to thoroughly drool over its contents, Mariah watching on in amusement as her friend pestered Ryenne with every question under the moons, the queen finally excused herself. Ryenne informed the two women that dinner would be brought up to Mariah's rooms within the hour before she slipped out the white and gold doors to the suite.

Ciana had tasked herself with digging through all of the cabinets in the kitchen, her occasional exclamation echoing through the room, which left Mariah alone in her new bedroom. She glanced down at herself and realized with a jolt she still wore her shimmering golden gown, her strappy heeled shoes still on her feet. In a rushed movement, she slipped off the shoes, discarding them into a corner, before padding back into the closet to do some rummaging of her own. She wondered for a moment when—if—she would be able to retrieve her belongings from Beva. The thought had her freezing in her tracks.

Beva's inn. Her father. Mariah had told the queen he'd traveled with her and where he'd been staying, expectantly awaiting her return. She was sure Ryenne had sent a messenger to inform him of the events of the day, but Mariah desperately wanted the chance to speak with him. To listen to his laugh. To hear his advice on what was now to be her future, whether she wanted it to be or not.

Mariah pushed away her rising panic. She *would* get to see her father again. If this afternoon had shown her anything, it was that she wasn't a prisoner here.

She was to be a *queen*. It wasn't what she'd wanted, but she couldn't deny the advantages that kept materializing before her.

Grabbing two sets of soft leggings and two oversized cotton tunics from some drawers in her ridiculous closet, Mariah stripped out of her golden dress, leaving it in a gilded pile on the floor. She slipped into one pair of leggings and a tunic before grabbing the other set in her hands and padding out into the living room.

"Hey, I think that's enough," Mariah said to her friend, a laugh in her voice. Ciana's golden head popped up from behind the island, her hair wild and her amber eyes bright. Mariah tossed the extra leggings and tunic over the back of one of the couches. "I found some extra clothes for you, if you have any desire to get out of that monstrosity you keep calling a gown."

Ciana ignored the insult, pushing her golden waves out of her face. "Thank you! I was just about to ask." She stood and walked out of the kitchen, grabbing the leggings and tunic from the couch. She stopped in front of Mariah for a moment, her expression so bright and full of excitement that Mariah couldn't help but grin back.

"Mariah," she said, "I found a *waffle-maker* in this kitchen."

Mariah giggled, just once. "By the Goddess, I fucking *love* waffles."

Ciana squealed. "Me too!" And then she took off towards Mariah's rooms to remove herself from her too-big gown, stepping back out twenty minutes later, red-faced and breathless but dressed finally in the comfortable clothes Mariah had lent her.

As promised, their dinner arrived about an hour after Ryenne's departure, a warm beef stew with carrots, potatoes, and onions, a loaf of fresh baked bread and an assortment of steamed vegetables on the side. It was clear the palace chefs were leaning heavily on the abundance of the harvest season, the meal an ode to this time of plenty that would last until winter swept its way across the continent.

Mariah and Ciana sat together at the kitchen island, eating their fill and chatting, building the bonds of true friendship between them as the sky darkened with the passing hours. It was decided that, just for the night, Ciana would stay with Mariah in these suites; tomorrow, she would move into a suite of her own in the next hall over, the wing reserved for the Queen's Ladies.

"You're not mad, are you? That I've now made this your home, too?" It had been a question nagging at the back of Mariah's mind, a steady guilt that had grown and grown as the hours passed since she'd spoken Ciana's name to Ryenne in that office.

Ciana was thoughtful for a moment, her face uncharacteristically serious, before she turned and met Mariah's gaze.

"No," she said, her voice quiet. "I'm not mad. Truthfully, I never had any intention of going home after the Choosing. I'm glad that you gave me an easy way to stay, so I wouldn't have to run."

Mariah's blood chilled at the tone in her friend's voice. It sounded so unlike her, so lacking in her usual luster and sparkle. She swallowed hard before answering.

"It seems you and I have more in common than just our new home."

Ciana gave her a sad, somber smile. "While I'm beyond grateful that I'm now here with you, I also sincerely hope that our new home is the only common thing that we share."

Mariah held her gaze for a moment before blinking down to look at her food.

Everyone had a past. There was no point getting caught up in it now, not when everything had just changed, their futures rewritten by the gods themselves.

So, Mariah changed the subject, and chose to ignore the pain she'd seen in her friend's eyes. Instead, she opted to laugh and talk with Ciana into the late hours of the night, eventually falling asleep on the plush gray and white couches adorning the living room. Moonlight streamed in through the wall of windows, its soft caress like silver and gold fingers on Mariah's cheek as she faded into unconsciousness.

CHAPTER 11

Popping oil and soft movements, along with the salty-sweet smoke of what could only be bacon frying, pulled Mariah from the clutches of sleep, sunlight streaming through the walls of windows.

She groaned as she rolled onto her stomach on the plush couch, her legs tangling in a soft blanket, her hair a mane of darkness around her head. She opened her eyes to see Ciana rustling on another couch in the sprawling living room, her golden eyes blinking open, reflecting the same feeling of disorientation Mariah felt swimming in her head. Scrubbing at her eyes, Mariah stretched her limbs, her arms and legs sore and tight after the days spent on the road.

The night on the couch hadn't helped, either.

With another grunt, Mariah heaved herself into a sitting position, and finally turned her head towards the source of the sounds and smells that had awoken her. Her gaze was pulled to the kitchen, and she realized with a sudden jolt that they weren't alone.

A small man wearing a chef's apron around his front was

bustling around the kitchen, his wild, curly strawberry blonde hair pushed out of his face by a thin strap of worn gray cloth. He sported a youthful face that made it hard to tell his true age, his skin heavily freckled, his eyes creased with smile lines.

Mariah quietly stood from the couch as he continued to labor in the kitchen, her eyes darting to where she'd discarded her grandfather's dagger on the kitchen island the night before. It lay there, that precious piece of steel, right behind where the small man was hard at work. She watched him for a few more heartbeats, holding herself as still as a statue, before deciding her curiosity outweighed the potential threat.

After all, who could possibly touch her here, deep in the heart of the great palace? She was likely safer here than she'd ever been in her entire life.

She padded on near silent feet into the kitchen, eyes never leaving the newest arrival. As she neared, traversing the massive living space, a jaunty tune filtered over the sound of crackling bacon—*humming*. The man was humming to himself, his body swaying slightly to his music, the tune off-key and unrecognizable. Mariah continued to move closer until she stood before the kitchen island, the dagger now within an easy arm's reach. The man was oblivious to her approach, however, too immersed in the preparation of the, frankly, *glorious* breakfast coming together in that kitchen. There was even a full carafe of what appeared to be coffee, the rich aroma tickling at Mariah's nose. After a few increasingly awkward minutes, Mariah finally cleared her throat as softly as she could.

The man jumped at least a foot in the air, the utensils in his hands flying from his grip and clattering to the ground. He whirled around, meeting Mariah's gaze, his own eyes widening as he realized, finally, that he wasn't alone.

"Oi, darkness between the stars! Ya scared me half to death!" The man pressed a palm to his chest, breathing deep as his wide eyes took in Mariah, whose own expression slowly morphed from curiosity into one of pure incredulity.

"I'm ... sorry?" Mariah said, twisting her hands in front of her. "I didn't mean to startle you, but ... who are you, and what are you doing here? Did Queen Ryenne send you?"

All valid questions.

The stranger's eyes widened even further. "You ... you wouldn't happen to be Her Majesty Mariah, would ya?" His accent was thick, clearly not Onitan, but not one Mariah could place.

Not that she'd much experience with different accents.

Mariah blinked slowly at the man. *Her Majesty Mariah.* She hadn't expected that.

While she found it excessive ... she didn't hate the respect it commanded. And that shocked her more than anything that'd happened the day prior at the Choosing.

She composed herself before answering the small man. "I am, actually. Pleased to meet you, I suppose. And you would be ...?"

The man flushed a bright ruby red before bending deeply at his waist, his head nearly disappearing below the countertops. "My Queen!" He rose ever so slightly, so he could peer up at her from beneath thick strawberry blonde lashes. "Please accept my humblest apologies for the intrusion and my lack of manners. I believed ya to be in your sleeping quarters, but clearly, I was gravely mistaken." He lifted himself up fully from his bow, his head still dipped, eyes still peering up. "My name is Mikael, and I'm your appointed chef, an honor I hope to spend my entire life living up to. I'd thought Queen Ryenne had informed ya I may be coming this morning, but it appears I was mistaken. I, again, sincerely apologize for the blunt intrusion."

An appointed chef? It seemed the longer she remained here

in this palace, this place where only yesterday she dreaded beyond measure to enter, the more opportunities and amenities opened their doors to her.

If she was to give up her version of freedom, at least she'd get a personal chef in exchange.

Mariah visibly relaxed, a smile spreading across her face as she met the man's gaze. "Please, Mikael, call me Mariah. I'm sorry for startling you; Ryenne must've forgotten to inform me you would be coming, but you're welcome all the same."

The man—Mikael—finally lifted up his head, his own smile touching his merry face. "It is my deepest honor ... Mariah." And with that, he turned back to the crackling pan behind him, flipping the slices of bacon as they continued to fill the room with their salty-sweet aroma. "There is fresh coffee, imported straight from Vatha, ready for you in the carafe on the island. I do hope that bacon and omelets are acceptable to you. Does ham, cheese, and tomato sound appetizing?"

Right on cue, Mariah's stomach grumbled, the sound traveling around the kitchen. Something about this palace made her ravenous; she'd always loved to eat, but never had an appetite quite like the one she had now. "Yes, that sounds absolutely wonderful." She turned away, allowing Mikael to continue his crucial labors, only to find Ciana finally staggering up from her couch, her blonde hair framing her head like a golden halo, her eyes and lips parted slightly as the smells from the kitchen reached her nose. She yawned once, stretching her arms above her head, before she spoke.

"Did someone say bacon?"

Hunger finally sated after what Mariah perhaps considered to be the best breakfast of her life, she and Ciana dressed for the day, finally utilizing Mariah's new outrageous bathroom. Ciana was a few inches shorter than Mariah, but was able to find a gown within the deep depths of the closet to fit her more petite frame. Mariah, on the other hand, dug through a few of the drawers until she found what she was looking for: another pair of soft, wool leggings and a decadent red cashmere sweater that hung loosely off her shoulder, baring a swath of her golden tan skin.

From the vanity, Mariah found a drawer stocked with several hairbrushes. She tossed one across the room to Ciana, who immediately began working through her tangled curls. Picking up a second, she turned back to the mirror and set to work on her own appearance. She ran the brush through her straight, dark hair until it was smooth, and then began sectioning portions off into a braid that ran down her back. Pulling a few tendrils free to frame her face, she tied the braid off with a strap of elastic, which she then wrapped in a single chain of gold she'd found in the vanity drawers. The contrast of the gold was stark against her near black braid, the added weight to her hair forcing her to hold her head high. She stared back at her reflection in the mirror, and didn't think for a second that she looked like a queen apparent.

She looked like herself. And she loved it.

Mariah and Ciana emerged from the bedroom to find Ryenne sitting, patient and elegant, at the dining table. Beside her sat Kalen, his broad frame folded into the chair, relaxed as he spoke softly to his queen. Behind them both, however, standing just in the foyer entrance as rigid as a pillar, was High Priestess Ksee, garbed in those same pale gold robes she'd worn yesterday, her expression pinched and tight. The queen and the high priestess whipped their gazes to Mariah at the same time, just as she emerged from her bedroom.

"You look beautiful—"

"What in the Goddess's name are you wearing—?"

Ryenne and Ksee spoke at the same time, the differences in both their tone and their very words clashing in the air like swords. Ksee's eyes widened slightly and darted to the queen, who'd tensed nearly imperceptibly in her chair. Kalen only huffed a breath as he watched his queen's gaze frost over slightly. Ryenne broke her stare from Mariah, speaking over her shoulder at Ksee.

"I shall remind you, High Priestess, that while your place at court is vital, Mariah is now your queen apparent. As such, she may wear as she pleases, as has been the way since Xara's reign."

Mariah watched as Ksee stuttered over herself, attempting to regain her composure, her eyes nearly bulging out of her face. "Of course, Your Majesty, I understand. But she wears *trousers*. Like a man. Never has a queen strode through these halls in such attire."

That statement caught Mariah's tongue before she could hold it. "Never? Truly, no other queen has ever worn pants ... *ever*? And tell me, High Priestess, what would you have me wear instead? A ballgown? As I understand it, today will be spent learning and training, not holding court. So, please, tell me why I can't be comfortable in a place I'm supposed to now call my home?"

The room was utterly silent, Kalen's chair creaking as he shifted uncomfortably in his seat. Ryenne simply watched Mariah with a look of cool curiosity. *Shit. Think before you speak, Mariah. A lot may have changed yesterday, but she's the high priestess, and you're still ... just you.*

But even as she thought that, it didn't quite feel right. For the first time today, that deep, dark place within her stirred, flashes of metallic light suddenly coiling through her veins, a sudden and instant reminder that she might never be *just her* again.

Fighting back her unease, Mariah turned her gaze to the queen and was shocked to find that Ryenne's face had broken out into a very un-queen-like grin. Beside her, Kalen appeared to be doing everything in his power to keep from bursting out laughing. Mariah heaved a breath before looking back to the priestess, who continued to stand in the foyer entrance, floundered and flustered. "*You—*"

"Again," Ryenne said, interrupting Ksee again. "Mariah is Queen Apparent of Onita. She may wear what she pleases. I will hear no more about it in my presence, Ksee."

The high priestess's mouth snapped closed, her golden eyes glowing like wrathful embers, and Mariah wondered briefly if fire was her gift, the magic that had called her into the position she now enjoyed. Without another word, Ksee turned on her heel and strode down the foyer, the doors to Mariah's suites banging closed loudly behind her. A feeling of momentary triumph washed over Mariah, chased quickly by a wave of apprehension. She was by no means making a strong first impression upon a woman who was supposed to be one of the closest advisors to the Queen, the closest bridge to their Goddess.

A part of her couldn't help but wonder whether her words to the priestess would eventually come back to haunt her.

CHAPTER 12

Ksee, as it turned out, hadn't truly left them and waited in the hallway when they emerged, quiet and stewing. The priestess had been able to quell the fiery anger that flared in her gaze before she'd left Mariah's suites, now appearing content to maintain an air of cold indifference as she, Ryenne, Kalen, Ciana, and Mariah embarked on a formal tour of the palace.

In all honesty, Mariah couldn't be bothered to care much about how the priestess felt towards her. Not now, as she walked awestruck through the palace hallways.

It was truly more beautiful within than it appeared from the streets of Verith.

Ryenne led them all through stunning, gilded halls filled with archways which opened to either the Attlehons above or the city below. Everything about the palace was massive in scale, and the way portions of it were constructed into the foothills of the mountains themselves gave every room a cavernous feel. Ryenne led the group through aureate receiving rooms, an incredible domed library, and no fewer than five courtyard gardens, each one teeming with more life than the last. Their path eventually led them back to the main palace entrance, back through those massive, gold-plated doors, and down those grand, daunting steps. With a tinge of curiosity, Mariah realized that Ryenne was leading them to the stables. As they neared the buildings, as the sounds and smells of horses brushed over her senses, the queen glanced back over her shoulder at Mariah, a soft smile on her lips.

Mariah met Ryenne's gaze with a look of confusion and an inquisitive smile of her own. Her eyes then drifted past the queen, landing on two horses in the large saddling area of the stables: one pitch black and massive, the other a gleaming golden buckskin. Beside them stood a tall, lean, middle-aged man with graying blonde hair, engaged in a rather animated conversation with a youthful looking stable hand.

Wex Salis. *Her father.* With her buckskin gelding, Kodie.

A laughing sob escaped Mariah's lips as she broke into a sprint, breezing past Ryenne and Ksee. Wex turned from his conversation with the stable hand just in time to catch her as she crashed into him, her arms wrapping tightly around his waist as he gripped her shoulders. Once in his arms, Mariah let out a shuddering breath, breathing in his familiar scent as he squeezed her gently and chuckled, his breath warm on the top of her head. He released her slightly, looking down at her with warmth in his gold-hazel eyes.

"I should've known they would have a hard time making you wear a dress on your first day."

Mariah let out another sob-laugh as she met her father's gaze. "I like to think the Goddess knew what she was getting into when she picked me."

Wex grinned down at her, a grin which quickly faltered, a shadow of sadness fleeting over his eyes. "Your mother ... she knew. Somehow, she knew something would happen on this trip. That was why she pushed you so hard to go."

A heavy wave washed over Mariah as she processed his words. The wave carried with it hurt, a sour twinge of anger. Her mother ... *knew*? Mariah's mind was blank as she stared up into her father's weather-worn face, the pieces of her trust shuddering apart as the implication of her mother's betrayal.

Her mother had known. Her thoughts drifted for a moment to the book she'd given Mariah on her last night in Andburgh, about the words she'd told Mariah. "*If—when—you ever feel lost, truly lost, when you need a reminder of who you are and what you are capable of ... that book will tell you everything you need to know.*"

Had that been a warning from her mother? That she would soon be faced with an insurmountable obstacle, a course that would change her life forever?

Before she could formulate her response, Mariah felt the approach of her companions at her back. Her father, also noticing the nearing group, hesitatingly released Mariah, breaking his gaze away at the last second to dart a glance over her shoulder. In a smooth, practiced movement, he dropped to his knee, his head bowing in respect just as Queen Ryenne appeared by Mariah's side.

"My Queen," said Wex. "I am honored to be graced by your presence and for the invitation to your home."

Ryenne smiled lightly at Mariah's father. "Rise, soldier. I am warmed to see that none of the habits have been lost during your years of retirement."

Wex lifted his head, smiling broadly at Ryenne, and rose to stand once again. "A soldier never forgets his training, Your Majesty."

Ryenne nodded her head once to him, her expression thoughtful. "I thank you for coming to the palace on such short notice. Your presence is most welcome. I'm sure you are, by now, well-aware of what has transpired here with your daughter. You must be very proud and honored."

Wex hesitated for a moment, his brilliant smile fading slightly as he glanced quickly at his daughter. "I'm not sure *pride* is the best way to describe what I'm feeling, Your Majesty. I mean this with all the respect in the world, but ... I feel no pride at having raised a future queen. In fact, I care very little about what titles she now carries." He paused for a moment, a blend of several unidentifiable emotions on his face. "I would say that I now feel excitement, joy ... and, if I may be honest, a healthy dose of fear. Power may be extraordinary, but always carries burdens with it as well."

Ksee chose that moment to step forward, her cold expression taking in the patriarch of the Salis family, her lips tightening before she spoke. "That is a fascinating way to describe it, soldier. Do you not feel surprised, then?"

"No. I feel no surprise at all. I always knew she was meant for something greater in life than what we had for her in Andburgh," Wex answered, his tone neutral and controlled as he addressed the priestess. "She was always far too wild and strong to be happy there. Independence courses through her veins, and now that the Goddess has lifted the curtain, I'm no longer surprised as to why."

"It is curious that you describe her independence with such positivity," Ksee responded. "It has long been the way of Qhohena that her queen be dependent on the advice of those that surround her at court. Of course, I have no doubt your daughter will be able to learn the proper restraint, with time. As the daughter of a soldier, I expect obedience will come to her naturally." Her smile turned sickly sweet, her gaze still piercing.

This fucking bitch.

Mariah knew she should hold her tongue, that making an enemy of this priestess so early was a terrible idea. However, she had no interest in befriending those who chose to treat the people closest to her with such disdain.

Mariah turned her attention directly to Ksee, her own sweet sneer on her face.

"Well, I guess we'll just have to see what the Goddess has planned, won't we?

Ksee's answering glare was burning ice.

CHAPTER 13

Mariah's reunion with her father was short-lived. She didn't even get the chance to pull her father away, to ask him what in Enfara's depths he'd meant when he said her mother *knew*. Too quickly, too soon, Ryenne was there, telling her it was time to move on, that they had many other things to do that day.

Mariah turned back to her father, let him wrap her once more in a fierce hug, even as her heart still stung with her mother's deception. Releasing her too quickly, her father picked up three saddle bags from the ground, pushing them into Mariah's hands. Then, without another word, he turned and strode to his warhorse, mounting the stallion in a single, practiced movement. Her father gave her one last, lingering stare, a look filled with pride and sadness and all the words they hadn't had a chance to say before spurring his mount away and out the palace gates.

Shoving down all the anger and confusion and heartache burning through her, Mariah turned on her heel, following

Ryenne out of the courtyard. The bags her father had handed her, the bags containing the last remnants of her quiet life at the crossroads, were handed to a member of the palace staff with instructions to deposit them in her rooms. As the servant scurried off, Mariah and Ryenne continued their walk back up the steps to the palace and through the massive doors, Ksee, Ciana, and Kalen trailing just a few steps behind. Ryenne wordlessly led them into the throne room, then hooked a left into one of the many hallways spindling off the massive, central, glass-ceilinged space. This path led deeper into the palace, the floor sloping up gradually as they walked, and eventually they found themselves pushing through yet another set of double doors into a great, open space carved directly into the side of the mountains.

The floors of this new room were smooth and flat, and three of the four walls were non-existent, a simple guard rail the only thing to serve as a barrier to a drop-off that had Mariah's stomach twisting into knots. The cliff was sheer, and far below was a great, forested valley, a hidden vale sitting between the palace and the rest of the Attlehon foothills. Despite the harrowing drop, Mariah inhaled deeply, reveling in the scent of the mountain breeze tinged with early autumn, and shifted to look at Ryenne.

"What is this place?"

Ryenne continued further into the room—if it could even be called that—to sit in one of two chairs placed in the center. "It is a place for us to exercise our gifts—the magic from the Goddess flowing in our veins—without fear of leveling another part of the palace." She smiled back at Mariah. "It is not much of a concern for us with the Goddess's light in our veins, as our magic is more ... symbolic in nature. And serves more purposes beyond just its physical manifestation." Ryenne then looked to

Ksee, who'd chosen to linger in the shadows by the entrance. Kalen had remained outside the room, ever watchful by the double doors, and Ciana found another chair along the wall, far from the priestess, where she'd promptly sat with curiosity dancing in her amber gaze.

"But for the priestesses, this is a place for them to connect with their gifts safely. Our high priestess, for example, has the gift of fire, and she and her acolytes frequent this place." Mariah followed Ryenne's gaze to Ksee, only to find the priestess studiously ignoring them, inspecting the engravings within the double doors instead.

Mariah turned back to look at Ryenne. She *knew* that Ksee had fire magic. Her brother had it, too, after all. She knew she'd seen that spark in her tarnished gold eyes.

But where her brother's fire was all playful life, Ksee's only seemed to be low, flat smoldering of coals.

Ryenne gestured to the chair across from her, long, blonde hair shifting as she nodded. "Sit, Mariah."

Mariah did as she was commanded. Now, seated in the center of the circle, she couldn't help comparing this space to a landing, almost like a roost for some great beast of the past. The stone beneath their feet was scored with ancient scratches, worn and faded with age. Mariah had never heard of someone in Onita with the ability to wield earth, but she supposed the gift was possible, and that those marks could've been caused by a young wielder still learning the depths of her strength.

Or they could've been made by something far larger and wilder than a mortal priestess.

She pulled herself from those thoughts with a shake of her head, meeting the queen's ocean-blue gaze once again. Ryenne smiled at her, softly, kindly, before she spoke.

"Now, Mariah, this will be a lesson in learning to speak to your magic. It is not a matter of control, not truly; the magic is a part of you, yes, but it still ultimately belongs to the Goddess, and at many times will serve its own purposes. The queen's gift is different from all other magic in that way—we do not bend and warp our power to our will, but instead seek a partnership with it, a unified bond." As she was speaking, Ryenne had lifted a hand, and from her fingers delicate drops of golden light spilled out, wrapping in a thin rivulet around her hand and fingers before soaking back into her skin, leaving behind a lingering glow. The queen looked back to Mariah, smiling at the awe Mariah didn't try to hide.

"The magic manifests itself—both physically and internally—differently to each queen. As you can see, the magic has always been like water to me. I can pull out single droplets, a stream, or a wave, depending on the need. And when it is —*was*"—Ryenne faltered slightly before composing herself, continuing—"at rest within me, it felt like a lake or an ocean. Some great body of water.

"To start, I want you to close your eyes. Focus your attention and energy *inside* yourself, beyond your physical being. Find that place deep within where that power now resides. And I want you to tell me what you see, what you feel."

Mariah closed her eyes, obeying the queen's demand. It didn't take much thought or focus to find what Ryenne referred to. She'd felt that place the queen spoke of since the day she'd received the letter on her twenty-first birthday.

And, no more than a few seconds later, there it was—an inky black pit at the center of her being, and within it two spheres of glowing light. She drifted her consciousness a bit closer, closer, trying to get a better look at what those clusters of light were made of.

Then she saw it and was able to make out each and every individual strand of both silver and gold light.

"Threads," she said, her eyes still closed. "It looks like threads. All wound together in a massive ball."

Mariah expected a reaction from the queen, some sort of praise, but instead ... nothing. She cracked her eye back open to find Ryenne regarding her with a stunned expression.

"That was ... quick." Ryenne smiled slightly, but her shock made the movement stiff. "And ... threads? That's what you feel? Are ... are you sure?"

"I'm positive," Mariah answered firmly, her confusion at the queen's reaction like pin-pricks in her belly. "Is ... That's not a bad thing, is it?" Of course, it would be just her luck to not only have her life upheaved in a single day, but also for the magic that caused the very disruption to be wrong in some way.

However, Ryenne quickly regained her composure, the shock vanishing from her face. "No, there is nothing wrong with that at all," she assured Mariah. "If anything, I'm jealous it has manifested for you in such a physical form. You cannot *imagine* how difficult it was for me to learn how to grab onto and build a bond with droplets of water." She laughed, the sound only slightly forced as it tinkled from her throat.

But Mariah wasn't convinced. She did not, however, push the issue, content to accept the simple explanation for what it was instead of giving herself yet another thing to lose her sleep over.

Ryenne met Mariah's gaze again, her smile still tight, before she pushed forward with her lesson. "Now that you have found your magic, I want you to try to do exactly what I did earlier. I want you to reach into that place and coax out a single thread, draw it up through your veins, into your skin, and then to your fingers. Remember—it is not about control. You make the request, and then build the bond."

Mariah nodded once before again closing her eyes, turning

her attention back to that dark place illuminated by silver and gold light within her soul. She dove down, the masses within her growing larger and larger the deeper she went. She looked first to the great tangle of silver, its wildness eager and *alive*. Something about it called to a feral part of her, a part that craved blood and ruin and vengeance but also sought freedom and joy and laughter—

She turned from the silver mass suddenly, whipping her attention away and towards its golden twin beside it. Those feelings ... they would consume her, devour her, and she would let them.

She couldn't let that happen. For some reason, the longer she stayed in the palace, the more determined she was to make the most of her situation. To take these new obligations seriously, to earn her place here amongst those who ruled their kingdom behind gilded doors and raised daises.

So, Mariah moved closer to the mass of golden threads dwelling deep in her soul, the lengths of magic coiled so neatly compared to the chaos of its silver sister. She reached a part of her consciousness into that golden mass, and the threads instantly leaped to her, as if they'd been eagerly awaiting her invitation and arrival. A bundle of gold wrapped around her consciousness, twining into her being, warming her with comforting light that chased away all thoughts of wickedness.

Where the silver threads had emitted feelings of wild darkness, these golden threads felt only of tamed light.

Just one, she thought to herself, to the threads crawling around her. *I only need one.*

Slowly, those threads peeled off her, almost reluctantly, leaving behind a single, shimmering thread of golden light. Alone, in her mind's eye, Mariah marveled at its beauty, studying it just as it studied her.

At her metaphysical back, she could feel threads of silver licking at her with curiosity.

She ignored them. She was curious, but ... something told her to explore that part of her in private.

It was difficult to predict what might happen if she were told to procure golden threads for Ryenne, only for that light to manifest as silver.

Shoving that aside, she wrapped herself around the single golden thread, and rose out of the void inside her and back into her physical body. She became aware again of her breathing, of the breeze swirling her hair, of her heart beating steadily in her chest.

And then there was that thread.

It followed her up, sitting just in the pit of her stomach, in that same spot where she'd felt so much roiling in the days after her birthday. Remembering Ryenne's words, she beckoned it into her veins, pulling it forward to her arms, to her skin, and then opened her eyes just as she gently coaxed it into her fingertips.

Her breath whooshed out of her lungs as she beheld that delicate golden thread twisting and winding between her fingers, around her hand, the feeling as it moved along her skin both foreign and familiar.

"Holy shit," she breathed, a true smile finally touching her lips. "It's ... beautiful."

"Yes," Ryenne's voice was soft and sad. "It is."

Mariah raised her gaze from her hand, still ringed in that subtle golden light, to look at the queen, her own blue eyes locked on Mariah's hands. Her face held that same wistful sadness that had been in her voice as she continued. "You mastered that much, much faster than I did. I had a feeling you would." She smiled sadly. "I remember it took me at least a week to be able to get a strong enough grip on the liquid of my magic in order to summon it to the surface. But I am glad you took to this much more naturally than I did."

Mariah was silent, watching Ryenne, unsure what to say to the queen and opting for nothing at all. She suddenly noticed Ryenne, while still filled with supernatural youth, looked ever so slightly older than she had yesterday. What had been flawless, smooth skin around her eyes now bore soft smile lines that hadn't been there the day before.

Wrenching her gaze from the magic still glowing on Mariah's skin, Ryenne looked her right in the eyes. "You are ready, just as I had planned. We will proceed with your Selection tonight."

"Is it really that simple? I speak the words, I summon my magic, ask it the question, and then let it ... what, get to work?"

Ryenne chuckled. "Yes," she said, "it really is that simple."

Mariah inhaled, held her breath for a heartbeat, and then let it out in a deep exhale. "Okay." She paused, thinking. "I just have one other question."

Ryenne's eyebrows show up. They were now alone in that training space, and the sun was beginning to move into the afternoon hours. Lunch had been brought up while they'd worked, Mariah learning both how to create that partnership with her magic and what would be expected of her tonight. Ksee and Ciana had long since left them, giving them the privacy to discuss one of the more intimate rituals of a queen. Mariah assumed that Kalen still remained, though, still standing just on the other side of those double doors. Ciana had excused herself to formally get settled into her new chambers, exclaiming that she was *sure* her belongings had arrived at the palace and she needed to begin unpacking. Ksee hadn't given a reason for her departure, only slipping silently out of the training room, her face a rigid mask after Mariah's display with her magic. Mariah could only assume she'd left to prepare for the Selection, which would take place in Qhohena's temple there in the palace.

"Well, please. Ask away." Ryenne's eyebrows were still raised in amused curiosity.

"I just have to ask ... why? If I—the queen—has all this magic, why do we need to select and bond with seven men for the Goddess's gift to become fully matured? Not that I'm opposed to the concept in any way—I'm actually quite curious about that—but it just seems a bit ... antiquated, is all."

Ryenne's face relaxed as she smiled. "I was wondering when you were going to ask that." She thought for a moment. "It's ... complicated. And even I don't know the full truth of it. But from what I've learned of our history, the queens' history, it was something Qhohena wanted when she blessed the first queen, Xara, with our gift. I suspect—and these are only my thoughts—that our Goddess knew giving one single person that much power, without surrounding her with others who could help shoulder those burdens, could create a monster better suited to razing kingdoms than ruling them." Ryenne paused again. "And even our Goddess leans upon her Consort, Priam, for support. Perhaps she also wanted for her queen to find that same comfort during the loneliness of her extraordinarily long life. It may also be the most valuable lesson we have to learn from Qhohena: that every sword needs a shield, every great power must be grounded, and even the strongest need protecting."

Mariah was silent, her mind churning over the words. They made sense to her, she supposed. But then a new question leaped from her mind to her tongue before she could stop it.

"What of the other goddess? Zadione?"

All of Ryenne's warmth instantly vanished, and her face paled. She almost seemed to age even further in a matter of heartbeats.

"It isn't wise to discuss the Goddess of Death here, Mariah. Especially before you have fully bonded with your Armature and ascended your throne. Even then, doing so could still carry with it heavy risks. She vanished from the world thousands of years ago, and it's far wiser to pretend she never existed, because as far as we are now concerned, she might as well have not."

Cold silence descended upon the room, the whistling of the wind off the Attlehon's brushing talons over Mariah's skin. Her heart and mind raced with adrenaline and fear at the queen's words. *What in the Goddess's name was that about?*

"I apologize, Ryenne. I was just curious. I won't bring it up again; you have my word."

Color slowly returned to Ryenne's skin, and she relaxed back into her seat with several deep inhales. "It is alright, Mariah. You did not know. There is nothing to apologize for." Several more breaths from the queen before she turned the ever-composed mask of the Queen of Onita back to Mariah. "Do you have any other questions about what is in store for you tonight?"

Mariah shook her head. "No, I understand. I still have plenty of questions about what, exactly, it means to 'bond,' but I also understand that is something I will have to learn from my Armature directly, not from you. But as far as tonight … it seems simple." She paused, then asked the one final question that had been lingering on her tongue. "Have you seen them? The men who were Marked for me?"

Ryenne's composure cracked again at that, this time with humor as a laugh escaped her lips. "Of course, they've lived and trained here at the palace since they were boys." Her eyes glinted with coy understanding. "I would be very excited to meet them, if I were you."

Mariah knew her answering smile was more akin to a flirty smirk. "And what am I to wear? I can only imagine Ksee will never approve of anything I would pick for myself."

Ryenne's answering smile could only be described as foxy. "Let me handle Ksee. I have the perfect dress for you."

CHAPTER 14

"So, you're telling me Ryenne, Her Royal Majesty and all that, *personally* picked out *this* for me to wear tonight?"

Ciana's answering grin was wicked. "I don't know why you're so surprised. She told you that she had a dress for you. And then she handed this one to me herself."

Mariah could only stare at the full-length mirror in her bathroom. "It just doesn't seem very ... queen-like, does it?"

Ciana's face was suddenly serious as she held Mariah's gaze in the mirror. "Oh, quite the opposite, Mariah. I think this is exactly the dress needed to bring every man in the kingdom to his knees."

Is that what I want? To bring them all to their knees? Mariah couldn't hide the dark place deep inside her that flickered with excitement and curiosity at the idea. But ... *no*. She'd seen firsthand, in Andburgh, what tyranny and control did to a people.

She was better than that. She would *be* better than that.

"But isn't the point tonight to bring only seven of them to their knees?"

Ciana rolled her eyes. "Look, Mariah, if you don't want to wear it, just say so. But if you *do* want to wear it, then please by all that the Goddess has blessed, would you stop complaining and just appreciate this outfit for a moment ... because, well, *shit*."

Mariah couldn't help but smile as she refocused her attention on her reflection. She should've known better than to fear Ryenne would pick one of those thick, heavy ballgowns Onitan women seemed to prefer—especially given the look on the queen's face when she'd told Mariah she had something for her to wear. And, Mariah thought, she had yet to see Ryenne wear one of those massive ballgowns herself.

Even still, what she now wore was the *last* thing she would've expected. And, truthfully, Ciana was right.

This *could* bring men to their knees.

The dress was made of black lace and almost entirely sheer. The neckline cut a deep *v* down her chest, plunging to her sternum, highlighting the curve of her cleavage. The straps were about three inches thick and made of more black lace, and the back dipped even lower than the neckline, revealing the expanse of tanned skin between her shoulder blades. The bodice clung tightly to her body, and was mostly sheer, except for black paneling over her breasts to offer the slightest modicum of decency. It cinched tightly just below her waist before spilling into the skirts, which were really just panels of more sheer black lace, split up all the way on the sides to her hips. Sewn into the bodice of the dress were black shorts of the softest material, the only opaque portion on the entire bottom half of the gown. The black lace pooled at her feet, swishing against the ground softly, her tan legs on full display. On her feet were black heels, simple but wicked, much like the dress itself. Her hair had been softly curled, spilling over her shoulders and down her back, a simple sweep of kohl across her eyes and her lips painted blood red.

A slow smile spread across her face, her features igniting. The dress—if it could even be called that—*was* incredible. She felt a little like a dark goddess, and she swore she felt that tangled silver mass within her sing at the thought.

She gave into it, just a little bit. Let those silver threads mix with the gold as they slid into her veins, the power offering her a strange, foreign comfort against the nerves for what was to come.

A loud knock suddenly sounded outside the bathroom, coming from her chamber doors. Ciana whirled away from Mariah, grabbing her own red skirts in her hands and hustling away with a grumbled, "I knew we were running late."

Mariah continued to stare at her reflection, using that moment to compose herself and the coiling power now snaking through her in pure anticipation. Movement in the mirror pulled her attention away, and she met the reflection of Ryenne's ocean-blue stare. A smile graced the queen's lips.

"You look just as I thought you would: magnificent."

Mariah simply inclined her head respectfully before her question pushed past her lips.

"How do you even own something like this?"

Ryenne's face twitched, her expression amused. "I was a young queen once too, Mariah. I remember what it was to select and bond with my Armature. These are duties that are expected of us, but by no means should you believe them to be a chore."

Mariah twisted her mouth in wry amusement. She still had so many questions about the bond—how it was done, what was involved—but Ryenne staunchly refused to tell her more, repeating that Mariah needed to learn from her Armature herself. Part of building the trust between them, and all that.

"Is it expected that I ... that I bond with one of them tonight?"

Ryenne's amusement dimmed just slightly. "I forget, sometimes, how new this all is for you. How you were not raised with the knowledge that this could be your life, as I was. You just take to it so well." She paused, inhaling. "No, that is not expected of you. Not tonight. The idea of the bond is ... daunting. You may take your time, get to know them first. Tonight, I want you to focus only on the now. On selecting these men who will become closer to you than anyone else on this earth."

Right then, as if on cue, there was a knock on the bathroom door. In the mirror, Mariah saw Kalen lean his head in and then step inside. His eyes, as always, went first to his queen before settling on Mariah. A rakish grin, one that suited his face all too well, spread across his face.

"Those poor boys have no idea what they're getting themselves into."

Mariah smiled at Kalen and the compliment. "But ... they don't really have a choice, right? All this has been planned out by the Consort God since my birth."

"Just because it wasn't explicitly their choice doesn't mean they will not choose you, Mariah. There is something in us that calls to our queen, something deep in our souls. Maybe it's caused by our Mark; maybe it's just Priam's touch in general; maybe it's who we are at our very essence, the reason we were Marked in the first place. But trust this, Mariah: even without the intervention of the gods, I would've fallen upon my sword for Ryenne the very moment I laid eyes on her, whether she selected me or not. She is mine, and I am hers. Forever."

His gaze had drifted back to his queen, a look of such love and devotion etched upon his face. That look pulled at something deep within Mariah's soul, something that had her recoiling from the exchange.

Love is weakness.

That voice whispered into her mind with the same quiet power it had all her life. She silently prayed to whatever god would listen—whether Qhohena or Priam or someone, some*thing* else—that her Armature would understand.

They could be her armor, but they could never have her heart.

Ryenne and Kalen's attention slowly shifted back to Mariah. Ryenne took a deep breath. "Well. Are you ready, Mariah?"

Mariah lifted her chin and shifted her shoulders, feeling the long waves of her dark hair brush across the exposed skin of her back. "Yes. Let's go pick an Armature."

Ksee met them all outside Mariah's rooms, her pale robes substituted for those of brilliant white trimmed in gold, her gray-blonde hair pulled into a high, tight bun atop her head. Her cold, tarnished stare perused Mariah with blatant disapproval, the flames that resided in her veins dancing in her eyes. She flicked that fiery gaze to Ryenne.

"The Marked are already hers by decree of the gods. There is no need for seduction such as this."

Mariah spoke before Ryenne could answer.

She had a sudden desire to not let the queen fight all her battles for her.

"There is always a need for seduction, High Priestess," she said, her voice dripping with a mockery of tantalization. "Nothing quite inspires men and brings them to their knees before you like the promise of something *more*." She stole

Ciana's words from earlier, and out of the corner of her eye, she saw the smile that tugged at her friend's lips.

That burnt gaze turned back to Mariah. "Indeed. Let us hope, however, that you learn to use more than sex to inspire your people, *Queen Apparent*." And with that, the priestess turned on her heel, striding away down the hallway with the clear expectation that they would follow.

Ciana stepped to Mariah's side, looping her arm through Mariah's, much like she had just yesterday in the palace courtyard. Right before both of their lives changed forever. "Old hag," she grumbled into Mariah's ear. "She *obviously* needs to get laid."

Mariah let a giggle bubble out of her, earning her a look from Ryenne. It was clear from the shadow in her ocean-blue eyes that Ryenne was troubled by the rising strife between Mariah and Ksee. Mariah tucked the look away, curious as to why Ryenne bothered to keep Ksee around when the two clearly didn't see eye to eye on much. She shook her head, not interested in dwelling on that for now, and took a step forward. Arm in arm, the two young women followed after the priestess, the queen and her consort close behind.

CHAPTER 15

Qhohena's temple sat at the far side of the palace, closer to the city and the citizens who dwelt there, the one part of the sprawling castle freely accessible by the residents of Verith. It was a place those in the city could seek comfort from their gods, a place of refuge to the Goddess's people.

The closer Mariah drew to it, the more her heart began to race.

She could feel those two orbs of power within her, now fully awake after her earlier training with Ryenne. They twisted and wound their way around her gut, mixing with her nerves until it felt like worms had settled in her stomach and crawled into her chest. She tried to focus, tried to whisper to those threads, *Soon, just wait, just a few more moments*, but it was still so foreign. They all but ignored her pleas, continuing their writhing as if amused by her discomfort.

Eventually, they approached yet another set of great, gold-plated doors. So much gold in this palace, in this entire city. It was absolutely beautiful, but Mariah could already feel it beginning to grate against her like rough wool. Maybe it was the stress of the past day, the past *week*, but she suddenly wanted nothing more than to see a room in a color that *wasn't* gold.

I should paint a few walls black after my coronation. I'm sure Ksee would love that. The thought made her smile, just slightly, a welcome reprieve to distract her from the turmoil beneath her skin.

So welcome that she didn't even pause to think about how easily she'd just contemplated her coronation. How natural it had felt.

The group came to a halt just outside the gilded double doors. Ksee turned to face Mariah and Ryenne, the queen standing quietly at Mariah's side. Ciana released her friend's arm, falling back to join Kalen. The two of them would remain outside the temple for this particular ceremony.

This was a night for the queen, the high priestess, the queen apparent, and the Marked. No others—not even consorts—were permitted to join.

Mariah had to do this task alone, with only those touched by the Goddess herself to bear witness.

She turned her head to Ryenne, the queen as regal and composed as ever in her golden gown and gilded snowdrop blossom crown. Ocean eyes met those of forest green, and Mariah took a steadying breath, calmed by Ryenne's presence.

"Are you ready?" Ryenne's voice was soft but expectant, excited.

Mariah nodded her head in a single dipped movement. With the affirmation, Ksee turned her dark gold glare away from Mariah and the queen, whirled on her heel, pushed the temple doors open, and the three women strode through.

The temple was dark, so dark that Mariah could hardly discern the shape and size of the space itself, lit only by candlelight placed throughout its depths. The flickering light those candles afforded was only enough to make out the shape of the twenty-one tall figures standing in the room, their forms cloaked and hooded but clearly male. They stood with their backs to the door through which Mariah entered, and in the dim light she could see that they faced a raised dais, a smaller replica of the one in the throne room. Atop the dais was what looked to be an altar, something large resting atop it.

Mariah followed behind Ksee and Ryenne as they moved down a pathway around the gathered figures, Mariah's heart pounding heavily in her ears, forcing inhales and exhales through her lungs. The room was so quiet, so tense, and she could almost feel every other emotion rolling through the air.

So much anticipation and excitement and a tinge of fear that it nearly choked her.

But she kept forcing those breaths, and kept following after the queen and the high priestess.

They approached the dais and climbed the steps. As she'd been instructed, her mind somehow remembering her task despite the revolt happening in her body, Mariah went to stand before the altar, situated so she now looked out at the group of men before her. Even from this new angle, their deep hoods were still drawn, none of their features visible to her in the flickering candlelight.

She looked down at what she'd seen atop the altar from the doorway. It was a book, and with a flash of annoyance at herself, she remembered her instructions from Ryenne on this part. The tome was Qhohena's ancient texts, a collection of entries from the High Priestesses of Qhohena dating back to the days of Xara herself. The book was already opened to a page, the delicate writing containing the words to be spoken over this particular ritual.

Mariah drew one last shaky inhale, sending up a silent

prayer to Qhohena for strength. She carried the Goddess's own power in her, after all; maybe now, for the first time in her life, she would be listening.

She looked back down to the open page, at the words she'd memorized earlier that day, and began to speak.

"I am Mariah Salis, Chosen by the Golden Goddess as the Queen Apparent to the Onitan throne." Even though the words were still foreign to her, Mariah's voice came out far stronger than she'd expected, and with a swift exhale of relief, she continued.

"You were all Marked with a symbol of my reign by the Consort God, tied to my life by the powers that created this world. You have trained to become my armor against the world, the permanent shield around my throne, and tonight seven of you will be selected by the Goddess to forever bind your life to mine." Mariah glanced up and imagined, for a moment, that she was making eye contact with every man in that room, even though their faces were still completely concealed from her view. Then she did something she'd told no one about, not even Ryenne.

She deviated from the ancient words on that page, instead voicing something that suddenly bubbled out of her with wild urgency.

"If you are Selected, and if you don't wish for this to be your life, you may refuse. I will understand. You didn't ask for this, something I'm intimately aware of. I'm giving you the choice that I never had. I don't want anyone serving in my court who doesn't wish to be there." Behind her, fiery anger boiled off Ksee, cool shock emanating from Ryenne. Neither of them spoke, however; this night was Mariah's show, and these were her Marked. It was her right to do with them as she wished.

Though the men gathered before her did not react heavily,

she could sense their surprise as it thickened the air, the slight shuffles and raising of cloaked heads the only sign that their interest was now focused wholly on the dark-haired woman standing on the dais above them. Mariah gathered herself, the lace of her dress brushing softly against her legs and the feet of the altar, before stepping out from behind it and moving to the top of the dais stairs. With a single glance over her shoulder at Ryenne, the queen's eyes glistening with something that Mariah tried to convince herself was pride, Mariah turned once more to the men before her. She closed her eyes, and with a deep breath, dropped herself into that place in her soul where her magic lived.

Her consciousness swirled amidst those threads of silver and gold magic, stunned at how much more alive they'd become today as she'd coaxed them out, forging the partnership Ryenne had spoken of. Now, instead of tightly woven masses, both masses were loosened, relaxed, freely winding around her and each other as they awaited her question.

She let them, threads of both silver and gold, coil closer to her, before she finally asked the question Ryenne gave her earlier that day.

Who is my shield?

The magic paused, its movement halting for the briefest of moments. Suddenly, the silver threads retreated back within itself as a bundle of gold shot out, wrapping around Mariah and pulling her back up into her body. It filled her veins for a heartbeat as Mariah opened her eyes, reeling, unsurprised to find her skin glowing in the dim light, before the light leaped out of her fingertips and into the air in front of her.

The brilliant threads of light paused for a moment before diving off the dais, twisting and winding down the steps and through the men gathered below. They came to a sudden halt in front of one of the tall, cloaked figures, a rope of light connecting Mariah to her first Armature.

Mariah let out a shaky breath, her hands falling to her side. She stepped down the dais steps, one at a time, and walked slowly through the crowd, following the rope of light until she stood before the magic's first pick.

She still couldn't see his face, and with a snap like a whip, her magic dove back beneath her skin, content with its choice. It still lingered there in her veins, watching, waiting, and her skin glowed faintly because of it.

Oh, well. *Maybe he'll be flattered for making his queen glow.*

She inhaled once, exhaled deeply, then spoke the words Ryenne had instructed her on earlier.

"Soldier, Marked by Priam. Qhohena has requested your service to me and my court, to be my armor against the world and to guard my back against those who might wish this kingdom harm. Do you answer my call?"

The tall figure before her slowly kneeled, one booted foot scuffing across the floor as he rested it behind him. Even kneeling, his head came to Mariah's torso, his face still veiled from her view. Hands slipped out from under his cloak—calloused, warrior hands—and grabbed the edges of his hood, pulling it back to finally bare his face to his queen.

His hair was short and medium brown, and the planes of his face were classically handsome. His face was clean-shaven as he titled it up to meet Mariah's gaze, a solemn look filled with both unequivocal joy and unquestionable determination filling his dark hazel eyes as he spoke back to her.

"On this day, and on every day of my life, I will answer your call, My Queen. I swear my life, my sword, my shield, and my soul to you. I promise to be your armor against the world and to guard your back against those who might wish this kingdom harm." His voice filled the room with a rich timber, the sound offering to Mariah a calmness she leaned into, willingly.

She felt a smile spread across her face. "What is your name?"

His answering smile was soft, compassionate. "Sebastian, My Queen."

She extended a hand to him, slowly, before speaking again. "Then welcome to my court, Sebastian."

With a shaky breath, he reached out his hand, gripping hers and rising. The feel of his skin against hers was rough, but warm and comforting, much like the rest of him. As she looked up into that hazel stare, she started to feel the steady strength he could offer her; like a rock beneath her feet, he began to feel like the only thing keeping her standing in that dark room.

Hand in hand, she led him back to the dais, releasing his grip just before ascending back up the steps. As if on instinct—and, perhaps, it *was* his instinct—he moved to stand at the feet of the dais steps, alert and watchful, despite the utter lack of threats that this room posed to her.

That wasn't so bad.

One down, six to go.

Breathing deep, she shut her eyes again, returning to the home of her magic. The threads of silver and gold magic again leaped to greet her, welcoming her back like an old friend. And again, she asked that question.

Who is my shield?

This time, though, the magic was slower to react. It slowed its dancing movements around her, retreating to its respective mass of silver or gold. Mariah watched, and it appeared as if the threads were ... *conversing*. Which was impossible. But Mariah remembered what Ryenne had said—the magic had a mind of its own, and would never be a slave to her will. And as those silver and gold threads mingled closer, as if reaching some sort of agreement, she started to realize exactly what the queen had meant.

Lost in thought, she didn't notice the strands of silver threads that started to band together. Didn't notice them as they formed a rope of silver light that wrapped around her mind and pulled her back to body, just as the golden threads had done before. Before Mariah could stop it, her eyes were flying open, panic gurgling in the back of her throat as the wild silver power filled her veins, clawing its way to her skin, ready to reveal this secret to the world.

But what she saw instead shocked her more than the rope of light now dancing in the air before her.

The light of that magic—it looked no different than the golden threads had. Even in the near darkness, it just looked like brilliant light, gleaming with supernatural intensity that hid its true color. She could *feel* the difference, and if she focused closely, she could see the silver threads forming that rope of light, but that was it. She wondered, distantly, if Ryenne could feel the difference, could recognize this wasn't the same magic that once dwelled within her.

Problem for a later time, she thought. So, she took a single step off the dais, and the silver rope of magic leaped forward, weaving through the crowd just as its sister threads had done for Sebastian.

This time, it led her to the other side of the temple, stopping before a figure standing a bit closer to the dais than Sebastian had been. This magic, just as it had in Mariah, felt more playful, wild, full of glee at its choice. Once she was standing before her second Armature, that light again spooled back inside her, the glow once again lingering on the surface as it watched in anticipation.

Standing before this new male, she repeated the same words she'd spoken to Sebastian. And again, without hesitation, he dropped to his knee before her, pulling back the hood to his cloak.

His medium length, shaggy hair was a bright red, his skin freckled so thoroughly it gave him the appearance of a golden tan. Eyes of bottle green met her own, and a fiery grin spread across his roguishly handsome face.

"My name is Quentin, My Queen. And on this day, and on every day of my life, I will answer your call. I swear my life, my sword, my shield, and my soul to you. I promise to be your armor against the world and to guard your back against those who may wish this kingdom harm."

The way he spoke, with an earned arrogance and fierceness, had her eyebrow ticking up slightly.

She liked this one. He seemed like a cocky bastard.

She smiled back at him, letting some of her own wildness seep into her gaze.

"Welcome to my court, Quentin."

Quentin didn't wait for her hand before rising, instead extending his arm to her. She couldn't help the slight giggle that left her lips as she slipped her hand into the bend of his elbow. Together, they walked back to the dais, and just like Sebastian, he left her at the foot of the steps, moving to stand opposite Sebastian at the altar. The two men nodded slightly to each other, slipping into the roles they'd trained for their whole lives.

Mariah selected her next four Armature much as she had Sebastian and Quentin. The gold and silver magic within her alternated which warrior it chose, but the light filtering out of her skin still never changed. After Quentin, the golden threads selected a younger man with shaggy, tawny hair like a lion's man, his rich brown eyes filled with steady, watchful strength as he introduced himself to his queen as Drystan. Next, another man with dark hair and hazel eyes who looked very much like Sebastian, only slightly younger, was chosen by the wild silver magic and called himself Matheo. Gold took back control with the next pick, selecting Trefor, whose short blonde hair and sea-green eyes easily placed him as having ties to the coastal peoples of Ettervan. Finally, Feran was selected by the silver threads, a caramel-skinned man of obvious Kreah heritage, his braided dark hair pulled back loosely at the nape of his neck.

The first six selections breezed by Mariah, the magic flowing so smoothly to her, to her new Armature, and then back again. It wasn't long before she was back standing upon that dais, her six selected Armature standing at its base, their eyes already trained on her in the same way she'd seen Ryenne's Armature watch her.

It was now time for her final selection. One more, and she would have her full Armature, that last barricade to make her near untouchable in this new world she'd found herself in.

As she plunged back down into herself for the last time, ready to be greeted by threads of gold to make that final pick, she found something she wasn't expecting.

Where those threads of magic had, before, been conversing, working together to make alternating selections, it was as if they suddenly couldn't reach an agreement, now appearing to almost bicker together as silver and gold wound around each other in the depths of her soul.

It almost reminded her of how siblings fought.

Mariah pushed the thought down, forcing her mind to focus on the final task at hand.

Who is my shield?

When before, those threads of magic had responded instantly, this time they didn't stop their squabble, or even notice her presence there with them. They continued to twist and turn around each other, fighting for the power of that last Selection.

As she watched them bicker and swirl, an image flashed through her mind. An image of a dark-haired male with wild blue eyes leaning against a wall in the shadows of the palace stables. Of the look of shock that had passed across his face, quickly covered up by cold ambivalence.

Right then, just as the picture of those tanzanite eyes blazed into her mind, everything around her stilled. The silver and gold threads ceased their warring, turning their attention *outward* to look at Mariah where she peered in. Mariah flashed her eyes open, wanting to escape the chill crawling across her skin.

Not that it helped.

Internally, she felt the magic examining her, peeling apart the layers of her soul, digging into her very essence to reach a place she didn't know existed. She had no wards, no barriers, nothing to prevent the intrusion, and had no choice but to stand there, frozen as she was torn apart by the threads that were supposed to defend her from all harm.

Suddenly, it felt like a decision was made.

The silver and gold threads, wound together in a single rope of light, filled her gut and then the veins beneath her skin, eventually pushing out in the air in front of her in a flood of brilliant light. Watching the magic move in the air, Mariah wondered if anyone else noticed how much brighter it burned than it had for the previous selections.

The magic danced, twisting above the remaining men to the very last line of them, the space shrouded in shadow, nearly untouched by the candlelight. It eventually dropped to rest directly before a dark, tall figure who stood utterly still, the entire room now lit up by the brilliance of the light connecting him to Mariah.

Mariah steeled herself with all the resolve she had left and stepped off the dais for the last time, walking towards the back of the temple to stand in front of the male that had, somehow, been selected by both those threads of magic dwelling in her soul.

Before giving herself a second to doubt, she began to speak.

"Soldier, Marked by Priam. Qhohena has requested your service to me and my court, to be my armor against the world and to guard my back against those who might wish this kingdom harm. Do you answer my call?"

There was a heavy pause, where even the gods held their breaths. Mariah let her eyes dart up and realized her magic hadn't yet retreated back within her. She reached a mental hand out to that light, and it slowly fed back into her skin, settling just beneath the surface to light her up like a torch against the darkness shrouding this back corner of the temple.

She hadn't remembered it being this dark. Perhaps with the passing time, the light from the candles had grown weaker.

Her attention returned to the tall figure before her. Just like the others, she couldn't make out his face underneath his hood, but there was something strikingly familiar about him, like stepping back into a home that you had been away from for far too long.

Slowly, almost painstakingly slow, the figure lowered to his knees before Mariah. As if he were fighting the urge, but simply couldn't, not with her Mark burning upon his skin and her magic lighting the darkest parts of that room. Just like the other Armature, tanned, callous hands slipped out from under his cloak, pulling his hood back from his face.

And on his knees before her was that same stunning, dark-haired male from the palace courtyard, his eyes of ravenous tanzanite burning up at her.

CHAPTER 16

"Soldier, Marked by Priam. Qhohena has requested your service to me and my court, to be my armor against the world and to guard my back against those who might wish this kingdom harm. Do you answer my call?"

Her voice was strong, clear, hypnotic. It burned him, razed through every wall he'd worked so hard to build against this exact, impossible moment. He had trained to remain firm and unwavering against temptation. Instead, he felt that shimmering voice wrap its way around his neck, usurping every ounce of his free will with a single question.

And in that moment, he knew he hated her.

Since the day he was Marked, the day his father had sent him south to Verith bearing a single promise, a solitary threat, Andrian Laurent vowed that should he ever be Selected, he would refuse. He would agree to serve this new queen in the capacity that would suit his rank and station, leading her armies or protecting her city. But he would never allow himself to swear that oath. He would never—*could* never—bind his life to hers.

That all changed the moment the woman before him opened her mouth, her words spilling into the air like a liquid drug to which he was instantly addicted.

He hated that voice.

He was watching from the outside looking in, a passenger in his own skin, his body no longer in his control. The shadows dwelling beneath his skin, magic that was unlike any other in Onita, a cursed gift from his mother's Leuxrithian blood, were quiet for the first time since they'd stirred in his gut no more than a few years after his arrival in Verith. It seemed even they were unnerved by the light of the woman before him, retreating deep within the darkest parts of his soul—or whatever soul he had. Slowly, he sank to his knees before this siren, his mind screaming at him to *stand up, turn around, walk out.* Never look back.

But no matter how much he shouted in his head, no matter how much he yanked and pulled at the noose growing tighter around his neck with each heartbeat, he couldn't break through. She'd somehow managed to lock away his free will so quickly, so thoroughly, with only a few simple, regurgitated words.

And he fucking *hated* her for it.

Andrian's hands reached up, gripping the edges of the deep hood he wore. He slowly pulled it back, exposing his face to the still air of the temple, his eyes taking a moment to adjust to the dim, flickering candlelight. When he finally lifted his gaze, he fed all his anger and betrayal and loathing into his stare, hoping it would do *something* to break this spell.

But when his eyes met hers, he forgot, for the most fleeting of moments, that he hated her.

She was the most beautiful woman he'd ever seen. That same thought had drifted through his mind when he'd first seen her in the palace courtyard, just before the Choosing, stepping out of that cabby wearing a dress of molten gold. Now, her gown was made of sinful black lace. Sheer paneling revealed sweeping expanses of tan skin that shimmered faintly in the dull candlelight of the room. Her hair was dark, nearly the same as his own onyx black, and fell around her shoulders in thick waves. Suddenly, he had the strange urge to leap up from where he knelt, to bury his fingers into those near-black tresses, to know exactly how good it would feel to wind his hands in the lengths and *pull*—

Fuck. Not good.

He thought he could save himself from those thoughts by moving his attention to her eyes.

Gods, he had always been such a fucking idiot.

Those eyes stole his breath from his lungs and pulled apart the last threads of his shredded free will. They were so green, the color and life of a rich forest bottled up and placed into the eyes of a creature with the power to consume him.

Andrian hated her eyes most of all.

He felt his mouth begin to move, his tongue loosening as words began to flow, the recoiling in his mind doing nothing to stop them from spilling into the room. He was a puppet on a string, a marionette dancing for a beautiful master.

"On this day, and on every day of my life, I will answer your call, My Queen." His voice was deep, gravely, grating against his ears as it was pulled from his throat. *Fuck, why can't I stop this?* "I swear my life, my sword, my shield, and my soul to you. To be your armor against the world and to guard your back against those who wish this kingdom harm."

Her green gaze glowed brighter, and his shadows tremored in response, deep in their hiding place within the pit where his soul should be. He could hear his father's voice in his mind, echoing through his skull as if the man were standing right beside him.

"Weak, Andrian. You are weak."
And then she was speaking again.
"What's your name?"
Don't answer her.
"Andrian, My Queen."
FUCK.

At least his voice was tense and his words short. It was enough for her expression to turn slightly wary, her head cocking just slightly to the side as she assessed him. Intelligence and cold calculation shimmered in her eyes, and a quieter piece of him twisted with a sudden desire to know how her mind worked, to see what she hid behind the face of the wild, untamed enchantress.

But the louder piece of him, the more rational part of him, forced those thoughts away.

He wanted to know nothing about her. Only things that would help him grip onto his hatred.

She continued her silent assessment, and though he tried to hang fiercely to his resolve, he felt his soul as it was stripped bare in the dark quiet of that temple. A wave of raw anger and despair and frustration rose in the wake of her stare, trying to lock her out, trying to hold on to something, anything that he recognized as him ...

But he was fooling himself. He was nothing. Worthless. Things that were worthless couldn't be protected, especially from assaults by wicked little females.

He was pulled from the dark pit of his thoughts by movement across her face. Movement that he absolutely did not expect.

She *smiled*.

It wasn't a kind smile. It was a smile that burned and stole more than she'd already taken. Somehow, someway, this girl who had to be just barely twenty-one gave him a smile that screamed of knowledge, power, and dark promises.

It was positively terrifying and beautiful all at once. A dark goddess stood before him.

A goddess he hated.

"Then welcome to my court, Andrian." She extended a hand to him, the skin still faintly glowing, illuminating her tan skin. He stared at that hand and that skin for seven long heartbeats, every piece of him warring with another. Nothing was stable anymore. Up was down, left was right. Right was wrong.

Right was wrong.

And it was on that last thought that he finally lifted his own hand, placing it into hers, the skin of their palms meeting in the faintest of touches.

Yesterday, when he'd seen her step out of that carriage, when their eyes had locked and his ears had rang so intensely he'd thought his mind might collapse like a dying star, he'd written it off as an anomaly. A chance headache. Nothing to dwell on.

Now, though, when his skin met hers ... it was as if he'd been struck by lightning, burning through his veins and searing his skin from the inside out. It was finally enough to stir his magic from the dark pit where it had hidden, slithering out beneath his skin like a dark serpent. Only years and years of training kept him from ripping his skin from hers, from flinching away from her touch and her gaze and her presence. The only acknowledgment he allowed himself was a slight narrowing of his eyes, his world pinching just slightly smaller around the edges.

If she'd felt that too, she didn't react. Not a single muscle twitched in her frustratingly perfect face.

Interesting.

The quiet side in his head used that as an opportunity to speak out again: that, perhaps, he would be better off fearing her than hating her.

He brushed that side away, yet again.

No matter what, life had taught him that hatred was preferable to fear. Preferable to anything.

After all, hatred was the only thing that guaranteed survival in this world.

Finally, slowly, Andrian rose to his feet, his body again moving without his permission. Once he'd risen again to his full height, he noted with feigned disinterest that she was taller than he'd expected. He also noticed toned muscles beneath the bare skin of her arms and legs, and the hand that held his was rougher than it appeared, her palms calloused in a way that suggested training in swordplay.

He still hated her.

But he couldn't deny that he was curious.

His guard dropped for just a second, and that was—apparently—all it took. She tightened her grip on his hand and yanked hard, her strength yet another surprise, pulling him until they stood close enough to share breath. His heart pounded in his chest as her scent touched his nose. She smelled of eucalyptus and cedarwood and a hint of jasmine, heady and sweet and delicious.

Utterly intoxicating.

He forced his eyes to blink, forced his mind to snap out of its reverie or whatever the *fuck* was happening to him.

So fucking weak.

She drew him even closer, craning her head up just slightly until her lips brushed lightly against the shell of his ear. Her soft breath whispered against his skin, the hair at the back of his neck standing on end, as she spoke words only for him.

"I look forward to learning more about you, Andrian. I am

especially eager to hear why you said those words, when the only emotion I can see on your face is contempt."

He'd fought enough to make his disdain noticeable, then. He was still weak, but at least he wasn't completely useless.

If he was going to disappoint her, he might as well start now.

"And I look forward, *Mariah*," he growled, pushing her name through clenched teeth, leaning further into her space, "to seeing just how much you'll come to regret this decision tonight. To seeing how much I *don't belong here*." With that, he leaned away, just enough to meet her gaze, and smirked at the confusion and shock he found written in those hypnotic green eyes.

She thought for a moment before narrowing her gaze. "This wasn't *my* choice. And I gave you an out, remember? *You* are the one who had the choice. You didn't have to swear the oath."

"Did I not?"

They were silent for too many heartbeats, their gazes suddenly locked, neither wishing to back down first. He wanted nothing more to do with her, but by the Goddess there was something about those emerald eyes that made him want to rise to her challenge, to meet her head-on, to break her and make her *his*.

Wait ... what?

She released his hand just as that last thought filtered through his head, pushing away from him too quickly. He watched as she tried to twist her lips back into a smile, managing an expression that only resembled a grimace. He watched her, holding his features still as stone, trying desperately to get control of himself and the shadows twisting just under his skin.

Finally, blessedly, she turned on her heel, putting her back to him as she strode to the altar at the front of the room.

Andrian ignored the way she moved with athletic grace over the ground. Ignored the way her hips swayed with each step. Ignored the way the black lace of her dress caught and pulled and swirled around her legs.

He followed after her, passing over the stares of the six other men who now stood around that altar. They were as close to him as brothers; they'd been Marked as children, moved to the capital together, trained as a single unit to protect a queen they hadn't met—or, for most of them, would never meet. Not the way seven of them would.

Andrian should've been part of that majority. The odds were in his favor.

But he'd never been particularly lucky.

He loosened the damper on his magic, just enough to release the pressure building beneath his skin. As he stepped into a dark corner beside the dais, wreathed in the same shadows that crawled beneath his skin, tendrils of darkness spindled off his shoulders and into the blackness above.

Hidden, dark, quiet.

Just how he preferred to keep his curse.

Unlike most magic, this was no gift. Or at least, it hadn't been bestowed by any god or goddess of Onita. Only a few knew of it—the other men in this room being part of that select few—and he'd only been able to grapple with the gift after reading those dusty old manuscripts he'd found in the library.

His only other connection to that side of his blood—the mother from the northern kingdom of Leuxrith—was lost to him not long after he'd been Marked.

Andrian hated thinking about his mother and the accident that stole her gentle soul from the world.

Distantly, he heard the high priestess, Ksee, say a few pompous words to bring the ceremony to a close. She and Queen Ryenne dismissed the lucky men who would go forth with the rest of their lives, bearing the Mark on their chests but with their necks free of the noose of the Selection oath. Andrian felt almost wistful as he watched them file out of the room, followed closely by Ryenne and the priestess.

His feeling vanished as his attention settled back on Ksee, watching her back sharply as she strode out of the temple doors. He'd never liked that priestess. Something about her set his teeth on edge, made him uneasy in much the same way his father and the other lords of the kingdom always had.

And now, he would never be free. Of her, of the Royals, of his father ...

Andrian found, in that moment, another reason to hate his new *queen*.

Unbidden, as if pulled by the thought, his eyes darted to where she still stood on the dais. Another crash of lightning raced through him when he found her staring back at him.

She had that smile on her lips again, the one that made his skin crawl. She was a dark witch hiding in a young woman's skin.

He ignored the knot in his stomach. Narrowed his eyes. Smiled wickedly back.

Her grin faltered, just slightly, before she wrenched her gaze from his. Her attention drifted over the remaining men gathered around her—her new Armature, he realized with a sudden jolt.

Of which he was now one.

He used her distracted attention to survey who was to be his eternal brother, to join him forever in this damnation within the walls of the palace. He spotted Sebastian, along with his younger brother, Matheo. Then there was the one whose father had been Kreah—Feran—and beside him was quiet, ever-brooding Drystan. Finally, there were Quentin and Trefor, both of them usually more interested in fucking around than taking anything seriously.

Not that anyone could tell that now, though. Not with their chests puffed out in pride as they waited patiently for their new queen to speak, already lost to her spell.

It made Andrian sick.

Finally, Mariah broke the expectant silence.

"If I'm being honest ... I'm not exactly sure what to say right now." Her voice was the same it had been earlier: soft and strong and flirtatious. Quentin, Matheo, and Trefor chuckled, and smiles touched the faces of Sebastian and Feran. Only Drystan remained quiet, but amusement glimmered in his eyes in the flickering candlelight.

Andrian only seethed.

"I'm ... very excited to get to know each of you," Mariah continued, meeting each of their gazes—even Andrian's, a fleeting glance that moved past him as fast as it could. "I'm sure you all know that you're now expected to move into the quarters in the queen's wing—"

"Everything will be handled, My Queen." It was Sebastian who spoke. Sebastian, who had always been their level-headed and self-assured leader. On most days, Andrian considered him his best friend.

Right now, though, he only wanted to strangle him. And he wasn't exactly sure why.

The only thing that kept Andrian rooted in place was his glance at Mariah; at the blush that slowly began to crawl its way up her cheeks. It filled her features with a curious sort of innocence, an innocence he suspected she'd not had in years. Suddenly, his mind was filled with a myriad of images, ideas, ways he might one day get her flushed with that color all the way down her pretty little neck—

No. He would not entertain those thoughts now.

He would not entertain those thoughts, *ever.*

The blush still on her cheeks, Mariah responded to Sebastian, "Oh ... okay. That's great. I, um ... I think I'll return to my rooms now. This whole day ... these past two days, in fact ... have been overwhelming, to say the least." A sheepish grin. Another wave of chuckles. Even Drystan smiled softly this time.

Andrian gritted his teeth so hard he worried they might crack.

"Of course, My Queen." It was Sebastian again. *By the Goddess, could he please stop talking to her?* "Please, let me escort you."

Andrian lurched at those words, almost driven out of the comfort of his shadowy alcove.

But he halted himself just in time. Regained control of his body, his mind, his fucking senses.

This was good, he reminded himself. It was good for her to focus on the others.

It would keep her attention off him. And he wanted nothing more than to remain in his darkness, shrouded by his shadows.

So he held himself still as he watched her smile at Sebastian.

"Mariah," she said, in that lilting, musical voice. "My name is Mariah. I want you all to call me by my name."

And even though it was the first order issued by his queen, Andrian vowed to never follow it. He wouldn't call her by her name, not to her face.

Not until the stars winked out and the moons fell from the sky.

A grin spread across his face again just as Sebastian nodded.

"We would be honored ... Mariah."

Andrian choked back a snort.

Ignoring him in his dark alcove, Mariah smiled brilliantly at Sebastian, stepping forward to take his offered arm. She let him turn her, lead her toward the temple doors. Right before they passed through the doorway, though, she twisted her head back over her shoulder, immediately finding Andrian's gaze. Her smile turned dark, the face of the temptress again ghosted over her face, before she whipped her head back to face forward, disappearing through the open doorway.

Andrian let loose a growl, low and deep in his throat, as his brothers filed out after them. He was soon alone in the darkness of the temple with nothing but his shadows and his thoughts.

She was intoxicating, dangerous, beautiful, the source of new obsession he couldn't quell even if he tried.

And he hated her for it.

CHAPTER 17

Mariah reveled in the burning in her lungs, the feeling of sweat dripping between her shoulder blades, the sound of her feet rhythmically pounding the soft earth beneath her.

She'd awoken before the sun had even crested over the horizon, pulled from the clutches of sleep, her mind on fire, memories of the past week flashing by like shooting stars. Last night, Sebastian had deposited her into her rooms before excusing himself to move into his own neighboring quarters.

Finally alone, Mariah had showered quickly, the water hot and scalding against her skin, before dressing in a long, soft cotton tunic and curling herself into the outrageously comfortable bed.

She'd tried to rest, tried to shut off her mind, but sleep had evaded her. She'd sat up in bed, moonlight filtering in through her bedroom window, and suddenly her attention was drawn to the discarded saddle bags still strewn about her floor. Clothing spilled haphazardly onto the floor, along with a few sheathed throwing knives, a flask of her father's whiskey ...

And there. The book her mother had given her that last night in Andburgh. Mariah slipped out from beneath the thick comforter, padding to the pile on the floor. In a smooth movement, she'd picked up both the book and that flask of whiskey before settling herself on the seat below the window, pulling a heavy gold blanket over her legs.

She'd stared at the book for a long moment, taking a heavy swig of the whiskey. The burn of the liquor settled low in her stomach, dulling the edges of the unusual nervousness that had swept over her the second her fingers touched the smooth leather binding. She'd read that strange word inscribed onto the cover in silver foiling—*Ginnelevé*—over and over and over until the twists in her gut settled and the whiskey buzzed around her vision.

It was only then that she dared to open the book, to fan through the pages until her fingers caught on a single page. She'd taken another swig of whiskey, and then began to read.

> *I had a dream last night.*
> *I dreamed of silver and gold flames, of leathery wings, both blazing and shadowed.*
> *I dreamed of that which was feared, saving us all.*
> *And I dreamed that without darkness, we can never experience the light.*

She'd sighed. Of course, she should've known. Her mother, the airy dreamer she was, would be the one to give her a book filled with nonsensical gibberish. But even as Mariah thought those words, something in her recoiled. Her mother's words from that night by the fire flashed through her mind for the second time that day.

"If—when—*you ever feel lost, truly lost, when you need a reminder of who you are and what you are capable of ... that book will tell you everything you need to know.*"

Well, she certainly didn't need a reminder of that at this moment. She was exhausted and shocked, and more than a bit unsettled, but somehow had never felt more like herself than she had in that temple. It startled her, to feel so comfortable in a position she'd only expected to hate.

She took another swig of whiskey and turned the page.

This page...it was very different, but still very much the same. The writing was gibberish still, but even more chaotic, the words scrawled haphazardly across the fine cream paper. They overlapped each other, making it difficult to make out exactly what they said, but as Mariah continued to study it, she suddenly realized with a jolt what it said.

Repeated, over and over again across that page, was the phrase, "*Love is my strength.*"

Mariah instantly felt sick and slammed the book shut. She tossed it on the ground, far away from her, and had stared at it as feelings of horror and unease sifted through her like sand.

When she'd regained control of the bile that had clawed its way up her throat, when she'd forced her hands to stop shaking and her palms to stop sweating, she'd stood from the bench, picked up the book, and tucked it firmly beneath her mattress before settling herself back into the plush depths of her bed, exhaustion finally nipping at her heels.

As she'd faded into sleep, that familiar voice whispered its familiar mantra, a soothing dictum she was much more comfortable living by:

Love is a weakness.

Suddenly choking on her heaving breath, Mariah was

thrust back into the present, the smell of fall leaves burning her nose as she slowed herself to a walk. She'd heard that voice again, just now, as clearly as if someone had whispered into her ear, its sudden reminder ripping her from her memories of the night. Her eyes wandered idly as her mind returned to her body. She took in the woods around her; the sounds and smells and sights were so familiar, reminded her so much of the forest around her family's cottage it almost *hurt*.

The palace game park was situated behind the stables, and after a few pointed questions to a young stable hand, Mariah found the trailhead with ease. The woods were nestled in a valley between the western walls of the palace and the great rise of the Attlehon mountains, the ground slowly sloping up as the elevation increased into the foothills. Despite the bustling modernities available in both the palace and in Verith, it was clear to Mariah that the early queens—perhaps even Xara herself—had wanted to keep a small piece of the true wildness of Onita close to their home.

She continued to catch her breath as she walked along the forest trail, losing herself in the sound of birds and the rustle of the light fall breeze through the trees. The weather was cooling rapidly with each passing day, and while Verith was a coastal city, the Attlehon Mountains swept cold weather from their heights down towards the palace and the mountain district. Her run this morning was a bit of an impulse—when her mind had pulled her from sleep, all she'd craved was a chance to release some of the cornered energy starting to fester in her body.

Familiar sounds suddenly filled her ears. It was not the sounds of birds or winds or anything that belonged there in the depths of the woods.

No, it was the sound of warriors training.

Curiosity spurred her feet back into a jog, following the sounds of clashing metal and shouting voices.

Male voices, specifically.

Mariah rounded a corner and found herself standing at the edge of a large clearing, halting abruptly to keep herself concealed within the shadows of the thick tree line. The clearing was outfitted as a training space, complete with racks of dulled training weapons and equipment. A large pit had been dug up in the center of the clearing and filled with packed sand, a ring to practice hand-to-hand combat, and another ring was marked in the grass, clearly for sparring. Targets were arranged in a line across the clearing, more racks of longbows and recurve bows and crossbows ready for target practice. And those male voices she'd heard ...

It was her Armature.

All seven of them were there, dressed in training gear. Sebastian and Quentin circled each other in the sand pit, dodging each other expertly, a wild smile on Quentin's face that matched his fiery hair. Drystan, Matheo, and Trefor were leaning against one of the weapons racks, watching the two in the ring, letting out a shout or a jeer every so often whenever one of the sparring males got close enough to the other to land a blow. Mariah's gaze continued to idly wander, pulled away from the sand pit to the dueling ring by another clash of steel on steel.

It was there that she found Feran and Andrian, locked in a fierce duel, sweat dripping from their faces. Feran wielded two Kreah shortswords, much like those preferred by Mariah herself, but with blades curved into a wicked sickle shape. Andrian carried a single double-edged longsword, but the way he moved with it ...

Mariah was mesmerized as she watched the two men circle each other, their years of training evident in every move. Feran was fierce and fast, his dark skin flushed with exertion and slick with sweat, his skill with the twin blades of his people clear with every swipe and parry.

But it was nothing compared to the way Andrian moved. He wielded his sword as if it were an extension of his own arm, anticipating every move Feran handed him, easily blocking and twisting in the morning air. Despite his height, he moved with an animalistic grace, his movements a near blur. Suddenly, he dropped to the ground, Feran's slash missing right over his head just as Andrian's leg shot out, swiping at Feran and forcing him off his feet. Feran tumbled to the ground, losing his grip on his blades just as Andrian rose, pinning Feran where he lay, the tip of his sword touching the vulnerable skin of Feran's throat.

Feran's chest rumbled as if he were chuckling before he spoke to Andrian. Mariah was too far away to hear his words, but she saw the laugh on Feran's lips as he extended a hand up, as Andrian lowered his sword and took it, pulling Feran to his feet.

A genuine smile then touched Andrian's face. Mariah was nearly knocked sideways by the force of it. Not just because of how surprising and unusual it seemed ... but of how inhumanly *attractive* Andrian looked in that moment. The twist of his lips lifted his defined cheekbones, the angle of his chin softening, his white teeth flashing against his tan skin.

What unfortunate thoughts to be having. There were six other men in this clearing to occupy her time with; there was no need to concern herself with that *prick*.

But watching him there, in the clearing as he trained with Feran ... He was so comfortable with his fellow Armature. He was almost a different man here: open, warm, inviting. A leader.

And with that thought, his gaze slid to hers, instantly

finding where she stood hidden in the shadows of the woods at the edge of the clearing. Those tanzanite eyes hardened immediately, everything about him going tense, his easy comfort vanished.

Well, Mariah thought, *I guess my spying is over.*

She took a single, deep breath before stepping out of the trees and into the clearing.

The attention of the other six Armature snapped to her, their chatter instantly ceasing. Sebastian and Quentin halted mid-spar, the former not hesitating to step out of the sand pit and take a few steps toward her, a warm smile of greeting upon his handsome face.

Mariah met his smile with one of her own. "I hope I'm not intruding on anything." She glanced around at the clearing, the weapon racks lining the edge, the sparring pit. "Although, I have to say, I'm a little disappointed I didn't receive an invitation."

Trefor, who stood closest to her leaning too-casually against a tree, was the first to speak. "My Qu-Mariah," he corrected himself, grinning sheepishly. "Not that we aren't glad to see you, but … what are you doing here?" His short blond hair was spiked with sweat, his pale cheeks flushed with color.

Mariah turned her smile to Trefor. "Well, I was just out for a morning run, but this is looking much more interesting." She shot a glance around at all of her Armature, purposely avoiding a set of distracting blue eyes, and watched as amusement and curiosity sparked in their expressions. Sebastian was the next to speak, taking a few more steps in her direction, obvious confusion written on his face.

"Mariah … do you wish to train with us?"

Mariah met Sebastian's stare, rolled her shoulders once, and stretched the muscles in her neck. "Yes. Why not? It's been over a week. I wouldn't want to get rusty."

Sebastian's confusion extended itself to the rest of her Armature as they darted their eyes to each other. "Maybe we could arrange a separate session where we can each dedicate time to work with you ..." Quentin's question faded as a shit-eating grin spread across Mariah's face.

"Oh, Quentin. I don't know you yet, and I'll forgive you just this once because you don't know me yet, either." She paused. "But my father, a former special reserves fighter in the Queen's Seventy-Seventh Legion, has been training me since the day I took my first step." Leaning into ... whatever it was she was doing, she turned from the group and pulled the hem of her tunic over her head in one smooth movement, dropping it to the ground beside her. She now wore only her tight undershirt, the thin material designed to wick away her sweat, its length cropped to just below her navel. The cold air felt refreshing on her burning skin, still hot from the frantic pace of her earlier run. She turned back to her Armature, meeting the gaze of the one with fire-red hair.

"Now, Quentin. Since you seem the most concerned with my training, I'd like you to get into this pit with me. I'm assuming your sparring with Sebastian was just a warmup?"

She moved forward and brushed past the gathered men, Quentin following after her, that same fiery grin back upon his face.

"What, *exactly*, are you wanting to do, Mariah?"

She knew the grin she threw him was more a baring of teeth than a true smile. "I want to spar."

Sweat poured down her face, her lungs burned, and her teeth were still barred in that same grin as she circled Quentin, his red hair dark with sweat and his freckled skin flushed with exertion.

She knew he'd started off going easy on her, but the second she delivered a powerful roundhouse kick to his chest, sending him flying back on his ass, he'd woken up, fire dancing in his eyes.

She'd wondered, briefly, if the element lived in more than just his hair and gaze. If it ran in his veins, just as it ran in her brother's.

Just as threads of light now lived in hers.

Since then, they traded blows evenly and regularly. She felt the attention of her Armature on her as she moved, an unfamiliar weight on her skin she didn't mind. Quentin darted in, aiming a hook to her gut, but she dove out of his reach before driving her elbow into his side. He grunted, trying to twist, but she was one step ahead of him. Now behind him, she leaped onto his back with a nimble jump, one leg swinging around his neck. Her sudden weight and the momentum twisted him off balance, and they dropped instantly to the ground. In a heartbeat, he was beneath her, lying facedown in the sand, her knee pressed against his shoulder blade. She leaned her head down and whispered into his ear.

"If you tap out now, I promise I'll teach you that move."

Quentin's bottle green eyes darted up to hers in a joking glare, pausing only a few heartbeats before patting the ground beside him twice. Shit-talking chuckles arose from the rest of her Armature as Mariah stood up, letting Quentin go. She was still breathing heavily as she walked to her discarded tunic, wiping the sweat off her brow.

Quentin stood up and quickly dusted himself off before following her out of the pit, giving her shoulder a playful shove. "You weren't kidding, girl. That was impressive." He froze suddenly, obviously worried he'd pushed it too far.

No matter how impressed he might be with her, she was still his queen.

But Mariah only let out a tinkling laugh, shoving him playfully back. She was thankful he treated her like how she used to be—ordinary, normal, with nothing in her veins that set her apart from all the rest. "Keep working, *boy*, and one day maybe you'll be able to pin me back."

And just like that, Quentin's grin returned. He tossed her a wink before turning towards a pile of water canteens resting against a tree at the edge of the clearing.

Mariah let her gaze follow him, lost in her thoughts for a moment before she felt the heavy weight of several stares on her. The rest of her Armature still stood there, watching her, most of their expressions a blend of mixed awe and blatant interest. Even Andrian, though he lingered as far from her as he could, couldn't hide the disdainful surprise in his tanzanite eyes.

Suddenly, she felt an urge to move. Standing there, idly, a specimen being watched ...

It hadn't bothered her before, when she'd been in the pit with Quentin. But now, standing leisurely, it was making her skin itch. She turned toward the targets at the other end of the clearing; her feet, desperate for movement, carrying her quickly.

"I'm assuming there are arrows over here, as well?"

But before her question could be answered, a feminine cough sounded behind her. Mariah whirled to find Ciana standing on the edge of the clearing, dressed in leggings and a long cloak, unabashedly eyeing every single one of the men around Mariah. She had no idea when the other girl had arrived, or how long she'd been standing there, but Mariah nearly broke into hysterics at the expression on Ciana's face.

Her friend turned her gaze to meet Mariah's, swallowing once before speaking.

"Goddess-*damn* you, Mariah! One day with your new boyfriends and you're already abandoning me. Next time, the least you could do is extend an invitation."

CHAPTER 18

"Absolutely not, Ciana. No. Not a chance."

Ciana huffed, popping a hip and crossing her arms over her chest. "Ksee will be pissed if you don't."

Mariah barked a laugh before shrugging at her friend. "Ksee is always pissed at me. Wearing this ... *monstrosity* isn't going to change that."

Lying on the bed before them was a massive emerald ballgown, the bodice consisting of a paneled corset, capped sleeves, and full tulle skirts. Mariah had hissed the second Ciana walked out of the closet with it, staggering under its weight, then had promptly sworn to Qhohena herself that the atrocious article of clothing would never touch her skin.

"Well, then, by all means, what do you want to wear, Your Majesty?"

"Don't call me that," Mariah grumbled, her fingers idly scratching at the layers of green tulle covering her white comforter. "It's just a personal preference. For example, you like gin; I prefer whiskey." She gestured to the dress. "This is another one of those preferences. Except, instead of this being gin, it's backwoods piss-water that someone out near Tolona tried to call ale."

Ciana only stared at her, her amber gaze thoroughly unamused.

"Don't look at me like that, either," Mariah said. "If green is the color Ksee wants me in today ... then I might've seen something in the closet that will work. And don't worry; you can assure the priestess it was all my idea."

An hour earlier, Mariah had strode back into the palace, still sweaty and flanked by Ciana and her Armature, her tunic dangling from her fingers. And, naturally, the first person they'd encountered upon entering through one of the side-entrances nearest the stables was Ksee. The priestess had landed a crushing glare on Mariah, fires dancing in her eyes, and issued a pointed remark about the heightened expectations of Mariah's new position. Mariah had nodded once before stalking away, not in the mood to enter another sparring match after the training that morning. She'd felt the priestess's gaze burning a hole between her shoulders as she'd rounded the hallway corner, the feeling only vanishing when she was finally out of Ksee's sight.

A part of her knew she should reconsider her approach to dealing with the priestess.

But she also had no interest in treating with a woman who clearly believed her to be inferior, just because of the circumstances of her birth. As if that were something she'd been capable of controlling.

Mere moments after she'd closed the door to her suites, stretching in the morning sun filtering in through the wall of windows, Ryenne had come bustling in, followed closely by Mikael, his strawberry blonde hair again pulled back by that strip of brown cloth. The chef went to work in the kitchen, the sounds and smells of breakfast food filling the space as Ryenne settled herself at the dining table. Mariah had excused herself to quickly shower, and when she'd reemerged had found a plate with poached eggs, fresh toast, and tomatoes waiting for her on the island.

Ryenne had spent no time waiting to quell the happiness that rose in Mariah at the spread of food.

"Today, you will be introduced to the heads of the Onitan Royal families."

Mariah's blood had run cold, and those twin balls of thread in her soul had roiled in response. They'd been resting so quietly all morning, content to lie dormant as she'd trained with her Armature. Now, though, at the mention of the Royals, they leapt and cracked through her veins as whips of burning light. Despite how delicious the food in front of her looked, she suddenly had no desire to eat any of it.

Ryenne had waited in silence, watching as Mariah stared blankly at her plate. When several long moments had passed without a response, the Queen spoke again.

"You knew this was coming, Mariah. They are the closest to nobility that the kingdom has. The Royals have always been important advisors to the crown, and it is important for the queen to heed their advice when she can."

Mariah still didn't respond. Eventually, Ryenne had heaved an aggravated huff and stood.

"This is expected of you, Mariah. The Royals arrived last night and will be ready to meet in an hour. You will attend; your queen commands it." Mariah's gaze had snapped to Ryenne, the Queen's ocean eyes looking more like icy depths. And in that moment, Mariah knew she wasn't speaking to the woman she'd come to respect, come to think of as a friend; she was speaking to her *queen*. While the magic behind the crown now resided almost entirely within Mariah, she didn't yet hold the true power within those palace walls.

THREADED

So, Mariah heeded Ryenne's words, and a little under an hour later, she stood with Ciana in her bathroom wearing the dress she'd pulled out of the depths of the closet.

"Alright," Ciana said. "You win. This is a million times better."

The dress was made of soft green velvet, the same shade as the ugly mess Ksee had wanted Mariah to wear. However, instead of a full skirt and capped sleeves, it was form fitting, hugging Mariah's curves as if it was painted on. The neckline scooped down Mariah's chest, just enough to highlight her collarbones and a hint of cleavage, but not enough to be scandalous. The sleeves were long, ending at Mariah's wrists, and the material clung off her shoulders and dipped low on her back to create a stunning silhouette. There was a single slit up the left leg, ending near the middle of her thigh, and a short train pooled beneath her feet. As Mariah surveyed the material closer, she found that the entire gown was adorned with delicate golden designs, swirling up and around the dress, making the material shimmer when she moved.

Ciana's warm amber gaze met Mariah's in the mirror. A simple sweep of kohl along Mariah's lash line had the green of her irises blazing. "Go get 'em, My Queen." Ciana winked.

Mariah groaned, but a smile touched her lips.

Mariah's Armature waited outside her chambers, all dressed in clothing fit for the occasion. Mariah allowed herself one appreciative sweep of the group, and a few of them—Sebastian, Feran, Drystan—nodded their heads as her gaze briefly met theirs. She ignored the dark figure lingering near the back, the prickle of his blue gaze raising goosebumps to her skin. It wasn't until she felt that attention drop from her face and sweep down her form and the dress she wore that she finally decided to acknowledge him. Mariah locked her eyes on Andrian then, waiting for his gaze to rise. When their eyes collided, she couldn't help but smirk.

Caught you.

She turned on her heels and began striding off down the hall, feeling his burning glare as she chuckled softly to herself. Her steps faltered slightly, however, as she remembered his words to her last night.

"I look forward to seeing just how much you come to regret this decision tonight."

Her mind still whirled from those words.

What had he meant by that? And if he meant it ... why had he sworn the oath?

Shaking the thoughts from her head like cobwebs, she strode further down the hallway, finding Ksee, Ryenne, and Ryenne's Armature waiting for them at the end of the Queen's wing. Ryenne smiled at Mariah, looking relieved, but Ksee's glare sparked with flames. Making a point to not look at the priestess, Mariah approached Ryenne and dropped into a graceful curtsey.

"Good afternoon, My Queen."

Ryenne bowed her head in return, the snowdrop crown of Onita nestled within the golden waves of her hair. Mariah couldn't help but notice the faint streaks of gray that now slightly dulled the brilliance of that gold as the queen spoke. "Queen Apparent. You look stunning. And, I must say, quite a sight with your new Armature guarding your back."

Mariah smiled. "I'll admit, I'm impressed. They do clean up nicely." She turned her head to Sebastian, who now stood on her right, and winked. She caught his soft answering grin in the periphery of her vision as she turned back to face Ryenne, nodding once.

"Shall we?"

Ryenne watched Mariah, her gaze guarded. Whatever the queen was thinking, her expression revealed little. Finally, the queen dipped her head before turning on her heel, leading them down the winding palace corridors.

The Royals waited for them in a cavernous meeting room, the monstrous table within covered with all manner of fine foods: cheeses, fruits, eggs, meats, and even fish fresh from the boats that moored in the docks along the Bay of Nria. Mariah's mouth watered as her stomach silently grumbled, suddenly wishing she'd forced herself to eat more of her breakfast after that morning's workout. Especially as she took in those who also occupied the room.

Seated around the table were six men, all of varying ages. Some appeared younger, around the age of Mariah's Armature, some middle-aged, and one grizzled man who looked to be nearing seventy. And every single set of those male eyes were trained on her, scrutinizing, judging, dissecting. Mariah met each as she followed Ryenne to the head of the table, where two high-backed chairs were placed. Mariah sat to Ryenne's right, the queen taking her seat in the larger of the two chairs as both their Armatures spread themselves around the room. Mariah could feel their watchfulness, their wariness, as they assumed their posts. The Royals instantly quieted, their attentions turning fully to Ryenne.

"Good morning, My Lords. I trust your travels to Verith were smooth and you have all settled comfortably into your rooms." Ryenne's voice rang through the room with practiced ease. The Royals answered with their mumbled thanks, the occasional, "Your Majesty" and "My Queen" interspersed throughout. Not one rose from their chairs or so much as inclined their heads.

Mariah felt her magic stir further in her gut, agitated and

frustrated. It was then that she realized the slight, the insolence of these lords to not bow to their queen. She wondered how—or why—Ryenne tolerated it. The queen continued, the lack of decorum shaking her little. "Wonderful. Well, I am conscious of the reason for your journey, so I will not keep you waiting any longer." She paused, shooting a warning glance at Mariah. Mariah read the words in those ocean-blue eyes as if the queen had spoken them to her directly.

Play nice.

She swallowed hard and dipped her head. But her magic ... her magic only twisted harder, rebelling against the order. It was all still so new, so foreign. Mariah shot up a silent prayer that she had the control to keep it restrained within her veins.

Ryenne spoke again, "I would like to formally introduce you all to Qhohena's Chosen, our new queen apparent, Mariah."

Mariah dipped her head respectfully to the gathered Royals and the movement ... it nearly brought her physical pain. The threads in her veins wrapped around her muscles, her bones, and Mariah fought against them just to bend her neck.

She pushed back the urge to grit her teeth. This meeting was important to her reign. The queen needed the support of the Royals in order to rule.

Her reign. Still such a foreign concept, yet one she unwillingly grew more accustomed to with each passing hour she spent in that palace.

"It is an honor to meet you all, My Lords."

There was no response to her greeting; only continued stares from the men in that room. Mariah bit her tongue, annoyance rising fast, and bringing with it the silver-gold of her magic. She felt sparks in her mouth and clenched her jaw closed, her vision flashing with light.

Ryenne, thankfully, took over once more. "Mariah, I

would like to introduce you to Lord Campion of Kasia, Lord Beauchamp of Sacale, Lord Hareth of Ettervan, Lord Cordaro of Tolona, Lord Laurent of Antoris, and Lord Shawth of Khento."

Recognizing that as Ryenne's own family name, Mariah shifted her attention to the Lord of Khento. He was not young, but certainly not old either, with wispy blonde hair, watery blue eyes, and the growing hint of a gut. His entire presence was slimy, and the slight, pervasive sneer he directed at Mariah made her want to crawl out of her own skin.

The Royals each inclined their heads in turn as Ryenne introduced them, still watching Mariah but also refusing to directly meet her gaze. The queen eventually moved on into a conversation of pleasantries, drawing the attention of the lords away. Even Lord Shawth pulled his gaze away, yet Mariah still noticed the lingering cruel smirk that touched his pallid face.

Mariah hardly listened to the words being exchanged between Ryenne and the Royals, focusing instead on keeping her temper and her magic in check. It still pulsed against her skin, clawing just below the surface, pushing forth outrage she was sure didn't belong to her ... or, perhaps, it did. She nodded and smiled when Ryenne did, using the Queen's actions to lead her own as she lost herself in the whirlwind of her mind. Suddenly, she felt the heavy weight of eyes on her, and her gaze was pulled to the dark stare of Lord Beauchamp. Mariah remembered distantly that he was the Lord of Sacale, a southern coastal city nestled within the cliffs of the Attlehon Mountains, and was the birthplace of her father. Lord Beauchamp was the oldest amongst the lords, his skin wrinkled, body hunched, hair white.

"My Queen ... a question, if I may." The room grew silent as Ryenne turned her attention to the elderly lord.

"Of course, My Lord." Ryenne dipped her head respectfully, urging him to continue.

The old man nodded at Mariah without looking at her. "What is her family name? I do feel like one of us would have remembered a face and body like that if she were of our own stock, even if she hailed from a distant branch."

The entire room froze.

Behind her, Mariah felt more than saw the step forward that Sebastian and Quentin took. Across the room, in a corner wreathed in more shadow than the rest, Andrian perked up, the touch of an interested smile on his full lips.

She ignored them all as she locked her gaze on the old lord, his own still focused on Ryenne, as if Mariah were not even in the room.

Mariah saw Ryenne take a breath to speak.

Again, she decided she didn't want the queen being the one to fight her battles for her.

"My family name, My Lord, is Salis." Her voice was as cold as the cataclysmic anger now freezing over in her belly. She knew her eyes glinted with a hint of the magic coiling unchecked through her veins like a thousand snakes. "My father's family hails from Sacale, just as you do. I am common born, but I am as much Onitan as you." She paused, seething for a moment as she planned her next words carefully. "I'm also my own woman and am sitting at this table, just as Ryenne is. So please, do your future queen the simple *courtesy* of directing your questions to her, and not speaking of her as if she weren't seated no more than ten feet from you."

The room was silent for several heartbeats, frozen as each player watched and waited for the move of the other. The world held its breath, the powers inside Mariah writhing to her skin as the last of her control vanished like mist. Threads of silver and gold ached for freedom, prodding their way into her fingertips, scraping for a chance to rip their way into the world.

Another aging lord—Lord Campion of Kasia—broke the silence. But instead of addressing Mariah, he chose to speak to the other gathered Royals, ignoring the blazing green gaze of the dark-haired woman with light pushing out from under her skin.

"Well, this is very much unfortunate, and I dread for the future of this kingdom. But there is naught to be done now. She wasn't raised properly and will need to be trained before we can allow her to ascend the throne. Ryenne—"

The room erupted in burning light, silencing the Lord of Kasia.

CHAPTER 19

Light and power poured from every inch of her, sweeping through the room in a wave of undiluted wrath. Somewhere, in the distant recesses of her mind, Mariah thought she heard someone scream.

Burning, burning, burning. She'd kept that magic forced down for too long, her still-weak grasp on her control not enough to hold it back when the Royals had set her anger on fire, those twin spheres of power unleashing themselves through her. Both the silver and gold threads of light craved freedom, to exact her will, to solidify the place the Goddess had chosen her to hold. And she gave in to that urge, letting the magic burn through the remaining shreds of her humanity.

Ryenne hadn't warned her, hadn't spoken of this feeling, this wild hunger and rage.

And truthfully, she wasn't particularly keen to let it go.

Mariah thought she felt someone grab her arm, thought she saw a pair of ocean-blue eyes filled with panic flood her vision, but it all quickly faded away into the background of the hurricane of power enveloping her. All she could see, all she could feel, was silver and gold full of both death and life, spinning through the world as if different sides of the same coin.

It felt so good, felt so *right*. And she had no intentions of reining it back in.

That is, until a figure exuding solid strength gripped her arm, the hands on her skin firm yet calming, soothing. She couldn't see much beyond eyes and auras, but when she turned her head in idle curiosity, she was met with hazel irises shrouded in a cool gray. A name filled her mind, a name that blocked out some of the vengeful chaos still flowing freely through the air.

Sebastian.

She repeated his name to herself like a chant, as if it were an anchor to bind her amidst the magic exploding from her. Mariah felt those threads of light slowly begin to retreat, pulling from the very edges of the room, seeping back to where they rested, hesitantly, under the surface of her skin. Sebastian's form began to take the place of that dark shroud: olive skin, handsome face, dark hair, the black dress clothes detailed in gold that he and the rest of her Armature had donned for this meeting.

And that was when Mariah remembered.

Her blood ran cold as she felt herself regain just enough control to pull her gaze from Sebastian, glancing around the room as her magic began to filter back into her skin.

As she took in the devastation she'd wrought.

The Royals still sat around the table, but their eyes had dipped, arms thrown up to cover their faces to hide from the inferno of light that had poured from Mariah. Slowly, Mariah watched Shawth, Laurent, Cordaro, and Hareth drop their hands from where they'd been gripped tight over their eyes, blinking rapidly as if to clear the blinding light still lingering in their gazes. A part of her, the part that was less vengeful, more cautious, was relieved to see the lords relatively unharmed.

Her relief was fleeting, however, as she realized the same couldn't be said of the two remaining lords. Her insides turned to ice as she turned her attention to Campion and Beauchamp. Campion was breathing, but his eyes ... He'd clearly not been able to cover his gaze fast enough before Mariah erupted. The whites of his eyes were shot through with red, the eyelids frozen as if they, too, hadn't snapped shut fast enough. A mist-gray shroud was slowly dropping over his irises, and his chest heaved as he snapped his head to and fro, trying and failing to focus his gaze on something, anything.

He was *blind*.

Mariah's light, a force which was supposed to be harmless, had *blinded* him.

But that realization wasn't the true reason why her panic began to creep in like a thorny vine, twisting and digging its way around her heart.

Because across from her, slumped in his chair, completely unmoving, eyes still wide in shock and pain as they stared back at her, was Lord Beauchamp. His chest didn't rise or fall, and a line of spittle already began to drop slowly from his agape mouth.

Her explosion of light had done far more than blind a Lord of Onita.

It had *killed* one.

Suddenly, Ryenne stepped into her line of sight, pushing her back from the edge of the table, desperation rampant in her blue gaze. She searched Mariah's face, likely looking for some hint the magic might return, but was placated quickly. Those threads of magic had shrunken back into the dark place in Mariah's soul, the tension released, content with their work.

Over the past two days, she'd felt no fear towards that power growing within her.

Until now.

Ryenne darted a look over Mariah's shoulder to where Sebastian stood, his hand still gripped on Mariah's arm. Her voice was cold as she spoke to him.

"Get her out of here. Now."

Mariah didn't hear Ryenne's next words as she let Sebastian pull her away, leading her through the doors and down the winding hallways toward her chambers. Her sworn guards followed them, eyes watchful and wary, hands on the hilts of their blades until she stepped through the safety of her suite doors. They remained in the hallway, figures tense.

All except *him*.

Mariah was too lost in the spiral of her emotions to notice fully, but a part of her still caught his movement as Andrian peeled away from the group not long after leaving the conference room, blending into the shadows against the hallway walls and vanishing from sight. She couldn't process it then, but when she would reflect upon that moment later, she would recall what seemed to be the hint of a dark, wild smile on his full lips, his tanzanite eyes gleaming with something far from fear or worry.

CHAPTER 20

Mariah sat on one of the couches in her suite's living room, the past few minutes a haze. She knew little about how she'd gotten there, only that Sebastian now knelt before her, worry thick in his hazel eyes.

She still wore that stunning green gown, her hair still fell in waves around her face in loose, dark tendrils. She thought for a moment that it looked like whispers of shadows, of the darkness that must be seeping steadily into her soul.

Or, perhaps, that darkness had always been there, lurking beneath the surface, desperate for a chance when she would be uprooted just enough for it to be set free.

For how else could she have killed a Lord of Onita, simply because he'd *insulted* her?

Mariah felt herself falling again, spiraling into that place of darkness and silver and gold, tendrils of her magic whispered words that promised more death, more pain, should she continue to be denied that which she—which *it*—was owed.

And the same dark part of her that reveled in the power

she'd unleashed begged her to listen, begged her to want those things, too.

She was still lost to the shadows and anger when she faintly heard Sebastian's voice filter through the haze of her consciousness.

"Mariah. My Queen. Come back to me. It's over now; we're safe." He squeezed her hands tighter before he repeated, "Come back to me."

She blinked her eyes once, twice, three times, struggling to clear away the fog before meeting his gaze. The punch of his calm hazel eyes was almost immediate, washing away what remained of her maelstrom of anger and fear. She fell headfirst into it, losing herself in the steady gaze of the man who still knelt before her, her hands gripped in his.

They stared at each other for several heartbeats as the drum of magic continued to fade from her veins. Her entire body settled as she forgot for a moment what had just happened, what she'd done. Sebastian must've felt the shift in her; his jaw relaxed slightly, his hold on her hands loosened, and his shoulders sagged an inch in relief. He rose from where he'd knelt and moved to sit beside her on the couch. She watched him carefully as he sat close enough for her to feel the warmth from his shoulder and thighs. That nearness, the presence of another being, only grounded her further, settled her enough that she was able to press her own feet to the floor, twist her toes into the plush white carpet.

She wasn't sure where her mind wandered to right then, but as she continued to hold Sebastian's hazel stare, she felt her mouth fall open, and words she couldn't source spilled from her lips.

"I miss them."

Sebastian cocked his head. "Who?"

"My family." Mariah turned her head away, gazing out the windows to the Attlehon Mountains. She didn't understand why this was what her mouth had chosen to speak at that moment, when there were so many greater issues rearing their ugly heads, but ... she couldn't help but lean into it, nonetheless. "It may sound childish, but ... I miss them."

Somehow, Sebastian immediately understood, even when she didn't. His voice was gentle as he spoke. "Tell me about them."

And so she did.

She told Sebastian about Ellan and how much he both amused and annoyed her; the way fire burned in his veins but did little to temper his soft kindness. She told him about Wex, the father who'd raised her, trained her, and taught her to never let this kingdom or its people change who she was. And she told him about Lisabel, the mother who carried herself with such a strong, steady grace, but hid so many secrets behind her eyes Mariah had never quite been able to tease out.

"She gave me this ... book. The night before I received the summons from Ryenne for the Choosing," Mariah said. "My father told me she'd known I wouldn't be walking out of the palace after the Choosing. I tried to read some of it last night, but ... it was gibberish. Nonsensical. And yet, I can't shake this feeling that I'm missing something. My mother told me the book would help me when I felt lost, but I can't possibly see *how*." She sighed. "And because of that, I feel as if I'm ... failing my mother somehow. I know I'm not, but that thought is still there, lingering in the back of my mind, pestering me that if she knew I hadn't figured out her gift yet, she would be disappointed. In *me*."

Mariah hadn't noticed that tears had welled up in her eyes and spilled over onto her cheeks. Not until Sebastian reached a hand up, sweeping a rough pad across her skin, smearing the tracks of moisture dripping down onto the green of her gown. She darted her gaze back to his, and he smiled gently down at her, soft smile lines wrinkling around the corners of his eyes.

He was so kind, so gentle, so beautiful. She could lose herself in that easy smile.

"There's no chance that she's disappointed in you," Sebastian said. "I don't know her, but I can't imagine how proud of you she must be." He paused before continuing. "But...if you are convinced there is more to that book than meets the eye, and if you ever want help searching for it, I am at your disposal." His grin widened then. "I'm sure the other guys will bring this up eventually in a way meant to be to my detriment, but I do consider myself to be quite an avid reader. The palace library has long been my favorite place in the city since the day I moved here."

Mariah couldn't stop her answering grin. "I didn't take you for the bookish type, but now knowing that, I absolutely see it."

Sebastian let loose a chuckle, low and warm. The sound melted her chest, chasing away the last lingering remnants of that cold darkness. He'd demonstrated such devotion today, such steadfast support despite what she'd done, without even truly knowing her at all ...

Before she could let herself think too much about it, she leaned into him further, twisting her body so she leaned fully against his side. She nestled her cheek into his shoulder, breathing in his clean scent, his warmth, her head resting against the hollow of his neck. His arm, as if on instinct, instantly circled around her, clutching her shoulder and holding her close.

"Tell me about you. Please." Mariah felt Sebastian shift

beneath her at her request, his head turning to meet her gaze. She smiled up at him. "I want to know more about the well-read boy who came to be Marked, left his home for the capital, and now serves a homesick, unstable queen." She felt another chuckle rumble through him and couldn't stop her eyes from closing, just for a moment. She inhaled another breath of his clean scent, noting there was something else beneath it; something that reminded her of worn leather, of ink on parchment, of nights spent around a hearth lost in the magic of written words.

Which was odd, since she'd never once had a night like that in her life.

"While today was certainly a ... challenge, you are far from unstable, Mariah." She felt him tense, just slightly. "I, for one, am glad you made clear to those lords that—"

"I don't want to talk about that," Mariah interrupted him. "I want to hear about you."

Sebastian paused for a moment, still tense, before exhaling, relaxing with his breath. He didn't apologize—she wouldn't have wanted that, anyway—before he spoke again, obliging her request.

"I was born in Sacale, the first-born son to a family of successful merchants, our wealth attributable to old money that has long been maintained by connections with the fickle spice traders of the Kizar Islands. Much like you, I love my family. My parents were kind and doting, my father the ideal man for me to learn from, my mother as kind and compassionate as the Goddess herself.

"I was three years old when Matheo was born, and our childhood was filled with about as much chaos and fun as you could expect from two brothers so close in age who were growing up in obnoxious wealth without the expectations of being a lord or Royal. He was always wilder than me, though.

On some days, he would want to go on some tryst around the grounds of our family's estate, desperate for an adventure. But even at a young age, I only wanted to stay in our family library, reading dusty books about the swashbuckling pirates who'd founded Sacale so long ago, the same pirates my father told me we were descended from." Sebastian paused, and Mariah glanced up to see a soft smile on his lips. "It seemed that while Matheo sought to write his own stories, I was content to simply read them. We grew apart because of it, for a time."

So, Matheo is his brother. Mariah had noticed how alike they looked, but she couldn't deny her curiosity. What were the odds the Goddess chose two Marked brothers to serve in her Armature?

Sebastian continued. "But then ... the Mark appeared." He halted his speech again, something unsaid in his silence. Mariah felt him shift, his movement almost hesitant as he moved his arm from her shoulder to her upper back, his fingers curling through the ends of her dark hair. Mariah let her eyes drift back shut, the steady movement and the rumble of his voice in his chest nearly enough to rock her to sleep.

"I'm not sure how much you know about how we come to be Marked, but it appears when our queen apparent is born. I was ten; Matheo was seven."

Mariah stilled, her eyes flying open, all thoughts of sleep vanishing like smoke.

She hadn't realized how *young* they all were. Not now, but when that Mark had appeared on their bodies, when they'd been forced away from their families to a strange city, to serve a queen they would have to wait over two decades to know.

At the same time, she also was struck with the other piece of information he'd shared: Sebastian had been ten when she'd been *born. I did not realize they were so much older than me*, she thought. She guessed it must be for the strength and maturity that no amount of training could instill, especially when it came to men.

"We were terrified to tell our parents, of course," Sebastian went on; if he was aware of Mariah's sudden alertness to his words, he didn't reveal it. "Not only had one of us been Marked, but *both* of their sons, the futures of their family ... we didn't know how to tell them. But we knew we had to—tell them, that is. Even as boys, we knew this wasn't something that could or should be hidden from the world.

"So at dinner that night, with the autumn breeze blowing in from the windows in our house along the coast, we broke the news, hoping the fine weather and good food would serve as a peace offering to the blow we were about to land."

Mariah wasn't sure if she'd drawn a breath in several minutes. She again tilted her head back to look at his face, but instead of the pain she'd expected to find there, she found him smiling back down at her, his hazel eyes warm with the memory.

"I don't know why we were ever nervous. Our parents ... they were ecstatic. Not only had one of their sons been blessed with the honor of the gods to serve a new queen, they had said, but *both* of them were deemed worthy. They told us they could imagine no better future for their sons than the one we were given." His smile grew even wider, warmth permeating every inch of his handsome face. "So, they packed us up and escorted us to Verith, all the way to the palace gates, and here we've lived ever since. They visit us from time to time, and of course Ryenne has always been a gracious hostess. I miss them, but the assurances they gave Matheo and me that this was the path we'd always been meant to walk ... it has made the distance easier. And it makes serving you feel like the greatest gift I could've ever been blessed with."

Mariah knew she was crying again, but she didn't care. She

reached up with a free hand, wiping away her tears with a messy sniffle. Suddenly, she was struck with an idea—an idea that shocked her with how perfect it was, something she wanted to slap herself for not seeing and asking earlier. She sat back suddenly, meeting Sebastian's stare head on. He blinked in surprise, his lips parted slightly as he watched her.

"Bond with me. Next week. You should be the first."

Sebastian's surprise morphed into pure shock. "Mariah—are you sure? The first bond...it can be intense. It's always the most vulnerable. I don't—"

"Exactly. It's the most vulnerable. And you just saw me cry my eyes out. Do you know how many people, outside of my family, have seen me cry?" Sebastian didn't answer her, only stared at her with wide eyes. She continued, "None. No one outside of my family, except for you, has ever seen me cry. So if I have to go through a *vulnerable* ceremony with someone for the first time, a ritual that might rattle my entire worldview, I want it to be you."

He watched her for a moment and then exhaled heavily. "You don't know anything about what the bond entails, do you?"

"Nope. Ryenne has been frustratingly tight-lipped about it."

Sebastian rubbed his face, and then met her gaze, his hazel eyes sparkling. "Of course I will bond with you. It's not even a question." His voice was so kind, so gentle, Mariah felt her heart squeeze in her chest. She smiled at him broadly, glad to have accomplished at least one good thing today.

Especially since she'd killed someone earlier.

That reminder had blood rushing into her ears, and she dipped her head down, resting it back on Sebastian's shoulders, desperate to hide the sudden wave of anger and fear washing through her.

"Your parents," she said, clamoring hard for a distraction. "I think I would love to meet them one day."

Sebastian's smile was so broad, she felt the shift of his cheeks against the top of her head. "You will."

They remained there, curled on the couch, well into the night. They talked about their lives before Verith, about the families they both loved so much. At some point, Mikael had snuck in and deposited dinner, leaving as quietly as he'd arrived. Mariah had finally remembered how hungry she was, before ... everything. Each time she was faced with a reminder, her chest would lock up, panic springing a trap closed over her heart and her lungs. And each time, Sebastian responded to her panic with a gentle squeeze of her hand, a reminder that he was there, that she was safe, that somehow Ryenne would find a way to fix the damage Mariah had wrought. Sebastian brought the food over to her on the couch, and with a few more lighthearted stories, Mariah felt her appetite return. She finally ate her dinner, ignoring the relief reflecting back at her in Sebastian's face with each too-large bite she stuffed in her mouth.

There was another feeling she saw starting to flicker in his hazel eyes, but she didn't allow herself to even so much as acknowledge it. She was content tonight with his companionship, his calming strength. She appreciated his gentle touches on her hands and hair and back, how they kept her grounded on this plane of existence, but there was nothing more she could offer him.

He was too good. *Especially* for her.

As the twin moons, now spheres of silver and gold, rose high in the sky, Mariah found her eyelids growing heavy. They'd eventually spread themselves across the L-shaped couch, each sprawled on a section, Mariah's head resting on Sebastian's chest where they met in the center. His fingers were still curled into her hair, stroking it idly. Just as she felt herself finally fading into the clutches of sleep, a single thought flitted through her head.

I have got to stop sleeping on this damn couch.

CHAPTER 21

It had been one week since the meeting with the Royals.

One week, and Ryenne was still struggling to placate those lords, trying to contain the disaster Mariah had wrought in a single fit of uncontrolled anger. Since her outburst, her magic had come alive in her belly in a way it hadn't been before, a constant whirling and twisting mass crawling through her like serpents.

Mariah should've known that taking to the magic so quickly would become a curse of its own. She could hardly sleep, could barely rest. It was beginning to drive her mad. Irritation and frustration and exhaustion scratched at her mind in a place she couldn't itch.

"They are still ... upset, to say the least." Ryenne's voice was weary, her face sagging with both exhaustion and ... *age*. In that past week, a week without the well of magic that had given her long life, Mariah noticed time crept up on the queen, stealing back what had been withheld from it for so long.

All things, Mariah supposed, come with a price.

That same magic coiling in her gut was no different.

Ryenne continued, "Upset ... but I believe finally willing to put this entire matter to rest."

Mariah's attention shot up from the meal she'd been picking at since the queen had strode into her suites, her already nonexistent appetite vanishing as she took in the stoic face of Ryenne and the sour one of Ksee behind her.

"What? They are? How?"

Ryenne heaved a sigh. "It has taken many conversations and great effort on my part, but I believe they've come to acknowledge that Beauchamp and Campion displayed an unforgivable level of disrespect towards you. Through me, they wish to extend their most sincere apologies, for any and all offense you experienced. I've been assured that such disrespect will not happen again."

Mariah watched Ryenne carefully, dissecting her words. *Many conversations ... great effort on my part ... Through me...*

These words were not those of the Royals, but of Ryenne. And Mariah would be a fool to believe otherwise.

"So, what you mean to say is they believe me to be nothing more than an insolent child who takes offense to every slight she's dealt." Mariah met Ryenne's gaze with a hard stare of her own before shrugging a shoulder. "At least they don't want me dead."

At that, Ksee finally spoke up. "You *did* behave like an insolent child, Mariah. They failed to address you, and in response you lost control, blinded one lord, and stopped the heart of another. I have never once in my life questioned the decisions of my Goddess, but—"

"But what?" Mariah interrupted, silver and gold magic snapping like whips through her veins. They pushed against her lungs, wrapped around her heart, fueling the flare of rage at Ksee's tone. "But now you think she made a mistake in Choosing me? It's far too late for that now, Ksee. Either you can respect *your* Goddess's wishes and my future place here in Verith, or you can leave. And don't forget, I didn't want this for myself, either. I've been forced to accept this just as much as you. However, I'm determined to fulfill whatever it is Qhohena has planned for me, and if you intend to stand in my way, then you may see yourself out."

The room was so silent, a pin drop could've been heard. Ryenne held her breath as she watched Ksee, whose own face grew increasingly more red, her eyes blazing with the fires in her veins. Finally, the priestess spoke.

"If you don't wish to seek my counsel, *Your Highness*, then I should like to return to my prayer."

Mariah only glared at Ksee as the priestess rose from the table, not waiting for a response, and stormed from the queen's suites, embers sparking under her heels against the white marble floors.

Once the door clicked shut behind Ksee, Ryenne let loose her sigh, turning to stare hard at Mariah. "You need to stop provoking her, Mariah. She can be … difficult, but she has offered me sage counsel on more than one occasion. If you could simply try to earn her trust, she may one day do the same for you."

Mariah turned her fierce glare to the Queen. "Why should it be *me* trying to earn her trust? What if *I'm* the one who doesn't trust *her?*"

Ryenne's gaze softened, but she still stared at Mariah shrewdly before shaking her head almost imperceptibly. She sighed again, and when she spoke, she opted to change the subject.

"As I was saying earlier, the Royals are willing to move past this. Truthfully, I think a driving motivation for them is that they no longer have to deal with the old Lord Beauchamp anymore." Mariah blinked in surprise, her magic withdrawing in curiosity as Ryenne gave a wry smile. "His son and heir is half his age and has been close friends with Lord Cordaro since they were boys. With another younger Lord now taking up a Royal seat, I could see the Royals being more willing to accept your rule than they were before—an unexpected positive to this ... situation."

Mariah only stared at the queen, her expression close to vacant, before nodding once and dropping her eyes back to the plate of food in front of her. When she finally spoke, her voice was soft, but far from weak.

"I may regret it, but ... I will not apologize for it."

"I know, Mariah. I know." Ryenne's own voice was weary, resigned. There was a brief silence, both women lost to their thoughts, before the queen spoke again.

"How are you getting on with your Armature?"

The question wrenched Mariah away from the situation with the Royals, spurring her thoughts into wandering through the events of the past week. She'd been lying low around the palace, both upon Ryenne's request and on her own initiative. Her few moments spent outside her suites had been in the mornings, which she'd gotten into the habit of starting with a run. Running had always been a favorite of hers whenever she felt the urge to clear her head, something she needed quite a bit these days.

And every morning, her run would end in that clearing in the game park to train with her Armature. Despite everything —the uncontrolled power she'd unleashed, the repercussions of her lack of control—they and Ciana were the only ones in that palace who didn't fear her. Instead, they all grew steadily more comfortable in her presence, sweating and sparring and bantering with her freely as each day passed.

All of them, that was, except one.

Andrian continued to avoid her, arriving at the clearing

early and leaving before the rest. When she'd asked what his problem was, Sebastian and Feran had assured her not to dwell too much on it. Andrian had always been an enigma, they'd said, but they believed he would come around, eventually.

Despite his cool aloofness, she would sometimes catch his wicked tanzanite stare on her, his onyx-black hair wreathed in shadow and a cold, cruel smile on his face. She would whip her gaze away as quickly as she could, and she'd be lying if she denied the slight tremor of fear that lanced through her gut at what she felt in those chilling stares.

She knew they were playing a game of cat and mouse, and it was only a matter of time before someone was caught.

"I think we're getting along great," Mariah said, finally responding to Ryenne. "I know Ksee doesn't approve of this, either, but I train with them every morning in the clearing in the game park."

Ryenne smiled at that. "I know that clearing. It used to be an empty space in the game park until your Marked arrived. They decided they wanted a space just for themselves to train, away from the prying eyes of the barracks, so they spent weeks outfitting and converting it to suit their needs. Kalen and my Armature helped them, of course, but I believe it was Andrian who coordinated most of those efforts."

Mariah blinked, confusion and something *else* catching her off guard at the mention of Andrian's name. From her interactions with him so far, he didn't seem to be one who would take such initiatives. She tucked that knowledge away and moved on before her mind escaped her control again.

"There is something else?" Ryenne looked at Mariah expectantly, and she realized this was likely what the queen had been hoping she would reveal to her.

"I intend to complete the bond tonight. With Sebastian."

Ryenne's face flashed with shock before morphing into

excitement. "That is fantastic, Mariah! An excellent first choice. I believe everyone in this palace can see how devoted he is to you. I will be sure to pray to the Goddess that your first bonding ceremony goes perfectly."

Mariah answered Ryenne's brilliant smile with her own, though it wasn't nearly as bright. While excitement fluttered like butterflies in her stomach at whatever tonight with Sebastian might entail, she couldn't shake the image of burning tanzanite and tendrils of shadow from her mind.

Goddess damn him.

CHAPTER 22

The knock was soft, but Mariah still felt it echo through her bones.

She strode quickly to her suite doors, pulling them open on quiet hinges to find Sebastian, dressed in soft, black cotton pants and a plain white shirt. He was clean-shaven, as always, his short dark hair neat and his hazel eyes glowing warmly in the hallway light.

The sight of him had her shoulders dropping, her muscles relaxing, the threads of magic in her belly calming.

"May I come in?"

His voice was soft and amused, everything about him kind and calm. She smiled at him, stepping out of the doorway. "Sorry—yes, of course. Please come in. Mikael just left and I was about to sit down to eat, if you wanted to join me."

His answering smile was radiant. "Of course. I'm starving."

They sat at the dining table, plates of food scattered around them. They chatted conversationally as they ate, something about it so natural and easy Mariah forgot for a moment that she'd only known this male for just over a week. He already felt so familiar, his presence grounding her like solid earth beneath her feet. Even her magic was quiet around him, for once, something that hardly happened anymore since the events of the meeting with the Royals. The silver threads stayed wound up like a sleeping cat, but those of gold peeked at him with pacified curiosity, content to watch through Mariah's eyes.

She'd relaxed into her chair, her mind blessedly quiet, until a short lull in their conversation had her nerves waking and her mind racing as she suddenly remembered, with a slight jolt, why he was here tonight.

And she knew why she was suddenly nervous.

It had nothing to do with the ritual itself. She still had no idea what to expect, and truthfully, the mystery of what was to come only gave her a little excitement. She wasn't even concerned about the possibility that this could turn into something intimate. The Goddess knows she'd never shied away from sex.

It was Sebastian, the person she'd picked to go through this with first, the person who always made her feel so at ease, who was suddenly making her nervous.

As she sat here, eating and chatting and enjoying dinner, she realized this was a man she could so easily fall in love with. And that alone terrified her more than anything.

She'd resolved to keep him at arms length. She was confident she could do that. But she was nervous, because she feared that regardless of what happened tonight, she would end up causing this too-decent man pain he didn't deserve.

If she was a better woman, she would scrap these plans now. Would ask one of the other Armature who she didn't know as well to do this first bond. But, of course, she was selfish, and because of how unsettled she'd felt this past week, she wanted—*needed*—it to be Sebastian. She needed the strength this bond could bring her. And if that made her a despicable woman, if knowing this night could end with her hurting him ...

Then she could live with it. She had to.

"So," Mariah said, her voice far stronger than she'd expected it to be. "Are you sure you want to do this?"

Sebastian leveled his steady hazel gaze on hers. "There's not a single doubt in my mind, Mariah. I waited twenty-one years to meet you, knowing you would be worth the wait, hoping beyond hope I would be offered the chance to bind myself to you forever."

Her heart twisted. *Well ... fuck.*

Mariah couldn't stop the nervous giggle that escaped her. "And how many of those twenty-one years were spent rehearsing those lines?"

He smiled. "Every single one."

Qhohena, give me strength.

She took a deep breath, closed her eyes, and swallowed once. She shoved away all of those feelings of fear and nervous anxiety, focusing instead on this singular moment before her, what she had to gain. When she opened her eyes, she felt resolve settle over her like a blanket.

"I'm ready. But ... I'm not entirely sure how to do this."

His smile softened, and he stood from where he'd been seated beside her at the table. He then extended a hand to her, and she took it, rising as well.

"That's okay. I've got you."

When Sebastian led Mariah out onto the massive balcony of her suite, she was too stunned at the sight to speak. Distantly, she wondered who'd set this all up, and *when*.

And, of course, how she'd been too distracted to notice it.

In the center of the balcony, completely open to the night sky above and bathed in the bright silver and gold moonlight, was a large circle of lit candles, the flames flickering softly in the gentle night breeze. A large midnight-blue blanket laid flat in the center of that circle, and Mariah would've been enthralled by how truly romantic the whole setting appeared if she hadn't glimpsed the wicked knife that also lay on the blanket, the reflection of both moons and the candlelight glimmering on the polished steel blade.

Sebastian, noticing her wary expression at the sight of the knife, halted and drew her attention back to him. "Hey," he said, voice calm as she met his gaze. "Stay with me. Do you trust me?"

She nodded, and she meant it.

She *did* trust him.

He smiled. "Good. You'll understand after this first time. It's all just a test, for both you and me—us. It's imperative to the Goddess that if your Armature is with you, then there's nothing for you to fear." He moved again, his hand finding hers as they stepped closer to the ring. They paused right at the edge before Sebastian took a step over the candles, moving inside the fiery barrier. Mariah followed, feeling the heat of the flames kiss the soles of her bare feet.

Now standing within that circle of fire, the blanket on the ground in front of them, Sebastian turned back to her, his hazel eyes gleaming gold in the dancing firelight. Mariah glanced around, her curiosity washing over her as she took in the scene and looked back to Sebastian.

"So ... what's next?" She knew her question was blunt, but she couldn't hold it in. The blanket, the candles, the *knife* ... to say she was intrigued would be an understatement.

Sebastian flashed her his easy smile, a flicker of something new in his eyes. "Well ... now, we must bare ourselves before each other and the Goddess in order to complete the remainder of the ritual."

Bare ourselves ...

"And by 'bare,' you mean lose our clothing, don't you." The inflection to Mariah's voice was flat, more a statement than a question—she already knew the answer just by the glimmering in Sebastian's eyes. He nodded once before taking a small step back, the cool night breeze whirling into the gap between them.

"I'll go first." His voice was just barely deeper, rougher. "Then you. Then...we'll sit. And from there, just follow my lead, and remember that no matter what, I've got you."

She nodded her understanding, and her curiosity sharpened into something far hotter as Sebastian gripped the hem of his soft, white shirt, pulling it over his chest in a single smooth movement.

She suddenly realized that she hadn't seen him—or any of her Armature—shirtless before. She'd thought that was a bit odd, considering how much they'd all trained together over the past week, and how quickly she'd always shed her tunic the moment her sweat began to stick the material uncomfortably to her skin.

Now, though, as she stared at him in the flickering candlelight, her musings became obsolete. Beneath his shirt, inked across his chest, just over his heart, was a tattoo ...

Her Mark.

She stepped forward just as his hands dipped to the waistband of his pants, his hands freezing as he noticed her movement and the focus of her gaze. Sebastian remained as still as a statue as Mariah raised a hand up to the tattoo, her fingers lightly tracing the delicate, swirling Mark. It was circular in shape and abstract in design, but she couldn't help but see something incredibly familiar in the curling lines and swooping pattern. The more she stared, the more she saw dark wings curled in a crescent, a tail tucked around itself, and a bowed head with flames leaping from an open maw. There was also a single, straight line cutting through the center of the Mark, its rigidity so at odds with the rest of the image.

She flicked her gaze back up to his, his hazel eyes dark and wide.

"It ... it looks a lot like a dragon, doesn't it?" Her voice was low and steady.

His own voice was rough, and he cleared his throat once before answering. "Yeah—yes. That's what we've always thought, too. For a time, it made us wonder exactly what kind of queen we might one day find ourselves bound to." He reached his own hand up now, brushing a wisp of her dark hair away from her cheek. "After meeting you, though, I no longer wonder. I think it fits you perfectly."

He withdrew his fingers, returning to the lacings of his trousers. Mariah forced herself to keep her eyes locked on his, his hazel gaze burning hotter than the flames that flickered in the candles around them. He bent slightly, removing what remained of his clothing, never once breaking her gaze.

And despite the temptation, she didn't either.

After a moment of silence, Sebastian loosened a slightly shuddering breath. "Now— "

"I want you to do it," she interrupted him suddenly, her voice husky. "I want you to undress me." The hint of a smile tugged at her lips.

She still knew this might hurt him. But this was a game she'd played many times in her life, a game she'd gotten quite good at.

And despite how much had changed ... she had not. Not yet.

Sebastian froze, watching her carefully, before nodding

slowly, the gold in his gaze smoldering brighter. Without another word, he gripped her shoulders, gently turning her body so her back was facing him. She now looked out over the candles, past the edge of the balcony, at the Attlehon Mountains beyond. Her breath hitched in her throat as she felt his fingers trail lightly down her arms, goosebumps rising in their wake. She felt his hands grip the hem of her maroon sweater, and in one smooth movement he lifted it over her head, her arms rising with the soft material until it was freed from her body. She heard him turn and toss it aside, outside the candlelight circle, before his hands were on her again, resting on her shoulders and sliding down her upper back. She felt his fingers brush aside the length of her dark hair, pushing it over her right shoulder, his deft fingers quickly undoing the clasp of the lace brassiere she wore with a soft *snap*. The material fell forward, the breeze brushing over her exposed and sensitive skin, and she held back a shiver.

Then his hands were back on her skin, and her breath caught in her throat as they traveled down her sides, over the curve of her waist and hips, not stopping until they reached the hem of her own cotton leggings. Mariah felt him kneel behind her, hooking his thumbs into the waistband as he pulled down in one smooth motion, taking the silk underwear she wore with them.

And suddenly, she was fully bared before both Sebastian and the Goddess burning in that golden moon in the night sky above them.

Sebastian rose from where he knelt behind her, and she sucked in a breath when she felt his hands again on her shoulders, turning her back to face him. His eyes now smoldered like embers, and the wind whistled off the mountains as they stood there, chest to chest, drinking each other in for several heartbeats.

Sebastian broke the moment first. He leaned in to her, taking one more step closer, his forehead dropping to touch hers as he held her stare.

"You are ... so beautiful." His voice dropped another octave, and he brushed a featherlight kiss to her cheek. She told herself she wasn't one for sweet gestures, but she also couldn't stop the rush of warmth and heat that swept through her at his words. She took her own step closer to him and became suddenly *very* aware of the hard length of him now pressed against the skin of her stomach.

That contact had him pulling back, just slightly, just enough to meet her gaze as the glow in his eyes dimmed, as if caged by his waning self-control. He stared at her intently, reading her face for whatever she might be thinking.

And what am I thinking?

She couldn't even begin to guess.

"I want you to know," Sebastian started, his voice still low, rough. "That nothing—and I mean *nothing*—you do tonight could disappoint me. However far you want to go is how far we'll go. And I'll be eternally happy in whatever role you ultimately assign me to in your life, whether that be as friends, or ... lovers, or even a mixture of both." He gripped her hand in his, eyes dropping to their twined fingers. "I just ... need you to know that. Before we continue."

Tears threatened at the back of Mariah's eyes. This man ... she could hardly believe he was real, that he existed in her world.

That voice filtered in through her subconscious.

Love is weakness.

Yeah, yeah.

She smiled up at him softly. "Thank you."

Sebastian tilted his own lips up in answer. Still holding her hand, he led her to the blanket in the center of the candles, pulling her so they were again standing face to face. He then tugged her down, kneeling with her on the blanket. Soon they both sat there, knees touching, the gleaming steel knife lying beside Mariah's right thigh. She felt warm fingers grip her chin just as her gaze snagged on the blade, her attention pulled back to honeyed hazel eyes.

"Remember, Mariah. With me." She nodded slowly, just once, and then the smooth leather hilt of a blade was pressed into her palm. She held his gaze just as the corner of her mouth quirked up into a half-smirk.

"Sebastian, I know we're still getting to know each other, and I'm into a lot … but I'm not sure knife-play falls into that category."

Sebastian looked at her. Tilted his head. Blinked once. And then *rolled his eyes.*

"Well, it's a good thing I'm not either."

Mariah couldn't hold back her snicker.

He chuckled once. "By the Goddess, Mariah. You're already making this difficult enough as it is." He drew in a deep breath, and Mariah schooled her face back into seriousness. "Ignore the knife for a second. I need you to draw out your magic. Not all of it, just … a tendril. A thread." He met her gaze again, a slightly sheepish smile on his lips. "At least, that's what Ryenne told me it would feel like to you."

Mariah grinned back at him, but also kicked herself internally. *Is that something I should have told them all about this past week? The nature of my magic?* "Ryenne sure does like to talk, doesn't she?"

Sebastian shrugged. "She's been a queen for over three hundred years. I'm sure she has gotten quite used to having a hand in everyone's business, and I imagine it's hard to suddenly stop. She means well, though."

Mariah agreed, and then turned her attention to that dark

well within her, calling forth a single thread of golden light. The silver magic, she noticed, had no interest in her in that moment, at total odds to the coiling gold power. The shimmering aureate tendril whispered its way through her soul, her skin, until it filled her very being. She saw her skin begin to glow, the hint of gold pulling out the matching color in Sebastian's gaze, his expression morphing to one of awe.

"Sebastian. What now?"

He shook his head slightly, as if snapping from a trance, the short strands of his dark hair falling across his forehead. "Sorry. You're just … incredible." He took a deep, steadying breath, then reached to grab the wrist of the hand holding the curved knife, drawing it up so it gleamed in the air between them.

"On the Mark, do you see that solid black line running through the center of the circle?" Mariah nodded. Sebastian held her stare. "You'll need to make a cut right over it, deep enough to draw blood. It won't hurt me, I promise." He paused. "And then you'll make a similar cut on your own palm. Next, you'll focus that thread of magic into your hand, right into the cut, and press that hand to my Mark. The magic should take things over from there."

Mariah could only stare at him, blade still in her hand.

"*That's* what no one would tell me before now? A bunch of prudes, all of you."

Sebastian grinned at her, but said nothing.

He dropped his grip from her wrist, and without hesitation she leaned forward, pressing the cold steel of the blade to Sebastian's chest, right over the line in his Mark. Bright red blood immediately welled from the wound, spilling down the planes of his chest and stomach. She caught her eyes before they could follow that ruby trail any further.

Focus, Mariah.

She inhaled once, her hand surprisingly steady as she

withdrew the blade from Sebastian's chest. Switching the knife to her left hand, she looked down at her open right palm and pressed the sharp edge down into her skin. She winced slightly at the sting as she dragged the blade across her calloused hand, watching her own blood well up and drip onto her bare thighs. She tossed the knife off to the side, skidding slightly across the blanket and then the marble, the only sound besides the wind and their heaving breath.

Mariah returned her gaze to Sebastian, his stare wide and watching. With a breath, she focused that tendril of golden light on her skin into the cut on her hand, the glow on her body fading as the blood that dropped from the wound began to glitter with shimmering power. Looking back at Sebastian, he smiled again at her, nodding once, clear devotion in his hazel eyes.

And when she pressed her glowing, bleeding palm to the Mark on his chest, her mind exploded with light and every emotion imaginable.

She floated through time and space, unsure of where she was or where to land.

The tidal wave of light that had swept her away faded rapidly, replaced by thick, inky blackness. Suddenly, out of the darkness, she became aware of a shimmering golden thread, its twisting and beckoning through the void like a call from home. She latched onto it, following it without a second thought as the world around her began to solidify, the darkness retreating just enough for her to see a great chasm yawning open before her.

A chasm where a bridge of golden thread began to weave

itself into existence, forming out of the nothingness around her.

She drifted forward, onto the shimmering bridge of light. It wasn't complete, still forming over the pit, but she wasn't afraid. No, even in that vacuum of existence spanning beneath her, she felt nothing but safety here. She drifted further and further along that glittering arch, and soon the light had raced so far ahead of her that she could see the other side, the world there also growing more solid and real.

And there, waiting on the other side of the chasm, was a figure, a shroud of soft gray, golden hazel, and the warm brown of fresh-tilled earth. It was solid, comforting, steady. *Familiar.*

The golden bridge was near complete now, that single thread continuing to grow in length as it wound and wound itself together, the resulting link stronger than any metal or chain known to their world. Then, the bridge was complete, and she floated off it, settling herself into the space beside the other shape waiting for her. A golden tendril, the same one that had built that bridge, twisted into the air between her and the figure, circling once around them both before shooting itself straight into the gray shroud, not hesitating to meld itself to the very fabric of the being sharing that space with her. The thread wove itself into his very soul, until all she could see was a subtle golden thrum, deep in the center of the shape.

Mariah knew that feeling well, the claiming the magic could have on you.

Mariah. Her name. Even in this strange place, reality began to rush back in, chasing away the fog that made her forget even her own name. And deep in the gray shroud beside her, she could've sworn she saw the wisps surrounding it fade slightly, the hazel forming itself into the hazy shape of eyes looking out at her with a look that chased the breath from her lungs.

Her lungs.

She didn't have lungs in this place, but she had them somewhere. She didn't belong here. She turned back to the way she'd come, to the golden bridge she knew would remain open to her forever. With a final glance back at the figure—*Sebastian's*—ethereal form, here in this strange place between their minds, she moved back onto the bridge and flew across it, retreating to the safety of her own consciousness.

With a gasp, Mariah's eyes flew open, chest heaving as she met Sebastian's heated stare.

Her hand was still pressed to his chest, but she no longer knelt before him. While her mind had floated through that void, she'd moved impossibly closer to him, her legs now straddling his, her body suddenly *very* aware of their proximity and of every inch pressing against her, both hard and smooth.

She stared at Sebastian, sharing breath with him for several heaving exhales, her emotions still fractured and spiraling. She'd just been *inside his soul*, and she could still feel that bridge between their minds, could feel his consciousness brush against her, the feelings of arousal and shattering self-control rolling down the fresh bond in waves. Mariah knew the only thing keeping him still, kept him from grabbing her and *claiming* her, was his incredible respect and devotion to her and what she desired. She shifted slightly; the movement eliciting a soft groan from her mouth as the most intimate parts of her pressed closer to the length of him, and watched as his pupils dilated, his nostrils flared.

Fuck it.

Not letting her mind catch up to her body, she crashed her lips to his, ripping her still-bleeding palm from his chest and plunging it into his hair. Blood smeared down the back of his neck as he returned her frenzied kiss with his own gentle fervor, his tongue parting her lips as he wrapped his well-muscled arms around her back, lifting her up and even closer to him. She dipped her left hand down between them, wrapping it around his length, her blood thrumming and pounding through her body. She stroked him once, twice, and his answering groan into her mouth turned her feral.

"*Fuck* ... Mariah ..."

She rocked herself harder against him, desperate for some kind of release to quiet the screaming maelstrom of emotions rattling through her soul. The bond between their souls raged out of control, the intensity of the moment capturing every animalistic instinct she had and then cutting them loose.

Mariah had been warned the bonding could be intense.

Nothing, however, could have prepared her for *this*.

Sebastian pulled his lips from hers, dropping his head to the crook of her neck, panting hard as she continued to move over him, around him, inching him closer to the place she wanted him most. Suddenly, he growled against her, the sound low and rumbling, and then he was pulling her off of him, pushing her down so she lay on her back on the soft blanket. He moved over her, his strong, solid weight settling on her and pressing deliciously against her skin. Still spurred by feral desire, Mariah wrapped her legs around his hips, trying, *begging*, to pull him closer. He was strong, though, and instead of pushing into her like she wanted, he captured her lips in a quick, gentle kiss, a rough laugh in his throat.

He released her mouth and pulled back, staring at her with the candlelight dancing in his hazel eyes, his expression ravenous as he spoke.

"I'm not sure if this is the only night you'll give me. And

since it very well may be, I intend to take this opportunity to worship you fully."

Her own blood raged with fires she didn't have as he proceeded to do just that.

He skimmed his mouth over her jaw, down her neck, between the swell of her breasts and the smooth expanse of her stomach. He eventually came to rest between her legs, his hands on her thighs and her hips both strong and gentle, just like he was.

And as he'd promised, he worshiped her, so thoroughly and completely she thought she might fly into the stars that glittered in the night sky above them. They joined together there under the light of the twin moons, the raging in her body caused by the intensity of the bond finally receiving what it so desperately craved. Soon they both found their release, her mind fracturing and splintering with threads of golden light so bright and vivid she thought she might be blinded.

But as she felt herself slowly returning to the earth beneath her, to her body lying on that blanket in the ring of candlelight, to the incredible man whispering words of affection she neither wanted nor deserved, an image flashed into her mind, reflecting off the back of her still-closed eyelids.

Less an image, actually. More like a *color*.

As the picture of shadowed, wicked tanzanite lanced through her mind, Mariah was filled with a sudden and infuriating anger at the demon named Andrian for tainting what had very likely been the best night she'd spent with a man in her life.

CHAPTER 23

Groggy with sleep, Mariah shifted, rolling her body over and flinging out an arm ... smacking Sebastian in the face.

The contact shocked away the lingering tendrils of unconsciousness, and Mariah shot up, unable to stop the quiet laugh that spilled from her mouth.

"Shit ... I'm sorry." Glancing down at her errant arm, she realized with a jolt that she was also utterly naked, and decidedly flopped back onto the bed, pulling the heavy comforter up and over her head.

How very queen-like, Mariah.

Sebastian's low chuckle, still thick with sleep, vibrated from beside her. "Good morning to you, too."

His voice triggered Mariah's memories; images and sensations from the night before racing into the forefront of her mind. Sweat. Calloused hands. Gentle kisses trailed down necks.

Hazel eyes burned away by tanzanite.

Goddess, damn it all, straight to Enfara.

She was sore in the best possible way, her body perfectly sated. But her mind ... her mind was wrought with frustration, wringing itself with dread at the conversation she felt looming.

Mariah felt hands touch the duvet over her head, gripping it gently and pulling it from where it covered her face. Hazel eyes filled her vision, along with dark, unusually messy hair framing a classically handsome face. She couldn't stop herself; she reached a hand up, running her fingers through the tousled strands. Sebastian's eyes closed at her touch. She withdrew, but his eyes stayed closed, his face unmoving.

"Sebastian." Her voice was soft, far softer than she knew she could be.

Finally, he moved, blinking his eyes open and staring at her with a look that both stopped her heart and filled her with a confusing fear she couldn't bear.

This ... this was too much. She couldn't risk this pain, this heartache she knew she was about to cause him.

But she also knew she had no other choice.

"I ... about last night." She paused, her voice now showing signs of the tremor she felt, and took a deep breath. "I ... you're amazing. Perfect. Everything women pray to the Goddess to have one day. But ... I don't think last night can happen again. I'm so sorry, I don't want to hurt you, and I truly don't think I'll be able to survive here, in this city, in this *palace,* without you, but ... I can't give you what you deserve. I shouldn't have given in last night, but ... it was all just so much, and you're not bad to look at, either, and now ..."

He silenced her rambling with a calloused hand to her temple, his fingers shifting lightly into the roots of her hair. He leaned down and touched his lips to her forehead, as light as a feather. "I know."

Her mouth popped open, and she blinked up at him, not quite sure if she'd heard his soft voice correctly. "You ... know?"

Who was *this man?*

He smiled down at her. "Yes. I know. I know last night was ... *just* last night. And I think I distinctly remember telling you as much." His smile broadened before his expression shifted to something fractionally more serious. "The first bonding has always been warned to be the most intense for a new queen. We're all told of it, all know it in a theoretical sense, but ... it's something else entirely to experience it. And even with last night, and how thrilled I am to spend this time with you, I know I'm not your consort."

Confusion and slight unease again churned through her. "You do? How?"

The corners of his eyes crinkled with his smile. "Trust me, Mariah. You'll just ... know. You wouldn't have to ask me, and I wouldn't have to tell you. From what we're taught, it will be ... unmistakable," he said.

Mariah pondered that for a moment. "Does every queen have a consort?" *What if I don't have one?*

She couldn't deny the twinge of relief she felt at the idea. To not be shackled by a bond even more intense than the one shared with her Armature ... *that* was what she wanted.

But then Sebastian's next words tore all that relief to shreds. "Yes. Every queen has a consort. Just as Qhohena has—and always will have—Priam by her side."

Mariah twisted her face into a look of incredulity. "And you're *positive* it's not you?"

Sebastian's chuckle was low and deep. "Yes, Mariah. I'm sure. While you will always be so much more than I could've ever expected, and as incredible as last night was, it was only what I'd expected from the bonding—nothing more."

Mariah let her lips curl into a joking pout. "I'm not sure if I should be flattered or insulted at that."

Sebastian huffed a laugh at her, catching the amusement

that was indeed radiating down that new bridge between their souls. The reminder of it was a bit of a jolt to her, the sudden realization her consciousness was now linked forever to his. She'd worried it would feel odd, uncomfortable, like putting on a pair of shoes that didn't fit quite right. But ... it felt nothing like that. Instead, it felt like she was on a raft, and the bond was a tether, holding her firmly to shore.

"Stop that," he said. "You know damn well what I mean."

She released her pout and smiled, still not quite over the shock of ... well, *everything*.

"So, you swear that you're alright? That we'll be good? That nothing will change?"

That hazel gaze was so incredibly gentle. "Of course, Mariah. Do I seem any different to you now? Do you feel any less comfortable with me?" She shook her head, feeling and *knowing* from that bond he was right. "Then there's your answer. I'm bonded to you—for *life*. And not just for my previously short, insignificant one, but for the long one that's ahead of you, as well. And I couldn't be more honored and ready to serve you in whatever capacity you deem suitable for me."

Tears again burned behind her eyes, and she fought to keep them from spilling over. She didn't answer him, instead screaming silently to the Goddess, the gods, to *anyone* who might listen, begging why she couldn't find it in herself to feel romantic love for this man.

That dark voice which had been her companion all her life whispered back the answer from some inky void.

Because, Mariah ... love is weakness.

Mariah and Sebastian sat at her dining table, their comfortable conversations filling the room while Mikael busied himself in the kitchen, wiping down the countertops after preparing another perfect breakfast. Mariah had invited the cook to join them at the table and eat his fill of the food he'd crafted, but Mikael declined, saying he would be unable to do such a thing with the kitchen looking as it did. "Besides," he'd said, "I don't much enjoy my own cooking. Always judge myself too harshly." Mariah only scoffed and smiled, but hadn't pushed the issue further and left him to his cleaning.

She heard the doors to her suite click open, too casual steps on heeled shoes sounding down the foyer. Mariah turned in her chair just as Ciana strolled into the room, a comfortable set to her shoulders as if these were her chambers and not Mariah's. She chimed a pleasant greeting to Mikael before turning to the dining table, eyeing both Mariah and Sebastian with a suspicious gleam in her light amber eyes, her eyebrows rising in blatant curiosity as she sidled closer.

"Good morning, Ciana." Mariah smiled at her friend, slightly wary about the next words that might come from her often-unfiltered mouth.

"Mariah. Sebastian. Good *morning* to you both." Ciana's emphasis on the word "*morning*" was full of so much suggestion that it made Mariah grit her teeth and Sebastian shift uncomfortably in his seat.

"Did you need something, Cee?"

Ciana grinned, obviously enjoying the reaction she was eliciting from them both. "Actually, yes. Ryenne sent me."

"I will take that as my leave to go, then." Sebastian spoke, pushing his chair back from the table and rising to his feet. Mariah twisted back to look at him, and he met her gaze. "Reach out should you need me." Mariah smiled at him, and he returned the same warm expression before stepping around the table. As he passed Ciana, heading towards the exit and the hallway beyond, he shot the golden girl a blinding smile and a wink.

"Always great to see you, Ciana."

Ciana's face flushed beet red, not deigning to give him a response.

It was now Mariah's turn for her eyebrows to rise to her hairline. *Curious.* She was hoping Ciana's response would grant her some reprieve from the onslaught she feared was coming. That hope was dashed in an instant when she met Ciana's stare again, finding the girl's expression had returned to normal, her eyes gleaming with twisted curiosity.

The two women stared at each other for a few moments, Ciana searching Mariah's face for something Mariah didn't want to show. Finally, her friend rocked back on her heels and crossed her arms over her chest, a smug look on her face.

"You fucked him, didn't you?"

Mariah groaned and dropped her head into her hands, but she couldn't suppress her smile. She again wondered, briefly, about Ciana's response to Sebastian just now, wondering what might truly be going on in the hidden depths of her friend's mind. She hadn't known the other girl long, but over the past week and the great deal of time they'd spent together she'd come to see a softness in Ciana, a tenderness that her friend kept hidden from the world behind a wall of sarcasm and boisterous bravado. Mariah had thought long about what had put that barrier there, what pain or heartache Ciana must've experienced to keep an entire portion of herself so shut away.

She would ask her one day, when the time was right.

Not today, however. Mariah, though, was now slightly concerned whether she would discover a hint of jealousy in her friend's eyes as she finally lifted her head from her hands.

"What do you think?"

Thankfully, there was no envy in Ciana's expression or answering laugh. "I knew it! I mean, given what I've heard about the bonding, and how *hot* he is, I knew you wouldn't be able to resist." Ciana moved to the chair beside her, sitting in a flurry of movement, resting her chin in her hands as she stared at Mariah. "Tell me everything. I need all the dirty details."

At that, Mikael coughed an uncomfortable laugh, quickly dismissing himself from Mariah's chambers with an awkward, flourishing bow. Mariah couldn't hold back her giggle.

Nor could she hold back the question that slipped past her lips.

"He's *'hot'*, is he? Care to elaborate on that?"

Again, to her shock, Ciana blushed furiously. "I ... I mean ... your entire Armature is ridiculous. Just look at them. It's outrageous. And as your best friend in this Goddess-blessed palace, I require—no, *deserve*—all the behind-the-scenes information from you so I can try my best to live vicariously. It's the least you could do for stealing me away from my family and sequestering me here in the palace."

Mariah's grin was wide and bright. This was a conversation they'd had before, and Ciana's attempt at a guilt trip couldn't goad her into a response.

"Isn't the queen waiting for me? I think it's best we get ready and not keep her waiting."

Ciana slapped her palms on the table, throwing her head back in exasperation. "Ugh! Alright, fine, bitch. Play coy with me. I will, however, expect a full debriefing with all the details that would make our ancestors roll over in their graves later this evening." She rose from her chair, grabbing Mariah's arm and dragging her up as well. "Let's go get ready, then."

Quickly, Mariah dressed in her favored soft black leggings and a shimmering gold sweater, teasing Ciana the entire time for caring far too much about the clothes she chose to wear. "I can dress myself, you know," she told her friend, rolling her eyes at her in the mirror.

Ciana only waved her off. "Yeah, sure you can. But don't deny that you love having a friend help take these decisions off your hands."

Mariah couldn't, and she was glad of it.

CHAPTER 24

Mariah's run that morning was more frantic than usual, the turmoil in her head nearing a breaking point.

The past week since she'd bonded with Sebastian had been much of the same: her days were spent with Ryenne, practicing her magic, learning the inner workings of how one rules a kingdom. She'd been taught more about the *allume* that powered Onita and the *lunestair* pillars beside the throne that housed it, about the Solstice and its importance to the kingdom.

It all bored her to tears.

It wasn't that she didn't care about the information or didn't want to know more about how, exactly, those pillars functioned, how the queen played her role when *allume* was harvested on the Solstice, or why the light flickering in the opaque stone was so weak compared to the depictions in the ancient texts Ryenne had her poring over. Instead, her boredom stemmed from the feeling that she was back in school, a place she'd never truly enjoyed and had been more than thrilled to finally put behind her.

Her only true escapes, where she was able to experience a morsel of the freedom she'd always craved but still managed to elude her, were in the early mornings with her Armature, deep within the thick trees of the game park.

Her feet pounded the packed earth below her as her mind wandered to the cabal of men who now called themselves hers.

After her bonding with Sebastian, she'd told herself that now she knew what to expect, she would be able to keep her impulses in check. She wouldn't again allow herself into a situation where she might be forced to hurt one of these men, asked to give them something she never could.

She'd gotten lucky with Sebastian. She didn't think that luck would hold.

So, last night, when she'd tapped Quentin as the next to complete the bond, she'd told herself she was ready.

She could almost laugh at herself now for how wrong she'd been.

The ritual was, thankfully, less intense, but … not by much. And while she'd been able to control most of her physical impulses, had kept herself from crawling into his lap, one look at him with his fiery hair and wicked grin had her throwing all her self-control off that candlelit balcony.

She hadn't allowed him inside her, but she'd let him between her legs all the same.

A shudder skittered down her spine, a shudder not entirely attributable to the brisk morning air, and she almost missed a step as she recalled the feeling of him … *everywhere*. He was all chaotic fire, nothing about him tamed or controlled. Even as she remembered his wicked laugh, his breath rough against her skin, she got the feeling that while he would always serve and protect her, he would *never* obey her.

And she was beginning to suspect why.

Before the ceremony, when she'd dipped within her soul to

collect the thread of magic that would forever bind him to her, she'd attempted to coax forth some of those golden tendrils. But this time, they'd all but ignored her, choosing to stay quiet and dormant.

But the silver threads ... they were all too fucking happy to oblige.

That silver magic had leaped forward, twisting and winding around her, and just as it had at the Selection, it had gripped her soul tightly and drawn her up, back to where her body and Quentin waited. When she'd opened her eyes, she'd been far more annoyed and confused than scared, to find her hand glowing silver in the flickering candlelight. She'd looked at Quentin, expecting him to notice, but he'd stayed silent. Perhaps to him, just as it had at the Selection, the two different magics looked the same.

Not that it mattered much, since he now carried a piece of that silver power in his own soul.

Mariah was tired of the wondering, the questioning of the strange, foreign magic dwelling within her. She felt like she was being forced to tiptoe around something that would never go away, and it exhausted her.

No more.

It was high time, Mariah thought, for her to figure out what, exactly, she carried in her veins, and what it might be able to do. She needed answers, and she also knew she needed help in finding them.

And she knew exactly who to ask.

The crisp water in the canteen cooled the pounding in Mariah's throat as she drank from it deeply. She was drenched in sweat, her muscles aching from exertion, but was thankful that the run and training had taken the edge off the anxiety rolling through her that morning. She glanced around the clearing, watching her Armature retreat to the various corners for their own water breaks. Sunlight warmed the clearing, the cold frost of dawn long since chased away by the break of day.

They were all there ... except for one, of course. Mariah was unsurprised to note that Andrian had long since left the clearing, stealing away into the shadows as he always did.

Good. She was glad he chose to make himself scarce. He trespassed into her thoughts far too often for her liking, those disgustingly incredible eyes eating away at any pleasure she was ever able to find for herself. She was thankful that at least she hardly ever had to see him in the light of day, his self-imposed exile a welcome reprieve from the torment he caused in her dreams.

Or perhaps she should call them nightmares.

Mariah sucked in a breath, shaking her head to clear those thoughts from her mind. Looking back around the clearing, she raised her voice, calling out to two who stood on opposite ends.

"Sebastian? Quentin? Can I speak with you both, just for a moment?"

She knew she hadn't needed to call out as she did; she could've simply tugged on the bridges now built between their minds. Sebastian's was still slate gray imbued with gold, while Quentin's was burning flame touched by silver.

But with this many men in her court, she still had her games to play. Best to keep the rest of them guessing, wishing they were on the inside, wondering when it might be their turn to bind themselves to her for eternity.

Everyone except Andrian, that is. She outright refused to give that subject, with *him*, any space in her thoughts. She preferred to keep him on the outside, and she was perfectly content for him to remain there willingly.

There was enough for her to concern herself with.

Like the silver magic writhing in her soul.

Sebastian and Quentin jogged over to her, their sweat still gleaming on their skin. While the days were starting to shift into the cold bite of early winter, the sun was still strong enough to leave them all warm and drenched by the end of training. They watched her expectantly as she stood, glancing once behind them at the rest of her Armature. She watched them cast curious glances their way before filing out of the training clearing and into the darkness of the trees. No more than a few seconds later, she was alone with her two bonded Armature.

Taking another deep breath, she turned to face those two men, meeting their curious gazes of hazel and bottle green.

"There are some things we need to discuss. About ..." She inhaled, steading herself. "About my magic."

"So, you're telling us that not only do you carry Qhohena's magic, but you somehow have ... *other* magic? Something in addition to the gift of the Queen?" Quentin's voice was incredulous, and, truthfully, Mariah couldn't blame him.

"Mariah," Sebastian said, his own voice hesitant, processing what she'd told them. "It's not that I don't believe you, but ... how is that *possible*? Only unmarried, magic-less women are invited to the Choosing, and even then Qhohena's magic doesn't—has *never*—chosen someone who already bears another gift." He paused. "Qhohena is generous, but she's also not a goddess who gives away pieces of herself twice."

Mariah exhaled through her nose, trying to keep her

patience. She needed their help, needed to make them understand. She turned to Quentin first.

"Yes, Quentin. That's *exactly* what I'm telling you." She moved her attention to Sebastian. "And Sebastian—trust me, I've asked myself those same questions repeatedly over the past two weeks. And my answer is *I don't know*. I don't know what this is, or why it's in me ... I don't even know if it's a gift from Qhohena." She paused as she let that sink in, their confused stares as they gazed back at her only aiding her exasperation. "All I know is that on my twenty-first birthday, I not only received this letter, but this ... *otherness* awoke in me, and I've been grappling with this secret ever since. And now I'm telling the two of you."

The guarded looks they both wore had her gnashing her teeth in frustration.

Men.

"Look, Quentin, you should know what I'm talking about and that I'm telling you the truth. Don't tell me last night you didn't notice that my hand, my magic, was glowing *silver*, not gold. And, by the way, that very magic is in *you* now."

That finally jostled him awake. Quentin blanched, glancing down at her hand, at the cut on her palm that was just barely clotted. He swallowed heavily, swaying lightly on his feet, before composing himself with all the frustrating swagger he could conjure.

"Honestly, I was too distracted by the fact that you were naked—your tits are *fantastic*, by the way—to notice exactly what color your hand was glowing before you sliced my chest open and built a mind-bridge with me."

Mariah breathed a heavy sigh, squeezing her eyes shut as she clenched the bridge of her nose.

Goddess, give me patience.

Her prayer must've been heard, because Sebastian

thankfully spoke up. "Quentin, keep your dick in your pants. Now is not the time." He then spoke to Mariah, "Mariah, I hear what you're saying, but ... it just all sounds so impossible. Are you *sure* that's what happened? How are you able to distinguish them? You just told us that they feel nearly identical."

Mariah huffed. "Fine. I'll just show you." She opened her eyes just as she reached inward, plucked a single strand of golden magic, and willed it into her right hand, her skin instantly igniting as the light danced in the air.

"What color does that look like to you?"

Sebastian's answer was calm. "It doesn't really have a color. It just looks like light."

"No, I need you to *really* look. And I need you to tell me: if you were to give it a color, what would it be?"

They both were quiet as they studied her hand. "I mean ... if I had to guess, it looks gold to me." Quentin's voice was confused and reluctant.

"Great. That's right. And now ..." She dipped back inside her, calling forth a thread of silver, pushing it into her left hand. To her, the color difference between her two hands as the light thrummed in the air was so stark, so distinguishable, she was shocked that no others had noticed it yet. "What do you see?"

When she looked back at Sebastian and Quentin, she knew her demonstration had the effect she sought. *Fucking finally.* The color nearly drained out of Sebastian's face, but Quentin ... her red-haired Armature only grinned wickedly at her left hand before locking that bottle green stare on her.

"Looks like I got the freaky, new, potentially blasphemous magic, baby. Only for you."

Mariah rolled her eyes *hard,* a scoff in her throat as she prepared a retort to him about calling her "baby" when a dark presence suddenly prickled at her back, burning through her awareness, setting all her senses ablaze. She froze, her magic vanishing back under her skin, as she slowly turned, already knowing exactly what—or, rather, *who*—she would find. Her eyes clashed with those of blazing tanzanite, the same eyes that haunted the darkest recesses of her mind.

Andrian leaned against a tree at the edge of the clearing, still partly wreathed in shadow, as he smiled at her wickedly.

"Keeping secrets, are we?"

CHAPTER 25

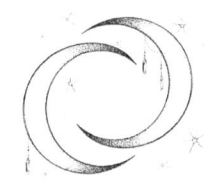

Those eyes.

They both consumed and filled her with a burning, irrational anger.

Mariah met Andrian's gaze without hesitation, her ire rolling through her and into her own stare as she lifted her chin at him defiantly.

"How much of that did you hear?"

Andrian's smile turned impossibly crueler. "All of it. And I must say, those are quite some secrets you're hiding, *My Queen*." He sneered her title, the words an insult on his lips.

She felt her own mouth pull back from her teeth into a feral snarl, her magic licking its way to her skin and flickering menacingly in her eyes. "I'm not sure who, exactly, you think you are, eavesdropping on *your queen*," she said, returning the same snideness he'd used toward her. "But I can assure you, I'm far from pleased with it."

"Oh, I'm so very afraid. What shall you do, *murder* me like you did that old, pathetic lord? Although, after watching that display, I might one day be able to find you at least halfway tolerable. You keep that up and you'll have the entire ruling class calling for your head in no time."

Mariah saw only red.

At least it blocked out the blue of his eyes.

Distantly, she felt a tug on her mind, a gentle pull down the bridge of smooth, gray stone. Sebastian's voice sounded in the clearing.

"Enough, Andrian. What in Enfara's depths is your problem?

Beside him, she heard Quentin laugh. "By the Goddess, Andrian, I hope she kicks your ass for that."

Andrian spoke again, and his voice grated against every fiber of her being. "I'm surprised you both are so quick to defend her after what she did with the lords, and especially now that she has revealed this *tantalizing* new secret. I mean, if you were like me, I would understand"—there was a bitterness in his tone that pulled back the haze of her fury, just slightly, curiosity lapping at the back of her consciousness—"but given that the two of you are ... well, *you*, I must admit I'm shocked."

"We are quick to defend her, brother, because we've seen her and who she truly is. And because of that, we trust her." Sebastian paused, shifting his gaze to Mariah, something akin to nervousness in his expression. "Just like how I'm about to tell her right now to trust you."

"*What?*" Her incredulous tone was one of pure venom.

"You heard me, Mariah." Sebastian was as calm and steady as ever. "You can trust him. You *need* to trust him. He now knows, and while eavesdropping was probably not the best decision he's ever made"—Andrian shot a dark glare at Sebastian—"he's now a part of this, whether you wanted him to be or not. He is also, I might add, a member of your Armature, a fact that you *both* seem to be forgetting."

Mariah leveled her heated green stare on Sebastian,

challenging him with it for a few heartbeats before shifting to Andrian. She tried to burn away his cold, shadowed exterior, tried to strip him down in order to see whatever it was he was hiding underneath. This man, this devil, had secrets of his own, and she wanted to know them. He held strong, though, and returned her glare with a fierceness that equaled hers.

Suddenly, just as it had that first day in the palace courtyard, and again at the Selection, a bolt of *something* whipped through them, raw and powerful. It forced their stares apart as they both staggered back, chests heaving, looking anywhere but at each other as they fought to regain their balance.

Sebastian and Quentin both looked on, startled, but wisely kept their mouths shut.

Mariah quickly regained her composure, rising back to her full height. She looked at Sebastian, contemplating for a moment. He was right, she supposed. Andrian already knew. And it was likely best now to keep him close, where she could keep a watchful eye on him, than to cut him loose to spread her secrets all over Verith.

"Fine," she said to Sebastian. "I hope you're right and he can make himself useful."

Of course, the one she didn't want to hear from spoke.

"Oh, I certainly think I can do that. In fact, I think I know just where to start to try to figure out the origins of that fascinating little party trick of yours." His voice was cool, and as much as Mariah didn't want to hear it, she couldn't deny her interest in what he was about to say. "You say you have two magics in you—one gold, one silver. Now, you all seem to have at least moderate levels of intelligence. Tell me, what else in our world are there two of, with one being gold and one being silver?"

Mariah jolted with the realization, and a part of her wanted to kick herself for being so obtuse.

"The moons," she said.

How could I be so blind?

Andrian gave her another cold smile. "I knew you were more than just a pretty face, *nio*."

She blinked at the name, confusion sparking. "What did you just ca—"

"And what is said about the ties and origins of those two moons?" he interrupted, not letting her finish her question.

Absolutely infuriating.

"Much has been lost to history. It is all mostly folklore at this point." Sebastian was staring at Andrian, his brilliant mind turning at what his dark companion was suggesting. "It's said that Qhohena rules over the golden moon and has since the dawn of time. But the silver moon ... for some reason, I cannot recall." A look of bewilderment crossed his hazel eyes.

"Ah, but *brother*, what would you say if I told you that I have found some texts from the time of the First War, texts that speak of legends they don't teach us in school, stories that may even shed some light on a certain silver moon and the power it contains?"

There was silence in the clearing.

"How do you ...?" Sebastian's question trailed off as he continued to stare at Andrian, thoroughly perplexed.

"Let's just say that growing up, getting lost in history was far more enjoyable than the present for me." Mariah could've sworn she saw a flicker of something other than cold hatred or boredom in those tanzanite eyes, but it vanished like smoke caught on the wind. Andrian's signature snark was back as he turned again to Sebastian. "You're not the only one who reads, *brother*."

Goddess, he was such an asshole.

Sebastian—her calm, steady Sebastian—looked nearly as annoyed as Mariah. Judging by the way he clenched his fists at his side, she wouldn't have been surprised to see him leap forward and land a punch on Andrian's annoyingly perfect jaw.

The more that image played in her head, the more she wished it were reality.

She shook her head to clear the thought, the more pressing matters at hand refocusing her mind. Mariah met the gazes of all three men—two of them bound to her for life, one just a massive pain in her ass.

A pain in her ass whose nose she had a slight desire to break. A demon had no right to look as he did; he needed to be marred, given at least some sort of imperfection that would shake him from her thoughts.

"Let's all save the sword fighting for training. I have to meet with Ryenne this morning, but I want you all to meet me in the library after lunch. Andrian, I don't actually care if you show up, but Sebastian and Quentin, I'll need your help."

Not waiting for a response, Mariah turned on her heel and jogged her way back to the palace.

Mariah realized, somewhat belatedly, that she'd only ever walked past the doors leading into the palace library. She'd never actually stepped through them.

She didn't consider herself much of a reader, preferring to lose herself in the physical world around her rather than those contained within words on a page. She'd done well enough in school, doing the minimum to learn what she needed and advance through the years and courses. She'd been carried by a natural level of intelligence, but reading and learning were never her passion. Mariah found her true joys to be with things she could touch, feel, and taste in the world around her.

Or perhaps she'd just never picked up the right book.

Either way, this library was glorious and decadent enough to make her want to give reading another try.

The heavy oak double doors, inlaid with delicate golden inscriptions of books and words in the ancient language of Onita, opened into a great cavern of a space carved directly into the side of the mountains. High above, the roof was domed and made of glass, the light from the late autumn sun beaming down and filtering around the rows and rows and *rows* of books, volumes, tomes, and texts beneath it. The main area of the library was shaped like a circular atrium, and in the stacks that lay in that direct sunlight were most of the modern texts—books written for pleasure and escape rather than for knowledge or learning. Branching off the main atrium were several hallways, some darker than the others, and she spotted several large tables and workspaces for patrons of the library to conduct their research in peace.

Mariah stalked through the shelves in the center of the atrium, running her fingers along the neatly organized spines. As she started to read the titles, she noticed with a jolt that she'd found herself in a section dedicated to romance. Spurned by a wave of curiosity, she grabbed a random title from the shelf—its spine read *The Passion of Snowfall*—and let the binding fall open to a random page. As she began to read, her eyebrows slowly creeped into her hairline, heat rushing in a wave to her face and core.

"I felt the groan leave my lips, his answering growl at my back as he pressed me forward, onto my hands and knees, and then I felt him pushing into me, stretching me, claiming me—"

"My, my, *nio*, what is it that you've found here?"

That dark voice skated down Mariah's spine, pooling low

in her already molten stomach, the flush on her cheeks creeping even higher. She froze, and then slowly closed the book before placing it back on the shelf, turning to meet Andrian's vivid blue stare.

She'd expected to feel like she'd been doused with a bucket of cold water the second she laid her eyes on him.

What she felt instead, though, was *far* from that.

Her breath caught in her throat as she looked at him, leaning against the bookshelf, no more than three feet from her. She had no idea how he'd crept up on her, but there he was, so close that if she took but a few short steps, she would be able to *touch* him.

And by the Goddess, she wanted to touch him.

You want to do far more than touch him.

A small voice somewhere in the back of her mind tried to remind her that she despised him. Tried to remind her that he was a disrespectful asshole, a bane to her existence, someone who'd even promised to make her life *miserable* since the day he'd sworn his oath to her. He was a constant headache all wrapped up in a tall, dark, and painfully attractive package.

And with that one final thought, she promptly forgot about how much she loathed him. All she could think about was the molten heat coursing through her veins, the way his incredible tanzanite eyes burned into her very soul, the way his nostrils flared almost imperceptibly as she shifted slightly where she stood, desperate for any sort of friction between her legs.

And when his eyes darkened even further, his gaze slowly perusing down the length of her body, when the tip of his tongue darted out and ran slowly along his full lower lip, she almost felt her control slip from her completely.

"Mariah? Are you over here?" Sebastian's voice pierced her lust-filled haze like an arrow, jolting her back to reality and away from the nightmare she'd almost fallen victim to.

By the Goddess, Mariah. What the fuck *was that?*

She ripped her gaze from Andrian's as she whirled in place just in time to see Sebastian poke his head around the shelves. Spotting her, he stepped into the aisle, his eyes darting warily between her and Andrian. He stopped a few feet away, eyes settling on Mariah as he spoke again. "We found some historical texts that may be helpful. Or, at least, they'll give us a place to start. Come, follow me."

Just as Sebastian turned to leave, a voice muttered from over Mariah's shoulder, "*I* found them."

Mariah shot the burning retort over her shoulder before she could quiet her tongue, suddenly furious at him for whatever reaction he'd forced out of her no more than a few moments before. "Insecurity is unbecoming, Andrian. Be careful when showing it or else we might all begin to think you're compensating for something."

A large, warm, calloused hand suddenly grabbed her upper arm, twisting her around so quickly her vision blurred with the movement. Her mind froze when she found herself chest to chest with Andrian, his breath warm on her cheek, so close that their lips could touch, if only she were to lean forward ...

Stop that.

"Don't tempt me, *nio*. I'm not compensating for anything, but I don't think you want me to prove that to you."

He let her go abruptly, stomping past her after Sebastian. She composed herself just enough, plastering a scowl to her face, to call after him.

"That name you keep calling me. Tell me what it means."

A glancing smirk over his shoulder. "'Bitch.'"

A string of curses fell from her mouth like water, his answering chuckle low and cruel.

CHAPTER 26

A headache pounded against the back of Mariah's skull like a drum.

"Mariah, stay with me. What do you remember about the First War?"

Sebastian's question cut through the dull thudding in her head. Mariah groaned and dropped her face into her open palms, her elbows resting on the solid oak table in front of her. "Not nearly enough, it seems."

Mariah was drained, and it was only partly attributed to her and Andrian's ... *heated* exchange amongst the racks of books. Her training with Ryenne that morning had been particularly strenuous, as she'd practiced her control over more than a single thread at a time. She'd already demonstrated she could wield such power in moments when her control left her, but to do it consciously was proving to be an incredibly difficult task. It was toiling, mentally taxing work; those threads of magic, both silver and gold, truly had a mind of their own, slipping through her fingers as if they were coated in a layer of liquid. The harder she tried to wrangle them, the more they resisted her. Ryenne continued to assure her it would get easier, that her control would strengthen with time, but when Mariah had left the training room she'd felt less in control of the raging pit in her soul than she had since the day it awoke in her.

At least Ksee had been absent. Mariah wasn't sure she could've withstood the straining lesson with the bitter priestess breathing down her neck, commenting on her incompetence as if Mariah weren't already *painfully* aware.

She'd thought this afternoon would bring a welcome reprieve from the stress of the morning.

Of course, she'd forgotten Andrian was now involved.

A black, musty, leather-bound book was suddenly shoved into her line of vision, snapping her out of her reflections.

"Okay, well, this one is a great place to start." Standing behind her, his warmth permeating through the cotton of her pale sweater, Sebastian leaned forward and flipped the book open to a page. Words were scrawled in an ancient script, the title written across the top in the old language of Onita:

D'abord Issil.

The First War.

Sebastian tapped the page before stepping away. "Read, Mariah."

So she did.

Mariah read, and while some of what she read was familiar, much of it was new to her.

The pages before her told the story of the Scourge—Flétrir, as he was called in Old Onitan—the demon king of Enfara, the great abyss of their world and home to the worst of the gods' creations. Long ago, in a fit of jealousy for what his realm lacked, Flétrir had led an army of his demons, or *mudae,* as the texts called them, out of Enfara and into their world. The wicked darkness they brought with them threatened to overwhelm everything, to wash away the beauty of the lands the Goddess had created while mankind was still in its infancy. That invasion by the Scourge was eventually what led to what those of their world called the First War.

The War raged for many years, and the race of men struggled against the never-ending onslaught from the darkest pits of Enfara. The War eventually came to a crest when a simple medic in the armies of men, a young woman named Xara, was approached by Qhohena in a dream. The Golden Moon Goddess, the Goddess of Life, gifted her a piece of her own essence, magic that bound itself to Xara's soul, a power that gave her people, Qhohena's people, a chance at survival.

The same magic that now flowed in Mariah's veins.

"We all grew up with these stories, Sebastian," Mariah grumbled. "Carrying Qhohena's undiluted power, Xara rallied her people, called down dragons from the very stars, and met Flétrir on a great battlefield, where she—"

"Where she lost." Andrian's voice rumbled through the room, cutting her off.

Mariah and Sebastian whipped their heads as Andrian sauntered out from the shadows between the shelves, carrying another leather-bound tome in his hands. Its binding was a rich red, the color of freshly spilled blood, and just the sight of it had the hairs on Mariah's arms standing on edge. Quentin, seated to Mariah's right and busy picking at his nails with a short bronze dagger, only flicked his eyes to Andrian in mild disinterest before continuing to toy with the deadly blade.

"What in the Goddess's name are you talking about?" Sebastian's normally calm voice carried a tinge of annoyance.

Mariah wondered, briefly, how they'd fared as boys.

Wondered if *she* was to blame for any of the tension she now felt rolling off Sebastian.

Andrian ignored his fellow Armature and stalked forward, dropping the red leather book onto the table with a soft *thud*.

"Oh, nothing. It's just something I read." Andrian shrugged before tapping the cover of the book. "Here, in this: an original recording from one of Xara's own Armature."

Mariah turned slowly, looking at Andrian, her eyes blinking once in astonishment. Dumbfounded, Sebastian dropped his gaze to the book, staring at it for three heartbeats before surging forward, snatching it into his hands and opening to the first page, reading the author's inscriptions. His eyes widened as he took in the words, his jaw hanging slack. "But ... this is impossible. That would make this book nearly five thousand years old, and it hardly looks older than a decade."

Andrian shrugged again. "I'd say it's totally possible, especially if Xara herself enchanted it with her magic to prevent it from aging. I'm sure our little *queen* could confirm that for you."

If her stare were daggers, Andrian would be pierced in multiple places, bleeding out upon the smooth tile floors. The image brought her some peace as he flashed her a grin that showed too many teeth to be friendly.

Slowly, she extended her hand to where Sebastian had set the book back down on the table, opening her senses as she did so. Sure enough, there it was, that same feeling that had raced through her when she'd first seen the text in Andrian's arms: a faint thrum of power, woven into the leather and the pages themselves, a power her own recognized, called to, but was too embedded in the tome to leap out.

Mariah's face must've reflected what she found. "Shit," said

Sebastian under his breath before turning his attention back to Andrian. "Where did you find this?"

Andrian gave yet another infuriating shrug, gesturing over his shoulder with his chin as he crossed his arms. "Back there, somewhere. I'm not entirely sure. And as I said earlier, you're not the only one who frequents these stacks." He chose that moment to turn his attention to Mariah and wink, slow and devilish.

She couldn't stop the flush that crept up her neck.

She despised him. *So* much.

Andrian grabbed the back of the chair in front of him, turning it around so its back now faced the table, and sat in it, his strong thighs straddling the mahogany wood. Mariah swallowed as she watched his smooth movement, and when he caught her gaze, she yanked her eyes away to stare intently at a swirl in the wood in the table in front of her.

There was a heavy, expectant pause. Finally, Andrian spoke again.

"If you all would like me to share the details of what I found while reading from this fascinating little piece of lost history, I would be happy to continue."

Sebastian sighed, moving from behind Mariah and taking a seat in the chair beside Quentin, clearly exasperated. "Yes, by the Goddess, Andrian, please share. You've got us all on the edge of our fucking seats." He paused, before muttering under his breath, "*Asshole.*"

Mariah tried—and failed—to suppress her grin.

There was another pause before Andrian's voice rumbled again through the room.

"According to *this* text, Xara and her forces lost to Flétrir, and the casualties were severe. Even the great dragons, creatures of myth and legend themselves, weren't enough to stop the Scourge as he ravaged his way across the earth. But it was after his victory, when hope was all but lost, that Flétrir revealed his war had never been waged because he desired to rule or to decimate the realms of men. No, he told Xara as she stood on that final battlefield, the last of her people around her, that he'd done all of this, had crawled his way out of Enfara for one thing —or, rather, for one *being*. The one entity whose attention he'd so desperately craved, but who'd evaded him for eons."

Mariah's blood ran cold as Andrian met her gaze, the glint in his eyes shadowed.

"He wanted the sister of Qhohena, the one who ruled beside her in a moon of glimmering silver. He wanted Zadione."

The room descended once again into silence, Mariah's heart pounding in her veins. She'd known Zadione was Qhohena's sister, but had never once heard her name in reference to the second moon that hung in the sky.

And if Zadione was connected to that silver moon, then it, somehow, meant that ...

No. I won't think of that.

It was Quentin, the conversation finally interesting enough for him to pay attention, who broke the silence next. "No *shit*. Zadione?" There was a *clink* as he set his bronze dagger on the table. "What happened next?"

Andrian was silent for a few more moments before continuing. "This particular history says that Zadione went to him willingly, and he left this world with her. The end."

Mariah's eyes snapped up, clashing with his. "But if she went with him, if she *loved* him, then why did she wait until the very end of the First War when hope was all but lost? Why not avoid that devastation all together?"

Andrian smirked at her. "Who said she loved him? Besides, she's a death goddess, princess." Mariah gritted her teeth, but he continued, "Perhaps all she craved was the loss of life and destruction she caused by hiding away from the Scourge." He paused again. "But this story does seem to suggest that the First War was an act of defiance on her part against her sister. She'd refused to go to Flétrir at the beginning, letting him ravage the continent, and then vanished with him once the damage was done, leaving Qhohena and Xara to pick up the pieces of a broken world.

"And that's exactly what they did. Xara, with the aid of Qhohena's magic and what was left of the dragons, helped to rebuild the land. But Xara was no longer strong enough to rule over all the world's inhabitants, as Qhohena had initially planned. So, the countries we now know were established: Xara settled in Onita, building Verith and this *ridiculous* golden palace as a shrine to her Goddess who'd tried and given everything, but was ultimately betrayed by her fickle and devious sister. The northern mountain people"—Mariah watched a shadow again flicker over Andrian's eyes—"settled what is now Leuxrith, the people of the western desert oases founded Kreah, the seafaring warriors made their home in the Kizar Islands, and the southern tribes went south to Vatha, where an internal war many years later led to the formation of Idrix." One final shrug from Andrian as he pushed back from his chair, standing again and turning the chair the right way around. "And now, here we all sit, reading dusty old tomes and forgetting our history with a queen apparent who would rather drink and fight than learn how her country came into existence."

That last bit earned a deep scowl from Mariah, but a glance at Sebastian's expression of thought and worry temporarily washed away her anger. He caught her eye, and through the bond between them flowed his tension, his concern, and his confusion. She knew what worried him, as it worried and terrified her, too.

Zadione had betrayed the world for a petty sibling rivalry. But that still didn't conclusively answer her one burning, desperate question.

"So ... what is this magic in me?"

No one could answer her.

CHAPTER 27

Ryenne held court that morning in a luxurious receiving room attached to the lower eastern courtyard of the palace.

Holding court, Mariah supposed, was a very loose way to describe the meeting she and Ciana strode into. The queen sat in a comfortable sitting chair, and around her in similar plush, feminine seats were seven women. Six of them were middle-aged, their hair showing hints of gray and features softened by a life well lived. The seventh woman, however, was much younger, closer in age to Mariah and Ciana.

"Mariah! Thank you for joining us. Please, sit." Ryenne's voice was clear and distinctly happy, far happier than Mariah had heard her sound in some time.

Certainly since the ... *incident* with the Royals.

"Ladies, I would like to introduce you all to Queen Apparent Mariah and Lady Ciana." Ryenne gestured around the room with a graceful, sweeping hand. "Mariah, Ciana, I'm pleased to introduce you both to the Ladies of my court."

Mariah's eyes widened as she dipped her head politely to

each of the women. "It's my honor to meet you all, truly." She remembered what Ryenne had told her about the Ladies of a queen's court. Mariah had appointed Ciana as her first, but she would one day have up to six women to serve her as close, trusted advisors. These women, however, as Mariah remembered somewhat sickeningly, weren't given the same longevity of life as their queen or her Armature. Ryenne had only smiled sadly when Mariah asked why the Ladies of the court remained mortal before explaining that while the arrangement made for several lifetimes of painful and difficult farewells for a queen, it was a necessary pain. The Ladies were valued for their advice and counsel because it offered the perspective from one with a fleeting, mortal existence, the type of life led by the rest of the queen's citizens. These perspectives, Ryenne had explained, kept a queen grounded, kept her priorities in check, and prevented her from getting lost in the daunting length of her existence.

"The honor is all ours, Your Highness," answered a woman with steady brown eyes, speaking for the group as the rest smiled and bowed their heads. "Although we have met you before. At the Choosing. But I know that day was a whirlwind for us all." The woman joined the rest with a smile. "We have been watching you these past few weeks. I believe I speak for us all when I say that we are excited to witness your future as queen."

Mariah shifted uncomfortably on her feet at the generous praise, her cheeks warming with that damn flush she could never control. "Thank you, My Lady. I hope I can live up to your expectations." She moved to an empty chair beside Ryenne, Ciana taking the last open seat on Mariah's other side. Just as she sat, the blood in her face drained as a sudden wave of memory of what had actually happened those past few weeks washed through her with urgent fervor.

The meeting with the Royals. The history she'd uncovered with her Armature. She doubted that if these women truly knew what lurked beneath her skin, what mysterious powers made her feel like a walking curse, they would be so generous with their praise. Those thoughts had Mariah casting a subtle glance at Ryenne, finding the queen watching her as well, her expression unreadable.

It would make sense for Ryenne to have informed her Ladies about the demise of Lord Beauchamp, seeking their counsel to maneuver through the most delicate of situations. Yet the brown-eyed woman who'd spoken had a sharp gaze, one that didn't miss much, and Mariah doubted she would've spoken such positive words if she'd known the full extent of Mariah's transgressions since arriving in Verith.

So, perhaps Ryenne hadn't informed her Ladies about the incident with the Royals. *Interesting*.

Ryenne, sensing the momentary lull in the conversation after Mariah and Ciana took their seats, spoke again. "Mariah, I invited you here today not only for you to meet the remainder of my court, but to introduce you to one person in particular."

Mariah's gaze snapped to the seventh woman, the one close to her own age. The woman met her stare steadily before smiling, rising from her seat, and dropping into an easy, practiced curtsy.

"Delaynie, My Queen. I'm honored to meet you."

The woman—Delaynie—was every inch the cultured Onitan beauty Mariah wasn't. With her porcelain skin, long auburn hair, and pale, icy blue eyes, she was someone Mariah would've normally looked upon with disdain, despised simply because she carried about her a polished perfection Mariah would never—could never—possess. However, a glimmer of *something* was in this girl's eyes, a shine of intelligence and something *more* beneath the surface that had Mariah wondering if this front she presented was nothing more than a pretty, painted mask.

"Delaynie has been here at court since her very first steps." Ryenne's voice was thick with emotion as she turned her smile to the auburn-haired woman. "How she came to be is *quite* a story. She's the daughter of my Lady Briella and one of my own Armature, Steven."

Ryenne's words stunned Mariah, her heartbeat suddenly pounding in her ears. They seeped into the air, and with it a slow panic filled her head.

If Ryenne's Armature could sire children ... Impossible.

She'd always been careful back in Andburgh. She had been adventurous, sure, but there wasn't much in the world that terrified her more than a child did.

A child would've been a very, very easy way to ensure she'd never free herself from the prison of the Crossroad City. Therefore, no matter how she chose to distract herself from the miserable monotony of her life, she made sure it would never lead to that.

However, last week, with Sebastian ... she'd been far from careful. So caught up in the new, explosive magic coursing through her veins, it was the last thing on her mind.

Somehow, Mariah found her voice. "It's an honor to meet you as well, Delaynie. And please, I hope I don't offend anyone with this, but ... how's that *possible*?" Mariah turned to Ryenne. "I thought you told me it was impossible for the queen or her Armature to bear or father children. That the magic of the Goddess prevents it."

"Normally, that's true," Ryenne responded. "And will always be true for us queens, since we carry the majority of that magic in our veins. However, Delaynie was ... conceived"—a dark-haired woman who must've been Lady Briella flushed just as Delaynie herself suppressed a giggle—"after I'd abdicated my power. The magic in Steven must've weakened just enough after that to allow him and Briella to create a miracle." The queen paused, her gaze frosting over with memory. "We were ecstatic for them. Briella was—*is*—Steven's last love, and I thank Qhohena every day that they were able to create something lasting from it. Even if such a gift also means that mine and Steven's time is nearing its end." Ryenne nodded to Lady Briella, her flush now receded and replaced with happy tears rimming her eyes. Mariah relaxed markedly at the assurance as she watched the heavy emotion flow through the air between Ryenne and Briella.

The two women were silent for a moment, a queen and her Lady, sharing the joy of a gift they both never expected to receive before Ryenne shook her head slightly. "Anyway. Mariah, I wanted to make this introduction to Delaynie in the hopes that the two of you could spend some time together. She is only about a year younger than you, and with her lifetime spent here at court, she may one day make a valuable asset to you here in the palace—"

"There's no need for that, Ryenne. If Delaynie wishes to serve me and join my court, the position as one of my Ladies is hers." The sureness in Mariah's voice was surprising, even to her. She'd recovered quickly from her moment of panic, and her instincts were now screaming at her to take this gift as it was offered, that this woman would be invaluable as she faced down whatever might lie ahead. Mariah still had no idea what she wanted out of this new life she'd been given, but she'd always leaned heavily on her instincts. She had no intentions of changing that today.

Mariah rose from her plush seat and walked through the circle of women. She stood before the auburn-haired girl, who met her gaze unflinchingly, the icy blue of her eyes sparkling.

"Lady Delaynie, daughter of Lady Briella, will you serve me

and my court, from now until the day the Goddess calls us home?"

The girl smiled, but it wasn't the practiced, pretty smile of a Lady of the court. It was a wide, toothy grin, the kind that had mischief glinting in her cerulean eyes.

Mariah's answering smile was just as feral.

"The honor would be all mine ... Mariah."

The use of her name, and not her title, sent a murmur ripple around the circle of women, but Mariah knew immediately she'd made the right decision.

Delaynie would be trouble, but not for Mariah. And as Delaynie rose from her own chair to clasp Mariah's hand in hers, to brace against a squealing hug from Ciana, Mariah sent up a wicked prayer to the Goddess.

Qhohena, save those who wish to challenge this new court. They'll need all the help they can get.

Mariah could feel a storm brewing, and she intended to weather it.

CHAPTER 28

All the gold in the palace was stifling.

Mariah wrapped the cream cardigan she wore tighter around her shoulders as she hurried through the halls, searching for something that didn't glint with the color of her kingdom, her crown, her future. Gold was certainly beautiful, but the longer she spent in the palace, the more it began to grate against her senses.

She'd awoken that morning to a welcomed day off from following Ryenne around from training to meetings. The reprieve couldn't come soon enough—she didn't know how much more she could handle of the politics, the parlor tricks Ryenne showed her with her magic, the subtle glares Ksee always shot her way when she spoke out of turn. At least her morning workouts with her Armature and her evening dinners with Ciana and Delaynie were there to break up the rolling monotony of her days.

Goddess, there were so many *rules*.

She wondered who she'd pissed off in a prior life to deserve such a rigid one now.

The only thing that made up for it was the ever-strengthening power that dwelled within her. As time progressed, and as she continued to work with her magic, the silver and gold threads slowly grew more and more intertwined. Each day, what had once been two separate balls of thread in her soul were slowly melding together, becoming one, and the feeling of power it brought her to wield them both at the same time was ... incomparable.

Yeah. Those feelings of strength, feelings she was coming to crave far too much, made all the other ridiculous tasks she was forced to deal with worth it.

Mariah continued her steady stroll down the long corridor, still looking for something, *anything*, that promised an escape from all the gold. Finally, she spotted a dark, worn oak door near the end of the hallway. Not a hint of gilding covered its surface, and in comparison to every other doorway in this palace, it appeared rather ... plain.

Perfect.

In Mariah's experience, the most interesting of finds could be discovered behind the most unassuming of doorways. The simple door in Lord Donnet's manor, a vision from a lifetime ago, flashed through her mind. So many stolen treasures behind that modest wood.

Her blood boiled at the thought, and she recalled another memory of a time a plain doorway opened so many interesting paths. Her favorite tavern had also been hidden behind a boring steel door. A place where she'd learned all the ways of pleasure, how her body could be used as a temporary distraction from how much she hated that town and the people who ran it.

Mariah quickened her steps toward the oak door, a sly grin on her face at the memories of that dark, ale-drenched bar. When she finally stood outside it, she placed her palms upon the cold, black door handles, twisting the metal and pushing against the wood with a soft grunt.

When she'd been given the news that she would have a day to herself, the first and only thing she'd wanted to do was explore this new, massive space she was now expected to call home. Her father would be disappointed if he knew just how little she'd gotten to wander those winding, gilded hallways. There was so much to be seen and found within those walls, and Wex had taught her long ago to never let stones go unturned or halls go unchecked. *"The only way something can ever catch you off guard,"* he would say, *"is if you choose to let it stay hidden."*

If she truly hated anything, other than the shit-stain of the lord who'd driven her to run from her home, it was disappointing either of the two people who'd blessed her with both a life and more freedom than most other girls in this kingdom would ever know.

At least, until those threads of magic had stirred in her chest and claimed her before a throne room of people.

She shoved those thoughts from her head as she again threw her weight against the stubborn oak doors. Finally they budged, swinging open on possibly the only set of rusted, noisy hinges in the entire palace. Stale, dusty air greeted her, and she coughed once, waving a hand in front of her face to clear the debris tickling her throat. The room before her was pitch black, but she blindly stepped in, moving toward the wall at her right in search of the light source.

She'd never been particularly scared of the dark. She'd spent enough nights in the depths of the Ivory Forest on hunting trips with her father and brother to be fearful of things she couldn't see with her eyes. The only threats that dwelled in the places absent of light were figments of imagination, and Mariah didn't like to afford hers much leeway. It was hardly productive.

Her fingers finally found what they sought: the *lunestair* panel on the wall, the smooth stone cool against her fingertips. She tapped it once, and the room filled with the brilliant light of *allume*. Turning around, she finally got a good look around the forgotten space she'd stumbled upon, hidden in the depths of the palace.

It was a gallery.

Mariah eased her way inside, her eyes going wide as she took in the dusty artwork hanging on the walls and statues that stood on stone pedestals around the room. She turned and followed along the right wall, allowing herself a moment of awe at the paintings that filled it. Despite the layer of dust, the paintings were still in excellent condition, and most were landscapes of the wonders of Onita: the palace nestled against the Attlehon Mountains, the looming darkness of the northern Everheim Mountains, the great, winding Ashtara River that carved its path so close to Andburgh. As she moved, the paintings increased in detail—a delicate sketch of a snowdrop blossom, the supernatural brilliance of the Emerald River, the waves of the Mirrored Sea crashing along the rocky beaches of Ettervan.

She rounded a corner and the artwork again shifted to historical depictions of the great events of the continent. One depicted the signing of the treaty between Vatha and what then became known as Idrix, a deal brokered by the third Onitan Queen, Iyana. Next, there was the coronation of Xara, Qhohena's first Chosen resplendent in a gilded gown, the snowdrop crown shown in marvelous detail atop her head, her hair made of spun gold.

It was the third painting, though, that had Mariah pausing. It once again featured Xara, but in a vastly contrasting setting. The first queen stood on a dark battlefield, dressed in worn and bloodied armor, that same yellow hair stained with black and red ichor. Behind her stood the human forces, their faces turned skyward to what hovered in the air above them. Mariah followed their gazes and sucked in a breath.

Everyone knew the dragons had aided Xara, that without their help the human forces would've been quickly exterminated from the earth. And, if that journal Andrian had discovered was to be believed, they still hadn't been enough, merely serving to even the scales as opposed to swinging the tides of the war. There'd been simple drawings all Onitan's were familiar with, the basic form of the dragons shown in black and white in most history books—two powerful hind legs, massive wings, whip-like tails, and long necks ending in a reptilian head filled with razor-sharp teeth.

However, Mariah had never once seen a painting of those great beasts in detail, and *especially* portrayed in color.

The sky in the painting was filled with seven of the winged creatures, and somehow the artist had managed to capture the raw power and strength of each. The first was a rich brown, the color of fresh-tilled earth; the second a stunning sea green with its extremities tipped in white, like the frothy caps of a tumultuous ocean. The third and fourth were both shades of blue, but vastly different: one was as light as the summer sky, the other a rich indigo, shades of perfectly blended blues and purples and blacks. The fifth was perhaps the most unique, most of its scales a deep midnight blue, but for the silver painted along its belly and the membranes of its wings.

The last two, however, had something deep in Mariah's belly, something hidden even beneath the vast well where her magic resided, stirring awake.

They were both slightly larger than the others, but it wasn't just their size that set Mariah's pulse racing.

One was a brilliant silver, the other untarnished gold.

A shiver chased up Mariah's spine as she wrenched her eyes away from the paintings of the dragons, looking back instead to the bloodied queen on that battlefield.

Where had those dragons come from? And how had Xara awoken them?

Mariah forced herself to step forward, away from the painting, before she could dwell too long on that question. She could stand there all day, but that would be a poor use of her temporary freedom. The dragons were gone; there was no point wasting her time trying to solve an impossible puzzle.

She continued towards the back of the lost gallery, the paintings again shifting from the historical depictions and becoming more ... vague. Abstract. *Interesting.*

It was the final painting along the back wall, hidden in the shadows of the room, that had her freezing up once again.

The painting wasn't an image at all. It was, truly, just a canvas, a blank template painted a single color, catching the weak light of the *allume* that managed to filter its way to this dark corner of the gallery.

Mariah stepped closer to the solid-silver canvas, her skin prickling with a feeling she couldn't place. When she stood directly before it, she noticed it wasn't as solid as she'd initially believed; upon closer inspection, she could just barely make out small flecks of darkness spread throughout the mass of silver.

The more she looked at the painting, the more that feeling lingered, and the more she felt like she was missing something.

That wasn't a new feeling. Ever since she'd acted on her terrible idea to flip through the pages of the *Ginnélevé* book gifted to her by her mother, she couldn't shake there was something glaringly obvious she was missing. Something her mother had wanted her to know, but she'd so far utterly failed to puzzle out. Mariah had kept the book hidden beneath her mattress, not wanting to remind herself of its unnerving words, but as she stood there in front of that painting a few flashed unbidden through her mind:

> *I dreamed of that which was feared, saving us all.*
> *And I dreamed that without darkness, we can never appreciate the light.*

The longer Mariah stared at the silver canvas, those words swimming in her head, the more frustrated she became.

"Mom, I just don't understand ..." Her voice was an exasperated whisper into the abandoned gallery, the soft whine she released at the end an attempt to claw down the mental barrier in her head, the words meant only for her.

And because of that, the *last* thing she expected was for someone to answer her.

Not just *anyone*.

A low, irreverent voice sounded behind her, a voice that instantly had her back going rigid, her blood heating, her magic unspooling through her veins.

"Unless your mother lives in that painting, I doubt you'll get an answer from her here, princess."

Mariah whirled, her brows pushing together in a scowl, to find Andrian standing no more than a few feet from her, his hands shoved into the pockets of his dark pants as he leaned against a tall marble statue of the Consort God, Priam.

"What're you doing here?" Her voice was biting as she narrowed her gaze.

Rage pounded in her skull, but not solely at him. She hated being snuck up on, and was more furious with herself for allowing him to get that close without her realizing.

Andrian chuckled darkly. "I saw the door open"—he

gestured behind him with a tilt of his head to where the wooden doors were still ajar—*shit*—"and decided to see who was interested enough in an abandoned wing of the palace to break in." He flitted his gaze down her body, an unreadable look in his eyes. "Imagine my surprise at finding none other than our little queen dirtying her hands in some old, dusty, forgotten gallery. Didn't take you for a fan of art or history, *nio*."

"Were you following me?" She didn't know why she asked the question, but … for some reason, she wouldn't put it past him.

His blue gaze flashed. "Trust me, princess, the last thing I want to do is follow you around this palace when I'm off duty," he growled, pushing off the statue and stalking a single step closer to her.

Mariah straightened her spine, tensing at his movement. "So you're telling me it's a simple matter of *chance* that you happened to find yourself in the same abandoned wing of the palace?" She scoffed. "Surely, you don't think I'm stupid enough to believe that."

Instead of answering her, Andrian only pressed his full lips into a thin line, meeting her glare unwaveringly. Before she could stop herself, she felt her eyes begin to roam over him, distracted by the sudden, tense silence.

Goddess, he was outrageously attractive. Toned muscle filled out his tall frame, the thin material of his long-sleeved gray shirt pulled taut over his skin. His brilliant tanzanite-blue gaze glinted with something she couldn't quite place but felt a lot like a challenge, and the longer he held her stare, the more the line of his mouth relaxed into a slightly crooked grin. She noticed his medium-length raven-black hair looked nothing short of roguish and even more unkempt than usual, as if hands had been run through it recently and repeatedly.

Either his hands, or ... someone *else's*.

The flare of jealousy that ripped through Mariah at the thought was enough to almost knock her off balance, swaying slightly where she stood. Andrian watched her subtle movement, but didn't say a word.

What the fuck?

She wasn't one to get jealous. *Ever*. She didn't want people to care about what she did behind closed doors, and she returned the courtesy. But the feelings washing through her like a damn torrent ... they were uncontrollable. A raging riptide she had to get a grip on before the devil standing before her caught on to what was racing through her mind.

Suddenly, the hands she'd imagined running through his hair to make it so tousled became hers. Just as quickly as it arrived, that wave of jealousy retreated, replaced by something *very* different.

Enfara, damn this.

"You seem distracted, *nio*. Something on your mind?"

Mariah again wished that voice could've been a bucket of cold water poured over her. However, all it did was further light the fires in her veins, her blood turning to molten lava as heat dropped swiftly into her stomach, *lower*.

Get a fucking grip, Mariah.

"I'm only wondering why, exactly, you chose to stalk me today. Considering you refuse to tell me what you're doing here, I have to assume that's what's happening."

Andrian bared his teeth at her in a cruel smile. "Maybe I don't want to tell you what I'm doing here, princess, because it's none of your Goddess-damned *business*."

Mariah shrugged. "Fine. Keep your secrets. See if I care." She cast her glance to the paintings around her, turning her back to Andrian with her best attempt at dismissive ambivalence.

Without warning, a warm mass slammed into her, spinning her around and pinning her shoulders to the wall beside the silver canvas. Andrian's eyes were blazing now, his mouth twisted into a snarl as he wrapped a large hand around her throat, his other arm resting on the wall behind them, caging her in. Mariah's magic instantly leaped into her veins, rising to her skin, subtle silver-gold light drifting into the air around them. Andrian's gaze darted swiftly from hers to the magic filtering off her skin, a growl rumbling in his chest as he again met her stare.

"You know *nothing* of my secrets, *nio*. All I wanted was some peace and quiet, away from the chaos you've brought into this city. But, of course, the gods are cruel and couldn't even afford me *that* today." He leaned closer to her, his warm breath tickling her cheek. "You have no idea how much your presence in this palace is driving me fucking *crazy*."

Goddess, save me.

The warmth in Mariah's core was back, and flames licked up her spine. She arched her back, pushing herself slightly closer to him, suddenly finding herself craving his heat, his unpredictability, his anger.

She'd spent so many years chasing after distractions.

And as she found herself pinned against the wall in an abandoned gallery, she also found herself craving a new one.

Perhaps it was time for a little ... *experiment*.

"Hm," she breathed, purposefully dropping her gaze to his full lips, the white teeth that were still bared in a snarl. "I wonder. How *crazy*, exactly, does me being here drive you?" She returned her eyes to his own, the wild blue blazing. "Crazy enough to show me?"

Her last words were barely more than a whisper, and for several, too-long heartbeats they stared each other down, sharing breath as she let him read every craving she felt for him in the pit of her stomach. She could've sworn she felt him leaning closer to her, pushing her further into the wall, the evidence of the effect of her words on him pressing firmly into her stomach ...

With a sudden, frustrated sound, Andrian released his grip on her throat, pushing off the wall in a single smooth motion before turning on his heel. Shoving his hands in his pockets, he threw his next words over his shoulder, as if careless where they might land.

"Never crazy enough for that, *nio*. Not even if the whole world was crashing down around me."

He continued for the door as Mariah slumped back against the wall, watching him go. She idly reached a hand up to her neck, tracing the ghostly feeling the imprint of his fingertips had left, watching the muscles of his broad back shift as he marched away. Confusion prickled under her skin, but she didn't let it surface; choosing instead to stare after him, not wanting to miss a single step until he left the gallery.

And, sure enough, just before he stepped through the ancient wood doors, he paused, turning just enough to shoot a glance over his shoulder, his dark hair falling errantly into his eyes. Their eyes clashed, just for a moment, but Mariah saw everything she needed to see. She smiled softly to herself as he stormed from the room, slamming the door behind him on those gods-awful hinges.

Crazy enough, indeed.

CHAPTER 29

The creaky fucking hinges on those ancient doors were almost enough to make Andrian turn and land a kick that would've splintered the wood into thousands of pieces.

Almost. But he didn't.

Because if he did, that would mean risking another glance at the heated look in those forest-green eyes, the light likely still filtering off her skin, making the cursed shadows in his blood sing in response ...

Fuck. He had to just keep walking.

It had felt so like that moment in the library, when he'd caught her with some ridiculously titled book. The heat that flared in her gaze had his own body responding like a damn horny teenager, the draw between them suddenly magnetic.

Not only was it fucking frustrating, but for him, it was forbidden.

That's probably why you can't resist the temptation, asshole.

He didn't know why he'd followed Mariah down that abandoned corridor. But when he'd spotted her stalking through the palace hallways, his shadows hiding him from her view, he'd been lured in by that curious look of determination on her face. It was like she'd been searching for something, but didn't quite know what.

He didn't let himself think about how accurate that feeling might've been.

However, he *definitely* hadn't meant to follow her into that old, abandoned gallery.

But he also started to realize his judgment vanished like smoke on a breeze around her.

He shook his head, growling low in his throat as he stormed down the palace corridor, desperate to put some distance between her and himself. He wound up staircases, through resplendent archways, past opulent gardens, until he was no longer sure where exactly in the palace he was.

Gods, this palace was fucking ridiculous. He'd lived here most of his life and the sight of all the gold and wealth made him sick.

And now, it wasn't the only thing that was making him queasy.

Get her out of your mind. You got yourself into this mess by letting yourself get Selected, but for gods-sake, you must *have the self-control to not make this worse.*

It was a speech he'd repeated to himself over and over, a litany he clung to with everything he had.

But every time he thought about how she'd bonded with Sebastian, and now Quentin, and how something may have, *must* have happened with one or both of them, irrational rage heated his bloodstream and twisted his stomach into violent knots.

He wasn't jealous. He was no fool; he knew as well as the rest of them what being a member of a Queen's Armature meant, how those bonds were formed, what feelings the ritual elicited. And he wasn't blind, either—he could see with his own eyes nothing romantic lingered between Mariah and the two who were now bonded to her.

But ... it was just the thought of someone else *touching* her. When he'd looked into her eyes, when his hand was wrapped around the soft skin of her neck, her cheeks flushed that infuriating shade of cherry red, he'd been overwhelmed with the feeling that she was his, that no one could touch her skin or see that blush except for him.

Fucking ridiculous, all of it.

He shivered, clenching his fists tighter as he pushed his steps faster, stomping up the latest flight of stairs. It was taking every ounce of his control, every mental wall he'd built for so long to keep himself from running back to the dark-haired girl with the glowing skin and forest green eyes and do *all* the things to her that were currently racing through his head. All she'd just teased him with.

That was the final straw. Andrian had to get out of that palace.

When he reached the top of the stairs, he turned right down the hallway and headed west. He was a little turned around, but he knew he would eventually find an exit, the stables, and a horse that could take him into the city. Once there, who knew; maybe he'd find a seedy tavern, drown out his miseries with shitty ale and poor company.

His pace quickened, his resolve set. Until the sound of voices stopped him dead in his tracks, all thoughts of distraction from a certain dark-haired queen fleeing from his mind.

"It's too soon, Victor. If we are not patient, we could lose *everything*."

That voice ... he would know it anywhere.

Andrian's shadows leaped out of his skin, filtering into the air around him, instantly blending himself into the gloom of the dimly lit hallway. He moved quickly to the wall, pressing his back to the smooth stone as he inched along towards the barely cracked door. He glanced around, and with a whispered curse under his breath, he realized suddenly where he was.

Every Royal family had both a collection of suites in the palace and a residence in the mountain district down in Verith. Normally, the lords would keep their residence at their manors in the city, opting for opulent seclusion over their comparatively cramped palace quarters. However, after Mariah's little explosion that had blinded Campion and killed Beauchamp—*good riddance, honestly*—the Royals had decided to remain a bit longer in the palace before removing themselves to their manors.

And, of course, that meant Andrian's father, Lord Julian Laurent, was currently living in the palace. And even once he decided to retreat to his manor in Verith, he wouldn't return to Antoris until after Mariah's coronation.

Which, if Andrian had anything to do with it, would *never* happen.

Lord Shawth's dark chuckle filtered out of the cracked doorway and pulled him from those thoughts.

"You say that as if we actually have anything at risk. We have the upper hand in everything here, Julian. There is not a single thing that hasn't gone our way in over two decades."

"While I see the positives to our situation, Victor, you know why I'm still unhappy with certain ... elements." Andrian's father's voice was brusque, a tone Andrian knew far too well.

That had often been the tone used right before his father would teach him a "lesson" that almost always ended with Andrian bruised or bleeding on the cold, hard floors of his family's ancestral keep.

"Yes, yes." Andrian could almost picture Shawth waving

his hand dismissively in front of his face, could envision the darkening anger setting into his father's expression. "I know you would have things differently. But all things considered, we couldn't have gotten luckier. He has truly blessed us."

He?

Another low growl from Lord Laurent. "Are things otherwise situated at Khento?"

"As I just told you, everything is in order. Julian, trust me; this is our time." A brief pause, followed by the sound of a soft creak, like someone was shifting in their seat. "The only obstacle left in front of us is ... well, *her*."

Andrian went utterly still.

Maybe they meant Ryenne. She was still the one who held the power in the kingdom. And as long as Mariah never ascended, Ryenne would remain in her state of limbo for ...

Well, he wasn't sure how long that could last, but he was determined to test it.

Andrian's father humphed. "What is it, exactly, that Kol wants?"

Who in the gods' names was Kol? Andrian knew Onita's history better than most, the lost words of the past his hidden passion. Losing himself in events that had already happened always seemed safer than dwelling on whatever horrors he might be subjected to in the present.

Shawth snorted. "He wants what he's always wanted— her." Another creak of a chair. "We have to move now. To bring her to him."

"*Not now*, Victor. It's too soon. Besides, we hardly have enough proof. Everything you rely upon is speculation; not enough to risk what you're proposing—"

"Did you not hear me before, Julian? There is no risk. They are weak, and we have a tool none of them would suspect."

Silence followed Shawth's words. Andrian's heart pounded in his ears, his shadows twisting tighter around him, pressing him deeper into the darkness of the hall.

Finally, Lord Laurent spoke again.

"No." His voice was low and dangerous. "Ryenne has faithfully served this kingdom for centuries. Because of that, we must give her a chance. Let her prove her worth to our cause. Let's see what we can get her to give to us willingly, and then we can discuss ... other alternatives."

The relief that flooded Andrian was immediate and sickening. *Ryenne. They were talking about Ryenne. Not Mariah.*

He hated himself for that relief. It was not something he should—could—feel.

Pulling his shadows back beneath his skin, leaving just enough in the air to conceal him as he slipped from the quiet corridor, Andrian finally continued toward the palace exit. He marched past the stables and stalked into the game park, trying and failing to shove the overheard conversation between his father and the other Onitan lord far from his mind.

CHAPTER 30

The clash of metal and the impact in her arms had Mariah clenching her teeth. She grunted softly as she pushed the soles of her feet into the earth, pouring her strength into her arms against the attack she was defending.

Well ... not truly an attack. She darted her eyes to Drystan's rich brown gaze, the hint of a smile playing on his lips as he stared down at her.

"You almost missed that block and let me in. Sloppy defense, Mariah."

She flashed him a joking snarl before shoving her blade against his, pushing him away. Turning with a grin and an eye roll, she walked out of the training circle, resting her dulled sword against a tree before grabbing her canteen and taking a long, deep pull of the cold water. She brushed her heavy, damp braid out of her face and off the back of her neck—it was a rainy morning, a fall storm having moved in from the coast in the early hours before sunrise.

She'd bonded with Drystan the night before, just before that same storm rolled in. And just as she'd expected, it had been the golden threads reaching out to him, weaving the bridge between their souls. This new bond felt like warm, fresh-tilled earth and sharpened steel, and while he may be the youngest of her Armature, he carried himself with an ageless maturity that Mariah had never known she needed.

When she'd sat with him last night at her dining table and explained to him that she knew of how intense the bonding could be, for both of them, she'd also made it clear there was a physical boundary she wouldn't cross with him. She'd further assured him that none of this had anything to do with him, and everything to do with her.

And, incredibly, he'd complied without so much as a question.

Once the bonding was complete, and they'd sat, bared and bleeding before their Goddess, their shared breath coming out in pants, he'd gently pulled her hand from his chest, placed it by her side, and pulled her to her feet, dressing them both in robes they'd laid out prior. He then proceeded to clean first the wound on her palm, and then the wound on his chest, all the while making comfortable conversation with her as they both settled back down to the earth.

His incredible self-control throughout the entire process had her watching him closely, his responses to her and to the bonding so *very* different from that of Sebastian and Quentin. She wondered if perhaps there were more to his quiet layers, if perhaps his true preferences lay with someone who looked very different from her. Not that it bothered her, of course—she needed her Armature to be loyal to her, to be willing to lay down their own lives to save hers.

She didn't, however, need them to crave her.

Actually, a part of her preferred it if they didn't. It made everything so much more incredibly complicated for her when they did.

After their wounds were cleaned and they were again fully dressed, he'd joined her in bed ... but not in the way Sebastian had. Offering her only steadfast comfort and companionship, they hadn't even touched, instead continuing their quiet conversations until she'd drifted off to sleep.

And this morning, when she'd awoken with him still beside her, she'd forgotten for a moment about the Royals, about Zadione, even about that magic in her soul.

The reprieve had been short, but welcome nonetheless.

"M! Get back over here. Sparring training isn't done yet."

A mix of a grin and a grimace touched her face as she was pulled from her thoughts: a grin for the familial nickname Quentin had fallen into calling her far too easily, a grimace for the soreness already setting into her arms and the thought of returning to that sandy ring. She set her canteen against the tree and walked back to her waiting Armature, loosening her stiff shoulders with a light roll. Just as she reached Quentin, about to step down into the pit, a shout and the sound of footsteps sounded down the game path leading to their clearing.

As one, her Armature turned toward the noise, years of practice becoming instinct. A dart of her eyes to the left revealed that even Andrian, his dark clothes similarly damp from the morning rain, had pushed himself from the tree at the edge of the clearing he had been brooding against and joined the ring of warriors that settled into alert stances around her.

They all instantly relaxed, though, as a golden female came bursting from the treeline, dressed uncharacteristically in leggings and a long-sleeved tunic. Ciana doubled over, attempting to catch her breath, her chest heaving in deep pants. Mariah, chuckling to herself softly, shouldered her way around Quentin and jogged to her friend. As she neared, Ciana was able to compose herself enough to lift her head, amber gaze meeting Mariah's, her face pale and signs of distress evident in her expression.

Mariah's grin instantly fell as warning bells began to ring in her head.

"Mariah … you're needed. Back at the palace. Now. Lord Shawth wishes to speak with you."

Mariah stood before the white and gold doors of the meeting room, dressed in her usual preferred black leggings and gold sweater. She'd changed quickly after being summoned by Ciana, and her hair was still plaited down her back in a tight braid, a few errant, sweat-damp strands framing her face.

She raised a hand and knocked on the door lightly, her eyes darting to either side to where she was flanked by Drystan and Quentin, their postures rigid. The three of them stood there quietly for a few long heartbeats, none daring to speak, before the double doors swung open to reveal Lord Shawth dressed in the blood-red of his house. His watery blue stare took in her appearance, and Mariah could've sworn she saw annoyance flash across his expression before shifting back to his normal slimy coolness.

"Welcome, Your Highness. Thank you for agreeing to join me at such an early hour. I intend to return to my city estate this afternoon and wished to speak with you before I departed."

Mariah nodded once to the Lord. "Of course, Lord Shawth. I'm happy to speak with you." The lie was thick as poison on her tongue, but she choked it out, nonetheless. She took a step into the doorway, Drystan and Quentin moving with her. Shawth's eyes darted to the two warriors, stepping back slightly at their advancement.

"I believe this conversation would be best kept between just our ears, My Lady. I can assure your Armature that you'll be safe. They may remain just outside the doors if you or they are at all concerned, however."

Mariah froze, hesitancy sweeping through her. She would rather vacation to the depths of Enfara than step into that conference room without Quentin and Drystan. But then she remembered Ryenne's words, the queen's voice tickling the back of her mind: *"You are on very thin ice with the Royals. Tread carefully, Mariah. They may have begrudgingly accepted Beauchamp's death simply because he was old and difficult, and they've found a gain in his loss, but that forgiveness may be withdrawn just as easily as it was given. And trust me—as despicable as they can be, ruling without those lords may prove to be an impossible task."*

She could also feel her grandfather's dagger that she'd strapped down her back, beneath the flowing material of her sweater. Its presence gave her a modicum of confidence, at least.

Mariah turned slowly to face Quentin and Drystan. "Stay here. I'll be fine." *And if I'm not, you'll know.* For good measure, she tugged gently on each of their bonds, communicating her unspoken order. They glanced at each other, wariness in their eyes, before looking back at her and nodding their heads. Together, they stepped back and took up positions on either side of the double doors. Mariah turned back to the waiting lord, smiling sweetly as she met his sour, smug expression. Shawth took one more step back from the doorway, inviting her in with a wave of his arm.

"Please, after you, My Lady."

Eyeing him, Mariah stepped through the doors and into the room. They closed softly behind her with a *click*, and she spotted another shape move out from behind a pillar against one of the walls.

A shape dressed in pale gold robes and graying blonde hair piled atop her head.

"High Priestess Ksee. What a surprise." Mariah's voice was tight as she plastered another fake smile upon her face.

The priestess smiled coldly back at her before beckoning with a pale hand for Mariah to take a seat at the table. Mariah's stomach roiled in disgust, her magic revolting with her, but she didn't argue as she sat. Shawth and Ksee followed, seating themselves across from Mariah. Once settled, Shawth leaned back, taking a deep breath as he looked at Mariah, his eyes shining with dark glee and his mouth twisted into a smirk.

"I do believe, Mariah, that we got off on the wrong foot, so to speak. It is my hope, and the hope of our High Priestess, that a meeting between us would help to ... bridge the gap. Ensure we are all on the same page."

"On the same page about what, exactly, My Lord?" Mariah's voice was far colder than she'd intended, but something in Shawth's voice had her trusting none of what he said. He spoke with the cool, too casual grace of a politician, his tone that of a man bred and raised for using words to manipulate and achieve exactly what he wanted.

"My, you are astute, my dear," Shawth said, his voice dripping with sarcasm. "Well, it's my desire to make sure you are well-informed as to my role in this court, in Verith, and throughout Onita. And, of course, to ensure you are well-informed of your own role, as well. And how the Royals and the Crown have long worked together to ensure future peace and stability throughout the kingdom."

Shawth's cold gaze locked on Mariah. She refused to flinch, refused to break, refused to let this man gain any ounce of traction over her. "Then by all means, My Lord, I'm listening. Please continue with your elaboration."

His sneer morphed into a cold smile that didn't touch his eyes. "As I'm sure you're aware, our lovely Queen Ryenne is of my own house. A great aunt, actually, although a few generations removed. And her reign has been lauded by many as one of the most peaceful and prosperous in all of Onita's history. Do you happen to know why, Mariah?"

Mariah ground her teeth at the casual use of her name but didn't deign to give him the satisfaction of a reaction. *Yet.* "Because she's an intelligent, fair queen who has long put the interests of her people and her kingdom before her own?"

His smile only grew colder. "That is correct, in a way. She *is* smart and puts the needs of her *people* first. Do you know how she does that?"

Mariah watched him, waiting for him to continue.

"When she first came into power and ascended the throne, she recognized that she, as a young woman, didn't know the first thing about running a kingdom, about ruling a people. So, she relinquished much of her control to her uncle, my great-grandfather, then the head of our house and Lord of Khento. *He* became the true wielder of power behind the guise of the throne. Ryenne became, and has been since, a beloved figurehead to the people, a symbol of the might and power of their kingdom, a beautiful rose without any of its thorns. And when my great-grandfather aged and passed from this earth, and was replaced by his son, and then his son, and then me, Ryenne never sought to take back any of that power. Because she knew allowing us to rule, while she oversaw the more trivial matters of the kingdom, was in *everyone's* best interests.

"And now, Mariah, her time as queen is coming to an end. And she's to be replaced by you. The arrangement she negotiated with her family—with *my* family—when she first ascended ... it was always her smartest move. The way of Qhohena's queens was great, long ago, but as our nation has grown and developed, it has come time for the monarchy to do so as well. We've evolved, adapted, and it's crucial that we not regress on that progression simply because the crown is now destined to pass to another."

Finally, the lord finished his speech, his blue gaze drilling into Mariah like twin ice picks.

Stunned was too simple a word to describe what lanced through her. She felt her magic again begin to unspool, both the silver and gold threads unwinding, curling together, spilling into her veins, responding to the building fury coursing through her. She couldn't, *wouldn't* believe it. This lord was lying, he *had* to be ...

... but deep down, somehow, she knew he wasn't. That the words he'd spoken were the truth. She'd been watching Ryenne over the past four weeks, observing the queen as she'd dealt with palace business, and not *once* had she ever witnessed the queen handle or address a real issue that truly mattered to Onita or the ruling of the kingdom.

Mariah let all the ancient power in her veins seep into her voice as she spoke.

"That may be how my predecessor chose to rule, Lord Shawth. And I respect her decision to do so. But as even you pointed out, it will soon be me to sit upon that throne. And while I certainly intend to hear your sage *counsel*"—she drew out the word into a snarl—"I intend to rule in the way Xara did, the way Qhohena intended. I intend to be the one in power. I'm the *queen*."

And as she spoke the words, she knew them to be true. She'd spent this past month wondering what, exactly, she wanted in this new place. But as she let her magic ripple through her, letting it fill her with an intoxicating thrum, she knew there was one thing she now craved far more than the freedom she'd once thought she wanted.

She wanted *power*.

A sharp voice suddenly interjected itself into the room. "Queen *apparent*."

Mariah's head whipped to Ksee, seated beside Shawth, cold flames licking in her stare. "You are the queen apparent. *Not* the queen. That title will not be yours until you bond with all your Armature and ascend the throne. As usual, you forget your place, *Mariah*."

Mariah snarled at the priestess, the untamed part of her slipping free, just a bit more.

Shawth chose that moment to speak again. "You're young, My Lady. Not yet ready for the business of leadership and all that the throne truly entails. You don't know what you speak. By the Goddess, you don't even know the true weight of your own crown. But I do. You were never raised to sit upon that throne. What I'm offering you is a lifetime of luxury, of comfort, without the burdens of power. I urge you—make the *right* choice here."

The silver magic suddenly forced itself up, slipping through her control, pushing out from under her skin and into the air around her, crackling like whips of wild lightning. The air felt static, pulsing in time with her hammering heartbeat, a caged beast growing closer to finding its true freedom and devouring those that sought to lock it away.

Mariah's display of power flashed and reflected in Shawth's eyes, his expression hardening into true disdain.

"You may have learned some circus tricks, my dear, but you don't frighten me. And until you are fully bonded, you would do well to remember that you are *replaceable*."

"Is that a threat?" The silver light around her began to form into physical threads, into solid-looking ropes, cords that begged to choke out the vile stare of the man who sat across from her.

Shawth only rose from his chair, thoroughly dismissing her and the power raging in the air. "But of course not, Your Highness. However, you forget—you're not in the Crossroad City anymore. Here in Verith, we deal in strength and power. As strong as you think yourself to be, with little bits of light magic and the indecent training with your Armature, you're naught but a mere speck on our chessboard. I encourage you to *tread lightly*."

Mariah shot to her feet, the screeching sound of her chair echoing in the room as it was shoved back with the force of her movement. That silver magic finally lashed out—not at the Lord, but at the table between them. And that light, that power that wasn't supposed to take any physical form, slashed across the wood, leaving a thin, smoking crevice in its place.

Shawth and Ksee glanced down at the mark in the table, their faces blanching, as Mariah's breath heaved from her lungs. Shawth composed himself the fastest, looking back to her with a look of pure venom and calculating awareness.

"Sleep well, Your Highness."

And with that, he turned on his heel and left, Ksee stumbling after him, leaving Mariah in turmoil.

CHAPTER 31

"You did *what*?"

Ryenne's incredulous question rang through the living room of Mariah's suite, the tone of her voice reflected on the faces of those gathered there—Kalen, Mariah's Armature, Ciana, and Delaynie.

And, of course, Mariah herself. But instead of bewilderment, her gaze was blank, tired and expressionless as she stared out the large windows facing the mountains. "Do you need me to repeat myself? I lost control and my magic sliced a cut into the conference table."

"While I can certainly appreciate more than most how ugly those tables are," said Delaynie, her quiet voice steady despite the tension in the room. "That seems ... *impossible*. Everyone knows the Goddess's magic is not physical in nature, except to its queen. It cannot actually harm or touch anything in this world."

Mariah lifted her eyes to meet Delaynie's cunning, soft blue gaze. "I know it's impossible. But I'm telling you all that it happened."

Ryenne shook her head once, twice. "I'm not saying you were mistaken, Mariah, but I agree with Delaynie; the magic simply does not work like that—"

"Is it true?" Mariah's voice was colder than the frost of the Everheim Mountains as she interrupted the queen.

Ryenne blanched at Mariah's tone. "Is ... is what true?"

Mariah didn't answer. She only locked the queen with a stare that would've sent lesser people running.

"Mariah," said Sebastian. "What, exactly, did Shawth have to say to you?" A tug of concern down that stone-colored bond. Of course, Sebastian would be the first to wonder not if what she'd said was possible, but what had caused it to happen in the first place.

And, truthfully, the last thing Mariah wanted to do was discuss Shawth's revelations with a member of Ryenne's own Armature present, but it was clear that those gathered in that room had now turned their full attention back to her, desperate to know the answer to Sebastian's question.

Fine.

"Shawth told me the truth. About the kingdom. About who really rules here in Verith. And he told me he has no intention of relinquishing that power, not after his family has grown so accustomed to it for generations. He expects me to be nothing more than a figurehead, a pretty face to lead the Solstice twice a year and use my magic to generate *allume*." Mariah kept her stare pinned on Ryenne as she spoke, and her anger slowly rose to the surface, all the feelings of betrayal and shock she'd felt at Shawth's words seeping back into her eyes. "I told him no."

The room was deathly quiet, Kalen stiff as he took a step closer to his queen. Mariah's own Armature were darting confused glances between the queen, her consort, and Mariah herself, shifting around the room with the growing tension.

Delaynie and Ciana sat still and held their tongues as the queen and her apparent held each other's stares.

It was Ryenne who spoke next.

"Leave us. All of you."

Immediately, Mariah's court stood from their seats or where they'd been lounging around the room and strode for the foyer. She heard the door as it clicked closed behind their shuffling steps. The only one who remained was Kalen, his hand resting on Ryenne's shoulder. Mariah didn't care, though; as much as she no longer trusted Ryenne, she also knew neither she nor Kalen were a threat to her, and she suspected the queen's consort already knew everything there was to know about Ryenne.

Including her failings in the role the Goddess had chosen her to fill.

Still holding Ryenne's ocean-blue stare, Mariah asked her question again.

"Is it true?"

Ryenne's solid expression finally crumpled, replaced with one of pure, undiluted guilt. Her voice was small and soft as she answered.

"Yes."

Mariah didn't even blink in surprise. She knew what Ryenne's answer would be. "Tell me. Tell me how it happened."

Ryenne closed her eyes as a single tear beaded up and spilled down her cheek, her once-flawless face now tired and slightly ragged with the life leeching from her, day by day. "I was young. Scared. And very quickly after arriving in the capital and being Chosen, things began to just ... spiral out of control. I didn't know how to stop it, how to do any of it—how to run a kingdom, how to ensure my people were fed, how to command armies, how to greet foreign dignitaries, how to negotiate with overly prideful Royals. And my uncle ... he presented me with an easy way out. And I let him. He told me he would rule in the way only our family knew how, but would do it behind the veil that the people saw, to keep the appearance of a powerful sovereign ruler. But ... the one in power would no longer be me.

"I let Lord Shawth rule, and I kept to the palace, appearing when I needed to, overseeing the Solstice and everything that came along with it. Then the levels of *allume* collected each Solstice began to dwindle, and our supplies began to wane, and I started to suspect that it was all because of *me*. Because of what I'd done. But I was even more terrified that if I were to retake control, I would do something wrong, and doom Onita to a far worse fate than it was perhaps already headed towards. So, when my uncle passed, and his son took his place, I let him continue to rule. And I did the same for his grandson. And now, four generations have passed, and I know to walk back my decisions would only cause more harm than what I'd originally created.

"But, Mariah ... the guilt of what I did is mine alone to bear. No one, *especially* not me, would fault you if you were to make the same choice I did. I was raised to be a queen, but ruling is hard, and what I chose was by far the easiest. And for you, being raised—"

"Being raised ... what? A commoner? A peasant from Andburgh? Regardless of our blood, Ryenne, the Goddess chose us—*both* of us—to be queen. And while I certainly didn't think I wanted that title at first, I'm here now. And I intend to rule."

Mariah's voice was harsh and punishing, her anger still thick and heavy on her tongue. Ryenne simply hung her head in defeat, Kalen's hand on her shoulder tightening once as he levied a cold look at the younger woman.

"You should know, Mariah, that you are no mere commoner to us." Kalen's voice, filled with an uncharacteristic chill, snapped her attention to him. "However, before throwing your anger like a knife, I would encourage you to think for a moment about what all is at stake here. This is not some mere play for power; perhaps it is for some, but is not—and has never been—for Ryenne or myself. The people of this kingdom are *real*. And a good ruler cannot afford to dismiss options that may help her in the name of pride."

Mariah kept her sharpened gaze on Kalen as he spoke. Once he was done, she simply stood, turning sharply on her heel as she strode towards her bedroom. She didn't yet possess the authority to dismiss the queen, or her consort, from her presence, but also didn't wish to remain sitting there for a single moment longer.

"A good ruler cannot afford to dismiss options that may help her in the name of pride."

No. This was not a matter of pride. This was a matter of taking back power from men who never deserved to wield it.

Before she slammed the doors to her room, Mariah chanced a glance back at Ryenne. Mariah watched her lips move, and despite the distance she could still hear the Queen's next words.

"Perhaps this is why the magic left me early. It no longer wanted to be kept a captive in this palace and wished to find one who possessed the strength to do what it had been created to do."

At those words, Mariah set her shoulders and turned back around, her bedroom doors closing behind her with a soft click.

CHAPTER 32

The night was cold, the stars twinkling above Mariah as she sat alone on her open-air veranda off the living space to her suite, the wind rushing off the Attlehon Mountains whipping her near-black hair around her face. She pulled her wool blanket tighter around her shoulders, taking a deep sip from the glass of ice-cold whiskey in her hand.

Sebastian and Drystan had poked their heads back into her suite as soon as Ryenne and Kalen left, but she'd promptly dismissed them, requesting the time to be alone. She felt her emotions, her anger, her stress rising in her like a tidal wave; all that which she normally suppressed and buried deep within her threatening to break the dam she'd been building inside her mind since her very first memories. She didn't tolerate emotions well—she preferred to remain unfeeling, hardened, ignoring anything beyond immediate gratification of the flesh and her instincts.

Love is a weakness.

Mariah thought about how much had changed in only a

few short weeks. No more than a month ago, she'd awoken with a hangover on her twenty-first birthday, expecting her only challenge to be how she would pull off her unnoticed escape from the town, grandfather's dagger in tow. Instead, she'd walked out of her room to a silent table, an unopened letter in her mother's hands that would alter the course of her life forever.

Now, she sat there, on a balcony in the queen's suite of the golden palace of Verith, feeling both that she was always meant to be here but also like she had no business calling this her home.

She tilted her head back, her green eyes shining in the starlight above, the bright light from the gold and silver moons bathing her in their glow. Her attention lingered on that silver orb, feeling the panic start to rise once again, but shoved it down before it choked and drowned her. That fear of what might lie inside her could petrify her, consume her, if she let it.

And there was no chance in all the heavens she would let it.

She then turned her gaze to the golden moon that hung beside its twin. And as she stared up at that golden sphere, she decided to do something she'd not done in a very long time.

Mariah prayed.

She prayed to Qhohena, to the golden goddess whose magic she carried in her veins, magic she'd not been born with but had been Chosen to bear all the same. She prayed that no matter what happened, no matter what she did or who upset her or how far she was pushed, she would never forget who she'd been on that night with her family, drinking whiskey around a fire crackling with the promise of change.

She hoped beyond measure that her prayer wasn't too late, that there was still a part of her left to save.

Despite the brightness of those moons above, she couldn't help but think that no matter how hard she prayed, how desperately she wished upon the stars above ... no one was listening.

Mariah slept soundly, falling into a deep slumber.

And as she slept, she dreamed.

In her dream, a silvery figure appeared, clothed entirely in light, its features concealed completely by the bright glare radiating from it. At first, Mariah could hardly tell if it was male or female, but as it moved closer to her, she caught the shape of hips, the dip of gentle feminine curves.

The female shape moved closer, Mariah's subconsciousness ensnared in a trance, until the being stood before her, silver light burning into Mariah's soul. The figure reached out, and Mariah could've sworn she felt a featherlight touch stroke softly down her cheek when a voice, a voice both ancient and youthful, feminine and masculine, a voice filled with dark power, echoed in her mind.

"*Wake.*"

It was as if someone dumped a bucket of cold water over her entire body. Mariah's mind went careening back towards consciousness; the ghost of that silvery touch lingering on her cheeks, her eyelids flashing open to reveal the darkness of her room. She remained motionless in her bed, adrenaline coursing through her veins, her senses and her magic reaching out into the space around her. When she felt the brush of the fall breeze across her face, her blood ran cold.

Her bedroom window was open.

A window she distinctly remembered closing, locking, and checking every single night before stepping into bed, with last night being no exception.

Forcing her breath to remain steady and her body still, she

slowly, carefully, quietly slid her hand under the pillow beside her, wrapping around the hilt of her grandfather's dagger.

The second her fingers touched the cool leather, she saw it.

Movement. A shadow creeping across the floor, a wave of slimy darkness permeating the aura around it.

Mariah's eyes tracked it as it moved through the shadows of her room, slithering along the floor. The shape moved into a patch of weak silver moonlight, just enough filtering in through the clouds that had moved in throughout the night. The silver moon was the only one even slightly visible—the clouds had clustered thickly in front of the golden moon, its light darkened completely. Lit by that faint light, Mariah saw what was there with her in her room, disturbing her rest. And she knew instantly what it was.

Her blood ran ice cold, her magic leaped instantly through her veins, the spools unraveling from the place within her in thick, banded threads.

It was an Uroboros. A serpent-like creature she'd only read about in history books, a creature crafted in the darkest depths of Enfara. Its two foul, venomous heads gleamed with wicked fangs in the pale moonlight, its ugly tongues flicking out to taste the air, taste the beating life in her veins as she lay there in her bed, her hand still gripping her family's dagger. Her magic thrummed, begging to be set free.

It was a demon straight from the legends of the First War. Mariah couldn't dwell on how it had gotten there, in what should've been the most protected place in the palace. All she could think of at that moment was saving herself, of getting *out of there*.

She shoved her magic down again, forcing everything in her to quiet. She couldn't risk her skin beginning to glow, to alert that creature in any way to the fact she'd woken. She kept her eyes locked on its dark form as it continued to smoothly slink across the marble floor, moving closer and closer to the foot of her bed. She stopped breathing altogether as it reached the post, arching its two heads off the ground and twisting around, winding its way up.

It kept coming and coming, and Mariah didn't move, didn't breathe, didn't dare look at it. She could hear its deadly soft hisses, could feel the slight dip in the mattress as it finally made its way onto the foot of her bed. It was massive, and she swore the smell filling her nose was one of death, decay, of rotten flesh and the misery of souls long since trapped away from this world.

She didn't let herself move, even as she felt it come up right beside her. She felt it arch up off the bed, those heads bearing the long, wicked, poisonous fangs that would bring her demise.

And then the Uroboros struck.

As it dove, its twin heads aiming for the soft, vulnerable skin of her neck, her hand whipped out from under the pillow, still gripping the leather hilt of her grandfather's dagger, the silver blade etched with dragon wings gleamed in the moonlight.

She moved as fast as the snake, all her magic pouring itself into her arm to lend it every pound of supernatural strength and speed she needed to strike her blow.

The winged dagger sliced clean through the heads of the Uroboros, black blood spraying her face and hands as the heads and body dropped with a heavy thud onto the mattress beside her.

Finally, letting the adrenaline coursing through her system take over, Mariah rolled from her bed, away from the creature of death and decay that now lay in pieces in the very spot where she'd been lying only seconds before. Staring down at her hands, covered in black blood, she took in the vile smell permeating the entire room and the bed in which she'd once thought herself safe. Her hands went loose at her sides, her grandfather's dagger clanging to the marble floor as she sank to her knees, her mind screaming with all the anger, fear, and panic her throat wouldn't let out.

CHAPTER 33

Andrian's chest heaved, his heartbeat thudding like the beats of a drum. His shadows wound uncontrollably through the air around him, a writhing mass of ebony ropes snapping in agitation.

He sat up with a jolt, sleep still heavy in his eyes, clutching his chest and his racing heart. His skin was slick with sweat, and his muscles trembled with adrenaline and *fear*.

Something was very, very wrong.

He didn't know what it was—instinct, magic, some sort of curse—but he could *feel* the vileness in the air, the evil licking against his skin, pulling him out of his bed.

Pulling him across the hall, to the rooms of the dark-haired siren who lived there.

The panic that hit him with the realization was like an icy dagger slowly sinking into his gut and twisting.

His mind shut off. Instinct drove his movement. Not bothering with a shirt, he slipped on a pair of black cotton pants, the soles of his feet barely registering the feel of the cool marble floor. Andrian grabbed a sheathed dagger from where he'd discarded it on his island, strapping it across his back before sprinting from his room, blood still pounding in his ears.

The entrance to Mariah's suite was directly across from his. When they'd all picked their rooms, he'd been the first to claim the one closest to hers, had glared daggers at his brothers in challenge. None of them said a word, though Sebastian had watched him with a wary question in his eyes.

He'd told himself the proximity would make it easier for him to avoid running into her unnecessarily.

But even he'd known that had been bullshit.

Slamming his body into the gold and white doors, he flung them open with a loud crash. His pace was still frantic as he was pulled toward her bedroom. Fear and panic still clawed at his belly, his stomach churning.

Andrian didn't want to know what he would find past those doors. Didn't want to know, but also *needed* to know.

If something had hurt her, if some*one* had *touched* her, had reached her there in the protected heart of the palace ...

He would tear this entire castle down, brick by golden brick. And then once he'd found who was responsible, he'd tear *them* apart, piece by piece.

Every rational thought had left his mind. Every wall he'd built was gone. He'd forgotten his hatred of her, the hatred he'd tried to convince himself he carried. He'd forgotten all she'd stolen from him, all she'd stolen from herself.

All he knew was that she was his, and someone had hurt her.

Andrian burst through her bedroom doors and froze in his tracks.

She was there, kneeling on the floor, dark hair falling in a curtain around her face. She wore a short, black nightgown, the thin material hiding very little of her smooth, tan skin—skin flecked and spotted with black blood. Her dragon-winged dagger was on the ground in front of her, its silver blade stained with the same ichor.

Andrian's feet felt rooted to the ground, his mind reeling. Slowly, as if sensing his presence, Mariah lifted her head, her hair falling back as she turned and met his gaze. Her expression was empty, devoid of light and life, so unlike her that she looked almost like a stranger. He tensed, his hands clenched, before chancing a glance at her bed.

His heart dropped from his chest, and he swore, low and vicious.

The creature that lay in pieces on her bed was straight from nightmares, a demon pulled from the history books he'd spent too much of his childhood lost in. It couldn't—*shouldn't*—exist. Those creatures were myths, beings that hadn't been seen in the world for thousands of years. He reached on instinct for his dagger, until Mariah spoke and froze his movement, her voice so hollow, so cold, so foreign.

"It's dead."

Andrian wrenched his stare back to her. She was still looking up at him, a broken shell of herself. And when he saw the rawness in those forest-green eyes, the pain and fear he could see beginning to creep in past the numbness etched in her features, something inside him cracked.

The urge was sudden. To go to her, to sit beside her. To pull her into his arms, to hold her close, to stroke that soft skin and breathe in that jasmine and cedarwood scent. It washed over him like a wave, a torrent pushing him to do anything, to *be* anything, she needed in that moment. He wavered on his feet, his limbs itching to move.

Until a thundering boom from the entry to her suite snapped the spell, and the rest of Mariah's Armature, led by Sebastian, came charging into her room. Andrian blinked, confusion rattling in his chest, and he watched Sebastian burst past him and sink to his knees beside Mariah.

Fury, sudden and hot, raced through him.

That should be me.

He yanked his gaze from them, looking back at the mangled creature in her bed. He forced himself to redirect that anger towards the hideous creature sprawled in pieces across her snow-white comforter; after all, it wasn't Sebastian's fault he'd been too weak to take that final step.

It wasn't as if Mariah would even want him to be the one to comfort her, anyway. Twisted self-loathing curled into his gut, pulling taut.

He could hear Sebastian's gentle crooning. "Mariah. Are you hurt?"

"No." Her voice was still so cold, so flat. Andrian's heart warped again in his chest.

"It was an Uroboros." His words surprised him. He felt everyone's attention turn to him, and then to the creature in the bed. Fists tightened, gazes hardened, temper's heated as they stared at the thing that had come far too close to killing their queen.

"It's dead." That same empty voice repeated once more.

Andrian still couldn't bring himself to look at her. His attention remained focused on the Uroboros, at the impossibility of the attack.

He remembered, just for a moment, the conversation he'd overheard between his father and Shawth. He knew, better than most, the ruthlessness of the Royals ... but nothing they'd said had hinted at threats to Mariah.

Besides, even they weren't stupid enough to attempt an assassination of the Goddess's Chosen.

There was more movement in the room, and Andrian watched from where he remained rooted in the doorway to

Mariah's bedroom as Drystan pushed forward, slipping into the bathroom just beyond the room. He grabbed a clean towel, dampened it under the sink, and then returned to the bedroom, kneeling beside her opposite Sebastian.

"Mariah," said Drystan, his voice soft. Andrian pushed down every urge he had to move, every emotion raging in his gut. He forced his mind to go blank, unfeeling, lifeless as he watched the golden-haired man press the damp towel into Mariah's blood-splattered hands. "Take it. Go into the bathroom. Focus on what you can control."

Mariah gazed at Drystan blankly for a moment, as if not seeing him. She nodded once, absently, before rising to her feet, a puppet on a string. Andrian didn't even blink, his eyes tracking her as she padded into the bathroom.

He could no longer see her, but his attention remained fixated. Around him, his fellow Armature moved quietly and efficiently, peeling the sheets from her bed and wrapping the corpse of the Uroboros within. But he didn't notice them as they worked, didn't care to join them. His entire being was focused on the rustling sounds that came from the bathroom, the sound of the faucet running, the brush of cloth against skin and soft, padding steps.

When she reemerged, no longer speckled in foul black blood, and changed into a different—but equally distracting— black nightgown, some of the light had returned to her eyes. Her skin was no longer sickly, color again starting to warm her cheeks. She stood there, at the threshold between her bedroom and bathroom, and watched Feran and Matheo as they carried her bulky, soiled bedding from the room.

Distantly, Andrian hoped they burned it.

It was Sebastian's voice that broke the tense silence settling over the room. He cleared his throat softly.

"We cannot let you stay here for the rest of the night,

Mariah. Not until we're able to do a full sweep and make sure the entire wing is secure."

Andrian watched her as she nodded again, that same absent movement she'd used earlier with Drystan, the heavy sheet of her slightly damp hair falling forward around her shoulders.

Sebastian glanced, almost nervously, around at the rest of the Armature, his gaze lingering for a moment too long on Andrian. "So ... you'll need to stay with one of us. It's the only way we can ensure you're safe."

Andrian instantly went rigid.

It was irrational, this feeling; overwhelmingly stupid. But in that moment, he knew he would rather rip out his own teeth than let her stay with anyone other than him.

The possessive anger was intense, but the pure terror that followed it nearly washed him off his feet.

He wouldn't tolerate her staying with anyone else. Wouldn't be able to survive it, not that night. But ... Andrian was also momentarily terrified that *she* would choose someone else. That he'd played his part too well, had actually managed to make her hate him as strongly as he'd convinced himself he despised her.

Gods ... he didn't hate her at that moment. Didn't think he'd ever actually hated her.

Sebastian continued speaking.

"You are more than welcome to stay with m—"

"No."

Mariah's voice, for the first time that night, was strong and clear as it cut through Sebastian's words. Andrian's attention whipped to her, his heart thudding in his chest. A war raged inside his heart as she slowly turned her gaze to him, the incredible forest-green glimmering with the same tantalizing shadow that had haunted him since the gallery, the question in them unmistakable.

A question ... an *uncertainty*. He read it on her face, as clear as the sky on a bright winter day. She was nervous, fearful that he would be the one to reject her next.

He should. If he had any strength left, any self-respect, a single decent bone left in his body, he would tell her to seek solace with those of her Armature who might actually be able to give it.

But he'd never been particularly good at being a decent man.

So, he pushed off from the doorway to her bedroom, his feet finally releasing him from where he'd been rooted. He stalked to her, watching her head slowly tip back as he neared, holding his gaze with that fierceness that drove him mad. Soon, he stood in front of her, jasmine and cedarwood razing through his mind. For three more heartbeats, he watched as her breaths began to deepen, the rise and fall of her chest becoming more and more pronounced. Then he bent down in front of her, swiped an arm behind her knees, and scooped her into his arms.

He almost grinned at the look of shock that flared across her face.

You asked for this, princess.

Andrian then strode back out of her bedroom, toward the exit to her suites, the sounds of the others beginning their sweep of her rooms already distant and muted to his ears.

CHAPTER 34

Andrian's rooms were directly across from hers. The realization struck her with a jolt, questioning how she'd never noticed. She wondered if he'd just been unlucky or if he'd actually selected that room for himself.

The former, most likely.

Gripping her tight, he moved forward, the hand under her legs reaching out and twisting the handle, pushing open the nondescript wood. Andrian strode into the room, nudging the door closed behind them with a gentle kick. The space beyond the entryway was lit softly by two *allume* chandeliers, just enough light to illuminate the space.

Andrian kept it tidy, but not pristine. It was open, with a door on the right wall Mariah assumed led to the bathing chamber. To the left of the entry was a kitchen, complete with a stovetop, sink, and storage. An island, much like her own, was currently adorned with an array of discarded weapons. Looking further into the room, Mariah saw a bed, its black sheets untucked and tousled, as if Andrian's sleep had been fitful and disturbed before he'd arrived in the threshold of her room no more than a few moments after she'd killed the Uroboros. Between the island and bed was a square dining table, complete with four chairs, and against the back wall was a comfortable-looking chaise and bookshelves lined with volumes.

The room wasn't large, and though she'd never been there before, something about the space felt familiar, comfortable. The magic and chaos still thrumming in her head and veins quelled, just slightly.

Andrian kept moving as she took in her surroundings, striding towards the island. He set her down, surprisingly gently, on the countertop, facing the bed and the rest of the room. Her back was to the kitchen, and the shock of the cold granite on her bare thighs had her suddenly aware of how little she wore, and goosebumps prickled instantly over her skin. He looked at her for a moment, his expression utterly unreadable —all traces of that little grin he'd flashed her back in her room nowhere to be found—before stalking to a crystal decanter on the end of the kitchen counter.

Mariah's eyes tracked him, watched as the muscles in his back shifted beneath his skin with his steps, as he poured two glasses of dark liquor and walked back to where she sat on the island. Her gaze dropped, just once, to the dragon-shaped Mark right over his heart, the black ink bold against his tanned skin. There was a faint dusting of dark hair across his chest, and another line of black hair on his lower abdomen, disappearing beneath the waist-band of his pants—

Her stare snapped back to his face as he handed one of the glasses to her. Andrian stepped back and leaned against the edge of the dining table, crossing his legs in front of him, eyes never leaving hers as he took a deep drink of the liquor.

Mariah's mouth went dry as she watched him. Nothing about him was real, was *fair*. No one had the right to look like that—especially now, in the middle night, no more than minutes after she'd just thwarted a fucking *assassination*. She raised her own glass to her lips, welcoming the burn of the alcohol.

At least he had whiskey.

They remained like that for a moment—seconds, minutes, Mariah couldn't be sure—staring, assessing each other. Mariah was first to break the silence, the whiskey now churning through her veins, loosening her lips and cutting through the ice filling her head.

"Aren't you going to ask me why I said no to Sebastian tonight?"

"I don't ask questions I don't need the answer to."

"Are you not curious?"

"Do you need me to be curious?"

"No."

Silence fell again, and they continued to stare at each other, tanzanite and forest green warring with each other in the soft light. They both lifted their whiskey glasses to their lips at the same time, each taking a sip without breaking their eye contact.

It was again Mariah who spoke.

"I almost died tonight."

Andrian was silent for several heartbeats, his gaze almost contemplative.

"Yes. You almost died tonight." A pause. "But you didn't."

The air thickened with his words. Mariah was unsure if the warmth in her core was caused by the whiskey or something else, something *forbidden*.

This time, it was Andrian who spoke next.

"What do you need, princess?" His voice was soft, dark, slightly rougher than it had been before. Even the inflection of the nickname, as insulting as it still was, was different. She answered without hesitation, without thinking.

"A distraction."

She could've sworn one side of his mouth ticked up, almost imperceptibly, into a smirk.

"And is that why you wanted me to bring you here?" His mouth twitched again, pulling into a half-grin. "Is that why you said no to Sebastian?"

Even though he asked the question she'd first brought up, she refused to answer him with words. Instead, she used her silence to speak for her. The heat settled low inside her, seeping into her gaze.

Those tanzanite eyes burned her, stripped her of everything from the inside out. His gaze darkened as he tipped his glass to his mouth, downing what was left of his whiskey in one smooth motion. Setting the glass behind him, he pushed himself off the table, his movement fluid.

"I remember when I caught you in the library last week with that romance novel. What a *surprise* that was. You were so full of fake innocence, so genuinely shocked by what you'd found. Tell me, *nio*—who were you thinking of to make your cheeks flush like that from reading just a few words on a page?"

The immediate warmth in her face and neck told her that same flush was back, an instant and wordless answer to his question. The smirk he wore grew even wider, more dangerous, his eyes gleaming with triumph.

And *that* pissed her off.

She forced her face into a twisted scowl, downing the rest of her own whiskey before slamming the glass on the island beside her, making a move to push from the counter.

"I don't know why I wanted you to bring me here. Why I said no to Sebastian. Obviously, a *severe* lapse in judgment. You are the most frustrating, annoying, *despicable*—"

"No. I'm not."

His voice interrupted her, stronger and louder than before,

freezing her in place. She brought her gaze back to him just as he moved, his pace somehow both quick and unhurried, the movement of a jungle cat stalking his prey.

No, that wasn't quite right. It was the movement of a jungle cat who'd already caught his prey, and was now toying with his meal, taking joy in the fact that she could not—*would not*—run.

It made her fucking *angry* ... but it also made her skin prickle in burning anticipation.

He pushed her whiskey glass farther away before moving into her space, pushing her hips back onto the island, forcing his body between her thighs as he stepped close.

Mariah leaned back on her hands as Andrian stared down at her, his sudden closeness both an irritant and a drug, his tanzanite eyes like blue flames. His hand reached up to her neck, his fingers trailing lightly down her chest, between the swell of her breasts and down the plane of her stomach, leaving a path of blazing fire and goosebumps in their wake. Mariah's traitorous body responded instantly to him, the thin material of her black nightgown hiding nothing.

She hadn't quite known what she'd wanted when she'd silently pleaded with him to take her with him that night. All she'd known was that none of the others looked at her the way he had, that moment he'd burst through the doors of her bedroom.

Mariah still couldn't shake that look. It was haunting, but was a lifeline thrown to her as she'd been floating through the sea of her nightmare, the only raft that had saved her from sinking fully beneath the weight of sadness and terror and fury.

She'd told him she wanted a distraction.

She supposed, in her own way, that's exactly what she now needed.

His hand settled on her hip, her nightgown riding up just

enough so his pinky finger rested on the skin of her thigh. Mariah felt his hot breath on her cheek as he whispered against smooth skin.

"You want a distraction, *nio*? I can give that to you." He paused, Mariah's breath catching in her lungs, her heart racing erratically in her chest.

"But that is *all* you'll ever get from me."

He pulled back from her slightly, just enough to meet her gaze with his own. His normally bright, intrusive eyes deepened to a rich sapphire, and she could've sworn she saw tendrils of shadow curling off his bare shoulders. She wondered, distantly, if perhaps there was something hidden in his veins, a gift that, like her own, he sought to keep secret.

Except ... he now knew about her second gift. She quickly vowed to unearth his.

It was only fair.

Mariah swallowed quietly, her mouth still hot and dry. Her gaze dipped to his full lips before speaking.

"Who says I want anything more." Not a question, a statement. A declaration. There were many reasons she needed this, but one thing was for certain.

She wasn't there for love, nor did she ever want to be.

Love was, after all, a *weakness*.

And after that night, she never wanted to feel weak again.

With her words, a rope was snapped, a tether unleashed. Andrian's lip pulled back further from his teeth into a smirking growl, his right hand digging deeper into her hip, his left latching onto the back of her neck.

And then he kissed her.

Mariah felt like she'd been lit on fire with a torch, every inch of her being set alight with immediate, craving *need*. Her mouth opened as he crushed his lips to hers, his tongue instantly sweeping in, claiming, *devouring*. He tasted like snow and smoke, something crisp and dark and *dangerous* all at once. Nothing about Andrian was gentle or kind—he was icy darkness, demanding, punishing her for something she wasn't yet aware of.

He was exactly what she needed, right at that moment.

She tilted her head back further, granting him deeper access to her mouth as his hand slid from the nape of her neck into the thickness of her hair. She arched her back, pressing her body into his, wrapping her legs around his hips. She felt *him*, the hard, impressive length of him, against her core, a soft, throaty groan escaping her lips.

He ripped his mouth away from hers at the sound, the darkness in his eyes near-feral, before dropping his lips and teeth to her neck. His mouth trailed down her neck, her chest, following much of the same path his hands had mere moments before. The hand gripping her hip suddenly moved up, right to her breast, pinching her nipple hard between his fingers through the thin fabric of her nightgown. She hissed at the pain, but couldn't stop from pushing into him, begging for more.

And then the low neckline of her nightgown was pulled down, her skin suddenly exposed. Andrian's mouth was hot and brutal as it wrapped around her breast, his teeth grazing the sensitive flesh of her nipple as he flicked it once with his tongue.

Mariah wasn't sure if the sparks she saw were in her mind or conjured by the magic in her veins.

She gasped a breath as he growled against her skin, his grip in her hair tightening, pulling her head back until her gaze met the ceiling of his rooms.

As immediately as he'd grabbed her, his grasp on her hair released, and as her head fell forward, her mouth was once again claimed by his. This kiss was even more ravaging than the first, a torrent of teeth and tongue and hair and nails. Her head spun, her heart pounded, and her control slipped further and further away.

As if she wanted to maintain that control. She wanted none of that power, none of that responsibility. Not tonight.

When his hand again returned to her hip, his fingers gliding slowly across the soft skin of her inner thigh, her control evaporated completely.

A slight shift of Andrian's hips had her legs falling from where they'd been clenched around him, his body pushing her thighs even farther apart. His hands were still moving, inching closer and closer to her center, the agonizing slowness of his pace driving her *mad*.

When she felt the rough pads of his fingers brush softly against her core, over her thin, lacy underwear, a shiver tore through her. A gasp escaped her lips as she broke their kiss, her head falling back further into his palm.

Andrian's mouth moved to her ear as he stroked her—light, teasing touches that evaded the bundle of nerves where she so desperately wanted him.

"Your body betrays you, *nio*. You say you despise me, that you shouldn't have come here tonight—yet you made that choice, not me. And now I'm *here*"—he slipped a finger beneath her underwear, pressing it ever so slightly into her as if in emphasis, drawing a whispered moan from her throat—"and I'm calling your bluff."

Her breath came out in ragged pants, but at his words she managed to lift up one of her hands she'd been leaning on, winding it into the silky lengths of his dark hair. She pulled, lifting his face away from hers so she could meet his gaze.

"Fine. Call my bluff." Her eyes took in his hooded lids, the lust in his eyes, the fullness of his lips. She pulled his head closer to hers until she was whispering against his mouth.

"But I'm calling yours, too."

Andrian answered her with a growl, his lips meeting hers just as he sank his finger deep into her.

Mariah's back arched, her breath gasping, but Andrian's other hand was again in her hair, holding her firmly in place as he moved his finger in and out of her, curling it to strike that spot deep within her.

When he pushed in another finger and finally brushed his thumb against her clit, she could've sworn light pulsed at her skin, her essence fraying at the edges. She couldn't stop herself from pressing herself into him further, begging him to touch every part of her, to rip the shreds of the night away from her soul until the raging in her mind was finally silenced.

His pace quickened, and she felt herself rising with it, chasing after the one thing she wanted, needed from him in this moment.

Suddenly, he withdrew from her, slipping his fingers out from inside her and leaving her feeling empty, pained, frustrated. Her eyes snapped open to meet his tanzanite stare, his expression heated, his chest rising and falling as fast as hers.

Without a word, he lifted his hand from between them and brought it to his lips, slipping the two fingers that had just been buried in her into his mouth. His eyes closed, a low groan rumbling from his throat before he slid them out and whispered a single word.

"*Svass.*"

Mariah was about to ask what that meant, her mind moving slowly from the near orgasm, when his eyes snapped open and his hands slipped from her head to under her thighs, pulling her off the counter and wrapping her legs around his waist. Her arms immediately went to his neck, gripping him tightly, before he stood tall and held her close.

"I'm not going to let the first time I make you come be on

the kitchen counter, *nio*. I have more plans for you than just that."

Mariah's breath caught in her throat, her blood heating to a near boil, as he turned around and strode for the bed against the far wall of the room.

CHAPTER 35

Mariah's breath whooshed from her lungs as Andrian dropped her, not ungently, onto the black silk sheets.

Then he was there, his body covering hers, the heat radiating from him scorching her skin. His lips again met hers, his hands creeping lazily up her thighs. His fingers found the silky hem of her nightgown, and a low, possessive growl ripped from his throat. He pushed up abruptly to stand beside the bed, his hands pulling her with him until she sat on the edge of the plush mattress.

Wordlessly, he gripped the lace trim of her nightgown and pulled it slowly, *teasingly*, up the length of her body. Mariah held his stare steadily as she lifted her arms above her head, as he peeled the scrap of fabric off her. Goosebumps pricked her skin the moment the cool air kissed her bare flesh.

For a moment, he just ... stared at her, frozen, chest heaving. In that same brief time, she swore she saw in his eyes everything he fought so desperately to keep repressed, hidden from her. It was the same look she'd seen flash in his eyes before —at the Selection, in the gallery, in the library. A look that demanded confessions be pulled from his throat, but begged her to look away and forget she'd ever seen them at all.

So, she just sat there, on his bed, hands braced behind her, as Andrian buried that look back down deep and knelt before her. His gaze drank her in, and her eyes widened in shock when he lifted a hand to her cheek, running the rough pads across her soft skin before gripping her chin. He held her firmly in place, his blue eyes blazing.

"I hated you from the very second you stepped out of that carriage on the day of the Choosing."

Mariah held her breath, watching him. Images of him in that courtyard flashed through her mind, memories of the intense *feeling* that had lanced between them curling her fingers tighter into the sheets.

Andrian's hand dropped from her chin and traced the same path it took in the kitchen, this time running down the outside of her chest, skimming under the swell of her breast.

"I hated the fire I saw in your eyes. I hated how that fire heated me, melted the wall of ice I'd worked for *years* to build. I hated how easily you were able to worm your way into my thoughts without even trying."

The feeling is mutual.

That tortuous hand kept moving down her side, caressing her skin with too-gentle touches, until it gripped her hip, just as firmly as before. With a yank, he pulled her even closer to the edge of the bed, standing just slightly until his forehead was pressed against hers. He dipped his head to her ear, hot breath tickling her skin.

"You will be my undoing, *nio*. Whenever you think it was you who lost control, remember—it was me who lost control first."

Those words. They were so simple, yet as close to a confession as she would ever get from him. The magnitude of what he said—that he felt this too, that he'd *always* felt this—had all logical thought evaporating from her mind, everything lost in a haze of heat and lust and light. His lips grazed the skin below her ear, and then he was moving again, kneeling once more before her, his mouth leaving a trail of fire down the planes of her stomach. By the time he reached her hips, gripping her thighs and settling himself between her legs, she was panting, her heart racing wildly in her chest.

Mariah managed to crack her eyes open, her eyelids heavy with desire and want and desperate *need*. She met his burning blue stare, darkened and gleaming in the dim, flickering *allume* of his room. Holding her gaze, he placed an achingly gentle kiss to the soft skin of her inner thigh, then one higher, and *higher*. A wicked grin touched his devilish features, the darkness in his face sparking a light in her chest just as he dipped down and licked her from bottom to top in a single, smooth sweep.

Mariah couldn't stop her eyes from fluttering closed, her body falling back onto the sheets, a breathless moan slipping through her teeth.

His answering growl against her most sensitive part was her undoing.

His tongue was both gentle and punishing, his teeth nipping at her clit, just enough to coax her back to the high she'd been nearing on his island countertop. She felt herself rising again, one hand fisting the silk sheets and the other winding into his hair, her fingers twisting into the dark strands.

That wave began to crest, higher and higher, when he slipped a finger into her, joining his tongue as he pushed her into the stars.

And when that wave finally broke, her release washed over her in a torrent of silver-gold light.

Somewhere, distantly, she thought she heard her voice cry out, but she couldn't be sure.

His tongue and teeth and fingers didn't stop moving right away, pulling every last drop of her orgasm from her body. It wasn't until she was breathless and shaking beneath him that he pulled away, his absence sudden and shocking. She forced her eyes to open.

Andrian stood at the edge of the bed, grinning down at her with a look dripping of pure male satisfaction.

Even in her pleasure-addled state, Mariah had a sudden and distinct urge to kick him in the throat.

He must've read the thought in her eyes, his grin widening even further.

"No need to look at me like that, *nio*. After all, you're much more tolerable to me like this. On your back and screaming my name."

Now, she definitely wanted to kick him. If her mind hadn't been frayed to its absolute limits, she would've told him to suck his own dick. She forced herself to swallow, desperately trying to pull herself together in order to tell him just that, when he hooked his fingers into the waistband of his pants, bending down to slide them off his legs, his eyes never leaving hers. When he stood, and she got a glimpse at him—at *all* of him—every conscious thought evaporated from her mind like mist.

Andrian Laurent was outrageously gorgeous when clothed.

Naked, he was *devastating*.

She took in every inch of him—the Mark on his chest, the evidence of his years of training written on the muscles beneath his skin. Her eyes dipped lower to his hips, to the hard length of him, her mouth suddenly bone-dry.

"Eyes up here, *nio*." Her gaze snapped back to his, a flush rising to her skin, to find that cocky grin still stretched arrogantly across his face.

"On second thought ..." He stepped towards the bed, placing his hands, then knees, on either side of her, slowly crawling up her body, pushing her further onto the soft mattress. His lips brushed hers, and she shivered when she tasted herself on them.

"You can stare as much as you want, as long as you promise to keep blushing like that."

Gritting her teeth, she pulled every ounce of her shredded dignity to her before pushing out her next words. "*Fuck you.*"

She felt his lips twitch against her cheek. "As you wish, *My Queen.*"

Mariah had no time to think, no time to hiss out a retort, before his mouth caught hers in a feral kiss. Words became an afterthought when she felt his hand move between them, guiding his length to her, and with one smooth, powerful thrust, he seated himself fully inside her.

She arched into him, pain blending into pleasure as he stretched and filled her. Her mouth opened as she gasped, and he bit *hard* into her bottom lip, the faint tang of copper filling her mouth.

"*Fuck, nio.*" Andrian's breath was hoarse as they shared breath, as he let her adjust to him.

Then he began to move.

His movements were slow at first, a painstaking withdrawal before pushing back in. Each time, it was as if he moved deeper, striking a spot that sent a wave of lightning through her, had more groans falling from her lips.

It must've been the sound of her throaty gasps that snapped the chain of Andrian's tenuous control.

With a snarl, he wrapped a hand into her hair, his lips again finding hers, as he began to pound into her with a vengeance.

Every ounce of hate, of frustration, of lust they felt for each other was set loose in that moment.

It was a flurry of hands and teeth and hair and nails, frantic grabs at the other's skin in attempts to pull closer, as if they were trying to meld the other into them.

Mariah began to rise again, the beginnings of a second release taking form deep within her. She was caught up in a surge of passion, carrying them both away to a place far away from that golden palace.

Sensing her rising climax, Andrian's lips left hers, moving back to her ear.

"That's it, *nio*. I want to feel you come on my cock."

She nearly came right then.

But she refused to give him the satisfaction.

She somehow managed to form words around her panted breath.

"If that's what you want, you're going to have to try a little harder than that."

Andrian's grin was fiendish as he pulled away, his chest leaving hers. He slipped out of her for just a moment as he rose onto his knees. He then pulled her right leg up to his chest, hooking her foot onto his shoulder as he placed his knee outside of her left.

Mariah felt completely exposed, bared, and utterly vulnerable to him.

She'd never admit it, but deep down ... she loved it. That surrendering of control.

Andrian's eyes raked down her naked form, the hand that had lifted her leg to his shoulder sliding down her calf to rest on her knee. He gripped his cock with his other hand, pumping himself once, before lining himself with her entrance and pushing into her in a single thrust.

This position ... it felt like *sin*. He felt impossibly deep, *too* deep, her muscles coiling in her legs and stomach and chest as she felt herself fraying around the edges. Her eyes rolled back into her head, her fingers desperately seeking purchase in the silk sheets, the lack of him to scratch and claw frustrating and maddening and *hot*.

Above her, she heard him groan.

"*So fucking good, nio.*"

Those words. They were all it took for her to open to him completely, everything in her going liquid. Her eyes shot open, meeting his stare, their shared look silently voicing a million words neither of them could say.

His pace was punishing, claiming, as if he wanted to mark her as his, to ruin everyone—anyone—who might come after him.

Somewhere, deep in the dark recesses of her mind, Mariah knew there would never be anyone else. Or, at least, anyone else who could make her feel like this.

The second he'd stalked into her life, she'd been ruined.

That rising tide within her began to quicken again, pulling her towards the sky with each thrust of his hips. She hadn't realized her eyes had closed again until she felt his other hand on her stomach, moving down, the rough pad of his thumb brushing her clit.

She met his gaze as he lightly swirled his finger over that cluster of nerves, light and magic crackling in her veins as she raced for the stars. Absently, she felt his name again slip unbidden from between her teeth.

Sweat shone on his brow as he murmured against the skin of her calf.

"Come for me, *nio.*"

So she did.

She felt herself fracture into a million pieces, a hoarse cry pulling from her lungs as the tsunami of her release buried her, washing away with it the memories and trauma and anger and fear that had threatened to drown her.

When she finally felt herself begin to drop from that high,

she felt Andrian's grip on her leg tighten, a growl escaping his lips as he found his own release. He dropped her leg to the bed as he collapsed onto her, his face buried into her neck. His hair tickled her cheek, the dark strands damp with sweat.

Breathing heavily, their eyes closed, they lay there together, still joined, their bodies riding out the last few waves of their pleasure, skin coated and dripping with sweat.

When Mariah finally opened her eyes, her breath caught in her throat.

The entire room was lit up by sparkling silver-gold light, the threads of her magic floating idly and peacefully about the room.

Noticing her stillness, Andrian lifted his head from the crook of her neck, his tanzanite eyes twinkling in the light of the room. As he glanced above them, at the light dancing in the air, his expression slipped into one of wonder, his normal walls still down.

Just as hers were.

Her heart sputtered in her chest when he turned his attention back to her. When he pressed a light kiss to the bottom of her jaw.

"*Reisligr, nio.*"

She didn't know what his words meant, but they felt like praise, his tone filled with something close to reverence. With a shaky inhale, she willed those threads back into her, the light winking out as her power returned to her veins. Its presence was now calming, soothing, no longer on edge and snapping at her mind with talons and fangs.

And there, wrapped in Andrian's warmth and covered in the evidence of his claiming, she felt something she hadn't felt in a long time. Long before the Uroboros, before the Choosing, before all of it.

She felt ... *quiet*.

CHAPTER 36

The trees outside bore leaves of burnished gold, red, and orange, the sign that fall was in full swing. The air pressing in through the window was cold, demanding.

Then again, there wasn't much about Antoris that wasn't cold and demanding.

Andrian was ten years old and couldn't remember a single day living in that northern castle when he hadn't been chilled to the bone.

He sat in the cold leather chair in his father's study, the marble of the floors and walls doing nothing to keep out the bite of autumn hanging in the air outside. Even the fire raging in the hearth behind his father's desk couldn't combat the stinging freeze.

Nestled in the foothills of the great Everheim Mountains, Antoris was the most northern Royal seat in Onita, and was by far the coldest.

As was its lord.

Andrian sunk deeper into his chair, seeking warmth, or even to just escape from whatever punishment he knew was coming.

His father, Lord Julian Laurent, and his icy temper had always utterly terrified him.

He was even more terrified right now, given the reason his father had summoned him.

The night before, Andrian had been woken by a burning pain on his chest, as if he were being branded, his skin lit on fire and scorched from the outside in.

For someone who'd spent all his childhood cold, the burning heat had at first been welcomed.

But then ... it hadn't stopped. It only grew worse, kept burning and burning and burning, *until Andrian had cracked under the pain, screaming into the night as he felt his skin melting off his flesh.*

His guards and maid had rushed immediately into his chamber, frantic by his panicked cries, desperate to find the source of their young heir's pain. Andrian could only clutch at his cotton tunic, at his chest, screaming, "It hurts" *and* "Please, stop the hurt, please."

Finally, one of his guards had managed to rip open his shirt while the others held him still, pinned beneath their arms.

Andrian remembered how the room had gone still, silent, as if a mudae *had walked out of his history books and into his bedchamber.*

Still pinned beneath his guards, his maid had run from the room to wake his mother and father. By then, the pain had slowly begun to subside; being exposed to the cold air had helped whatever was happening to him. When he'd stopped writhing, his guards had carefully released him, granting him back control of his limbs.

That was when he'd looked down at his chest, where the pain had come from.

Right over his heart, there was now a Mark. It looked like a tattoo—those inky inscriptions some of the older boys in training to join his father's guard had needled into their skin. It was shaped in a circle, curved into what looked to be a dragon, arched and roaring.

It was then his mother and father had come bursting into the room, both still dressed in their nightclothes. Andrian's mother, a frail, dark-haired woman with pale, amethyst eyes, had immediately begun to weep, falling to her knees as a sob had wracked her.

Andrian hadn't been sure why she was crying. The pain was going away. It wasn't so bad anymore. He was about to speak, to reassure her that he didn't hurt, until he glanced at his father.

Lord Laurent's face had been cold, colder than usual, icy fury blazing in his expression. He'd stared hard at his son for several chilling seconds before turning sharply on his heel, leaving his young son and weeping wife in the room behind him with a slam of the door.

Around noon the next day, Andrian had finally received a summons from his father to meet him in his private study. And now, here he sat.

Andrian's eyes snapped to the left as the door to the study opened, and Julian Laurent strode in.

The Lord of Antoris was a tall, muscular man, still young enough to be in his prime. His coloring was very much Onitan: golden skin, golden hair, golden-hazel eyes. Andrian supposed he looked more like his Leuxrithian mother, with her black hair and crystal eyes, and his lack of physical similarities to his father had only served to make him more terrified of the man before him.

No matter how many times Andrian called him Father, Julian Laurent still felt like a stranger.

Lord Laurent walked to his chair behind the massive marble desk, the expanse of stone between him and his son pushing Andrian to cower deeper into the leather of his own.

His father regarded him with glaciers in his hazel eyes. "Andrian. Do you know why I called you here today?"

Andrian nodded meekly. "You wanted to discuss last night."

Julian's eyes hardened. "Yes. That's exactly what I want to do." He paused, his fingers drumming on the arms of his chair. "Do you know what that Mark on your chest means? The one that appeared last night?"

If eye contact hadn't been drilled into Andrian from the moment he could speak, he would've dropped his gaze from his father's brutal stare. "No, Father. I don't know what it means. But it hurt so bad and—"

"Enough. I don't want to hear your whining." Andrian winced at his father's tone but wasn't surprised. He kicked himself internally for showing his father that weakness.

"It means that a new queen has been born."

Andrian felt his eyes widen. "Is there something wrong with Queen Ryenne?"

Laurent's own eyes narrowed. "No. At least, not yet. But that's not all it means. It also means that now, you will never be the next Lord Laurent. As of this day, you are no longer my heir. Thank the gods you have a brother."

Hurt—deep, soul-crushing hurt—tugged at Andrian, and tears threatened to spill over his cheeks. He kept his head high, though, and fought down the pain clawing at his belly, angry and thrashing as it tried to pull him under. He couldn't show that in front of Father.

"It also means this new queen was not born to our family. I would've known if any of your aunts or cousins were expecting. Which means this birth is outside our blood," Laurent paused, and his next words were nearly a growl. "Our family will once again be skipped for the ability to seat one of our women on the Golden Throne."

Andrian kept his mouth shut, knowing there was nothing he could say that his father would want to hear.

"And you, Andrian. With that Mark on your skin, your entire future has been changed. You must now move to Verith, permanently, to be trained by Queen Ryenne's Armature. And one day, when this new queen has come of age, you will be expected to participate in the Selection, where she will pick her own Armature. One of which may be you."

Andrian felt his breath whoosh out of him, too stunned to feel anything other than utter shock. His father leaned back in his chair, the leather creaking, as he turned his hard expression to stare out the frosted window.

"I would bet she's another Shawth. I don't know why that family is always Chosen to hold the monarchy. Victor is ruthless enough to do the job, but it's not as if there's anything particularly *special* about House Shawth."

"What if she's not a Shawth? What if she's not Royal at all?" Andrian blurted the words, unable to hold his tongue. It was like something had reached down his throat and hauled them out as soon as the thoughts had flitted through his mind.

As his father slowly, *too slowly*, turned his head away from the window and back to his son, Andrian knew it had been the wrong thing to ask.

"That would be ... impossible. But since you asked the question, Andrian, let me just say this: I will never serve, and will never allow a son of mine to serve, a non-Royal queen, someone of low-born blood who is not deserving of such privilege. If, somehow, she is not a Royal, and if you somehow *allow yourself* to be selected to her Armature, then I swear upon the depths of Enfara that she will meet a fate worse than death. And you, Andrian—I will make you *watch*."

A cool, thin layer of sweat covered Andrian's skin as the memory-turned-nightmare pulled him from sleep.

His ears rang with his father's words, given to him over twenty-one years ago, the time that had passed doing nothing to weaken their impact or the fear he'd felt that day.

The fear he *still* felt.

His face itched, and he tried to move, to brush away whatever it was tickling his cheek when he became instantly aware of the warmth beside him, the soft skin, the smell of eucalyptus and cedarwood and a hint of jasmine filling his nose.

He cracked his eyes open, just barely, discovering the thick tresses of Mariah's dark hair draped across his chest, their lengths in his face. He was wrapped around her, almost protectively, as if in sleep his walls had fallen and his instincts had taken over.

Nio. It was an old word given to him by his mother, a word in the language of her people she'd taught him each night before he'd left her for Verith. The borders between Leuxrith and Onita were as good as closed, and he treated it as his personal language. It was all he had left of that soft, gentle woman, a mother he'd been forced to leave too soon and who had suffered a mysterious, tragic fate, something he used when he wanted to speak without being understood.

He'd used the word mockingly at first, a dig at the power crawling beneath Mariah's skin that she flounced with such pride, not knowing the danger it brought her.

But when she'd lit up his room last night, that bright light burning the air around them, his own magic raking sharp claws down the inside of his spine in answer, begging to be let out ...

He shivered.

His movement must've been noticeable because he felt her shift slightly within his hold, stirring from sleep with slow, arduous movements. Her body was curled into him, every inch of her skin touching his, her ass pressed against his hips. He stifled a groan as she continued to move, stretching her lithe form ever so slightly, pushing the right parts of her further into the right parts of him. He felt his cock twitch and start to grow in response, his own hips shifting behind her.

How it even had the ability to do that after the night they'd just shared, he had no idea.

Maybe it was her. Everything about her drove him absolutely feral, burning through every wall he'd ever built with that infuriating spark.

She must've felt him, the hardness now digging into her lower back, and—Enfara *damn* her—she knew *exactly* what to do with it. Slowly, she tilted her hips up, sliding her ass up his body, until his cock rested against the firm flesh of her backside. She continued to move slowly, teasing him with the feeling of her skin on his.

It was making him ravenous, once again consumed with an insatiable need for *her*.

He slid the arm wrapped tightly around her chest down her body, tightening his hold on her arms with his other hand. Her skin was so unbelievably soft and smooth; just the feel of it beneath his fingers was addicting, a tactile drug as maddening as her scent.

He kept sliding his hand down her body, over the dip of her waist, the swell of her hips.

Without a second thought, he reached between her legs, the skin there softer than anywhere else. She was drenched, satisfaction rushing through him at knowing just his touch had her body reacting in much the same way his was.

He could already taste that wetness between her thighs. *Svass*, he'd said to her last night. Another word from the language of his mother's people.

It meant *sweet*. Like honey.

He drug his finger through her center, pulling one of those decadent, breathy moans he was beginning to enjoy far too much from her throat.

Just as he was about to dive in, to make her gasp and shake and whimper his name, his nightmare memory came screaming back into his mind.

His father's voice, the last voice he ever wanted to hear—especially in *that* moment—tore through the haze of lust that had settled over his vision.

"*I swear upon the depths of Enfara that she will meet a fate worse than death.*"

It was as if he'd been doused with a bucket of cold water. The icy chill from his childhood suddenly washed over him, cooling every ounce of heat the woman beside him had drawn to the surface.

With a stifled, frustrated groan, he pulled his hand from between her legs and slid his other arm from beneath her head, rolling onto his back and disentangling from her, his eyes moving up to stare at the ceiling.

The mattress dipped beside him as she shifted, his sudden absence rousing her further from sleep. Out of the corner of his eye, he saw her roll away from him and onto her stomach.

"Andrian."

That haunting voice pulled his eyes from the ceiling and back to where she lay on the bed beside him. She'd propped herself up, her head resting on her hand, her dark hair a heavy blanket across her shoulders, forest green eyes smoldering with questions.

Mariah Salis was ... stunningly, perfectly beautiful. He felt his heart constrict in his chest, his lungs squeezing desperately for air, just as they had on those days in the palace courtyard and in Qhohena's temple.

His father should've known. Never should've made that promise to him. Should've seen that the next queen would be so much more than just another woman, but a goddess made flesh.

Andrian had never stood a chance.

But ... he had to try. If not for him, then for the wicked siren beside him.

"Are you going to tell me what's wrong, or are you just going to make me stare at you all day?"

Despite the panic lingering in his mind from his nightmare, he couldn't help his smirk.

"Don't act like you don't enjoy staring at me, *nio*."

Mariah rolled her eyes. "You're insufferable."

He huffed a laugh in response, but then fell quiet, the smile falling from his face.

She was far too smart, he knew. He had to tell her *something*.

And the best lies were always those based in truth.

"Did you know that I was born Royal? Not just Royal, but the heir to House Laurent?"

Her eyes widened slightly, her nostrils flaring in slight shock. She shook her head slowly, and he waited for her to roll away from him in disgust.

But ... she didn't. She only continued to watch him expectantly, waiting for more.

He turned his gaze back to the ceiling, wanting to tell her what he needed to without being distracted by ... well, her.

Andrian heaved a breath. "My father, Lord Laurent ... he expects a great deal from the members of his house, myself included. And this ... this fate, me being Marked, moving to Verith ... it hadn't been what he'd wanted, to put it mildly. Of course, it's not like any of this was my fault—when I was Marked, I didn't have a choice. My future was sealed, and there was nothing he could do to change it. And he's not a man who takes well to not getting his way. But, as he made sure to remind me at every chance he could, at least he had another son." He couldn't keep the bitterness from leeching into his voice.

Some wounds never truly healed.

"He could live with me being Marked. He could live with his son and heir becoming a general or other military commander. But long ago, what he told me he couldn't live with was me being Selected and forced to serve someone who wasn't him." Lies by omission, all layered in truth. That was the only way he could sell this story without her learning the full extent of the danger he'd brought her, just by being there. Maybe one day, he'd tell her everything.

But it definitely wasn't going to be when she was lying naked in his bed.

The silence and tension radiating from Mariah was enough to pull his gaze back from the ceiling to her green gaze.

Her eyes were bright, her body thrumming with barely contained power, her skin beginning to faintly glow.

Finally, after a long pause, she spoke.

"I gave everyone a choice at the Selection. You didn't have to say yes."

The ghost of a smile touched his lips, his sadness seeping into his veins, the darkness of his magic prickling at his skin.

"Yes. I did."

She had no idea how much I had to say yes.

Mariah went utterly still.

He continued.

"The second I saw you, not just in the temple but in the palace courtyard, I knew I wouldn't be able to say no to you. I tried to fight it, trust me. But ..." He inhaled deeply, turning his gaze back to the ceiling before exhaling through his teeth.

"But you won."

They laid there, not moving, barely breathing, for several minutes, Andrian not sure what she would do next. He nearly leaped out of his skin when he felt fingertips brush down his temple, stroking to his chin before gripping tightly and turning his head to face hers.

"Don't shut me out, Andrian. Not now." A passionate, fierce demand.

He closed his eyes at her words. This woman, this creature who'd melted the ice that had long dwelt within him in only a few short weeks, had no idea how much danger she'd put herself in.

It was the reason a part of him still hated her. Would always hate her.

He wanted more than anything to keep her safe, and yet she was constantly pushing them towards a path that would only lead to her demise.

When he opened his eyes, his resolve was firm.

"I can give you only this. This, right now, in private, with no one anywhere near except your Armature. But don't ask anything more of me, *nio*. And *especially* don't ask me to make the bond. I can't ... I just ... at least, not yet."

He was scared that those green eyes would pierce through his half-truths and see what had been etched into his soul at the age of ten.

"Will you ever take it?"

Her gaze was searching as he answered as truthfully as he could.

"I don't know."

She nodded once before dropping her hand from his chin. She was about to roll away from him, off the bed, when his hand shot out and grabbed hers. She turned back to him, a question in her eyes.

"You have nowhere to be today. Sebastian and the others are still securing your rooms and investigating the Uroboros, and until they're absolutely confident in your safety, they want you to stay secure. You can check with them if you like."

Her gaze turned inquisitive. "How do *you* know all of that?"

He grinned up at her, overcome with a desire to make her squirm.

At least last night hadn't changed *that*.

"Wouldn't you like to know?"

Her answering glare started a pounding in his blood, as it always did.

Gods, he could spend the rest of his pitiful existence pissing her off and be perfectly content in doing so.

"Relax." He pulled harder on her hand, dragging her back into the bed and on top of him. She went willingly, her naked figure a warm weight that set every inch of him on fire. When she felt him, how hard he was, her eyes instantly heated, that beautiful flush spreading down her neck to the top of her breasts. He reached a hand up and tucked a long strand of her dark hair behind her ear before bringing his mouth to brush against the shell.

"Don't worry about how I know. We have this day, this one day, without interruption. And I don't intend to waste it."

With those words, he skimmed his lips across her cheek to her mouth, and with a devouring kiss, he lost himself in her.

CHAPTER 37

The stables smelled of hay and horse and leather and *home*.

The second Mariah strode through the barn doors, leaving Feran waiting patiently outside, she'd known this was exactly what she'd needed.

Even if she was *ridiculously* overdressed.

She glanced down at her black gown, the shimmering material clinging to her curves. It almost glowed like starlight, and delicate lines of gold were sewn into the material. The straps were thin, the neckline dipping between her cleavage, the back equally low.

She looked fantastic, and the dress was far too nice for riding.

But she wasn't actually here to ride.

Ryenne had given her a week after the Uroboros. One week away from her role as queen apparent, one week to piece a feeling of safety in her own home back together before she was summoned back to the politics of court.

That morning, her week had expired, and Ryenne had

asked Mariah to meet her in the queen's private council chambers. But after Mariah had dressed herself, staring at her reflection in her bathroom's full-length mirrors, all she'd wanted to do was visit the last piece of her old life lingering within the city walls.

Mariah still hated Andburgh, but at least with her family, she'd never felt terrified of empty rooms and too-quiet nights. Of things that might lurk in the darkness and hidden places.

She'd never felt terrified of being *alone*.

She walked through the rows of stalls, pausing every so often to pet the inquisitive noses and stroke the soft faces of the horses pushing their heads out at her approach. Rounding a corner, Mariah spotted a golden head, black mane falling into brown, intelligent eyes.

Kodie. Her horse.

He'd seen her, too, whinnying softly as he gently tossed his head. A soft grin spread across Mariah's face as she quickened her steps to him. She threw her arms around his neck, let his head drape over her shoulder, felt his warm breath against the skin of her back, not caring for one second about the dress she wore.

Stepping back, she continued to stroke his face, tickling his soft ears and velvety nose. Reaching into the satchel she'd slung across her shoulders, Mariah pulled out a carrot, breaking it into small pieces before offering the morsels to Kodie out of her open palm. His soft whiskers and breath tickled her hand, and the feeling of home, of safety, of simplicity burned away some of the chaos in her mind that took root every time she opened her eyes.

The only other cure for that chaos she'd found, annoyingly enough, was a dark-haired devil with tanzanite eyes.

Mariah continued to stroke Kodie's face as her mind wandered.

She still couldn't sleep in her own chambers. She'd walked in once, taking slow steps through the open kitchen and living space, forcing herself to stand at the entryway to her bedroom. Looking at her bed, the silk sheets now replaced, all evidence of poisonous black blood gone, her feet had felt rooted to the ground. The world had begun to collapse around her, shrinking in, paralyzing her with fear. Her magic had roiled up, the light dwelling beneath her skin seeping out, tendrils of silver and gold threads pooling at her feet. She was unraveling, the rising tide of her anger and terror threatening to swallow her whole.

Until a firm hand had gripped her shoulder, slowly spinning her away from the bedroom. Her forest green eyes had met those of wild blue, his shadowy aura drinking up her light, pushing it back beneath her skin. She'd made another mental note, to one day question what she was beginning to suspect lurked inside his veins.

She'd then followed Andrian back to his rooms and used him to help her forget, to feel some semblance of safety once again.

Still stroking Kodie's nose, she felt her cheeks heat as her thoughts shifted to those nights spent in his room this past week.

They couldn't keep their hands off each other. It was as if some tether had snapped, and now that they knew the feel of the other's skin, it was like a drug. A Goddess-cursed *addiction*.

But it was only behind closed doors. He'd kept his word to her on that.

Before now, the only other times she'd left Andrian's room and her wing of the palace were to join her Armature for training in the game park. Despite the ... activities with Andrian, she still craved that training—it brought her a feeling of safety and strength, a stability she desperately needed to find again for herself.

Her Armature knew about her and Andrian; it wasn't a secret that could possibly be kept from them. But while those training sessions were just with them, Andrian had still been his usual cold, aloof self, choosing to train on his own each morning. He refused to interact with her in any way outside their wing in the palace.

It pissed her off.

But she understood.

It wasn't as if she was interested in anything more, anyway. He was great in bed, a fine distraction, but that was it.

Love was, after all, a weakness.

Mariah continued to lose herself in her thoughts, the movement of her hand over Kodie's nose meditative.

Suddenly, she saw Kodie's ears twitch forward, his nostrils flaring ever so slightly. In that same moment, she spotted something move out of the corner of her eye, pulling her from the depths of her thoughts.

Her senses instantly reacted, her magic unraveling into wakefulness. She knew Feran still stood at the entrance to the stables.

Feran, however, wasn't yet bonded to her. And because of that, she couldn't link to his mind. She cursed herself for bringing him, but ... he, of all her Armature, understood the most about why she'd needed to come here. She'd often seen him stop by the stables after their training, wandering the hallways and greeting each horse like an old friend.

Sometimes, the companionship of animals felt more genuine than the friendship of people.

The shadow at the edge of her vision moved again, snagging her attention from her thoughts. Slowly, the silver and gold threads within her spooling out of where they normally dwelt, she turned to face the source of that movement in the darkness.

"I know you're there."

Her voice sounded weak to her own ears, shrill with foreign fear.

She *hated* it.

The shadow stilled and then moved toward her out of the darkness. Slowly, the shadow began to take shape.

And then a second shape morphed out of the first.

As she watched, two female figures emerged from the shadows of the stable, coming to stand before Mariah.

Both females were tall and lithe, with the same rich chocolate skin and jet-black hair. Their profiles were much the same, too—*sisters,* Mariah thought. Maybe even twins, identical but for the dark brown eyes of one and the gleaming hazel eyes of the other. They both wore short black shorts, barely visible under the panels of white cloth pinned at their shoulders and draped down around their bodies, one panel falling between their legs, the other at their backs. They each also wore a golden breastplate over the white cloth, the metal adorned with intricate designs and foreign runes. On their feet were golden sandals with long straps that wrapped up their calves, nearly to their knees.

They were Kreah.

"We're sorry if we surprised you. We didn't expect there to be others in the stables today." The one with dark brown eyes spoke, her accent strong, head tilting slightly to the side as her eyes darted past Mariah to Kodie before returning to hold her gaze.

"Neither had I. Are you looking for something?" Mariah was still wary, alert, but her magic no longer roiled through her, her senses shifting into confused curiosity.

"We were only ensuring our mounts were settled nicely.

Which, it seems, we're not the only ones in this palace with such priorities." This time, it was the hazel-eyed sister to speak, her eyes glinting.

There was a moment of silence that passed between the three women, each taking the time to observe and read the others.

Mariah felt her question bubbling out of her before she could stop it.

"You're Kreah, aren't you?"

The hazel-eyed sister's lips twitched up. "We are, yes. It has been many years since the Onitan border was tentatively opened, since any of our people were invited to the capital. We could not pass the opportunity to visit this city for ourselves. Who are you?"

Mariah tilted her head, weighing for a moment how much she should tell these women, before she settled on the truth. "My name is Mariah. Mariah Salis."

The eyes of the Kreah women widened slightly, each stealing a quick glance at the other before looking back at Mariah.

"You are the queen apparent?"

Mariah nodded, slowly.

Without further hesitation, both women sank to their knees in a low bow, dipping their heads.

"Oh, no, wait—please stand," Mariah said, laughing softly and nervously. "There's no need for that. Not here."

Both women looked back up to her and silently rose to their feet. Mariah was glad she didn't need to explain herself any further. The picture of these strange foreign women kneeling before her ... it sent her pulse racing, her ears ringing.

She didn't deserve that. Queen apparents weren't terrified of their own castles. Didn't hide from their own rooms.

"Our sincerest apologies, Your Majesty. We should've recognized you."

"No. You wouldn't have." Mariah let a soft smile touch her lips, pushing down the panic trying to rear its ugly head. "So… you were invited to the palace." They nodded.

A sudden wave of curiosity made it too hard for Mariah not to ask her next question. She had to know.

"What's it like? In Kreah?"

The two women shared a quick, confused glance, a touch of amusement in their eyes. "That is … quite a question, Your Majesty. We only arrived in Onita recently, but we can say that Kreah is very different. Magnificent, but in the way only a desert can be."

It was at that moment Mariah realized just how *little* she knew of her world.

"Do you have magic? Is it … is it the way we have magic and *allume* here in Onita?."

The sisters stared at Mariah for a long moment, several heartbeats passing without a word.

Finally, the sister with brown eyes answered.

"Yes, we have magic. But it is not the substance you call *allume*. Our blessings are something else, entirely. Perhaps, one day, you might visit our home country and see. We think there is much that we could teach each other." Her eyes darted to Mariah's hands, where her magic still pooled, the skin of her palms glowing faintly with both silver and gold. Mariah glanced down and saw the light flooding from her fingertips, quickly spinning back those threads into herself. "And, perhaps, once you ascend your throne, you might be able to use those teachings. Make some changes in your own kingdom."

Mariah looked back at the two women in front of her, their words making her mind whirl. She'd felt like such a pretender recently, hardly ever allowing herself to dwell on the future waiting for her. The reminder was sharp, but ... it woke something in her. Forced a shift in Mariah's soul she hadn't known she'd needed.

Mariah decided, instantly, that she liked these strangers from Kreah.

"Yes. Perhaps, one day, I will."

They both smiled. "Good. Now, Your Majesty, if you would please excuse us; we have an engagement we must attend."

Mariah dipped her head to them. "Of course."

On feet silent as a panther, the two Kreah women turned and strode from the stable hallway, blending back into the shadows.

Just when they disappeared, Mariah realized that she'd completely forgotten to ask them how they'd gotten past Feran, and what in Qhohena's name two Kreah warriors were doing wandering the grounds of the Golden Palace.

CHAPTER 38

Sebastian Riqueti always strove to be a good man. To make the right decisions, do the right things, set the right examples.

When he'd been one of the Marked, training every day with Ryenne's Armature and the nineteen others who bore the dragon tattoo on their chests, he'd taken instantly to leadership. Most of the others had been wrenched away from their families, thrown into a strange city and palace with the promise of a life they never could've prepared for. Of course, he was, too, but unlike the others, he'd been able to keep a piece of his family with him when he'd journeyed north to Verith.

Maybe it was the fact that he'd had to be there for Matheo that forced him to grow up far faster than any boy should've. But he would be lying if he wasn't thankful for the responsibility, the purpose it gave him in his life. He'd started off leading his brother, and because he was one of the oldest of the Marked, the others had simply fallen in with Matheo, taking Sebastian's leadership without push-back.

He'd worried things might change when those lucky seven of them went from being Marked to Selected as Armature, swearing oaths to a queen they'd spent the last two decades of their lives preparing for. But his concerns were for nothing, and his brothers had settled right into their usual patterns, accepting his leadership and guidance easily.

Well ... all except one. But he'd never really listened to Sebastian anyway, even before the Selection. Andrian was perhaps the best among them, but was always a bit of a black sheep.

It had been perhaps the best day in Sebastian's life when he'd been selected by Mariah.

That was, until the bonding.

He'd had his share of rendezvous with women in the past; there was no shortage of companionship either in the palace or within the walls of Verith. But after that one night ... he suspected a piece of himself would forever be tied up with the memories of his dark-haired queen, olive skin glowing from both the moonlight above and her own magic in her veins.

He wasn't surprised by her words to him the next morning. And he'd meant what he told her. He would fill whatever role in her life she needed, would support any choice she made, would *always* be by her side to protect her from anything that might wish to harm her.

Then the Uroboros attacked.

He rammed himself into the library doors, hard enough to swing the heavy wood open with far more force than he intended. He stalked into the hall beyond, away from his favorite place in the entire palace.

It had only been a week since that foul creature had managed to slip past all of them, right into Mariah's bedroom. One week since she'd awoken in terror and sliced the demon's hands from its body, all as he'd slept on peacefully, not feeling anything unusual coming from that bond between their souls. It was like she'd cut him off, closed him out, and it was only the sound of Andrian's door slamming closed that finally woke him and drove him from bed.

He'd utterly failed her that night. His job—his *one* job— was to ensure that no harm befell her. And when that promise he'd made came to be tested, he wasn't there, and she'd been left to protect herself. Sebastian was eternally grateful to the Goddess that Mariah trained every day, that she'd been training every day with her father since she'd been big enough to hold a bow, but ... she shouldn't have had to use those skills to protect herself. Not there, in the palace, with seven of them near who had a duty to keep her safe.

And he also didn't want to think about how he wasn't the one she'd turned to in the aftermath in search of a way to mend her pieces back together.

He ground his teeth together in frustration at the memory of seeing Mariah in Andrian's arms as he'd carried her into his rooms, kicking the door closed behind him. Of all the members of the Armature, she, of course, had to seek refuge with the only one who was as emotionally unavailable as one could be.

In the week that passed since then, he and the other Armature were busy trying to find something, *anything,* that would show who was ultimately behind the attack. Uroboros didn't just appear in the middle of the Queen's palace—they were demons of Enfara, but they weren't the most intelligent. Someone had summoned or captured it, had stowed it away as they'd walked right through the palace doors, and had somehow set it loose. Likely had even directed it towards the Queen's bedchamber. But despite all their training, all their searching and scouring and questioning, they'd all come up empty.

And in the meantime, Andrian had been keeping Mariah … occupied.

At least she was safe and not alone. He couldn't quite trust Andrian with her heart, but he could trust him with her life. And for now, that would have to be enough.

Today, with Mariah rejoining palace life and resuming some of her duties, Sebastian finally had some time to himself, and had taken the opportunity to indulge in his favorite method of distraction: losing himself in the fictional worlds that lived on smooth sheets of paper bound by leather.

The reprieve was much shorter than he wanted, though. It felt like no time had passed before the thoughts reminding him of his failure began to worm their way back in, forcing him to slam his book shut and stomp his way out of the library.

The hallways were near-silent, the only sound the *click* of the soles of his boots as he strode along the marble floors. The *allume* sconces on the walls gave off their pale yellow light, illuminating the gold foiling and plating that gilded the interior hallways of the palace. He noted soft sunlight shining in through the occasional window, its orangish hue telling him it was nearing sunset. That shocked him slightly; he hadn't realized he'd managed to spend so much of his day sequestered in the library.

He also hadn't realized he'd somehow managed to go most of the day without eating.

As if on cue, his stomach twisted painfully, and when he reached the next staircase, he took the steps leading to the basement levels of the palace.

Down here, the floors were no longer made of opulent marble, the walls no longer gleaming with gilded architecture.

Instead, the simple tile beneath Sebastian's feet was gray and durable, the walls painted a practical shade of taupe. It was on this level that the servants of the palace—at least, those who chose to live in the palace and not in the city—kept their quarters.

It was also where the main kitchens and storerooms were found.

Most of the larger suites in the palace had a kitchen, but it was only suitable for cooking some items, and only for a small number of people at a time. *These* kitchens were where the bounties for the great feasts that accompanied any grand event hosted by the crown were prepared, the teeming belly of life and loudness beneath the floors of the rigid royalty above. Sebastian had come here since he was a boy and had learned quickly that being friendly with the chefs was always the best way to guarantee the pick of the freshest desserts or the choicest cuts of meat.

When he stepped into those kitchens that day, however, he was greeted by a scene even more cacophonous and hectic than usual. There was even Mikael—who, as Mariah's personal chef, hardly ever assisted in the main kitchens unless the need was dire—sprinting back into the main kitchen from the cold storerooms, carrying bundles of what looked to be romaine lettuce, his usual bandana pushing his shock of orange hair back from his face.

Suddenly, Sebastian remembered what was happening this week.

The *Porofirat*. The presentment ball that would serve to formally introduce Mariah as queen apparent to not only Onita, but to the entire continent. The only time when Onita's usually rigid borders were opened, just a crack.

Shit. With all that had happened with the Uroboros, all the questions still unsolved, he'd completely forgotten. He wondered if anyone had even told Mariah of what was coming.

That would be fun.

His stomach grumbled angrily again, forcing him to push the reminder of the *Porofirat* from his head. He would deal with that soon.

After he managed to steal something to eat.

Sebastian slid to the right along the wall and grabbed a bowl from a rack of clean dishes. He then sidled up to the massive range, where several pots of various soups and stews were simmering, decadent smells twining in the air around him. One of the kitchen maids, a tired-looking woman named Myra, caught him as he dipped a ladle into the pot of what looked to be roasted mutton stew. He turned and smiled sheepishly at her, but she only grinned back before pushing a small loaf of fresh bread into his other hand and scurrying off to help with the chaos of the *Porofirat* preparations. Food finally in hand, Sebastian moved his way out of the kitchen and into the room attached to it.

Really, the space could only be described as a cafeteria. Still filled with the rich smells from the nearby kitchen, the room was long and open, the low ceilings making it a little cramped, and long, worn wooden tables and benches filled the space. This was where the palace staff took their meals, but Sebastian enjoyed eating here from time to time. *I should bring Mariah here sometime*, he thought distantly to himself.

Although, he had to wonder what the presence of the queen apparent would do amongst the servants of the palace. They would either love it, or ... they would be furious at him for spoiling their haven.

However, as Sebastian quickly scanned the room, something caught his eye that made him suspect that maybe

Mariah's presence wouldn't be as big a distraction here as he feared.

Seated at one of the long cafeteria tables, wavy golden hair pulled back from her face in a low, loose ponytail, was Ciana, her body hunched over her own plate of food as if she were worried someone might steal it from right in front of her.

Sebastian's lips ticked up into a slight smirk just as he felt his feet move, carrying him to her table. She didn't notice his presence until he'd set his bowl down across from her, the clatter of his spoon on the polished wood making her jolt.

"By the Goddess! Next time, tell a girl you're coming before scaring her shitless." She grabbed a napkin that must've been on her lap and wiped her mouth and hands with it—*ever the lady*, he thought with a chuckle—before leveling her amber stare at Sebastian.

Sebastian's smirk broke out into a full-blown grin. "Oh, come on, Cee. What have we all been trying to teach you? Always be on your guard." He slumped gracelessly into the seat across from her before promptly picking up his spoon and, without waiting to check the temperature, took a bite of the stew.

It was hot, but not enough to scald his tongue.

It was also delicious.

He was nearly shoveling the food into his mouth, using the bread to soak up the flavorful broth around the bites of mutton and vegetables. He could feel Ciana's eyes on him, but he ignored her.

If there was anyone in that palace who saw his true, unmasked self, it was her.

The two of them had spent a lot of time together in those early days after the Choosing. Ciana was appointed as the first Lady of Mariah's court, and Sebastian had similarly stepped forward as the first bonded Armature. It had almost been like an unspoken covenant between them, to be there for Mariah as she adjusted to life in the palace and as a queen. In that time, friendship had blossomed, and he knew without a doubt there was no one in the palace who would be willing to do more for her queen than Ciana.

She'd already given up so much to be here.

She'd been saved from so much, too.

Sebastian often wondered how much of her story she'd shared with Mariah. One drunken night, she'd confessed it to him, spilling her secrets and the ghosts that still haunted her even in the palace's hallowed halls.

She hadn't spoken of the night since, and Sebastian hadn't brought any of it up. After all, they weren't his stories to tell.

"You're eating like you haven't eaten in a day." Her tone was dry, yet teasing, in the way only Ciana could muster.

"That's probably because I haven't," he answered between bites, his voice muffled. He watched her golden eyes widen with concern.

"Sebastian," she said. "You're not still punishing yourself, are you? You have to stop this. It wasn't your fault."

He continued to devour the stew, pretending to be unbothered by her question. Finally, when the bowl was empty, every last drop of the broth soaked up by that delicious fresh bread, he set his spoon down and raised his gaze to meet hers.

"I'm not punishing myself. I was just in the library all day and lost track of time. That's all."

Her concern-widened eyes narrowed with suspicion. "And why were you in the library all day?"

Sebastian pursed his lips. There was no point in responding to her; she knew the answer already, anyway.

Ciana huffed a sigh. "Fine. Well, I'm glad to see you managed your way down here to eat something." She glanced around the cafeteria, her sharp gaze missing nothing. "You know, I've never actually been down here before. I like it. Smells incredible. I think Mariah would love it down here, too." She paused and looked back at Sebastian, who now wore a sad smile on his face. "But ..."

"But you worry about what the servants' reaction might be if their queen apparent suddenly decided to dine with them. I know." She grimaced slightly at his words, and then nodded, just once.

"I just think she would love the feeling down here. The ... normalness of it all. I know she misses it." She paused again, her expression pondering. "Feran told me that she went to the stables before she met Ryenne today. All she wanted to do was spend time with her horse. I think that with everything that has happened and just the fact that she's, well, *Mariah*, it's easy to forget that so much has changed for her in such a short time. And with her spending so much time with Andrian lately, I feel like I hardly ever get to see her." A wide grin spread across her face then. "Not that I think that's a bad thing. Honestly, good for her. Andrian is *gorgeous*."

"Great to have your opinion on *that* matter. I was dying to know," Sebastian said dryly, eliciting an even wider grin from Ciana. "But ... I agree with you. On everything else. I think it's easy to forget that, despite *what* she is, she's still ... her. The first-born daughter of a soldier and a healer from the Crossroad City."

They were silent for a moment, lost in their own thoughts. Sebastian re-broke the silence first.

"I'm actually glad I came down here, and that I found you in the process. I'm assuming you realized as soon as you walked in what all the chaos was about?"

Ciana nodded. "The *Porofirat*. I'd completely forgotten."

"As had I." Sebastian leaned back on the bench,

straightening his arms and breathing deeply. "So ... does Mariah know?"

She pursed her lips. "I haven't spoken to her about it. Like I said, I haven't really seen much of her in a week. Unless Ryenne or *he* told her, then I wouldn't care to guess how much she knows about what is coming later this week."

Sebastian knew which "he" she referred to without having to ask. "That feels like ... a problem." He met Ciana's golden gaze. "Perhaps one for a Lady to help resolve?"

Ciana snorted. "Nice try, pretty boy, but I'm not getting in the middle of those two just because you batted your eyelashes at me."

Sebastian shrugged. "Worth a shot."

"I think you should try talking to Andrian first. He may have spoken to her already; we just don't know. And if he *has* talked to her, and has already arranged to be her escort, isn't that something you, as the captain of the Armature, should know?"

She had a point.

He groaned deep in his throat. "Fine." He stood from the table, Ciana's eyes tracking him. He picked up their empty dishes before moving to the sinks lining the far wall. Appearing at his side as he cleaned the plates, Ciana accepted them to help dry as he finished. Once they were done, he turned back to her.

"I guess I have to go find Andrian. Wish me luck and pray to the Goddess he doesn't try to rip out my throat."

Ciana giggled, and the sound made him smile.

"So. This is how you've decided to spend your free time? I must say, Andrian, this may be a new low."

Andrian barely glanced back over his shoulder at Sebastian

before returning his attention to his glass of cheap whiskey, downing the rest in a single swig.

It hadn't taken Sebastian long to track Andrian to the dark, seedy hovel in Verith's market district. It was Andrian's favorite whenever he wanted to vanish, to get out of the palace walls and pretend he had a life beyond the one the gods chose for him.

Sebastian only knew this because Andrian had once confessed those feelings to him while exceedingly intoxicated. Sebastian wasn't sure if Andrian even remembered, and he wasn't stupid enough to bring it up.

He preferred his head attached nicely to his shoulders.

Sebastian moved to the bar, seating himself on the stool beside Andrian and raising a finger to the wizened barkeep. The man grunted in Sebastian's direction before placing a second cloudy glass on the counter and filling both it and Andrian's with two fingers of whiskey. The pungent odor wafted up to Sebastian, and he wrinkled his nose before taking a sip that burned through his entire body.

"By the Goddess, man. You're drinking straight sphinx piss."

Andrian only grunted in response before taking a swig of his own. "Tastes fine to me."

"You're many things, Andrian, but I've never known you to be a liar."

Andrian shrugged. "I find myself lying about many things lately. Mostly to myself."

They sat in silence for a long moment, Sebastian's mind churning over those cryptic words.

Questions for another day, maybe.

"I assume you know why I came down into the city to find you."

Andrian's piercing blue gaze burned the side of Sebastian's

face. "I try not to assume too much about anything. Always leads to disappointment."

Deep breaths. It wouldn't be a conversation with Andrian without a hint of frustration for everyone involved. He wondered for a moment how Mariah managed to put up with his incessantly maddening conversations.

Probably because they haven't been doing much talking.

He shut that line of thought down as quickly as he could.

"I know you're not an idiot. And I know that you're aware of what is happening this week."

Andrian lifted a finger to the barkeep, and the man responded promptly, again refilling Andrian's now-empty glass. He took another swig before staring at a whirl in the sticky, stained bar, refusing to meet Sebastian's gaze.

"Why should I care about the *Porofirat*? It's not like I'm the one hosting the damned thing."

Narrowing his eyes at him, Sebastian scoffed. "It doesn't matter to me if you care or not. What I want to know is if you've spoken to Mariah about it."

Andrian whipped his head up at the mention of her name. Sebastian saw a look in his eyes, one he'd never seen before. It was almost like … panic? But that couldn't be right. He blinked once, trying to control his surprise.

"Are you asking me if I intend to escort her? Are you fucking *mad*?"

"Seems like a valid question to me, considering that you've spent every waking moment of the last week with her."

Andrian grimaced—actually *grimaced*—before downing the rest of his drink. "Just because I've been fucking her doesn't mean I want to escort her to the damn *Porofirat*," he muttered into his empty glass.

Sebastian's blood went both hot and cold. "I know you better than that, Andrian. I know you don't mean that."

Another grunt. He was quiet for a moment, and then he muttered, almost to himself, "You know why I can't. *He'll* be there."

Of course. Sebastian did know.

The *Porofirat* was a presentation of the queen apparent to all the nobility of not only Onita, but the continent. And of course, that meant that the lords of Onita would be in attendance, including the Royals. Mariah had met the Royals before, but this would be on a much larger scale, and much more public.

It also meant that Lord Laurent—Andrian's father—would be in attendance. Would be watching Andrian's every move, and of course where Mariah was in relation to him.

Sebastian didn't quite know why his father's presence always set Andrian on edge, or where Mariah fit into that puzzle. But what he did know was that he'd never seen the man look more anxious, more vulnerable, more *terrified* than he did when his father was in the palace. Sebastian continued watching Andrian for a few more minutes; the two men—brothers, in every way it counted—sitting in silence at the grimy, destitute bar.

To Sebastian's surprise, it was Andrian who spoke next.

"You should do it. Escort her, I mean." He paused. "You're better for her than I am, anyway."

And with those words, it all snapped into place for Sebastian. Everything Andrian had done, had said, made absolute sense. Sebastian still had a piece of his heart with Mariah—always would—but any lingering traces of jealousy vanished from his mind. All he felt was a sense of true, bone-deep sadness for his friend, for the man who, for some reason, thought himself unworthy of anything that could bring him joy.

He sent a quick prayer up to the Goddess—to any god who

would listen, really—that Andrian would one day be able to find the happiness he seemed to believe he didn't deserve.

Sebastian clasped his hand on Andrian's shoulder, gripping him firmly. He pulled the other man off the bar stool, tossing a few coins from his pocket onto the stained and grimy bar.

"Come on. No more sitting here with your misery drinking shitty whiskey. Let's go home."

CHAPTER 39

Mariah rubbed at her eyes with her fingertips, the tension and exhaustion behind them like a lead weight.

Huffing a breath, she reopened her heavy eyelids, her gaze wandering around the table she sat at, avoiding the ancient texts sprawled open in front of her.

Most of her Armature, plus Ciana and Delaynie, were spread around the three expansive research tables in the center of the library, directly below the great glass skylight roof above. Everyone was entrenched in various tasks—some more so than others. Sebastian and Drystan sat beside Mariah, deep in a quiet discussion, not noticing her wandering attention. Quentin and Ciana were seated at the next table over, bickering over something likely unrelated to the books lying open on the polished wood. Then there was Matheo, strolling amongst the nearby stacks, restlessness urging him to his feet to stalk through the racks before returning to the tables, more volumes in his arms.

Mariah had bonded with Matheo the night before. After

the Uroboros, an inner urge had swept over her to take those next steps with each of her Armature, the power those bonds might bring her becoming almost necessary to her very survival.

Of course, there was one significant block to that plan, but she didn't often let herself dwell there for too long.

A part of her had dreaded completing the bond with Sebastian's younger brother, fearing what could've been an incredibly awkward moment for the three of them. She now realized, however, her fear was both unfounded and unwarranted. Even throughout the intensity of the bonding, her thoughts of Andrian had consumed her. The itch brought on by tanzanite eyes had been scratched, but she also knew there would be no going back. Because of that … complication, she was fully capable of keeping the bonding confined to a process that, while still incredibly intimate, was also wholly platonic.

Matheo, the youngest of her Armature but still six years her senior, had struggled slightly to hide his disappointment, but recovered quickly, nonetheless.

It also didn't escape Mariah's attention that, unlike the golden bond between herself and Sebastian, it was the silver magic in her veins that now bridged her soul to Matheo's. And she was still not quite sure what to think of that.

Which was partly why they were all now back in the library, poring over ancient texts and searching for answers about what it was that might lie beneath her skin.

"All I can seem to find is that Qhohena's magic summoned the dragons. That one thing is consistent across all the texts. But as far as more details, or any other sort of magic blessed by the Goddess, there is just … nothing."

Drystan's voice snapped Mariah out of her thoughts.

She'd almost forgotten that she'd instructed her court to look not just at information on sources of unusual power, but the other magic, the one she'd assumed there might be more records of.

Those golden threads in her veins. Qhohena's magic.

She should've known it would lead to another dead end. Should've known there would be no easy answers or automatic assurances. And Mariah wouldn't admit to any others beyond those who sat in that room that she was still plagued by nightmares of the Uroboros, fully unsettled by what the attack had truly been.

An *assassination* attempt.

She didn't do well when stagnating, stuck in place. She was tired of feeling so trapped. She had to know. Had to know why the queen's magic, why Qhohena's magic, was only semi-physical light, nothing more than a conduit for the Solstice, yet had still been used by Xara to somehow bring the world to heel. How it was so weak and believed to be harmless now, but it'd been used to face the Scourge on the battlefield and eventually establish the Onitan throne. Mariah had to believe there was *more* to it, more she should know, something that had been forgotten by thousands of years of peace and gentler times.

Her golden threads certainly felt like more as they crawled through her veins, unspooling and twining themselves with the silver magic that dwelt with them.

The more the weeks passed, the less Mariah was able to differentiate between the two. They kept winding closer and closer together, what used to be two massive balls of twine deep inside her slowly merging to become one.

A problem she didn't have the capacity to deal with at the moment.

"But ... dragons are extinct," Delaynie's soft voice chimed in from where she sat, alone at the third table, pouring over a wide collection of texts.

"No shit," quipped Quentin, his attention drawn from his debate with Ciana to the auburn-haired young woman. Ciana pierced him with a stare he refused to acknowledge.

Those two are far too similar, Mariah thought. Full of raging fire. Never a great mix when put too close together.

It was Sebastian, as always, who interceded. Ever the peacekeeper.

"Alright, enough. I'm sure there is something we missed. Quentin, why don't you and Ciana ..."

A movement from the shadowy depths of the library stacks drew Mariah's attention away from Sebastian's words, letting him continue his reprimand and give directions to her court. Her gaze snagged on a figure emerging from the darkness, her eyes drawn immediately to embers of burning blue flame.

Andrian stalked out from the stacks, halting while still partly concealed in shadow, his arms crossing over his chest as his gaze held hers.

Mariah felt her skin begin to heat under the intensity of his stare. She wondered, briefly, if she would ever not have this reaction to him; this magnetic draw, this visceral response that was becoming harder and harder to fight with each night they spent tangled together, escaping from the chaos of the world around them.

Suddenly, she realized the current scene before her—the heat in Andrian's wild blue eyes, the way her court was preoccupied with reading or bickering—presented a unique opportunity she couldn't pass up.

As they locked gazes with each other, she lifted her chin, almost imperceptibly, to Andrian. He watched her movement, quirking an infuriating eyebrow in response, and she saw something in his gaze that twisted her belly into knots.

The walls he usually kept built high seemed to have crumbled, the carefully maintained control he normally gripped to tightly slipping. A subtle manic energy coiled in the way he held himself in the shadows. She knew him—his eyes, his expressions, *him*—enough to know that to be true.

Perfect.

She also couldn't stop the heat from rising to her own skin, sinking low and heavy into her core.

Silently, Mariah rose from her seat at the table. Everyone was too engrossed in their other conversations and arguments to notice her.

Everyone ... except Sebastian. His eyes darted briefly to hers, his hallmark concern evident in his handsome, hazel gaze.

"Everything okay, Mariah?" Sebastian's voice was quiet, non-assuming, cautiously guarded.

She nodded to him once, quickly. "I'm fine. I'll just ... I'll be right back."

He stared at her for a long moment before dipping his head, a question in his eyes he didn't ask, and returned his attention to the book open in front of him.

On quiet feet, Mariah walked towards the darker corners of the library, vanishing into the same shadows where Andrian stood a moment before.

It only took a few minutes of walking through the stacks, the darkness increasing the farther she moved from the bright sunlight streaming from the glass roof of the domed library atrium, before she felt Andrian's presence at her back, permeating through the thick and heady air of the tunnels that wound into the depths of the Attlehon mountains themselves.

Mariah whirled on her feet, her eyes searching the darkness for his shape. When she saw nothing, the shadows around her far too thick to be natural, she remembered why she'd followed him into those stacks in the first place.

"Andrian," she whispered into the writhing darkness. "Cut it out. I can't see."

A quiet, deadly chuckle came from the shadows. "That's the point, *nio*."

A tendril of *something* brushed down her cheeks, freezing her in place. It was both cold and warm, alive and dead, soft and hard.

She shivered and swallowed audibly, struggling to regain her composure.

"About that," she began. "I've been meaning to ask you a question."

"A question?" That dark voice was closer now, a breath against her shoulder.

"Yes." Mariah inhaled once, pushing down the magic writhing in her own veins. She wanted the darkness in this moment; not only for her answers, to understand what she so desperately wanted to learn, but also because it felt *good*. To let go of her control. To no longer be the one in command of the room.

It reminded her of the freedom she'd chased not long ago in the seedy taverns of Andburgh. A freedom she'd come to terms with never knowing herself, but she still wanted to experience whenever she could.

Another exhale, this time at her other shoulder. A *humph* of a chuckle. "Well, by all means ... ask away, princess."

Mariah swallowed again, pushing the words past her teeth before she lost her nerve.

"You are one of the *reykr*, aren't you? One of the shadow-wielders from Luexrith?" Her words floated into the air as she paused for a moment before continuing. "There isn't much that passes between the borders of the different kingdoms of the continent. But I found a book recently that spoke of those from the Northern Wastes who could speak to darkness, could wrap it around themselves and bend it to their will. It said it's not a gift from Qhohena, and was considered by many to be a curse, something evil and foul and wrong."

A moment of silence before she suddenly noticed the darkness lifting around her, just enough to make out Andrian's shape in front of her, his tanzanite eyes blazing and a curious expression on his face.

"Very good, *nio*. I was wondering when you would make the connection. Took you long enough." Now it was his turn to pause, his head tilting slightly before he grinned, slow and cruel. "Do you think I'm cursed? That I am—how did you put it?—evil and foul and wrong?"

Mariah ignored the slight and the loaded question, only reveling in the momentary victory at gaining another piece to the puzzle that was Andrian Laurent. She shifted on her feet, cocking her own head back at him, parroting his movement.

"I think an argument could certainly be made about whether you're cursed or not. But ... no, I don't think you are. I think not all stories we read about in books are the truth." His expression was curious again, a strange mixture of guarded and vulnerable as she paused. "There's just one other thing I don't understand."

His eyebrow lifted.

She continued. "This magic—your magic—it's Leuxrithian. And you—you're Onitan. Not just Onitan, but the son of a Royal Lord. So ... care to fill the gaps for me?"

The shadows darkened around them again, his shape winking from her view. There was a growl somewhere in the air nearby, not quite against her skin, but close enough so she could feel the vibration through the dark.

"My father is Onitan. But my mother ... my mother was Leuxrithian. Let's just say I take after her."

My mother was Leuxrithian.

Was.

She wanted to ask, to know the tragic story she could feel snagging in his mind, but she held her tongue.

"There's something else you wanted to ask, isn't there, *nio*? That wasn't the last of your questions." His voice was still a growl. The tension that pulled at him earlier now weighed heavy in the air, presumably heightened by her questions and the mention of his mother.

She thought she might hate that he could read her so easily, but truthfully, she was relieved she didn't have to search for unnecessary words after the bit of himself he'd unintentionally revealed.

My mother was *Leuxrithian.*

"You bend shadows to your will," she began, focusing on what she was most curious about. "And my magic ... it more or less bends light." Mariah paused, searching the darkness blindly for him. "But yours seems to be so much more corporeal than mine has ever been. And I'm just curious. About how it works."

Her vision was suddenly filled with him as he pushed into her space, the tanzanite of his eyes flooding her vision. "You want to know what my magic is capable of?"

She could only meet his gaze and nod. *Yes,* she thought. *I want to know.*

He searched her face for a few heartbeats. "You want to know ... because you want to see if your magic may one day be capable of the same."

Mariah narrowed her gaze at him. "Let's just say that I have no interest in the parlor tricks I'm currently being taught."

Andrian's lip quirked up at that. "Alright, *nio*. I can show you how my magic works." He fell silent, watching her, his stare heating with the passing seconds. Mariah's breath hitched in her throat as he held her gaze, a languid heat flitting across her skin and settling low in her belly.

A part of her already knew what his words would be before he spoke them.

"How about a demonstration?" He leaned in closer to her, his mouth grazing the soft shell of her ear. "My shadows, after all, have been far too eager to taste you. I suppose it's as good a time as any to indulge them."

Mariah's throat went dry, her breath hitching in her chest. Somehow, she forced out her next words.

"Here? In case you hadn't noticed, this is a *library*, Andrian."

Another low chuckle against her ear before he withdrew from her, blanketing her again with living shadows now teasing and licking at her skin, sending goosebumps washing over her in waves.

"Do you remember when I caught you reading here in this very library?"

She couldn't pinpoint where exactly his voice came from, but she nodded, knowing that even in the darkness veiling her eyes, he could see her.

"The second I saw you standing there, cheeks pink and flushed, I became *furious*. Do you know why, *nio*?"

Mariah shook her head, not trusting her voice to speak.

"I was furious because I wanted to be the one to make you flush like that in this library. Where anyone could catch us, but only the books around us would hear."

Suddenly, she was slammed into the shelf behind her, Andrian's warmth seeped into her skin as his hand wrapped around the base of her neck, her sweater riding up her torso. At the same time, she felt one of those shadow tendrils, as real as another arm or hand, touching the now-exposed skin of her abdomen. It slipped under the burgundy material, brushing lazily up her stomach, sweeping languid circles around the swell of her breasts and across the peaks of her nipples. She pushed her head back against the shelf and the hand that held her neck, a moan threatening to escape when a second large hand suddenly clamped itself over her mouth.

"As you said, princess, this is a library. You must be *quiet*."

As quickly as he'd consumed her space, he released her, disappearing back into his shadows. Mariah gasped against the shelves, her body filled with roiling heat, the sudden absence of him dropping every ounce of temptation deep into her belly.

Goddess, he would be her ruin.

She was still heaving breaths into the dark, heavy air around her when his voice sounded again.

"Kneel, *nio*."

Her eyes snapped up, peering hard into the darkness.

She was a queen. No one ordered her to fucking *kneel*.

"*Excuse* me?"

His breath reappeared again at her right ear, his voice rumbling through her.

"For once in your Goddess-cursed life, princess, fucking *listen* to me. It's just us. You said you wanted to know what my magic can do, and all I'm asking in exchange is for you to *kneel*."

The world around them froze, time standing still as she contemplated his words. On one hand, she was still coming into her power, learning to crave it more than anything before in her life.

On the other hand ... the more carnal side of her mind raced with the possibilities of what might happen if she gave in and let him take the lead, much like he had that night of the Uroboros attack.

In the end, it was the second half of her that won.

Slowly, tauntingly, she sank to her knees, the material of her soft leggings meeting the chill stone floor beneath her. A sound of approval rumbled from somewhere in the darkness around her, her magic zapping along her skin in answer. She pushed it down before it could illuminate her skin.

At least right now, she still wanted to do this in the dark.

"*Good girl.*" A firm tendril of darkness gripped her chin, tilting it up. She couldn't see Andrian, but she could certainly feel him—his presence, his breath, the space he took up in that hallway between the bookshelves. "You will be rewarded for that. Is that what you want, *nio*?"

"*Yes.*" Her answer panted out of her before she could stop herself.

Not that she would've stopped herself.

Especially not when a ribbon of darkness began to carve a path down her body, joined by several other wisps that brushed against her skin, slipping beneath the hem of her sweater in smooth movements.

She'd been worried they would remind her of snakes, of the hellish creature that had turned her whole world upside down.

She couldn't have been more wrong. They were rope-like, of course, but they felt ... familiar. Natural. Sensual.

Like *him*.

When one of those tendrils teased at the waistband of her leggings, inching to and fro, her thoughts stalled in her mind. Then the magnetism pulled from her front, and knew Andrian was standing there, staring down at her as his magic teased and taunted her.

"My magic has always felt like both an extension of myself ... and its own being." Andrian's voice rumbled around her as those ropes of darkness continued to work their way lower down her body. "It certainly has a mind of its own, but ..."

Mariah's gasp was audible as dark magic suddenly stroked her center, dipping through her, the sensation indescribable.

Andrian's voice had turned to smoke. "I can always feel everything it does."

Without warning, a hand threaded through her hair, the shadow between her legs continued to curl through her, striking the *spot* that had her chest heaving.

"I may not be touching you with my hands, *nio*, but I can fucking *feel* you all the same," he growled, closer to her ear than she'd been expecting. "What a dirty little queen, so wet for my shadows here in this dusty old library." He tsked, the brush of his exhale against her temple as she panted through clenched teeth, her climax racing towards her. "Whatever will we do about that?"

His magic pushed into her, around her, consumed her *faster*, and she felt herself being taken away on that wave, letting it edge her higher and higher and higher ...

Until it all suddenly withdrew, vanishing into nothing. Mariah's eyes flew open to find the darkness surrounding them gone, her chest still heaving, a near *painful* feeling at her denied pleasure settled deep into the sensitive nerves between her legs. She was still on her knees, and she glanced up to meet Andrian's stare, his gaze a mixture of both heat and cruelty.

Letting out a growl of her own, she allowed her magic to finally filter into the air as she shifted where she knelt, pressing her knees closer together, desperate for any sort of friction. "What the actual *fuck*, Andrian?"

The asshole had the audacity to *smirk* at her.

"You wanted a demonstration, *nio*. I did as you asked. Just a taste, remember?"

She made a mental note then to never believe a word he said to her again.

"Fine," she said as she pushed herself up, stomping her feet as she forced herself to stand before him. She met his gaze again for a brief second before turning on her heel, thoroughly annoyed and frustrated and angry and wanting to be anywhere but there.

Until his deep voice stopped her again in her tracks.

"We need to talk about the *Porofirat*."

And there it was. The reason for his ... mood.

"What about the *Porofirat*?" Mariah's voice was flat and emotionless as she slowly stood, pushing down anything else that might give away the bottle of nerves she was quickly becoming. She'd been filled in by Ryenne earlier that day about the presentation ball rapidly approaching, about its importance both to the kingdom and her future reign.

He leaned back casually against the shelf behind him, as if he hadn't just edged her with his shadow magic in an ancient, revered library.

"My father will be there."

Mariah narrowed her gaze at him. "Well, I'd assumed that, considering he's currently residing in the palace and all. It would be exceptionally poor manners for one of the six Royals to be absent from the formal presentation of the queen apparent."

"Please refrain from the superiority complex with me, *my queen*." The way he always sneered her title boiled her blood. "I need to make sure we're on the same page about ... this." He gestured between them with a finger.

Mariah scoffed. "And what, exactly, is *this*, Andrian? Stress relief? A good fuck? I don't even know what to call whatever just happened here ... maybe a *distraction*?" Her voice was back to a growl. "We can be on the same page about whatever you want, but I remember *everything* you've ever said to me. And just as I said that first night after the Uroboros attack, I'm calling your bluff, too." She paused.

"And, if I recall, you said it, not me: that I would be your *undoing*."

His tanzanite eyes flashed with cold fire. Pushing himself off the shelf, Andrian stalked towards her, crowding into her space enough to force her to take three steps back until her shoulder-blades were once again pressed against those ancient wooden shelves, his body flush against hers. This time, though, his proximity didn't send heat lancing through her veins.

No, this time ... he *terrified* her.

"Do you think you know me just because you've had my dick inside you and know a story from my childhood?" His voice was dark and lethal and *quiet*. "Sorry if this is a disappointment, but neither of those things make you special. You know nothing about me, princess. I'm not a good man, nor have I ever pretended to be. I told you that you never should've Selected me, and I meant it; I will bring you *nothing* but pain." His voice nearly broke then, but he quickly regained his composure, and Mariah would've thought she'd imagined it if she hadn't seen the broken flicker in his gaze.

He continued his tirade.

"You ... you ... *trapped* me into taking that oath, and I can't take it back. But I can again vow that I will *never* make the bond with you. Yes, I told you I would be your distraction, but you seem to have forgotten the second part: a distraction is *all* you will ever be to me."

With that, the last of his words still echoing in the tunneling hallway, he stepped back from her, releasing her from his hold.

Just as hot tears began to prick behind her eyes, tightness clamping around her throat.

What the fuck? I do not cry.

Especially over hot, dark-haired assholes.

"Fine." To her surprise, her voice came out strong,

unwavering. "If that's really how you feel, I assume you won't have any issues with me seeking *distractions* from other members of my Armature." She paused, letting the bravado of her words flow through her, using them to fill out the cruel smile she let play across her face. "I know any of them would be more than happy to oblige their queen."

He'd hurt her, and she wanted to hurt him back.

Andrian only bared his teeth at her in a snarl. "You want to let the entire royal army fuck you? Be my guest; I couldn't care less. Just keep yourself far from me, especially at the ball, and you can do whatever—or whoever—the *fuck* you please."

His words hung in the air above them like a dagger poised at Mariah, aimed right at her chest. Without another sound, Andrian turned on his heel and stalked down the corridor, away from her and the stacks of books surrounding her, the silence deafening.

Mariah pushed off the bookshelves, trying desperately to compose herself as she listened to the sound of his retreating footsteps.

The second they faded from earshot, she sank to her knees, letting the roiling hurt in her gut wash over her.

CHAPTER 40

Mariah groaned into her pillow as the midday fall sunlight streamed through her window, burning her eyes despite its relative weakness.

She'd slept like shit the night before and refused to get out of bed until she absolutely had to.

With another soft moan, she rolled from her stomach onto her back, her arm flopping on the silk sheets beside her. Last night was the first night since the Uroboros attack that she'd slept in her own bed.

It was also the first night since the attack that she'd slept alone, but she refused to attribute her lack of sleep to *that* minor detail.

Turning her head to glance out the window and the autumn light filtering in, she guessed it was sometime past noon. Based on the angle of the light, she saw the sun had already peaked on its course across the sky, had begun its descent back towards the horizon.

All she wanted to do was lay there, in her bed, all day.

She also refused to think about how getting out of bed and

perhaps encountering a certain dark-haired, blue-eyed asshole made her stomach twist into tangled knots.

Don't be an idiot, Mariah. Remember, love is a weakness.

She cringed at the thought, gritting her teeth so hard she worried they might crack. *Not that you love him. He's not worth the time.*

Damn good fuck, though.

Heaving a sigh, she prepared to roll onto her side, but as soon as Mariah started the movement her body decided to revolt against her. A long, rumbling groan emitted from her stomach, reminding her of something she wasn't quite sure how she'd forgotten.

Mariah hadn't even gotten out of bed that morning to *eat*.

She turned her gritted teeth into a snarl. She would *not* let that asshole keep her from breakfast food.

Groaning one more time, she finally pushed the duvet back from her body and slipped out from under its decadent warmth. Mariah padded to the doors leading to the main living area, still dressed in the oversized maroon tunic she'd fallen into bed wearing, her dark hair hanging in a tangled mess down her back. Pushing open the doors, she was suddenly greeted by a rich, earthy smell emanating from the kitchen.

Her stomach let loose another low rumble just as she spotted the recognizable shock of orange hair pulled back with a bandana.

"Oi! Good mornin', lassie! Or should I say … good evenin'?" Mikael's head bobbed up from where he stood by the stove, stirring a pot that must be the source of the outrageously tantalizing smell.

Mariah smiled brilliantly at him. Right now, with her stomach panging angrily against her ribs, Mikael was perhaps the most important person in the world to her.

"Good evening, Mikael. You have no idea how happy I am

to see you." She stepped further into the living space, making a beeline to the kitchen and taking a seat at one of the bar stools as she watched him continue to stir the contents of the pot. "What deliciousness have you cooked up today?"

"Well, I knew that you slept right through breakfast—so sorry about that, I know how much you love my waffles"—she groaned at the thought of the incredible pastries—"and with tonight's upcoming event, I figured you could use a good, hearty meal. So, my family's special beef stew is what you're getting. And if you don't eat everything I put in front of you, not only will I be hurt, but I'm afraid *he* might try to force feed it to you."

He?

Mariah twisted on her stool, blinking in surprise as she was greeted by hazel eyes watching her from the couch, Sebastian's expression carefully masked yet still amused.

"How long have you been here?"

Sebastian shrugged, shifting slightly. "Most of the day. I wanted to make sure you eventually got up and ate something before tonight." He paused, concern filling his face. "Plus, I was worried about you after you left the library yesterday."

Mariah felt her own expression steel over as she nodded to him curtly, just once.

After Andrian had said his ... *words*, and she'd taken more than a few minutes to compose herself, she'd marched her way out of the library without a further word to anyone. Sebastian had tried to call after her, reaching out to her through their bond, but she'd closed herself off from him and all the others and had run to the one place she felt she could have a chance at pulling herself together.

She'd saddled Kodie and ridden into the game park, urging him deeper into the thick forest than she'd ever ventured on foot. She'd lost herself in the feel of her horse moving beneath her and the sound of his hooves on the soft dirt and fallen leaves underfoot, his breaths and heartbeat slowly bringing her back to earth. She'd returned well after dark and had found Feran waiting for her in the quiet of the stables, leaning patiently against Kodie's stall door. Without a word, he'd followed her back to her suite, where Sebastian and Drystan were standing guard outside of her door. She didn't say a word to any of them, striding into her suites and closing the doors behind her with a click, that door directly across the hall from her own burning a hole in her chest.

Mariah cleared her throat. "Yeah, well, thanks for checking on me, but I'm fine. Really."

The look on Sebastian's face told her he wasn't at all convinced.

Behind her, she heard Mikael shuffle to the island, the sound of a dish being set down on the marble drawing her away from Sebastian's concerned hazel stare. "Here ya go, lass. Eat up."

The savory smells wafting up from the dish were beyond decadent. Her mouth instantly salivated, her stomach rumbling a third time. Grabbing the spoon Mikael placed on the counter beside the bowl, she picked up the steaming dish and stood up from the island.

"I think I'm going to go eat outside on the terrace. Thank you for dinner, Mikael. It smells absolutely delicious."

Mikael smiled warmly back at her. "My pleasure, lassie."

With her food in hand, Mariah strode out to the glass table on the terrace, the view of the mountains beyond thawing the numbness in her heart just a touch.

She could live here for five hundred years, could live out the remainder of her now near-immortal existence, and never grow tired of that view.

Mariah heard quiet footsteps and knew Sebastian had

followed her out onto the terrace. Once she was seated, spoon poised over the bowl of stew, he sat in the chair across from her, watching her closely. His bright gaze sifted through all her omissions and half-truths, peeling her back until he saw exactly what was driving her out of her mind. She chose to ignore him, taking a bite of her stew, the tender beef melting in her mouth as the flavors exploded across her tongue.

She groaned and then proceeded to devour the entire bowl in a far-from-queen-like manner. Sebastian watched her for a few minutes as she ate before he finally spoke.

"I don't know what he said to you, but … he does care for you, you know. In his … own way."

Mariah froze, her eyes meeting Sebastian's, before she scoffed and set her spoon down next to her nearly empty bowl.

"I highly doubt that."

Sebastian only held her gaze. "Andrian had a difficult upbringing. Being Marked is not always a … joyous occasion, as it was for Matheo and I. Andrian had a lot to gain as the heir to a Royal house, and that Mark—*your* Mark—stole it all away."

Mariah's gaze shifted into a glare. "Trust me, if I could give it all back and wipe that Mark from his chest, I would. I would also remind you, and him for that matter, that I didn't choose any of this; not for you, not for him, not for any of the other Armature, and *especially* not for myself."

Sebastian's expression softened at that. "I know, Mariah. I know. We *all* know that. And deep down, Andrian knows it, too. His relationship with his father, though … it's complicated." Mariah averted her eyes from Sebastian and turned her gaze back to the stunning view of the mountains beyond.

Her next words were a grumble. "I shouldn't have slept with him."

To her surprise, Sebastian laughed, his deep chuckle

rumbling in the afternoon air. "You were always bound to do that, Mariah. While I certainly enjoyed our one night together and would be lying if I didn't say I quite often hoped for more" —Mariah snapped her eyes to his, finding them twinkling with amusement—"it has also been more than apparent to me, to *all* of us in your court, that there is something *else* between you two. Call it chemistry, hatred, anger ... whatever. But ever since you stepped out of that carriage on the day of the Choosing and your eyes found his, we *all* felt it. We're just thankful you gave in before you ripped each other's throats out."

Mariah could only stare at him, slack-jawed, which only made him chuckle again.

"Yes, I know he's a dick. And like I said, I don't know what he said to you yesterday, but based on the emotions I felt down the bond and your disappearance into the woods afterwards, it probably wasn't anything you wanted to hear. Not to mention, that shadow magic of his makes him a scary motherfucker. But ... don't give up on him just yet. He was an asshole before you arrived, and believe it or not, has become somewhat more tolerable since his Selection, even if he doesn't want to admit it."

After a few pounding heartbeats, Mariah finally found her words. "Where in all the gods' stars did you come from? How are you so ... perfect? Why couldn't I have been drawn to you?"

Sebastian just kept that sad, knowing smile on his face. "The gods had other plans for you, My Queen."

The conversation died out after that, but they continued to sit in silence as Mariah finished the last of her meal. At some point, Mikael stepped out onto the balcony to deliver some fresh-baked bread, and Mariah used the warm loaf to soak up every last drop of the stew. Once she was done, not a single bit of broth left in the dish, she put her spoon down, sighing contentedly before meeting Sebastian's gaze.

"Let's talk about the ball tonight."

He nodded once, attention again trained on her. "Do you know what to expect?"

Did she? "I think so," she said. "I know that it's my formal presentation as queen apparent. All the lords of the realm will be in attendance, not just the Royals, as well as representatives from the continent's other kingdoms." She felt like she was reciting a line from one of those dusty old tomes in the library, stagnant words with no true feeling behind them.

Sebastian nodded again. "Ryenne will preside over everything, so there isn't much for you to worry about. Just go where she tells you, shake the hands that are offered, and for the love of all the *gods*, don't try to stab anyone."

Mariah gave him a feral grin. "But that just takes the fun out of it."

He chuckled, shaking his head, the neat, dark strands of his hair brushing his forehead. "You can also select one of your Armature—or, really, anyone—to be your escort. Guide you in your first dance, stand by your side, all that."

"Dance?!" Mariah knew the basic steps, but she by no means considered herself someone able to step into a royal ballroom and stun a crowd.

"Relax," Sebastian laughed, his grin slightly crooked. "All your Armature are trained in the steps. Let us lead you and you'll be fine. Besides, dancing is not so different from sparring, and I know you're plenty good at that."

She only eyed him, cocking an eyebrow as his words stretched between them.

"Well, this feels like an easy choice. Obviously, you'll be escorting me."

His answering grin was blinding, but a steeled hardness lined his hazel gaze. "Are you sure? There's not ... someone else you'd rather try to make amends with by asking to escort you instead?"

A dry, humorless laugh pulled itself from Mariah's throat. "Trust me, that would be the *worst* decision I could possibly make at this moment."

Sebastian regarded her thoughtfully for one more moment before sighing heavily. "Of course, Mariah. I would be honored to escort you." He glanced quickly behind her. "Speaking of which, it's about time we begin getting ready." He stood, walking to her side of the table, offering his hand to her. She took it and rose, his warm and masculine scent wrapping around her like a blanket and the feeling of home.

He was so perfect; everything she could ever want and need.

And she despised the part of her that didn't want him. But she also knew he was someone who would be so easy to fall in love with, and she could never let that happen.

Love is a weakness.

She didn't want to think about how that weakness was starting to stare back at her with sinister shadows and tanzanite eyes.

Gazing at her reflection in the large, full-length mirror in her bathroom, Mariah hardly recognized the queen who stared back.

For that was what she looked like: a queen.

Her gown was floor-length, the long train pooling on the ground around her feet, the material the color of the night sky —a black that really was the darkest blue when hit by the light. The short sleeves fell off her shoulders, revealing the muscular slope of her shoulders and collarbones, highlighting the rise of her breasts. Sewn into the dark fabric, curving and threaded in all the right places, were swirling designs of shimmering gold and silver. Somehow, the patterns spoke to Mariah of starlight, loss, change, and power. She blinked, shaking her head slightly at the feeling, and returned her gaze back to the mirror.

"You designed this yourself?"

The young woman behind her, who'd tasked herself to reorganizing Mariah's collection of beauty tools, turned back around to meet her green gaze in the mirror. She smiled softly and nodded once to Mariah in answer.

"I did indeed, Your Majesty."

Mariah regarded the girl carefully for a moment. She was on the shorter side; her figure full, with curly, light-brown hair and creamy skin smattered with freckles. Her eyes were a light gray and twinkled with fire and intelligence and something *other* that Mariah couldn't quite place, but the threads of magic in her soul felt and strangely desired to reach out to.

"You said your name was Brie?"

The girl nodded again, hesitant, unasked questions lingering in her gray gaze. Mariah turned her attention back to the mirror and her gown.

"Well, Brie ... this dress is truly incredible. It feels like something very different than would be expected for an Onitan queen to wear, but ... I love it."

Brie's face exploded into a beaming smile, her chest almost puffing up with pride. "I'm deeply honored, Your Majesty. When I was tasked with making it for you by the head seamstress, I ... well, please take no offense to this, but I'd heard of you. And from what I'd heard, something told me you wouldn't be like any other queen in recent memory, content with dressing and flouncing about in gowns of all gold. So, I let the fabrics speak to me, and this is what resulted. I'm ... I'm happy you love it."

I let the fabric speak to me ...

Those words burned into Mariah's mind, her magic reacting just enough to pique her curiosity. She forced it to the side, however; later, after whatever awaited her this evening, she would find this girl again and ask her what, exactly, she meant by that.

That is, *if* she even survived this evening. She'd read enough about balls to know they were the perfect opportunity for scandal or betrayal.

Mariah heaved another breath and took in the rest of the appearance Brie had so artfully crafted.

Her dark hair hung down her back in long, gentle waves, each side pinned off her shoulders with golden clips crafted to resemble the same snowbell blossoms adorning the Onitan crown. A simple gold necklace in the shape of a crescent moon hung around her neck, resting between her breasts. Her eyes were shadowed with subtle grays and golds, the forest green of her irises stark against her tan skin. Rouge had been swept across her full lips, soft golden powder dusted across her cheekbones.

She looked like a fallen star, adorned in darkness yet still shining with light and power.

Movement behind her in the mirror drew her attention away from her reflection. Sebastian stepped into the room, dressed in fitted black pants and a matching jacket, the lapels adorned with gold and silver threading similar to that on her gown. His eyes widened slightly as he took her in before he bowed his head, his hand immediately going to his chest in a fist.

"My Queen. You are ... stunning."

Mariah smiled at him. "Stop that, Seb." She eyed him appreciatively as he raised his gaze back to hers. "You clean up nice yourself." His lips curved into a smile as she threw him a wink. Mariah grinned back and turned to address Brie one last time before they left her chambers.

"I would like to get to know you better, Brie. I hope this will not be the last time I see you around the palace."

Brie answered with another one of those brilliant smiles. "Of course, Your Majesty. It would be my honor."

"Mariah," she answered softly. "My name is Mariah."

The girl's eyes widened, but she didn't argue. Only dipped her head once to Mariah, her gray eyes shining.

With that, Mariah turned to Sebastian and placed her hand on his forearm, feeling the flex of his corded muscle through his jacket. He met her gaze again, an eyebrow lifting in silent question.

She only grinned wickedly in return.

"Let's go give them a show, Armature."

CHAPTER 41

"Royals and lords of Onita, esteemed guests, people of Verith. It is my absolute privilege to introduce Qhohena's Chosen, our next Queen of Onita, Mariah Salis."

The answering applause from the throne room thundered at Ryenne's words from behind the gilded doors, rattling Mariah's heart in her chest. She tightened her grip on Sebastian's arm, sucking in a deep breath as she steeled herself against the onslaught waiting for her beyond that solid white oak.

As the great doors swung open to reveal the cavernous, glass-ceilinged room beyond, Mariah's subconscious guided her feet forward, moving her out onto the dais behind the golden throne. A smaller, less auspicious twin was placed beside it, and she focused her attention on the back of that chair, pushing out the ringing of the room. The faces of all the gathered people faded away, the sounds of their applause distant as her heart pounded louder in her chest.

She recalled a time when she'd been one of those people, watching a woman walk through those same doors onto this very dais. Recalled a time when she'd thought she still had a chance at a normal, free life, that she would be able to board a ship and flee for the Kizar Islands with a satchel of stolen coin.

What a joke that had been.

The weight of the crowd's gazes pushed against her skin, clawing and scraping like thousands of hungry mouths eager for a morsel of her attention.

Don't focus on them. Focus on those you know, those you trust.

The words in her mind, not quite sounding like her own, dragged her away from the heaviness burning in her lungs and back to the others standing with her on the dais, dressed in the finery of the queens' courts. There was Ryenne, poised and elegant beside the larger throne, resplendent in a gown of shimmering gold. Kalen and the rest of Ryenne's Armature stood to her left, watchful but smiling softly at Mariah, their gazes lit with compassion and encouragement. She didn't know many of them, was too preoccupied trying to keep her head above water with her own new life, but she nodded once to them all the same, a silent *thank you*.

Mariah continued to walk toward the second, smaller throne, her eyes darting down the dais to where her own court stood. Her Armature stood closest: Quentin, Drystan, Matheo, Trefor, and Feran, all dressed in the same fine, tailored suits as Sebastian, all smiling at her with grins of varying degrees of wickedness and pride.

And standing at the bottom of the dais, as far as was acceptable for a member of a queen apparent's Armature to be from her, was Andrian, his attention fixed on the wall beside the door behind her.

She refused to look at him, too.

Further to the side of the dais stood the Ladies of her and Ryenne's courts, and it was there that Mariah let her attention wander. Ciana and Delaynie stood, shoulder to shoulder, eyes shining with joy and pride at their friend. Despite the situation, and the nerves still clawing through her belly, Mariah had to hold back an elated giggle when she saw Ciana's dress: an incredible, form-fitting gown of crushed maroon velvet, the skirts clinging tightly to her slender curves.

She deserved far more than being a cake-topper, anyway.

Pulling her attention from her friends, Mariah looked back to the two thrones, meeting the queen's sterling blue gaze. Ryenne's blonde hair was coiled high atop her head, the thick strands now streaked thoroughly with gray, her snowdrop blossom crown resplendent on her brow. A gentle smile spread across her lips, her eyes darting briefly to Sebastian before returning to Mariah.

There was a warning hidden behind the Queen's eyes as Ryenne hardened her stare at Mariah, glancing away to another corner of the dais, drawing Mariah's attention with it. Mariah schooled her face into neutrality as her eyes clashed with Ksee's burning, tarnished glare.

The high priestess stood behind Ryenne's Armature, her face twisted with contempt and disapproval as her glare soaked in the dark gown that clung to Mariah's body. Anger washed over Mariah as the priestess picked her apart, her skin warming with eager silver-gold magic that sought to snap free from her skin. Instead, Mariah inhaled deeply, settling herself for just a moment before she wrenched her gaze from Ksee and lifted her chin in the air, forcing the most regality she could muster into her posture. She removed her hand from Sebastian's arm before striding forward and joining Ryenne beside those two golden thrones.

Distantly, as if from underwater, Mariah could hear the crowd below her cheering. The realization snapped her back into the present, to the exuberance filling the air and dragging greedy fingers down her skin. Despite the cacophony, a sickly sweetness clung to the cheers, as if it were tinged with something ... manufactured. Synthetic. False.

They didn't want her, but curiosity drove them all here just the same.

Fine. She'd never cared much about the opinions of others. *As long as they didn't wish to harm her where she slept.*

Mariah's gaze darted to Ryenne, only to find the queen watching Mariah closely, her ocean blue eyes still carefully guarded. Ryenne then turned to face the gathered crowd beneath them, her hands raised just as they'd been at the Choosing. The mass of people fell instantly silent, eager and greedy for more.

"May Queen Apparent Mariah's reign be long and prosperous! Now, let us revel in this divine night before the shine of the golden moon and celebrate Qhohena's Chosen beneath her blessed light!"

There were more cheers as glasses were raised, toasts to the queen's words ringing out, soft echoes of "*To Qhohena!*" echoing through the cavernous throne room. On Mariah's right, a band began to play, and her attention wandered for a moment to watch the semi-circle of six musicians—three men, three women—as their instruments began spinning rolling melodies through the room. The music was traditional Onitan, and it pulled at her feet in a way that made it near impossible to resist the urge to stand and dance, to lose herself in the crescendos and diminuendos of the strings and percussions.

"My queen?" said a soft, deep male voice from Mariah's side. She turned her head further to meet Sebastian's steady hazel gaze, his firm presence a rock in the flowing din of the room.

Goddess, she wished—more than anything—that she could give him the love he deserved.

Seb extended a hand to her, bowing slightly at the waist, his other hand held lightly behind his back.

"Would you honor me with this dance?"

Mariah smiled at him, the warmth of his solid presence wrapping itself around her skin. "The honor would be all mine, Armature."

With that, she placed her hand in his and let him pull her from the dais, down the steps, and toward the empty, polished dancefloor.

CHAPTER 42

"We wish you a long and blessed reign, Your Highness." The reedy man standing before Mariah and Ryenne bowed deeply as he stepped back from the dais, the queen and her successor nodding to him respectfully in return.

"Thank you, Lord Fraser. It has been an honor to make your acquaintance. I pray that Qhohena's grace shines down on you in the coming years, and that you always feel welcome to petition my court for assistance, should you ever need it." The words, repeated over and over again by Mariah as she met lord after lord, Ambassador after Ambassador, had long since lost their candor, but she forced them past her teeth, regardless.

Mostly because she didn't want Ksee to ruin her night more than her incessant glaring already had.

The Lord of Tolona, a small southern town close to the Onitan border with Idrix and Vatha, flashed her a slightly haphazard smile. "I shall always do just that, Your Highness." And with that, he retreated fully from the space before them.

In his place, a group of six ascended the dais steps next—two dressed in finery, flanked by four guards. The two in the center wore a familiar white fabric pinned at the shoulders, a style instantly reminding Mariah of the two Kreah women she'd met in the stables. One was a man, thickly built, heavy silver chains hanging around his throat and resting against his broad chest. Beside him stood a woman, an elaborate headpiece woven into her thick, black hair, her kohl-lined eyes glittering with a fierceness Mariah recognized.

Reaching the top of the dais, the man dropped to his knee, his hand forming a fist that he rested against his chest. The woman beside him did the same, and their guards who'd remained at the base of the dais mimicked their actions.

"Queen Ryenne." The man's voice was deep, rumpling. "It is an honor to finally make your acquaintance."

Ryenne stood up straighter, taking a small step forward. "And you as well, Ambassador Enoch. I am deeply grateful to you for making the journey here to Verith. Please, rise."

At her words, the entire party rose to their feet. Ryenne presented her practiced, diplomatic smile before forging on.

"Ambassador, it is with great honor that I present to you the Queen Apparent of Onita, Mariah Salis."

Ambassador Enoch swung his head to Mariah, dark brown gaze meeting hers briefly before dropping again into a deep bow. "Queen Apparent Mariah. It is my greatest privilege to meet you. It is a rare occurrence indeed when Onita gains a new queen. We are blessed beyond measure to be here, witnessing your ascent."

"The honor is all mine, Ambassador." A genuine smile touched Mariah's lips. There was something about this man and the woman beside him that was so different from all the others she'd met that night. Something real, and authentic, not smothered with a layer of sticky superiority. "Forgive my question, but … you are Kreah, correct?"

Enoch flashed a smile, his teeth brilliantly white against his dark skin. "Yes, Your Majesty. I am the Kreah Ambassador to Onita." He turned to the woman beside him, her eyes a brilliant jade green that contrasted beautifully with her similarly dark skin. "I would like to introduce you to my wife, Satya."

Mariah dipped her head in greeting. "It's a pleasure to meet you, Lady Satya."

"Just Satya will do. I have no need of titles." The woman's tone was matter-of-fact and accompanied by the hint of a mischievous smile, her jade eyes sparkling.

Mariah immediately liked her.

Enoch beamed at his wife before casting a glance over his shoulder. He returned his attention to Mariah and Ryenne, now appearing a bit more flustered than he had before. "Please forgive us, Your Majesties. We had meant for you both to also make the acquaintance of our daughters, but it seems they have not yet joined us—"

"We're here, Father."

Mariah's head snapped up at that voice, recognizing it instantly.

Emerging from the congested crowd, as if they were there all along, the two women she'd encountered in the stables ascended the dais steps, moving to stand beside who Mariah now realized were their mother and father.

Of course, they hadn't been just *any* Kreah warriors wandering the grounds of the palace. They were the children of the Kreah Ambassador to Onita.

Enoch's smile grew impossibly wider as he turned to his daughters.

"Ah, *priya*! There you are. Thank you for joining us." He turned his dark gaze back to Mariah and Ryenne. "Your Majesties, if I may present to you my daughters. Kiira"—the girl with dark brown eyes nodded, her expression somber—"and Rylla." The one with hazel eyes grinned.

Ryenne smiled at the newcomers. "Welcome, Lady Kiira and Lady Rylla." The queen paused, her gaze turning curious. "What brings you to Verith? Besides accompanying your father, of course."

Rylla glanced briefly at her father, who gave her a slight nod, before answering. "We're the Ambassador's youngest, Your Majesty. And because of that, we are blessed with the ability to travel, to see the entirety of the world the gods have gifted to us. We've already seen so much of the continent, but have not had the opportunity to explore all the beauty Onita has to offer. Even after our father has concluded his visit, we hope to remain in your country, both to learn more of your ways and to share the ways of Kreah."

"What a wonderful opportunity for you both," said Ryenne warmly. "Please, feel free to remain in Verith for as long as you both please. I shall ensure you are both well provided for."

The entire Kreah party bowed their heads. "We thank you for your generous hospitality, Your Majesty," rumbled Enoch before glancing at his daughters. "Although, if I know my daughters well, I suspect they will desire to forge their own paths. But I also implore them to not ignore the offers of powerful sovereigns." Enoch tacked on the last of his words with a pointed stare. Kiira and Rylla dipped their heads respectfully, and Mariah didn't miss the hint of amusement that touched their faces.

"Well, I know there are many more here who seek an audience with Your Majesties, and we do not wish to take up any more of your time." Ambassador Enoch bowed again, Satya, Kiira, and Rylla following suit. The Ambassador raised his gaze back to Mariah, a curious look, one Mariah couldn't quite place, written across his kind face. "It has been an honor to make your acquaintance, Queen Mariah."

Queen Mariah. No one had called her that yet.

She decided she rather liked it.

"The honor has been all mine, Ambassador Enoch." With that, the Kreah party took their exit, stepping back down the dais and merging themselves once again with the throng of attendees. In their place, the next party to address the queens stepped forward.

One look at the approaching lord's face had Mariah's entire body tensing, all the kindness shown by Ambassador Enoch and his family instantly forgotten.

Lord Ernest Donnet. Lord of Andburgh and Protector of the Crossroads. Mariah's former liege.

The former liege whose room of stolen wares and coin Mariah had raided on her last night in Andburgh before racing furiously with her father for Verith. The bags of coin she'd stolen that night were still shoved haphazardly under her bed, the dagger she'd taken strapped to her thigh beneath her night-colored gown.

Her skin beneath that dagger began to itch just as her heart thudded heavily in her ears.

Lord Donnet clapped his hands together, full of the same male bravado as that night he'd stolen from Mariah's family all those years ago. "Ah! Queen Ryenne, you're looking as resplendent as ever. I'm always honored to stand in your presence." He took the hand Ryenne outstretched to him, planting a sloppy kiss on her knuckles and the golden rings adorning her fingers.

To her credit—or perhaps it was years of experience dealing with these pretentious lords—Ryenne neither flinched nor reached to wipe off the spittle flecking her hand.

"Lord Donnet. Always a pleasure to have you join us at court. Your presence has become far too scarce."

Donnet dipped his head to Ryenne. "My sincerest apologies for any prolonged absence, My Queen. Managing the complex trade routes of the Crossroad City is quite a consuming task. But it is, of course, all done in service to you and the crown."

The snort that slipped from Mariah's throat jerked the attention of both Ryenne and Donnet to her, the latter's beady black eyes narrowing. Mariah couldn't miss the recognition that flashed in Donnet's gaze. Perhaps he wouldn't have known her name, but of course, he'd recognized her face. His words from that night, the night that had solidified her desire to one day run from that town forever, echoed through her mind.

"I only wanted to let you know that your daughter is quite a beauty. It is too bad she was not born to ... better circumstances."

Her magic woke instantly, pulsing violently beneath her skin. Her eyes twinkled with faint silver-gold light, darkening the forest-green.

Ryenne's blue gaze darted rapidly between Mariah and Donnet, noting the palpable anger filtering from Mariah. Nervousness slipped past her facade, her shoulders tensing. Out of the corner of her eye, Mariah watched Ryenne twist her fingers around each other before she spoke, her voice tight.

"Ah, where are my manners ... Lord Donnet, it is with great pleasure that I introduce you to our new Queen Apparent, Mariah Salis." Ryenne paused, her demeanor shifting into one of careful assessment as she focused her attention on Mariah. "As I understand it, Mariah was born and raised in Andburgh. I'm sure it has brought you great pride seeing one of your own being Chosen by the Goddess herself."

Despite the rushing in her blood, Mariah forced her face into a mask of cool indifference. She took a steadying breath, pushing down the angry flush she could feel building from her chest. "Thank you for the kind words, Ryenne," she said, her voice far icier than she'd intended. "It's a true honor to bring some much-needed recognition to the Crossroad City here in Verith."

She knew she shouldn't have said it. The insult was thinly veiled, at best. But the temptation was too great, and when it came to holding her tongue, she was far from strong.

Lord Donnet's rotund face flushed a cherry-red. Spittle formed on his lips and his chest puffed out, an obvious retort on his tongue. Suddenly, he took a deep breath, the fight leaving his body as his black eyes cooled from hot anger to cold malignance. He tossed a too-casual glance over his shoulder, noting the close proximity of the crowd to the dais, before turning back to Mariah.

"Indeed, Your Highness. It is *such* a great honor to have a representative from our peaceful town now next in line to sit upon the golden throne. Especially one from such ... *humble* means. Perhaps I should pay your family another visit to that hovel at the edge of the woods they call a home."

Mariah's vision flooded with red, her entire body instantly filled with boiling rage. Her tongue loosened, preparing to defend her family and that perfect home they'd made together, and she would have unleashed herself if she hadn't caught the strangely confident look on the lord's face. She paled, fear washing over her like a wave.

He wouldn't admit he'd been robbed—not here, not with all of Onitan's rich and powerful within earshot. But if he knew—somehow, if someone had seen her slipping from his manor...

"Since you've left, so many ... *interesting* stories about you have begun to spread around our town. Tell me, is it true what they say?"

Mariah's mind stuttered, the question cooling some of her rage as it caught her completely unawares. "I'm not sure what you're referring to, My Lord," she said through gritted teeth.

Donnet grinned back at her, his teeth stained and tarnished. "That you can handle a sword as well as you do a cock? So many young men in Andburgh have been bragging about how they once fucked a queen. How many men were you with on the Summer Solstice ... Ten? Twenty? Too many to count? I understand the purpose of the holiday is to celebrate the creational power of our Goddess, but from what I heard, you've always been more than willing to take things to that next level. I must say, I'm a bit disappointed I was never invited to give you a try, myself—"

Her heart pounded in her ears, her magic unspooling and lancing through her veins. She was so distracted by her anger and pain and embarrassment, all of it ripping through her gut like a knife, that she almost didn't see what had cut Donnet's tirade short. A short, dark-bladed dagger pressed into the soft skin of the lord's throat, the sharp point just nicking his skin, and a tiny ruby drop of blood spilled onto the crisp white of Donnet's shirt. Mariah's eyes traveled from the blade to the hand holding it, to the tan skin that disappeared beneath the sleeves of a dark, tailored jacket, the lapels threaded with silver and gold. She finally reached his face, staring at the tanzanite eyes fixed on Donnet, the darkness dancing in their depths singing a song of death.

"Utter one more foul word about her and I will slit your throat from ear to ear. I'm sure the red of your blood will look like a work of art pooling at her feet."

Andrian's quiet words echoed through the throne room as if carried on a shadowy breeze. The music came to a grinding halt, the dancers stilled, and gazes turned to the dais and the Armature who held a dagger to a lord's throat. Mariah's breath caught in her chest, her anger and pain from Donnet's words fizzling out as she stared intensely at Andrian and the knife in his grip. She felt Sebastian move to her side as she took a single step forward, the eyes of everyone in the throne room blazing into her with a mix of blatant curiosity, fear, and—for some—thinly veiled contempt.

Donnet was one of their own; a lord, a member of the upper echelon of Onitan society.

She was not.

As if reading her thoughts, Andrian's eyes snapped to her, the rich blue still filled with the shadows of his magic. She could tell that his control was slipping, that he was far closer to the edge than she'd ever seen him before.

She met his gaze, and unlike the last time she'd been near him, she was unafraid.

"Stand down, Andrian." Her voice was soft and calm as her body fed off his rage, the barely leashed darkness in his eyes soothing the light in her veins.

Andrian hesitated for one, two, three heartbeats before stepping back from Donnet, dropping his black-bladed dagger from the lord's throat. Behind her, Ryenne shifted on her slippered feet, the sound of her skirts ruffling across the marble floors too loud in the silent, cavernous throne room. The room heaved a sigh as the tension dropped with the queen's movement, murmurs racing through the crowd.

Except for Lord Donnet, whose round face had turned red and hot with boiling rage.

Before he could explode, however, Ryenne intervened, stepping forward and placing herself between Mariah and the lord. "Lord Donnet, what a dear misunderstanding. Please, if you would accompany me to the refreshment table, I do believe the Kreah Ambassador has supplied us with an absolutely superb vintage for tonight's festivities …" She pushed herself into the lord, grabbed his arm, and nearly dragged him away from the dais, Kalen following close behind.

With the lord retreating quickly, Mariah felt her eyes gravitate away, pulled by a magnetic force she couldn't fight even if she tried.

Eyes of forest green and tanzanite blue clashed together, screaming silent words across the short distance separating them, words that wouldn't, couldn't, *shouldn't* be said.

Especially after the events in the library.

Especially here, with the whole continent watching on with morbid curiosity.

But then, Andrian moved, sheathing his knife smoothly into a scabbard hidden at the small of his back before striding to Mariah in two long steps. He halted before her, his chest rising and falling in steadying breaths.

Mariah was utterly shocked at what he did next.

Like the true, highborn gentleman she supposed he'd been in another life, he extended a hand to her, rough palm up, his other hand wrapping behind his back. Those tanzanite eyes burned her, stripped her down to a baser form, the silvery gold threads of her magic dancing along her skin.

"Dance with me."

It wasn't a question.

There were no thoughts in Mariah's mind as she grasped Andrian's hand and let him lead her down the dais toward the dance floor beyond.

CHAPTER 43

The band had taken their cue from Ryenne when she'd dragged Donnet from the dais, and the music instantly filled the throne room once again. The melodies leaped and swirled, rose and fell, a tumultuous wave Mariah could never hope to keep up with.

That was, until Andrian pulled her against him and began to move.

The feel of his body against hers instantly snapped her attention away from everyone else in the throne room, tendrils of his shadows whispering against the bare skin of her shoulders, their touch like a caress.

He set the pace, leading them skillfully through the steps of the dance, twisting and twirling, her skirts splaying out around her legs and *swishing* across the polished white and gold marble floor. Wherever she needed him, he was there, ready to grasp her hand or guide her body or catch her at the small of her back.

In those few moments, Mariah forgot about everything—

her past, the realities of her new life, the vile truthfulness of Donnet's words, the Goddess's magic thrumming in her veins. The way Andrian looked at her now, the way he watched her as she moved with him across the dance floor, made her feel so alive and so ... *worthy*.

Which was stupid, considering the words he'd shared with her only yesterday in the darkness of the library.

The spell snapped. The memories came screaming back into her mind before she could stop them. The crushing pain she'd felt at his words. That she would never be more than a *distraction* to him, that he would bring her nothing but *pain*.

And yet, here she was, getting lost with him while the entire continent watched on.

No. He may have defended her to Donnet, but she wouldn't let this happen. She *couldn't* let this happen. She could feel herself crossing into dangerous, foreign territory, her heart beginning to pull her in a direction she would not go.

Love is a weakness, Mariah.

At that moment, the song ended, the final notes dissipating into the open air of the throne room. Mariah and Andrian halted in the center of the dance floor, staring at each other as their breaths heaved with exertion. She yanked her eyes from his before she turned her attention to the rest of the room, to the crowd that had gathered around them.

They were the only pair on the dance floor, but the *Porofirat* attendees watched on, wearing expressions of curiosity and fear and anger. She could hear their words in those gazes, two sides to the same disapproving coin.

Is the queen apparent dancing with the Laurent heir? The one who looks too much like his foreign Luexrithian mother? Shameful. Qhohena's light has no business mingling with northern darkness.

Did you hear Lord Donnet's words? Disgusting. How could our Golden Goddess choose a whore like that? And Lord Laurent's lost son defending her and now dancing with her ... What shame that must bring upon that noble family.

It was unbearable, the mutterings of the crowd scratching down her spine like the claws of a demon.

Her heart thudding in her ears, Mariah frantically shoved away from Andrian before spinning on her heel. She pushed through the crowd, shouldering her way into one of the many hallways spindling off the throne room. Once there, she ran, not stopping until she found an exit from the stifling air of the palace, the glass doors to the hallway balcony clicking softly closed behind her.

The cool, late autumn air burned Mariah's lungs as she inhaled deeply, leaning heavily against the balcony railing.

She'd known—just *known*—this night would go poorly.

She hadn't exactly predicted she would be called a whore before the entire continent by the lord of her hometown, but ... given her luck, she supposed she should have.

Mariah dropped her chin against her chest with a sigh, fighting back the harsh tears that threatened and burned behind her eyes. Sure, Andrian had made things better for one brief, fleeting moment, but the reminder of what he'd spat at her yesterday still rattled around in her head. She'd told herself, over and over, that it shouldn't—didn't—matter what he thought of her. It shouldn't matter if he despised her or if he wanted to fuck her ... or if he might, unbelievably, feel something real towards her.

But yet, somehow ... it still did.

"Love is a weakness, is it not?"

Mariah froze, the breath rushing from her lungs in a startled exhale. The silver threads deep within her separated themselves from the gold and leaped to the surface of her skin, something they hadn't done in weeks. Power crackled along where they rose, tingling in her fingers as alarm slammed through her.

Slowly, Mariah turned to face the balcony doorway and the origin of that voice.

Standing in the dim light of the paneled double doors was a woman, dressed in a fine, yet simple, silver gown, the sleeves long and heavy. A veil of silver draped over her head and face, obscuring her features. By her dress, Mariah knew she was clearly not Onitan, but nothing about what she wore was familiar enough to firmly place her origin. The woman took one step towards Mariah, her movements flowing across the tiled floors, and unease prickled across Mariah's skin.

But ... Mariah didn't feel threatened. Her unsettled senses had nothing to do with a fear that this strange woman might harm her.

No ... she was suddenly afraid of what this woman might know. What this woman might say.

Especially since she'd greeted Mariah with the single, secret phrase that had been whispered to her all her life. *No one* knew about that.

Not even her mother.

The woman glided further onto the balcony until she stood at the railing, about three feet to Mariah's left. Her head tilted up to gaze at the night sky above, where the twin moons hung as thin waxing crescents, their light still enough to illuminate the air around them. Those moons would only continue to grow larger and closer as the weeks passed until the Winter

Solstice, when they would be at both their lowest and largest and brightest. Just as they were on the Summer Solstice.

There was pure, raw magic to be found on those nights when the moons were huge and blazing in the sky. Magic that was not just reserved for men or priestesses or queens.

"The moons are beautiful tonight, don't you think?"

The woman's voice was soft, yet strong and smooth. Mariah narrowed her eyes as she looked at her, opening her mouth to speak, when the woman continued.

"I think there is something so powerful about when they wax. They all but vanish from the sky during the Equinox, but watching them reappear as we move closer to the Solstice is such a marvelous thing to witness." Mariah swore she could hear a smile on the woman's words.

This woman was ... quite strange.

"Yes, it sure is ... something." Mariah paused, leaning forward, trying to peer beneath that thick veil. "I'm sorry, but ... can I help you? Who are you?"

The woman ignored Mariah's questions, continuing her monologue as if she'd heard nothing. "It is funny, I think, how your people worship and celebrate only one of those moons, when they both provide us all with light against the darkness of the world."

Her words skittered over Mariah's skin, goosebumps erupting in their wake. She stared at the woman, her mouth agape. Slowly, the strange woman turned away from the night sky above and finally turned to face Mariah. While Mariah couldn't see her eyes, she still felt the burn of the woman's gaze, the weight of it so heavy and intense she felt her soul shriek and crawl as it caved under the scrutiny.

She didn't particularly like that, being so seen.

"You know of the Ginnelevé, Your Majesty. Do not forget

her. The journal you have been gifted shall guide you, but let what is inside of it lead you."

Mariah's heart stopped in her chest as the mysterious woman turned, the silver material of her strange clothing whispering around her, and disappeared back through the balcony doors and into the shadows of the hallway beyond.

CHAPTER 44

The chill was instant as Mariah yanked herself from Andrian's grasp and pushed herself into the depths of the crowds, slipping away from him like mist through his fingers As she went, it felt as if a piece of him were being ripped from his soul, pulled out and carried away in her soft yet calloused hands.

He'd meant what he'd said to her in the library yesterday. Or, at least, he *thought* he'd meant what he said. Andrian knew she was growing too close to him, and he had to push her away, into the arms of Sebastian or literally *anyone* else who was more deserving of her than him. He'd meant to stand by his word and stay away from her tonight, to be present only because his position and the oath he'd unintentionally swore demanded it. He absolutely had not intended to do the equivalent of kissing her feet before every eye on the continent.

But the second that swine—*Donnet*—had opened his mouth …

Andrian had never felt such fury in his entire, angry life.

The darkness dwelling in his veins had swirled up and out, veiling his vision so suddenly that when he'd finally been able to recapture its reins, he'd found himself standing between Mariah and the lord, his dagger pressed against the man's sweaty throat.

And even with a semblance of regained control, it hadn't stopped him from issuing that threat for the entire world to hear. But that wasn't even what surprised him the most.

What shocked him to his core was that he'd *meant* it. Gods, he'd wanted to spill the blood of that poor excuse of a man right there on the dais, let it wash around Mariah's feet in a beautiful, macabre painting just for her. She'd worn that dress of sinful night; not a speck would have marred it.

He'd somehow wrestled control of himself enough to turn and meet Mariah's gaze just as her voice had spoken his name. It had snapped his bloodthirsty trance, and the emotions shining in her eyes hadn't been fear, or apprehension, or anything of the sort.

Mariah had looked at him with *appreciation*.

He didn't think anyone had ever looked at him that way before.

She'd taken in all his darkness, light magic sparkling in her incredible green eyes, alighting across her golden skin and in the near-black waves of her hair, and was utterly unafraid. That had been nowhere near as dark as he could go, but to see her staring at him like that, with so much acceptance ...

He still hated her, he'd reminded himself.

Hated her.

Hated her.

But words, when you start to repeat them often enough to yourself, begin to lose all their meaning. Begin to sound like nothing at all.

The sparkling brilliance of her magic in the air around

them had suddenly cracked something in the icy depths of his soul, splintering everything he'd fought so hard to keep locked down and frozen away.

Those cracks made it impossible to resist reaching out to her. To ask her to dance with him.

Even though he was a Marked man, he was also still a Royal's son, and he'd danced with plenty of women in his life. Had asked plenty of women to dance with him.

But nothing had shocked him more than when she'd said yes. Those cracks in his ice shattered even further.

He'd been close to her before: with her, on her, under her, *inside* her. But there in the throne room, dancing, their conflicting magic crackling in the air around them, the declaration he'd laid at her feet mere moments before swirling through the room in front of lords and ladies and ambassadors and emissaries ... something had felt completely raw and new and *terrifying*.

And now, as Andrian watched her dark head flit through the crowd, he could almost feel the warmth of her light seeping through the frozen cracks in his soul.

But she was always slipping away from him.

It was maddening.

And he was so, eternally, *fucked*.

He wanted to go after her the second she disappeared from view. His feet, previously rooted to the marble floor beneath him, suddenly loosened, and he took a lurching step forward. He was once again frozen in place, though, his gaze snagging on a pair of golden-hazel eyes set into a bearded face filled with cold, frigid rage.

Lord Julian Laurent met and held his son's eyes. Andrian, despite the three decades he'd had to accustom himself to his father, felt his heartbeat sputter in his chest. The Lord of

Antoris lifted a hand, gesturing to Andrian to follow him, his expression leaving no room for argument.

Choosing to ignore him and walking away at that moment would not be an option. It was time to face the consequences of his actions that night.

Filled with shameful weakness and rising dread, Andrian shoved his shadow magic down—his father never took kindly to the reminder of the Leuxrithian influence in Andrian's blood—and followed Lord Laurent out of the throne room and into the darkness of the hallways beyond.

Leaving the object of his *hatred* behind him.

The door to the private meeting room slammed shut behind Andrian, the boom reverberated through the room and rattled the *allume* sconces on the walls. His gaze lingered on the soft gold light filtering from them before turning to face his father. He refused to think about why he found that light familiar and oddly comforting.

Lord Laurent stood at the head of the dark, heavy table, his hands resting on the back of one of the white wood chairs, everything about him burning with the rage of a furious inferno.

In his entire thirty-one years of life, throughout both childhood and his years in Verith after being marked, Andrian had always known his father to be a raging maelstrom of fire, mirroring the elemental gift he rarely used that filled his veins nonetheless. Julian Laurent was lord of the most northern Onitan stronghold, his city once a major center for Onitan-Leuxrithian trade before the borders were closed. It was a place where frost and cold reigned most of the year except for those few sweet months in the summer when the longer days chased away the worst of the freeze. However, Lord Laurent let himself burn with just enough fire to melt some of that ice, keeping the farms standing and his people prosperous. All a ploy, Andrian knew, to keep the common folk beholden to him, meek and unquestioning.

The origins of House Laurent hearkened back to the earliest of Onita itself, when its people were still reeling from the First War and the new divisions between the kingdoms. Qhohena's blessings had still freshly inundated the land, and the physical appearances of those earliest Onitan peoples had taken on her gilded glow, their hair, skin, and eyes all varying shades of gold. Julian Laurent, and much of the Laurent line, still carried those strong golden traits indicative of pure Onitan breeding.

His oldest son, however, wasn't as lucky.

Andrian had always been colder, darker, and filled with far too much ice and shadow to make his father happy. He'd taken after his Leuxrithian mother, physically resembling the northern people who dwelt in the eternal cold beyond the Everheim Mountains. And because of that, he was always so easily burned by the inferno dwelling within his father.

"I am disappointed in you, Andrian." Julian's golden gaze was scorching.

If Andrian were still a boy, those words would've had him shrinking under the table.

He was not a boy anymore, though.

Andrian crossed his arms, straightening his spine. "For what? Not saying 'hello' earlier in the evening? I didn't strike you as one to be personally offended by a simple slip in manners, especially from your own blood."

"Save your snark with me, Andrian. You know *exactly* of what I speak."

"No, actually, I don't." Andrian scratched his chin, the

slight stubble growing there irritated his fingertips as he narrowed his gaze at his father. He was filled with a foreign confidence, one that most certainly flowed from a certain dark-haired siren who'd surprised him more than anything ever had with her acceptance of him that evening. "Care to enlighten me?"

The inferno in his father's gaze strengthened into a hurricane of flame. "I haven't spoken to you in many years, wanting to keep my distance, but I *know* you remember what I told you that day you were Marked. However, it seems you might need some sort of *reminder*." Julian paused. "You disgraced your family tonight, Andrian, by dancing with that *whore* bearing a name worth nothing that we are soon expected to call *queen*."

"*Is it true what they say about you? That you handle a sword as well as you do a cock?*"

Andrian felt the dark magic in his blood stretch its tendrils out from him, seeping into the air, a shadow come to life. His control faltered at his father's ugly words, at the reminder of Donnet's very public proclamation, and his voice came out of his throat in a low growl. It filled the air with all the ice and smoke in his frozen heart.

"How *dare* you call her that foul word."

Julian Laurent was unfazed. "Ah, yes, of course. How could I forget? That is, as it seems, an easy way to wind up with a dagger to my throat and—how did you put it—with my blood pooling at the feet of your so-called queen." His father's words were sneered, not a single hint of fear shown in his expression at his son's display. "You threatened a Lord of Onita tonight, Andrian. He spoke the truth, too. About her. All his words were true, and we'd all been thinking them."

Andrian's non-existent restraint slipped further, his

shadows desperate to choke off the words as they spilled from his father's throat.

But the sick, morbid twinge of curiosity ... of fucking *jealousy* that raced through him ... he couldn't hold back his next question.

"What do you mean?"

Julian laughed, a cold sound that conflicted with the fire blazing in his gold eyes, no real humor behind it. "You don't know about her? About what she truly is? This woman who you, for some reason and against all my express commands, allowed to Select you to her Armature? She comes from nothing and has quite the reputation back in her town. The daughter of a healer and a low-ranking soldier, a *slut* who slept her way through the entire town since her first Solstice at eighteen." He paused, a cruel grin spreading across his face. "I hear she even welcomed multiple men into her bed on the last Summer Solstice. Tell me, are you prepared to share her when she inevitably does the same to you?"

Andrian forced hard against the swell of anger threatening to sweep over him. It would do him no good to explode here, even though the implication behind his father's words nearly brought him to his knees.

Of course, he wasn't prepared to share her. He may have said as much in the library, yesterday, but that'd just been an attempt to push her away. He hadn't meant it.

But ... had *she*?

"Her past has no bearing on her present, on what kind of queen she might end up becoming. You don't know her. Honestly, I don't even know her ... but I'm starting to."

Julian laughed, a cold, hard sound. "So ... you're falling for her. Is that it? I will give it to you, she is beautiful. But then again, the queens always are. It is so they can wrap their weak little Armature around their fingers and trap you down with the sweetness of their Goddess-blessed pussies. Beauty and good sex do not make a good queen. But then again, you've always been weak, and I am not surprised you have confused the two."

For a moment, the conversation Andrian had overheard between his father and Shawth flashed through his mind. He'd been so sure the obstacle they'd been discussing was Ryenne, that whatever work they were planning involved the aging Queen. But now, hearing his father spew such hate ... he began to wonder if he'd been wrong. Began to realize just how much danger Mariah was actually in.

Shawth and his father had always craved power. And Mariah would never be one to share it with them.

Andrian knew if he remained in that room any longer, he would end up slitting his own father's throat. And as much as the man before him might deserve it ... he couldn't have that kind of blood on his already-marred soul.

Not yet, anyway.

So, he turned on his heel and strode for the door. "If all you wanted to do was insult my queen, I have no more interest in continuing this conversation."

His father's laugh was cold and scorching at the same time. "*Your* queen, is it? My dear son, what I wanted to do tonight was remind you what will happen to *your queen* should you continue to forget your blood and the promise I made to you all those years ago."

Andrian froze in his tracks. He tried to fight it, but his head tilted back over his shoulder, meeting his father's smoldering gaze.

"Hear me closely, Andrian. I do not care if you have been captivated by whatever it is about her you find so ... *appealing*. She will *never* be queen; I will make sure of that."

Everything in Andrian turned to ice. Even his heart stopped beating in his chest as his father spoke his next words.

"If you so much as *think* about accepting the bond from her, or of assisting her in any way towards the growth of that useless power she stole from a family far more deserving, then I will *personally* assure her death. In fact ... I will force *you* to be the one to serve as her executioner."

CHAPTER 45

"I can't *fucking* do this anymore."

Mariah collapsed onto the couch, the skirts of her black gown twisted in her legs, her hands covering her face and pressing into her eyes. She didn't care if she smudged the perfectly drawn lines of kohl; the night was over, and too much had happened for her to give a shit about her appearance anymore.

The couch dipped slightly beside her, and then a hand grabbed her wrist, wrenching her fingers from her eyes. She cracked her lids to meet Delaynie's wide blue gaze, her perfectly curled auburn hair cascading around her shoulders. Her voice was soft and calming when she spoke.

"Tonight was ... a lot. It is more than understandable to be feeling overwhelmed. No one will fault you—"

"*Overwhelmed*?!" Mariah pushed up, Delaynie recoiling from her like a startled hare. She knew the girl didn't deserve her coldness, but at that moment, she didn't care. Words and rage and fear were coiling in her chest, and she paced to the wall of windows, gazing out at the starry night sky and the Attlehon

Mountains. She focused her gaze on her reflection in the glass, noticing the fevered flush to her skin and the wild look in her eyes.

She hardly recognized herself. None of this is what she'd wanted. She didn't belong here. This didn't have to be her future. She was still her own woman, could still make her own future. Goddess be damned.

"'Overwhelmed' is an Enfara-damned understatement." Mariah's voice was a pained whisper, her rage and desperation clogging her throat. "You heard what Donnet said tonight, in front of every powerful representative on the *continent*. And you know what the worst part of it is?" She choked on her next words, wiping away an errant tear that spilled from her eyes. Not even sure if Delaynie was still listening, or if she'd been left alone in the room to confess her sins to the mountains and stars, Mariah continued, "The worst part is that it's *true*. All of it. I earned my reputation in Andburgh. I'd always thought I would leave when I turned twenty-one, would never see them again. So, what did it matter what—or who—I did? I took three men to my bed on the last Solstice. Fucked them under the stars that night in our own little twisted party.

"I deserve it. All of the insults they throw at me. And the longer I'm here, the longer I'm convinced the Goddess ... she must've made a mistake. I don't belong here. I *can't* do this." Her voice never wavered, despite the pain pulling at her throat, in her chest. "I shouldn't be here. It never should have been me. I have half a mind to just run away, like I'd always planned to do. I could go west, or set sail across the sea, and put this entire Goddess-damned palace and city and *kingdom* behind me. Everyone would be better off, anyway."

"Don't you *ever* fucking say those words again."

The voice, which sounded behind Mariah, back towards

the entrance to her suite, snapped Mariah's attention away from her reflection, whirling around on her feet.

And there was Ciana, leaning against one of the pillars framing the foyer entryway still dressed in her stunning gown of crushed maroon velvet, her golden eyes roaring and raging like a lioness. Mariah could have sworn she saw the ends of Ciana's hair lift as if on a phantom breeze, the whisper of a wind chasing through the room and across her own skin at the fury radiating off her friend.

Interesting.

Mariah held that golden stare, testing to see who would break first.

In the end, Mariah couldn't stand the harshness of the other girl's words, even if she was her closest friend.

"What if I mean it? You know it as well as I do, Cee—I don't *belong* here. Nothing in this palace is for me. No one except you, Delaynie, and my Armature even *accept* me. Everyone stares at me like a whore, an outcast, a traitor, someone who stole a crown I never fucking *wanted*. And the best part is that I am *exactly* what they say I am!" Mariah threw up her hands, taking a few paces closer to her golden-haired friend, Delaynie watching silently from where she still sat on a couch. "Do you know what that's like? To be *despised* simply because of who you are?"

"Yes."

Ciana didn't miss a beat when answering. The quickness of her response had Mariah blinking, taking a step back as if she'd been slapped.

Ciana heaved a sigh, hanging her head for a moment before lifting her chin proudly, meeting Mariah's stare without a shred of doubt.

"I know exactly what it feels like to be hated because of who you are. I spent most of my life feeling that way. But because of you, I got out, and I refuse to let you run away. Because if you run, then I go back to where I came from, and I would sooner *kill myself* then let that happen. Do you understand?" Ciana paused, her stare filled with burning intensity as she held Mariah's gaze unflinchingly. "If you don't wish to stay for you, or for this kingdom, or for the Goddess, then stay for *me*. Stay and fight so women like me can find the better future that I was able to find here, with you."

All words were zapped from Mariah's throat like a bolt of lightning. All she could do was stare at her best friend, her mouth gaping like a fish, as she processed Ciana's words.

And the more she thought, the more her anger built again, this time like slow-moving lava instead of an icy maelstrom. Beside her, she felt Delaynie's calm, gentle presence sidling closer, watching Mariah and Ciana with wary eyes.

"Ciana," Mariah finally choked out, her voice raspy with her shock. "What happened to you?"

Ciana's look of steely determination finally faltered, and behind that golden wall of resolve traces of pain flickered through. She drew in another shaky breath, her gaze darting from Mariah, to Delaynie, and back to Mariah, before she uncrossed her arms and nodded her head once.

"You'll want to sit for this. And ... we should probably get some wine."

"Kasia, being as close as it is to Kreah, was always hot, and you needed money just to survive there." Ciana's voice was soft, uncharacteristically muted, pausing as she took a sip of the chilled red wine Mariah scrounged up. "Money was needed to build the houses with the best insulation, install the most innovative *allume* cooling systems and fans, and, of course, pay for the necessities like water. Thankfully, my family had no shortage of money, and I never knew how deadly that heat really was." She took another sip. "That is, until my father got sick, and then died when I'd barely turned eight years old. They said it was something that grew in him—in his heart or his lungs, I don't remember—but it drained the life from him like a parasite until there was nothing left.

"My mother ... she loved him, of that I have no doubt. But she'd always been a bit of an airhead, which was fitting considering the air magic that was exceedingly common in the men of her family. In most Kasian's, in fact." Another sip from her wine. "Mother's family was also wealthy, just as Father and Father's family had been. But ... she hardly had any living family left; life was hard there on the cusp of the desert. And it was—*is*—even harder for a single, widowed woman who'd never worked a real day in her life, to continue to provide herself and her daughter with the lifestyle they'd always been accustomed to. So, the money soon ran out, and Mother was left with no other choice: she had to remarry.

"The man she married was from another excessively wealthy family in town, a widower whose first wife had passed away many years ago on the birthing bed. His riches were all that Mother cared about. And while he had money, he was *ugly*, in both personality and appearance." Ciana stopped, a shadowed look crossing her expression. She drained the rest of her glass, and Mariah stood from where she leaned against the kitchen island to grab the bottle of wine. Her friend extended her arm, putting her empty glass within Mariah's reach, and Mariah filled the glass back up to the brim before topping off her own. She offered some to Delaynie, but the auburn-haired girl simply shook her head once, her intense blue gaze fixed on Ciana.

Ciana took one more big swig before continuing.

"His sixteen-year-old son was just as ugly, in the exact same ways."

Mariah's blood ran cold at the hollow sound of Ciana's voice, the distant look that filled her normally brilliant, shining golden eyes.

"I was ten when Mother moved us into that house with my new stepfather and stepbrother. Two new, strange men, who I was expected to now call family."

Dread pooled under Mariah's skin, awakening her magic in her belly. She forced the threads of light to stay beneath the surface; she had to know—*needed* to know—all of Ciana's story, what had happened to her golden friend that made the mere thought of going home an impossibility.

Ciana cleared her throat before forging on.

"It started with just minor teasing: a pinch here, a flick there. Always in places where the tiny bruises that they left wouldn't be seen by Mother or anyone else. Not that anyone was looking particularly closely.

"I complained once, just once, about the touches and marks on my skin. About how they stung, about how he was *hurting* me. But all Mother did was act like it was my fault, like I'd deserved it, that I had to *play nice*. I was a girl, after all; nothing more than a burden to my mother, an extra mouth to feed. Girls are worth very little in a world where money and magic and power reign supreme. My accusations made Mother furious. 'We owe them everything,' she would say. 'Be a good little girl for them, Ciana. Make Mommy proud.'"

Chills raked Mariah's skin, and she was about to speak as she watched the first tear spill over Ciana's eyes and onto her cheek, but her friend only took another swig of wine and kept going.

"It wasn't long after that he began to visit me at night. He was seventeen; I was no older than eleven."

Mariah thought she would be sick, and even Delaynie's pale skin turned green as Ciana's expression hardened into stone, her voice monotonous, as if reciting a memorized play or the instructions of a science experiment.

"He would tell me that we were just playing. That it was a silent game, and I had to stay quiet. *'Our little secret,'* he would call it. And I played along, because I was a girl, and in this world—in *my* world—girls and women had no choice but to cope with the hand they're dealt and do the best they can to stay alive.

"That continued for ... well, until the day I received the Queen's summons. I patiently let Mother pack me a trunk with all the gaudy, ridiculous dresses she could squeeze in, gave her a hug, and then left the house that will always haunt my nightmares and never looked back."

There was a dead silence in the room. Mariah's breathing was ragged as tears streamed down her face. A glance at Delaynie revealed the same. Ciana, still stoic and stony, had only cracked slightly, just a few fat, full tears tracking down her bronze cheeks. Ciana set her wine glass—again empty—on the counter, filled it up once more, wiped those few lingering tears from existence, and then turned to fully face Mariah, her expression devolving from stone to fire.

"When I saw you in that courtyard, I saw a woman who had everything that I never had. You were free, confident, powerful in your femininity. Sure, I know I hide behind a convincing mask, but that's all it is ... a mask. Inside, I'm just a heaping lump of scar tissue, just like so many other women in this country without magic to protect them. Because at the end of the day, even if the priestesshood is nothing more than a prison, at least it gets girls like me *out*.

"But you, Mariah ... you're about to be the *queen*. Not just a priestess, not a wanderer, but a monarch. Someone with the power of a fucking *goddess* in her veins and who's about to sit upon the most powerful seat on the continent. Who cares if Ryenne gave away most of her power? *Take it back.* It's yours. And with it, you could have a real chance to offer to other Onitan women the same gift that you offered to me." She paused, the tears real and uninhibited as they poured down her face. This time, though, they were not tears of pain.

They were tears of silenced anger and undiluted rage.

"You can change everything about what this kingdom has become. Show Onitan women that they can be—that they *are* —more than just property or priestesses. That we have *power*. We don't worship a goddess because she's weak, and I think it's time this kingdom remembers that."

Mariah forced back her sobs as she stood from her stool, moving to stand beside her friend. She held Ciana's gaze for a moment longer, the faces of both women streaked with tears, before she opened her arms and pulled Ciana close, squeezing her beautiful friend tightly to her with all the force and pain and love and heartache she could muster.

"I am ... so, so sorry. I know that doesn't fix it—that nothing will ever heal those wounds—but—"

"I don't want your sympathy." Ciana pulled back from Mariah's grip. "That's not why I shared this. Plus, you're the one who saved me, remember?"

Mariah choked out a sobbing laugh. "Yeah, but ... I didn't know I was saving you. Not until now."

"It doesn't matter that you didn't know. What matters is that you did." Ciana's eyes darted past Mariah, and then she was grabbing Delaynie's hand, pulling her in close to stand beside Mariah. The three women stood there for a moment, letting themselves process and feel and just *be*, as friends, as sisters who'd chosen and found each other.

And as Mariah's emotions began to settle, her mind began

to swirl, to run through everything that had happened that night, that week, all the way back to when she'd arrived at the palace.

"*You can change everything about what this kingdom has become.*"

"*We don't worship a goddess because she is weak.*"

There was one very important, very public event fast approaching that served as a display of the Goddess's magic. And Mariah knew, because Ryenne had told her as much, that the ceremony and the magic it produced had been weakening for centuries. Maybe that was due to Ryenne's trade, or maybe it was due to the subliminal oppression which had been slowly taking place throughout the kingdom and unchecked for generations. Or, maybe it was a combination of both or something else entirely. But what Mariah *did* know was that if Ciana was right, if she now truly had the power to change this kingdom for the better, then that ceremony seemed like it would be the perfect place to start making some changes.

"I hear you, Ciana. I'll stay—if not for me, then for you, and for every other woman in this kingdom who is trapped and suffering." Mariah inhaled deeply, then looked both her friends in the eye as she let a slow, wicked smile spread across her lips.

"I was also just thinking. What better place to start a revolution—to remind the world of what the Goddess and the women of this land are capable of—then at the Winter Solstice?"

Ciana and Delaynie blinked at Mariah as they both processed her words. Finally, the answering grin that lit up Ciana's brilliant face could only be described as feral.

"M, if you're suggesting that we bring a little depravity to the palace, then I'm totally on board."

CHAPTER 46

Andrian lay awake in his bed as he stared blankly at the ceiling above, his father's words weaving a tapestry of hate through his thoughts.

He hadn't slept for more than a few minutes, his mind flickering between the feeling of Mariah in his arms, a look of pure, unadulterated happiness on her face as they'd danced through the ballroom, and the rage in his father's eyes as he'd issued the threat that had haunted Andrian for over twenty-one years. His feelings had always been a convoluted mess hidden behind a facade of ice, but now that crystalized front was failing him, and he was reeling.

He *had* to talk to Mariah. As the hours of darkness dwindled away and the early dawn rays filtered through his window, that was all he could focus on.

Andrian decided she had to know. Had to be aware of the danger she was in, the threat he'd brought to her simply because he hadn't been strong enough to resist her and couldn't seem to stay the fuck away.

Everything had gotten so fucking complicated, but he was

tired of keeping this secret from her. She'd proven herself to be smart and strong and capable. She could handle this, and she would help him, and they would figure out a solution that saved both their asses.

Together.

What a foreign word. Andrian had never allowed himself to even contemplate the possibility of an "us" that actually included him. But with his clear declaration of loyalty to Mariah at the *Porofirat*, followed shortly by his father's hateful words, he had no other choice but to run to her.

From the second she'd stepped out of that carriage, a part of him had known she would be both his damnation ... and his salvation.

And if yesterday had made one thing glaringly, painfully obvious to him, it was that he no longer hated Mariah Salis.

If he was honest with himself, he knew he'd never truly hated her. The anger he'd directed towards her was always just the loathing he felt for himself. He was weak; that much he knew. But he also recognized his flaws were not her fault.

Andrian was tired of running from the way she made him feel. He was tired of lying to himself, refusing to acknowledge it was more than just lust and great sex between them; it had always been more. While he still couldn't confess those feelings to her, maybe—just maybe—he could finally stop with all the lies that blanketed him heavier than the cursed shadows in his veins.

He tilted his head, noting the sunlight at his window had grown brighter. He knew the Armature—that *she*—would be heading down to the clearing to train soon.

Mariah had been confronted with a lot yesterday, and he knew her well enough to know she would want to blow off some steam. It presented him with the perfect opportunity to track her down and get her to listen, to finally make the confessions weighing heavily on his soul.

 Filled with resolve, Andrian pushed back the covers of his bed. He dressed himself quickly before slipping from his room. His eyes darted once to the gilded double doors across the hallway before he began his walk to that clearing in the game park.

Mariah was ignoring him. Andrian was sure of it.

 He'd never been a fan of the group style of training the others favored, preferring to work alone, as he did most things. Today, however, his determination to get close to her, to pull her away for just a minute, a *second*, had driven him towards the other Armature and the dark-haired female who laughed in their midst.

 Quentin and Trefor stared at him with expressions of slight bewilderment, but Sebastian, Drystan, and Feran gave him one look and tossed him a sparring sword, seamlessly working him into their training circle.

 Those three were always far too observant and empathetic for their own good. It was fucking annoying.

 Normally, Mariah could be found in the center of the sparring, joking and fighting with her Armature as if she'd been born to it, almost more than they had.

 In a way, he supposed she had.

 Today, however, when she'd stepped into that clearing a few minutes after them, she'd taken only a look at the sparring circle, her green eyes flashing over him, *through* him, before she moved quickly to grab Matheo. She pulled him away from the others to work through a cardio circuit and archery training. Matheo looked ready to grumble, up until the moment he realized it would be just him with her, just him receiving the full focus of her attention …

Andrian knew it was natural, woven into their souls and stamped on the very fiber of their beings like the tattoos that Marked them on their chests, the draw to her and the desire to seek as much time with her they could get. But that knowledge didn't stop him from grinding his teeth together angrily, his shadows curling at his feet, flooded by an urge to wipe the stupid, giddy grin from Matheo's face.

They'd gone about their workout, and Andrian had done his best to distract himself with the clang of steel and the sweet satisfaction of knocking Quentin on his ass three times in the sparring circle. Now, with the training winding down, Mariah and Matheo finally rejoined them. She sat on the ground, sipping slowly from one of the water skins they hauled out with them from the kitchens every morning, the rest of her Armature lounging around her in a loose semi-circle. She was dressed in all black, as usual for their morning training, and there was a faint sheen of sweat visible on her olive skin even in the chill late autumn air, her near-black hair braided down her back.

She looked fucking *delicious* like this. Raw, savage, feral. All the things about her that had taken him so off-guard, had set his world spinning on its axis.

In a smooth motion, she set her water skin down on the ground beside her and stood, the eyes of all seven men tracking her every move.

She had them all wrapped around her fucking middle finger, and Enfara damn her, she knew it.

The pull towards her was magnetic, and the second she was standing Andrian felt his feet begin to move. He took a single step towards her, easing himself closer to the edge of the semi-circle, no longer content to stand in the fringes, when her clear, melodic voice rang out across the clearing.

"I want you all to know that I plan to complete the bond with Trefor tonight. We've already spoken, and he's ready."

There were sounds of clapping and congratulations as the other members of the Armature turned to Trefor, his already-red cheeks staining even more pink as he looked at his queen, happiness shining in his blue-green gaze.

For Andrian, however, everything in his world stood still as his ears rang, a tidal wave rising in his blood.

She'd trained with Matheo all morning.

Not with Trefor.

When had she had time to speak with him? How much time was she spending alone with each of his *brothers*? Time he was completely unaware of?

Somewhere, a distant, more rational part of his mind whispered to him that he had no right to be jealous, that this was the way of an Onitan Queen and her Armature. They belonged to *her*, after all. The quiet voice even whispered a reminder to him that he'd pushed her towards them with his words in the library.

She did not belong to him.

But the words of his father, of Lord Donnet, filtered unwanted into his head.

"Whore."

"Slept her way through the entire town."

"Are you prepared to share her?"

Andrian's mind locked down on the last of those words, his fury seething to a boil.

No. *Fuck* that. There would be no sharing.

Fuck his role as an Armature. She was *his*.

And he would stake his claim.

Finally, while his brothers continued to pat Trefor on the

back and ooze their words of congratulations, Andrian caught Mariah's eye, her gaze surveying over him with an unreadable look. He let her read him, let all the dominance and rage and *things* he felt but wouldn't, couldn't, dwell on swirl through his own expression, loosening his shadows even more as they spilled into the air around his shoulders and twined further up his legs. They whipped and snapped like mini tornados, driven to madness by the chaos fueling his thoughts, spurred by the green-eyed she-devil standing before him.

With a deep inhale, he drew it all back into him, regaining his weak control. He pushed his shoulders back, rolling them once, before turning on his heel and stalking off into the deeper part of the woods, the parts that inched closer to the Attlehons, full of ancient secrets and empty of prying eyes.

The ruins were deep in the game park woods, likely some forgotten retreat of a long-passed queen. The structure was in a state of absolute decay, and the only sign it had once existed at all was the singular stone wall that still stood, vines and moss covering most of the gray surface.

Andrian walked right up to the wall, forcing his breath out through clenched teeth as his lungs heaved. His hands clenched and unclenched at his sides, every inch of his restraint melting away with each dragged inhale.

He froze as he heard soft steps behind him. It was the sound of someone who'd grown up in a forest, who knew how to move without so much as a whisper but wanted to be heard. He knew she'd been following him, of course, but hadn't heard her steps until now. Until she'd *wanted* him to hear.

Witch.

And then ... that voice.

"Andrian." She practically whispered to him, the sound surprisingly gentle. As if he was some wild beast in need of taming.

Yeah. Fuck that.

He held himself still, letting her take her steps closer, drawing her in to him like a moth to a flame. Then, when she was but a few feet away, he whirled, his shadows lashing out and wrapping themselves around her hands, her waist, her ankles, rooting her to the ground. As he finally let his eyes drop to hers, meeting the forest green gaze slowly filling with anger and a hint of confusion, a flood of questions, statements, and confessions went rushing into his head.

But he only asked one.

"*Why?*"

It was a simple question, but was also the only one that truly mattered to him.

Why?

Why Trefor?

Why had she been Chosen as the next queen?

Why had he been Marked and Selected?

Why couldn't she have been Royal?

Why was it that everything he wanted most in this life had to be so fucking *rotted* around the edges?

"Why what?" Her response was cold, the anger in her eyes now a simmering vat of green and gold and silver burning up at him.

Good. He would gladly take the heat of her wrath if it meant guaranteeing himself five minutes alone with her.

Not that he would let her know that, though. *Not yet.*

Andrian tilted his head slightly and stalked a step closer to her, watching her skin alight with the glow of her magic as her anger ran wild around her. The feeling of her silver-gold threads pushing into the air, twining up and out towards him, touching the slight wisps of his shadows he always kept loose around his shoulders had his blood instantly heating. It felt like someone was running a fingertip between his shoulder-blades, along his spine, scratching the places he could never quite reach. His cock twitched in response, his teeth grinding together as he clenched his jaw. He tilted his head at her and loosened the damper on his power just a little more, his shadows pressed harder against the light of her magic.

He had so many different ways he could answer her, but in that moment, he chose to go with the one that might actually succeed in opening the door for her to hear what he desperately needed to say.

The conflagration in her eyes began to soften to a mere candle, her magic also relaxed as it began to gleefully wind itself around his own. He took that as his sign; either she would answer him now, or she never would.

"Why did you run away from me at the ball last night?"

She blinked, her full attention fixated on him, the light of her magic pulsing stronger as it seeped into the brilliance of her irises. "Is *that* what you're so upset about?"

"No. Far from it. But I need to know the answer." He held her gaze, as wariness flickered over her expression. "Tell me where you went, and I'll tell you why I'm *truly* upset." His shadows squeezed her wrists, waist, and ankles harder at the word. She bared her teeth at him in response, just enough to crinkle the smoothness of her delicate, straight nose.

They stared at each other for several heartbeats, locked in a battle of wills. Finally, she broke first.

"Fine. If you're so *determined*." She paused, suddenly filled with a strange hesitation. "Donnet's words ... they got to me. I could ... could hear what they were whispering about me. About you. About us. Dancing there, together. And I ... I couldn't do it. I needed out, needed some space. So, I found some." Her gaze hardened once again as it clashed back with Andrian's. He knew his expression was slightly stunned, but he could hardly focus on controlling it; he was just glad she was speaking. "How nice of you to come check on me, by the way."

He knew she was trying to bait him. And if he was being honest, he would admit he almost fell for it. On any other day, he would've given in, played along with her little game of cat and mouse she appeared to love so much. He knew she wanted to pretend to be the alpha with him, the one in charge, all up until the moment she was caught and pinned in a corner, eyes wide and filled with lust.

Not today, though.

More of his magic seeped out from the darkness in his soul as he stalked closer to where he kept her rooted to the ground. It wasn't until he was standing over her, the sweet smell of her sweat drifting up to meet him, that he spoke.

"Yes, my *apologies* for that. I would've run after you, like a good little Armature, if only I hadn't been dealing with my father *threatening your life* because I had chosen *you*, and *only* you, before the entire continent. So please, *Your Majesty*, forgive me for the oversight. I'll try to be better next time."

Her jaw went slack, her eyes wide as they stared up at him.

A sick, twisted part of him was instantly aroused by her look of vulnerable confusion. She had never looked so ... open before.

"Your father ... threatened? *Me?*"

Andrian narrowed his gaze but loosened his hold on her, ever so slightly. "It wasn't the first time, either, princess. He threatened you the day I was Marked, the same day you were born into the world with your single thread of magic. He told me that if I ever let myself get Selected, he would make sure you never sat the throne. And now that I've proven myself too weak for even that, he has renewed his threat, except now it's that if I ever complete the bond with you, he'll not only end your life, but make me serve as your executioner."

He knew his voice had slipped into a gray-toned monotony; it was the only way he could force those words past his lips. But while he spoke, he'd taken a step closer to her, so he now stood close enough to her to feel her go utterly still. Even her breath caught in her throat, and her eyes shone with a mix of anger, frustration, and a new emotion that bothered him just as much as it had the first time he'd seen it in the library.

Fear. Fear of *him*.

He wanted to wipe it off her features, but ... he knew this was for the best. He knew she had to know what she was up against. She needed to be afraid of what would come for her here in this city, this palace, with *him*.

Andrian had woken that morning prepared to give her a reason to be fearful.

But he'd also been prepared to give her a reason to fight past it. To come out stronger than those who threatened her. Something deep inside him told him that if anyone could conquer that fear, it was Mariah Salis.

"But you know what, *nio*?" He leaned into her, slipping one hand behind her neck and the other to the small of her back, her toned body soft and warm as he pressed her to him. A silent thrill lanced through him when she did not fight him or draw away. "That is *never* going to happen. Because you are fucking *strong*, and more importantly, because the bond is something you will never have to worry about from me."

Andrian felt her tense in his arms, her muscles twitching as she prepared to shove him away. "Goddess, you are such a di—"

Before she could finish her sentence, he tightened his grip around her, securing her to him with his arms and his shadows, and whirled, spinning them in place so her back was now pressed against the ancient stone wall behind them, pushing her up into the worn surface as he caged her body with his own.

"I'm not done, *nio*. All that brings me to what *else* is wrong today," he continued, the feeling of her body pressed *just right* against his enough to threaten his sanity. He let a bit of that madness seep into his voice as he spoke again.

"I do not want you to bond with Trefor. I grew up with him, spent the last twenty-one years of my life training beside him as a brother, but just the *thought* of him being near you like that makes me want to slowly peel the skin from his fucking bones."

"Andrian ... what the actual *fuck* is wrong with you. Let me go—"

"*No*." The darkness that laced his voice, his soul, was all-consuming. He leaned in closer to her, pressing her further into the ancient stone, lowering his head so he could whisper against the soft shell of her ear. He could feel her pulse racing wildly, her breath panting against his cheek.

"Forget what I said the other day in the library. I've changed my mind. Just because I can't have you, doesn't mean the others—or *any* other—can." He pulled back slightly, looking down into the emerald of her eyes, burning like a forest fire. Her lips pursed into an angry snarl as she glared up at him.

"You have no *Goddess-damned* right to say that to me, Andrian. I am not yours. I have a duty to my kingdom. A duty I never wanted, but have been saddled with anyway, and I'm trying to make the most of it. So, if you don't *mind*, I would very much like to walk away now and forget that this conversation—that *you*—ever happened."

Distantly, Andrian knew he should've felt hurt by her words.

But because he was a sick, twisted fuck, all he felt was his dick pulse at the venom in her words, his impulse to press himself into her even harder, to claim her so she knew she was his without him having to speak those words. She seethed, and her eyes narrowed to slits, but he knew she felt it too. Felt him. Felt that incomprehensible spark leap between them, charging in the air, lightning and storm clouds all wrapped tightly beneath their skin. He leaned back down to her ear, his voice a molten rumble.

"You know what, *nio*? Fuck the kingdom. Fuck the Goddess. Fuck my family, too. I can't—*won't*—risk your life with some antiquated old ritual, but I won't share you either." Faster than a viper, he snaked a hand up and sank it into her hair. He yanked her head back, forcing her defiant stare to his once more. He snarled at her again, putting all his twisted longing into his next few words.

"And I don't care about your past, or your future, or any of it. Because you are fucking *mine*."

Andrian crushed his lips to hers, even though her teeth were still bared at him.

He instantly matched her fury with his own, their kiss devolving into a battle of teeth and tongue and lips and gasped curses.

Whenever he challenged her, she met him. She pushed back against his cold darkness with her brilliant light, and it drove him wild.

He knew then he would never stop craving this. Craving *her*.

He was just about to slide a hand down her body, slip a hand inside her wool and leather leggings to get to the hot wetness he knew waited for him, when the sound of *something* rustling in the woods ripped his attention away from her. Andrian froze, Mariah gasping beneath him as he pulled his mouth from hers, pressing into her even harder so she was all but hidden against that ancient stone wall.

No one should be out there, this deep in the game park.

That was, after all, the reason he'd led her here.

"What are you ..."

"*Shh, nio,*" Andrian whispered, his voice low, barely more than a shift in the breeze. "There's someone out there."

She went still beneath him for a single, long heartbeat, before she pushed against him, twisting around in his arms to try to get a look at the trees. He hissed at her through his teeth, but she only shot him a blazing glare. He could almost read her words in her eyes.

I've spent far more of my life in the trees than you. If there's something out there, I'll spot it first.

He held her gaze for another heartbeat, before rolling his eyes and relenting. He loosened his grip on her, and she turned and pressed her chest into the wall, peering her head around the corner, scouring the thick copse of trees surrounding them for signs of movement. There was nothing for several moments, and Andrian began to wonder if he'd imagined that sound. But then ...

There. A rustling in the trees, the sound of footfalls. A person running, trying to move quietly, but going so quickly that complete silence was impossible.

A woman burst from the underbrush, her features hidden behind a dark veil, her oddly styled silver gown gripped in her fists to keep it from tangling in her legs as she ran. She was obviously not from Onita, or anywhere Andrian had been in his lifetime.

Not that he'd been anywhere other than Onita, anyway. But her clothing was clearly *other*, the fashions unlike anything he'd ever seen. That wasn't what set him on edge, though.

What unnerved him the most was that Mariah had gone

utterly rigid beside him, a sharp inhale the only sound or movement she made. He chanced a glance away from the strange woman to see that her face was utterly pale, the skin pallid beneath her tan cheeks. She looked shocked, or maybe terrified.

But that made no sense; nothing about this woman sprinting through the woods seemed a threat, other than the fact she was currently in a part of the game park that no one ever wandered.

A shout wrenched Andrian away from his thoughts, his veins flooding with adrenaline.

That woman, it appeared, was not alone.

Mariah—and the woman—noticed it at the same time he did. The woman glanced over her shoulder sharply, and Andrian could've sworn that he heard her let out a low chuckle before she regathered her skirts and bounded off like a deer, heading deeper into the woods and toward the Attlehon Mountains beyond. Andrian watched her go for a second before his attention snapped back to the woods, another shout echoing.

He and Mariah held their breaths and their bodies utterly still as four guards, armed to the teeth and wearing the red and gold livery of House Shawth, barged through the trees, hacking off branches and brush. It was obvious their quarry was the silver woman, and they didn't even toss a glance in his and Mariah's direction before pressing onward into the woods, heading away from where the woman had bounded off not a moment earlier. Neither of them moved a muscle until well after the sound of those guards faded into the distance. It wasn't until the birds around them had resumed their chirping and the forest had settled back into its usual quiet activity that he finally relaxed the tension in his shoulders, the sunlight instantly pouring in around them as the shadows he'd unintentionally cast to shield them lifted. Mariah similarly stepped away from the wall, her hands shaking slightly, her skin still pale and seeped of color. She released a great exhale, dropping into a crouch before resting her head into the palms of her hands.

"Well," she said, her voice shaky. "Looks like I'm not the only one in this city someone wants dead."

Andrian didn't know whether he should laugh or growl in anger.

Instead, he chose to remain silent, not trusting his voice. He extended a hand to her, which she took, and led the way back towards the training clearing and the palace beyond.

CHAPTER 47

"If Ryenne actually believes I would ever be willing to apologize to that disgusting old *dick* who happens to be in control of my hometown, then she truly doesn't know me at all," Mariah seethed as she stalked along the expanse of windows in her living room.

Her *Porofirat*, with its strange and poor end, had been two days ago, and the queen was still working to placate the lords. Particularly Donnet.

But Mariah had no interest in placating anyone, despite her many frustrating conversations with Ryenne. Even Ksee seemed to recognize it as a lost cause, instead lingering in the corner of those meetings while watching Mariah with a disdainful look.

Mariah, now dressed in soft leggings and a black sweater, the entirety of her court gathered in the cavernous space of her suite, paced restlessly back and forth, every set of eyes in the room tracking her movements. Most of them were lounging about on the couches and other furniture, Feran and Delaynie the only two who perched instead on the stools at the island in the kitchen. Mikael was also in the kitchen, busying himself with assembling enough food to feed the hoard of people currently intruding upon Mariah's personal space.

Not that she truly minded their presence; all those in that room with her, both those Selected for her and those she'd chosen for herself, made her feel more comfortable than she'd felt since the night she'd drank too much whiskey with her family around a campfire in the quiet of the Ivory Forest.

Then, of course, there was *him*.

She refused to acknowledge him as he lurked in the shadows of one of the pillars at the edge of the living room. But she could feel his cold, tanzanite gaze on her, following her pacing steps as she worked her way through the events in the game park yesterday.

The silver woman, the same from the balcony at the *Porofirat*, running from guards in Shawth's livery.

The confession Andrian spat at her through clenched teeth. His possessiveness, his claiming, the all-consuming hunger written across his face.

That *kiss*.

She couldn't stop the shiver that raced down her spine, curling her toes and tightening her hands into fists.

Mariah stopped her pacing and fanned her gaze over the other's, momentarily snagging on Trefor, who sat on the couch closest to the windows and where she currently stood. His closely cropped hair was so pale it was almost white, and as she met his sea-green gaze, a grin burst across his face that nearly cracked her in half and had her giggling in return.

They'd bonded last night. She could feel that new bridge between their souls, beside the other four, his like gentle ocean waves, playful and restless. He was one of her youngest

Armature, right alongside Matheo at twenty-seven, yet the bonding ceremony had felt so ... *platonic*. Whatever reaction Sebastian had pulled from her during that first bonding hadn't replicated itself as intensely with the others. Or, perhaps it was only because she now knew what to expect, how to build the bridge between their minds without losing herself in the process.

Either way, she was glad. While the version of herself who'd run wild through the streets of Andburgh since her eighteenth birthday, desperate for freedom and autonomy and just *something* to make her feel like she was truly the one in control of her own life, would've gladly taken anything her warrior Armature would give her, the person she was now ...

It shocked her how much she'd changed in just a few short months.

Maybe it was because she'd become too fucked up by a dark-haired devil with shadows beneath his skin.

The continued feel of Trefor's stare on her pulled her back from her darkening thoughts. He was so full of light, of warmth, the opposite of Andrian in every way.

Down his bond, Mariah could almost feel the words dancing on his tongue. Finally, he spoke.

"Just so I understand ... why is apologizing to him completely off the table again?"

Mariah froze, her gaze turning molten.

"Trefor, I think if you weren't already bonded to me, I would chuck you off the balcony for that."

Twin tanzanite flames bore a hole into her back.

She ignored them.

Trefor went pale at her words, and Mariah felt immediate regret; he was too kind, too understanding. He didn't understand her plight with these lords. At least ... he didn't understand *yet*.

She spoke before he could. "But I think you'd be far too much of a hassle to replace at this point." She sighed. "Just ... trust me when I say that what he said doesn't warrant any apology from me. *Ever.*"

Mariah remembered that Trefor, who'd been stationed away along the edges of the throne room the night of the *Porofirat*, likely hadn't even heard the words exchanged between Lord Donnet, Mariah, and Andrian. He'd seen the commotion occur, sure; had seen Andrian draw his knife and elicit a sliver of blood from the lord's neck. But he'd not been privy to the words that caused the night to disintegrate into confusing chaos.

There was a moment of silence as the group processed Mariah's words before a flash of red hair in the midday sun drew her attention. Quentin leaned forward where he sat on the couch, running a hand through his flaming shock of hair, a cocky smirk on his face, and proceeded to break the tension in the air in a way only he could.

"So, those two Kreah girls. They're hot, right?"

Mariah only slumped her chin against her chest and heaved a sigh. Out of the corner of her eye, she saw Sebastian pick up one of the many pillows from the couch and fling it across the space, hitting Quentin squarely on the side of the head. Disgruntled noises rose in response from Quentin's side of the couch, but he quieted and his face returned to his usual grin when he caught Matheo's eye.

Matheo, who'd stood on the dais behind Mariah when the Kreah party was being introduced. Who, besides Sebastian and Andrian, had gotten perhaps the best look at Kiira and Rylla as they'd formally introduced themselves to Mariah and Ryenne. Mariah didn't miss the smirk that spread over Matheo's face. Nor did she miss the wink he cast in Quentin's direction as he nodded, just once, as if trying to send a subtle response to Quentin's question.

A frustrated sound ripped from her chest, something between a growl and a groan.

"Can you all please keep your dicks in your pants for more than five seconds?"

That voice immediately sent ice rushing through Mariah's veins.

"Well, that depends, Mr. Broody," Ciana responded, twisting in her seat to face Andrian where he still sulked in the shadows. "We will only if you can."

Mariah froze.

The entire room froze.

She could've sworn that everyone could hear the pounding beat of her heart against her ribcage.

But then Andrian did something she could've never expected.

He *laughed*.

It was more like a huff, the sound surprisingly warm, brushing across her skin in a way that heated her blood and left goosebumps in its wake, the ghost of a smile dancing across his full lips. His eyes darted almost imperceptibly to Mariah, something like humor in his blue gaze.

"Fair enough," his low voice rumbled, and that was that. Andrian moved out of the shadows and sat himself in the last open chair in the room, leaning forward on his knees and clasping his hands in front of him before leveling an expectant stare at Mariah.

This time, the sound she released was a full groan, confused and frustrated. She moved to sit beside Sebastian on one of the couches, sinking deep into the plush fabric as she leaned forward, her posture similar to Andrian's as she pressed her face into her hands.

Mariah allowed herself three full breaths before she lifted her head and began to speak to her court.

"There is much more going on here than just one pissed off lord."

"So, to recap," Trefor said. "The Royals pissed you off, so then you pissed *them* off, and then Andrian's father—*our* Andrian—issued a threat to your life. Not only that, but you have more magic than just what you received at the Choosing, and you still aren't sure where it comes from and what it is." He paused and looked around at the rest of the gathered court. "Did I miss anything?"

"Thanks for the summary, Trefor," Andrian said, his voice dry.

Sebastian spoke next. "But seriously, Mariah." His gaze darted once to Andrian before returning to her. "This is ... *serious*. There has been a threat made to your *life*. Are you sure we can't take this to Ryenne? Insist that Laurent be detained, or at the very least *questioned*? And Andrian, you're my brother; you know that. But you—all of us—swore an oath to protect our queen. If that is compromised, you must tell us. Now."

Andrian's cold, tanzanite eyes glinted, his teeth baring in a snarl as he turned his attention to Sebastian. Shadows danced and drifted around his broad shoulders, the entire room going dark in a matter of seconds.

"Enough of that." It was Drystan this time. "Sebastian, I know you mean well. But Andrian is one of us. With this threat, we cannot start suspecting each other—that will only make it easier for anyone who wishes harm to our queen to get to her." He paused, and then added quietly, "They already almost succeeded once."

No one had a response to that. Everyone could feel it in the air, and Mariah felt the emotions running down the five bonds: feelings, and memories of feelings, from that night, panic and fear that, despite their lifetime of training, someone—or, rather, some*thing*—had almost gotten to her.

Thank the Goddess she'd long ago refused to be dependent on the protection of men.

"We don't need to relive that night," said Mariah. "I survived. I'm safe. We're moving on from it." She paused. "As far as bringing this to Ryenne … Lord Laurent is one of the Royals. He carries almost as much power in the kingdom as Shawth. Certainly more than Ryenne herself. When it comes down to it, who do you think the politicians at court will believe: one of their own, or a girl they still view as an outsider pretending to be queen?"

Every Armature in the room averted their gaze, the air tense and silent.

Drystan, once again, was the one to break the quiet. "I will move on. However, we still want to help." A murmur of acquiescence ran through the room. "Maybe we aren't the ones to assist you in navigating the politics of being queen; that's what your Ladies are for. But maybe the mystery of your magic is something we *can* help with. If you'll let us."

Mariah raised her gaze to meet his brown stare. Drystan was so much like a lion—a natural leader, all golden strength and hidden wisdom.

"I'll always welcome your help."

Drystan let out a breath. "Good. Because I've had some thoughts." He paused. "We've tried to explore any historical bullshit that might lead us to something only to come up with nothing every time. But ... what if the answer isn't one found in history?"

Beside Mariah, Sebastian frowned. "I'm not following, Drystan. Explain."

Drystan's stare was dry, yet there was a feverish glint hidden in their tawny depths. "If it's not something found in history or from the sacred texts ... what if it's family magic? Something long repressed that, out of coincidence, happened to reemerge in you? Magic in Onita has always been a bit mysterious; no one quite knows how it works. Families can go generations without any gifts, and then suddenly a son will be born tossing fireballs from his cradle."

What if it's family magic?

That question struck Mariah like a blow, sending her reeling. The strange conversation with the silver woman on the balcony at the *Porofirat* leaped into her mind, the mysterious words twisting and snagging in her thoughts.

"You know of the Ginnelevé, your Majesty. Do not forget her. The journal you have been gifted shall guide you, but let what is inside of it lead you."

"Oh, Goddess."

All eyes in the room snapped to her. She could only gaze blankly ahead, her mind racing. Then, her movements slow, she stood from the couch and padded softly into her bedroom, heading straight for the side of her bed. She dropped to her knees and slid a hand beneath the heavy mattress, drawing out the *Ginnelevé* book where she'd kept it hidden, the gray cover embossed in silver.

Mariah hadn't opened it since that day she'd read from it, driven by a wave of curiosity, then chased away by feelings of terror at the words she'd found within. She'd fought desperately to push those words from her mind, but had still kept the book hidden, touching it only once to move it to a hidden recess in her closet while her room had been cleaned and cleared of all traces of the Uroboros. She'd replaced it back beneath her mattress on the same night she stopped staying with Andrian, some instinct urging her to keep it close and safe and hidden.

She walked back into the living room, the weight of the stares of her court like lead upon her skin, and when she stood back before them she flipped open the book to the page she'd first turned to, when she'd sat comfortably on the window seat in her room. Back when she'd still felt excitement for her new life, before lingering uncertainty and fear had crept its way into every shadow of her mind.

In a soft voice, she read the words out loud to the room:

"I dreamed of silver and gold flames, of leathery wings both blazing and shadowed.

I dreamed of that which was feared, saving us all."

The room was so quiet, the near-silent wing beats of Attlehonian Eagles, great birds of prey that prowled the skies just beyond the spires of the palace, could be heard filtering in through the open windows.

"Mariah," said Sebastian, his voice carefully controlled. "What is that?"

She lifted her gaze from the pages, her mind blank as she retold the story from the night before her twenty-first birthday, the night before her life changed forever, her voice lacking emotions as that careful wall in her mind threatened to crack and break and fall.

"It belonged to my mom. When she gave it to me, she said it contained wisdom accumulated over many generations. That whenever I felt truly lost, it would tell me everything I needed to know." She paused, looking back at the book, inspecting the binding and the pages more closely. "Although ... it looks to be in awfully good shape for a supposedly ancient book, doesn't it?"

No one answered her. They only watched her with steadily growing curiosity, waiting for her to piece together the missing links in her head.

"I met a strange woman on the night of the *Porofirat*. She found me on a balcony. Told me the journal I'd been gifted would guide me, but I needed to let whatever was inside it lead me." She glanced at a wild blue stare. "I then saw the same woman being chased by Shawth's men through the game park." Andrian narrowed his eyes but said nothing, even as murmurs of excited confusion raced through the rest of the gathered group.

Mariah supposed she was the only one who felt dread unspooling in her stomach, right there with the threads of her magic.

She fanned the pages, the words on them blurring together, until she landed on the final entry. She didn't recognize the handwriting, but tucked in the binding was a folded piece of parchment. She carefully removed the paper before setting the book onto the small table beside her, the room falling unearthly silent once again. With trembling hands, she unfolded it, and when she saw the words written neatly on the page, she felt her heart drop completely out of her chest.

The handwriting ... it was her mother's.

But that wasn't what shocked her completely. She'd figured her mother had left an entry or two in the book before passing it to her.

What shocked her was that the page wasn't a journal entry, but a letter.

A letter addressed to Mariah.

Mariah inhaled deeply, the air thick with heavy anticipation, and began to read the letter out loud.

To my daughter, the brilliant light of my life, Mariah:

If you are reading this, then everything I felt and thought from the moment you came into this world is true, and now a reality.

Until now, I have not even permitted myself to think it. Thoughts can be just as deadly as words, and those that lurk in the dark know how to draw even our most suppressed memories out to be used against us. So, to protect you, I allowed myself this letter, using the last drop of magic that I carry in my veins to create a place to tell you the full truth, a place to seal away all my suspicions and knowledge from even myself, until the day comes when you are strong enough to fulfill the destiny I saw for you.

The first of my confessions to you, my daughter, is about that magic. In our family, it has always manifested differently. Our gifts are remarkable, and utterly unique from any other on the continent.

This is because our magic is not a gift from Qhohena.

It is a gift from her sister, Zadione.

And everything that has ever been taught to you about the silver goddess, the Goddess of Death and Darkness, is a lie.

The name "Ginnelevé" belonged to my mother, and her mother before her, to me. It is the name of our female line, never spoken but never forgotten. The first Ginnelevé was Xara's equivalent, hand-chosen instead by Zadione to serve as advisor to the new Golden Queen, the first and only Silver Priestess. She was meant to be the physical embodiment of our Goddess on the earth, the other side to the same coin, the balance to the scales.

For Zadione is—and has always been—so much more than the Goddess of Death. She is also the Goddess of the

Wilds, of passion, of free will, of everything untamed. She is Qhohena's necessary equal, as important to the world as her sister.

For what is life, of living, without the knowledge and wildness and uncertainty of death?

But then ... Xara lost the First War. The true knowledge of what Zadione is to this world was lost, just as she was taken from it. The blame for the loss was passed to her, and the only reminder of her existence was her silver moon still hanging in the sky and the kernel of her magic still flowing in the first Ginnelevé's veins.

That same magic was passed down from mother to daughter, weakening with each generation but always there, guiding us and keeping us hidden from the darkness that has steadily been seeping into this world.

I am the last Silver Priestess. And you, my light, are our last heir.

The night you were born, I felt something change. The small drop of silver power I carried roared in exaltation, as if celebrating the return of something resembling itself. And when I held you in my arms for the first time, I looked into your eyes and I knew. Somehow, Zadione had come back into the world, just briefly enough to bless the last of her chosen line with a power I could not yet comprehend.

You carry something in your veins that our world has not yet seen, something that perhaps has been forgotten since the days the gods and goddesses walked upon the earth themselves.

I do not know yet what you will have to do, but whatever it is, you must succeed.

I love you more than I love the stars in the sky, my light. Never forget that.

Lisabel Ginnelevé Salis

A single teardrop slid off Mariah's cheek as she finished reading, the paper fluttering to the floor as she sank to her knees.

CHAPTER 48

The room erupted into chaos just as Mariah's knees hit the white marble floor.

Everyone was speaking at once, the sound a cacophony of resonant voices blurring together until they were indistinguishable from each other. She could sense the sudden nearness of other bodies as a few members of her court shot from their seats and clambered to her.

Numbness slid like sludge through her limbs, and she barely noticed the barrage of movement around her.

Mariah felt more than saw Sebastian and Trefor suddenly appear before her face, her vision blurry and unseeing. She forced herself to focus on the hazel of Sebastian's gaze, the haze lifting just enough for her to make out his panicked expression. Behind him, Ciana and Delaynie pushed as close as they could, the rest of her Armature standing from their seats and taking lurching steps forward. Concern was etched on every face, but all those looks did was spark a flame of annoyance deep in her gut.

That flame ignited into an inferno as her court kept

coming, coming, coming closer to her, crowding the space around her body. The air in her lungs grew thick and heavy, as if that blaze inside her belly was eating away all the oxygen available to her. It was becoming too much, *too much* …

Her lungs began to seize, her heart hammering in her chest.

Yet still they all pushed in closer, and she … she couldn't find the words to stop them. She needed air; she needed space; she needed …

Her eyes lifted, instinct and magic reaching out for the only one in that room who was not crowding her in rushing panic. Eyes of forest green collided with those of tanzanite blue, and for one fleeting second the world paused, and she could breathe, a momentary reprieve from the panic laying heavily over her skin.

The moment was gone too fast, and the peace around Mariah snapped, shoving her back into the chaos closing in on her. She gasped, the weight of those around her once again threatening to drag her under, and for the first time since arriving in the capital she let all of her walls and masks and facades fall away. She lifted her gaze again, giving Andrian a look of pure desperation, letting him see all the panic gnawing and clawing and cleaving her in two.

A rumbling voice answered her plea, cutting through the din of voices.

"*Get out*. All of you." Those words—that *voice*—were both Mariah's temptation and her salvation.

The room fell instantly silent, the bodies around her stilling in surprise.

Sebastian, still planted directly in front of Mariah, whirled on his heels and stood, visibly bristling as he faced Andrian.

"Who are you to order us out, Armature? You forget your place. I am still your captain. She needs us. She needs her *bonded* Armature." He nearly spat the word at Andrian, but the only sign of Andrian's answering anger were the tiny shadowy tendrils that leaked from his shoulders.

"Sebastian. Stop." Somehow, Mariah found her voice, shocked out of her stupor by Andrian's intervention and Sebastian's outburst.

Sebastian spun back around, glancing down at her with a look of incredulity in his eyes. "M, you can't be serious," he said, his voice turning panicked. "Let us help you. We'll figure out what this note means, what we can do, how we can bring it to Ryenne and Ksee, *together*—"

"Do not presume to know what I want or need, Sebastian," Mariah interrupted, her tone cold as she fought to regain some semblance of control. "I owe you so much—my life, my future, *everything*—but letting you dictate how I decide to cope with impossible information like this is not how I intend to repay you. So don't make me ask you again."

Sebastian paled slightly and leaned back on his heels as if he'd been struck, but he fell silent.

Ciana—bright, brave, observant Ciana—noticed the shift in the room, her amber eyes darting from Mariah to Sebastian to Andrian then back to Mariah. A look of resolve filled her face, and she shouldered her way past Trefor, coming to stand beside Sebastian, grasping the tanned skin and corded muscle of his upper arm.

"Come on, let's go. Trust her; it will be okay. She just needs space." She tugged lightly on his arm, attempting to wrench his gaze from Mariah.

Sebastian continued to stare at his queen for far longer and with much more intensity than Mariah wanted, but eventually he relented. He shut his eyes and turned, allowing Ciana to drag him from the room. The rest of the Armature, along with Delaynie, followed behind them, each casting worried glances over their shoulders at Mariah as they left her, kneeling and frazzled on the cold marble floor, her mother's letter still lying there on the ground.

The last of them filtered out of her rooms, Feran chancing one last glance back at Mariah before grabbing the handle to her door, pulling it shut behind him with a soft *click*. The sound echoed through the room with the reverberating *boom* of an avalanche.

And then it was just Mariah.

Alone, save for Andrian, who still leaned against the pillar across the room, arms crossed and expression unreadable.

They stared at each other in silence.

Mariah still knelt on the floor. She could feel the tips of her toes beginning to go numb, her limbs tingling from being folded for so long, but she didn't move. She held herself completely still as she met Andrian's gaze, refusing to be the one who broke the silence and stillness between them.

To her utter shock, he was the one to speak first, his voice far rougher than it was mere minutes earlier when he'd ordered the rest of her court from the room.

When she'd *let* him order her court from the room.

"How are you?"

What? She could only blink at him, shock evident in her gaze.

He sighed, hanging his head slightly before peeking back up through thick lashes and the black curtain of hair that fell over his forehead. His expression was almost ... *soft*, and filled with evident, genuine concern.

What in the Goddess's name is happening?

He released his crossed arms from his chest and stalked towards her, his steps light and silent. When he was before her, standing right in front of that piece of paper on the ground, he further stunned her into a silence she wasn't sure she would be able to come out of. He sank to his knees in front of her, her eyes tracking him the whole way down, a foreign feeling prickling beneath her skin.

Andrian picked up the letter with something almost akin to reverence and read it over to himself silently. Mariah's eyes never left him, not even daring to dart her gaze away for a moment, fearful that whatever was happening here would vanish in a whiff of smoke. With the same painful gentleness, Andrian set the letter back down on the ground behind him, leaving the space between them so empty that it scratched at Mariah's already frazzled nerves.

He then brought his gaze back up to hers, those stunning eyes still filled with that same strange, foreign expression as he cocked his head to the side.

When he spoke, it was with a voice that was so patient and gentle it hardly sounded like him at all.

"What do you need, *nio*?"

She felt her eyes widen, instantly going on high alert, searching his expression for any hint of what he might actually be after.

"What do you mean?" Her own voice was still flat and cold.

He sighed, his brows furrowing slightly. He reached out a hand, running the rough pads of his fingertips down the side of her face, tucking a loose strand of hair behind her ear before gripping her chin tightly, forcing her to hold his gaze.

"Tell me what you need." Not a question this time. A command.

Her eyes went from wide to narrow as she ripped her chin from his grip. "What makes you think you have anything that I need?"

"I see it on you, princess. You're barely holding yourself

together. You need help. So, I'm going to ask you one more time: what do you need?"

The air between them went tense and silent as she met his stare, her mind slowly spinning. It wasn't what she needed, not really, but there was only one thing she would let him give her.

"Fine. Do you know what I need?" She forced a coy smile to play across her lips, the familiar flirtatious mask she'd donned far too often back in Andburgh falling into place over her features. She rocked forward, onto her hands and knees, and crawled slowly across the small distance separating them. He didn't move a muscle as she slid up his body and into his lap, her knees falling to either side of his hips, pressing her chest to his. Sliding a hand behind his neck, her fingers tangled in the black strands at the base of his neck as she leaned close to his ear.

"You once told me you would be a distraction for me. In fact, you told me that was *all* you'd ever be for me." She slid out her tongue and slowly dragged it along the outer shell of his ear, a thrill racing through her when she felt him tense beneath her, felt him instantly begin to lengthen and harden where she was pressed against his hips.

"This is what I need, Andrian," she said, purring his name. "A *distraction*."

Sparks ignited where she was pressed against him, the tension in the air slipping into something viscous.

And then ... he *chuckled*.

He suddenly relaxed beneath her, a casual hand resting on her hip while the other went to the back of her neck, pulling her gently away from his ear.

She knew the shock she felt was as clear as day on her expression, but she didn't care.

"You're right," he said. "I did once say I would only ever be a distraction for you. But then you went and turned yourself into *mine*. And now, I think we both know that I will never just be a distraction to you again." He paused, a slow smile spreading across his perfect, full lips. "I also distinctly remember calling your bluff. Well, guess what, *nio*—I'm calling your bluff again, right now." As quickly as it had spread, his smile fell away. "A distraction isn't really what you need; not anymore."

Mariah could barely feel herself breathing. Somewhere, deep within her, his words were settling in, combining with the other events of that evening, that day, that week, of every single Goddess-damned moment since she'd received that summons from the queen nearly eight weeks ago.

And in that place within her, she felt her innermost barriers, those guarding the most vulnerable and desperate parts of her, begin to shake and crumble and fall.

Andrian brought the hand on her hip up and cupped her face, the rough pads of his thumbs sweeping across her cheekbones in a movement so achingly gentle that Mariah's heart nearly fell out of her chest. His eyes were like warm hearths of blue flame, filled with concern as he stared her down, the fire of his gaze burning away the fraying remnants of the barricades deep in her soul.

"What do you need?" His voice was impossibly quiet and warm and *safe*.

And with that repeated question, the last of the walls within her came crumbling down. A floodgate opened, and every emotion she'd ever shoved down came rushing out at once.

On a whispered sob, she told him the one thing she knew that could maybe make things right, the one thing she also knew she couldn't have.

"I need my mom."

CHAPTER 49

When he'd asked Mariah what she needed, Andrian had told himself he would rip apart the heavens until he found the gods and goddesses themselves to make her happy.

But when she shuddered apart in his arms and requested her mother, he suddenly realized that some needs were never meant to be met.

As he'd held her to his chest, rocking gently as she'd sobbed into his dark shirt, he thought about how easy it was to forget how young she was. Sure, she'd reached the age their society considered to be an adult, and she held herself with such fierce grace and determination that could command a room the second she entered it. But she was still barely twenty-one, still trying to figure out a life away from the only home and town she'd ever known.

Feeling his feet beneath him begin to grow numb, he stood, her long, tan legs wrapping around his torso as the emotional dam within her continued to quietly sunder. Gripping her even tighter to him, he padded from the great living space and into her bedroom, using his foot to push the door closed behind him with a soft *click*. He walked to the edge of her massive bed, laying her down gently on the plush white comforter, peeling her off him even as the sudden loss of her warmth struck him like a dagger to the heart.

She only rolled onto her side, clutching a pillow to her chest, and continued to cry.

Utterly unacceptable.

Andrian quickly shucked off his boots and crawled into the bed beside her, pulling that pillow from her grasp and letting her use him instead.

He wasn't sure when—or what—had changed within him.

Maybe it was when Lord Donnet had insulted her. Maybe it was when she'd been so ready and willing to get on her knees for him and his shadows in the quiet of the library. Maybe it was when she'd sought him out for relief after someone had tried to end her life with a demon born from the darkest legends of their world.

Or maybe, it was the very second she'd stepped out of that carriage, so resplendent and ethereal in a gown of liquid gold, a zap—of magic, of fate, of who the *fuck* knew—lancing across his skin as she'd met his gaze.

Not that the *when* really mattered, anyway.

All he knew now was that he would go to the ends of the earth for this wild girl crafted from moonlight and the darkness between the stars, even if it killed him.

That night, he waited until all her tears were shed, her wracking sobs calming into quiet, gentle shudders.

It was then that he finally spoke.

"Tell me about her."

And so, he let his queen tell him stories about Lisabel Salis.

Mariah spoke of long rides on horseback through the Ivory

Forest in the spring, of afternoon picnics in a glade of white birch trees as light filtered through a green canopy still young and new with the transformational magic of the vernal season. She spoke of Lisabel's remarkable healing skills, her touch with her patients the very best in the village.

"It was always a shock for people to discover that she had no magic," Mariah said, chuckling softly to herself before falling silent. "But I guess that wasn't entirely the truth."

She told Andrian of how her mother had always defended her daughter, even though the people of Andburgh never approved of Mariah's rejection of the boxes society tried to shove her in. Never, not once, had Lisabel forced Mariah to be anyone other than wholly herself, no matter how wild and unruly and fiery—and, sometimes, dark—that girl had been.

Rage boiled in his chest when Mariah told him the story of Donnet, how he'd stolen from her family that night when she was young under the guise of tax collection. How her mother had been forced to separate from a dagger long owned by her family ... and how Mariah had risked every shot at freedom she might've had by stealing that dagger back. For her family, for her future ... and, above all, for her mother.

Eventually, Mariah's stories grew further apart, until they stopped altogether. She'd fallen into a deep sleep, curled against Andrian's chest as if his presence were the only thing in the world that could bring her peace.

It was at that moment Andrian knew he loved her, heart and soul.

It was also the moment he knew he could *never* accept the bond from her. Could never be what she needed him to be.

Her life was far too precious.

As he slowly joined her in unconsciousness, content in both his new internal acceptance and the feel of the soft, warm shape pressed against him, he felt a presence both old and young, light and dark, flit along the edges of his mind just long enough to whisper words he would later convince himself were nothing more than a hallucination.

Love is a weakness, Andrian Laurent.

CHAPTER 50

The weakening early winter sun was hazy overhead, the chill in the air indicative of the colder weather rapidly approaching. Winters in the coastal capital of Verith were mild, but this was still Onita, and the cold was always a looming threat. Mariah, for the first time in weeks, sat astride Kodie, the warmth and smell and sound of his hooves on the paved street the only familiar thing around her.

Just like that day, which now felt like another lifetime, when she'd made her way to the palace for the Choosing, the procession she was now a part of felt eerily like a funeral march.

Funny enough, the entire purpose of it was to build excitement and anticipation for her impending coronation. To showcase the queen apparent to the people of the city, put her on display for all their judgment and curiosity.

Not that her coronation was set to happen anytime soon. She couldn't ascend the throne until she'd bonded with her entire Armature, until those bridges had drained the last of the magic from Ryenne and Mariah bore the full power of the queen. As it were now, she'd yet to complete her bond to Feran, and of course there was the matter of a certain dark-haired pain in her ass to contend with.

Although, he was *far* from a pain in her ass the other night, when he'd held her close and listened to her tell stories of her mother and her family until her voice was hoarse and she'd fallen asleep with the soft light of dawn filtering in through her window.

"Mariah." Ryenne's lilting voice pulled her from her thoughts. The queen rode beside Mariah on a white mare, resplendent in golden tack decorated with the sigil of Ryenne's reign: two black crescent moons, overlapping at their base, across a field of gold. Ryenne rode sidesaddle, her shimmering midnight-blue gown accenting the brightness of her eyes and the silver now streaking her blonde waves.

It wasn't lost on Mariah that each time she bonded with another of her Armature, the queen aged a decade.

Ryenne continued, "This parade is for you. Please, do remember to smile and at least *look* like you are having a good time."

Mariah grimaced, but the sharp glare from the queen had her turning her lips up into a forced smile as she gazed out at the gathered crowds.

Ryenne was right, after all. This parade *was* for her, even if she didn't want it. She'd been formally presented to the Royals, to the lords of Onita and the other nations of the continent, to emissaries and ambassadors and merchants. But the people she was to rule one day had yet to truly see her, to have their opportunity to mete judgment on their future monarch. So, Ryenne and Ksee had insisted on the arrangement of this parade, this presentation to the people of Verith so Mariah could be peeled back, layer by layer, and scrutinized by yet another group of people who would never truly know her.

The one thing she'd refused to concede on, however, was her clothes.

Ksee had made her best, sour attempt at forcing Mariah to dress similarly to Ryenne, in a dress which, according to Ksee, was befitting of Mariah's power and station in the kingdom. If the priestess had her way, Mariah would be dolled up in that gown, riding sidesaddle on a docile beast of their choosing as they dragged her down the winding, hilly streets of Verith.

Naturally, Mariah had agreed to no such thing, and with Ryenne staying out of the debate, Ksee had eventually conceded, a look of pure venom in her eyes as flames danced on her fingertips.

Which was why Mariah was now seated on Kodie in her worn, comfortable black leather saddle. She wore black riding leathers, tucked into ankle boots of thick and shining onyx leather, her grandfather's dagger strapped to her thigh with a new garter of dyed burgundy and detailed with gold threading. As a top, she wore a white tunic, more gold threaded through the fabric, its long, billowing sleeves comfortable and tapered to her wrists. A beautiful cloak of brilliant golden fabric was fastened across her back, draped over her saddle and Kodie's haunches, secured to her throat with a fastener designed to look like the wings of a dragon.

Wings just like those on her grandfather's dagger. Just like those of the beasts in that painting she'd found in the abandoned gallery. Just like the tattoo that Marked the chests of her Armature, directly over their hearts.

Ksee, of course, had hated every single detail of Mariah's appearance, calling it too masculine for an Onitan Queen and not far from an abomination of Xara's crown.

Ryenne, however, had only smiled softly.

Then there was Andrian, who'd grinned like a demon from Enfara at the sight of her.

Cheers from the crowd pulled Mariah back to the present.

"Long live the queen!"

"We love you, Queen Ryenne!"

"Please, don't abandon us, Your Majesty!"

All the loving cries echoing from the gathered Verithians were for Ryenne. No one seemed to recognize Mariah, or even know her name.

She thought she would be bothered by it, but really, all she felt was ... ambivalence.

Until she remembered her promise to Ciana, that she had the power to create a better world than the one they currently had.

It would be hard to bring about a revolution when no one knew who she was.

Ryenne must've also noticed the shouts and cries around them. They quickened their pace until the street opened into a massive crossroad; the road forming a circle around an empty, grassy knoll. The whole of the square was ringed in buildings of tawny stone that were favored in Verith, the air stuffy with the feeling of people pressing in too close. The queen led them forward until they reached the knoll, and then brought the entire procession—which consisted of Ryenne, Mariah, Ksee, and the Ladies and Armatures of both courts—to a halt, the group falling into place as Ryenne raised her head and hands to address the crowd.

As Mariah moved Kodie to stand beside the queen's white mare, the hairs along the back of her neck suddenly stood on edge, the magic in her soul unspooling and winding together into ropes of light in her veins. Her instincts, drilled into her by her father, were on edge and screaming, quickening her heart and sharpening her senses.

This place, no matter how safe Ryenne and Ksee claimed

the city to be, was far too exposed for so many people important to Onita to stand together on display.

Ryenne spoke, not seeming to notice the threat Mariah felt pulsing in the air around her.

"People of Verith!"

A cheer roared up from the crowd, lemmings begging for attention from their queen. Ryenne waited a moment for the cacophony to die down before continuing, her voice strong and echoing around the square.

"Thank you all for coming today to celebrate a momentous time in our nation's history, a moment which has only occurred nine times before."

The cheers this time were deafening, and Mariah's pulse ticked up faster.

Get this over with, Ryenne ...

"Today, you are all being given the first opportunity to set your eyes upon the queen apparent, the next bearer of the Goddess's magic, the one who will lead Onita into the new age of this world." Ryenne turned her blue eyes on Mariah, and Mariah could've sworn she saw a hint of sadness in their depths.

Maybe she, like Ciana, was hopeful Mariah would be the one to right the wrongs that had been allowed to fester in their world for far too long.

Mariah worried for a moment that all these people were starting to put way too much faith in her.

"It is with the greatest honor and privilege that I present to you the Queen Apparent of Onita, the next Lady of Verith, Mariah Salis—"

A soft *whish* and a *thunk* through the air cut Ryenne's speech short, her words falling like heavy raindrops over stunned, silent ears as they all took in the scene playing out too slowly before them.

Before Mariah could even twist in Kodie's saddle, Ryenne's blood-curdling scream carved into the air like a knife.

Directly behind Mariah was one of Ryenne's Armature, a dark-skinned, mountain of a man named Cedoric. He'd ridden behind the two women during the entire procession, seated upon a massive blood bay stallion, a great sword slung across his wide back and his dark eyes watchful. His presence was a comfort to Mariah as they'd paraded themselves through the exposed city streets.

Now, a thick arrow erupted from the center of his chest, its white fletching splattered with ruby-red blood. The sounds of his chokes and gurgles hammered against Mariah's ears. He reached a hand to grip the shaft, his eyes wide, before darting his dark gaze to his queen, her heart-wrenching cries still ringing into the air.

Just then, something whizzed past Mariah's head again, and a clang on the *lunestair* light post beside her had Kodie rearing up, startled into movement. With a choking shriek, Mariah leaned forward and wrapped her hands around his neck, gripping him tightly to keep from slipping from her saddle and down his back. Her eyes shot over her shoulder to the post, to the grass beneath it, and she saw another white-fletched arrow lying there, stark against the rich green. Another *whish*, and a third arrow embedded itself in the lawn at Kodie's feet, this time just barely missing its mark.

Which, she realized with a sudden jolt, was *her*.

Kodie's hooves slammed back down into the grass, his panicked snorts and whinnies stirring the other horses into a frenzy, as a fourth arrow blitzed again past Mariah, this time hitting a target behind her with another wet *thud* and a groan. Searing pain suddenly lanced through Mariah's shoulder, racing down a bond in her mind that whispered of the sea, and with another cry she grabbed hold of Kodie's reins, collecting him into her just like they'd practiced so many times, and whirled him around to meet Trefor's blue-green gaze, his expression twisted in pain.

Trefor—kind, gentle, young, patient Trefor—who now had a massive arrow protruding from his left shoulder.

Mariah was nearly doubled over from the pain racing down their bond, her breaths gasping, and she frantically reached for that bridge between their souls.

She wasn't sure exactly how she did it, but an instinct driven by self-preservation wrapped itself around the sea-green and gold bond connecting her to Trefor, slamming a wall down across the bridge. The second she severed their connection, the onslaught of pain finally ceasing, the only color she saw was red.

Mariah whipped her head up and twisted in her saddle, looking for the source of those arrows. Her eyes narrowed, and she scanned the roofline, threads of both gold and silver now snapped and spun through her veins and in the air around her. For the first time since that initial meeting with the Royals, when the uncontrolled brilliance of her magic had killed a man and blinded another, she gave in to the sweet pull and whisper of the magic. Its reins cut, those threads filled every fiber of her being, sharpening her vision and heightening her sense of smell, the sweet, metallic crisp of blood touching her nose and tongue.

Then, she saw it.

It was quick, but with her sharper vision, she somehow caught it. The flash of a black hooded figure, a quiver of white-fletched arrows strapped to their back, the sharp tip of a longbow. They sat atop one of the many buildings lining the square, the deep facade of the storefront offering the perfect slot of protection from the scouring eyes in the courtyard down below. Mariah's rage burned hotter than an inferno as she wheeled Kodie again to face the rest of her Armature, Feran and Matheo already tending to Trefor.

The placement of that arrow, while deep in his flesh, didn't appear to have struck anything vital. With quick attention from a healer, Mariah was sure enough he would live.

Which meant she could focus her own attention in that moment on what she truly sought.

"Matheo." His bright hazel eyes snapped up to meet hers, his hands drenched in Trefor's blood. "Get him back to the palace and to a healer. Now." Matheo nodded once before pulling Trefor up from the ground, slinging his uninjured arm over his shoulder, and with Feran's assistance, hoisting him back onto his horse. Trefor gripped the saddle horn with likely the last of his strength. Matheo grabbed the reins of Trefor's horse, mounted his own gelding, and took off down the street in the direction of the palace. As her eyes followed them, she noticed Ryenne and Ksee, surrounded by Ryenne's Armature, swords out and eyes alert. The queen was on the ground beside Cedoric's body, her harsh wails still echoing around the courtyard. The people who'd gathered to watch the parade were also dispersing, panicked shrieks and wails added to the jarring discord of the square as they filed quickly down the streets, city guards rushing from their posts to shepherd them to safety.

As she watched the movement in the square, Mariah felt as Sebastian moved up beside her, dismounted from his horse, and reached for Kodie's reins.

"Mariah, you have to get out of here. They're after *you*. Go back to the palace, *now*—"

"No." Mariah's voice was firm as she cut him off. A distant part of herself, a part that didn't currently govern her, whispered that he meant well. But the part of her in control, the wild darkness she'd given free rein, was nothing but annoyed.

She snapped her gaze to the remainder of her Armature, their expressions steeled and expectant, the fervor of the moment bright in their eyes.

Good.

"Feran, you will stay here with Sebastian, Ryenne's Armature, and the Ladies of both courts. Get them all back to the palace and protect them at all costs." She saw Sebastian open his mouth, trying to protest, making a second attempt to shut her down, to get her to run, but she steamrolled over him as her skin flashed again with silver-gold light.

"Drystan, Quentin, you're both with me. We're going hunting." Two grins from the two best fighters in her Armature answered her, their expressions nothing short of feral.

A prickle across her skin had Mariah turning to meet Andrian's familiar gaze. He'd dismounted his stallion and now stood on the other side of Kodie's head, his sword already drawn, a wickedly defiant look in his tanzanite eyes. Mariah thought she could hear his words, whispering to her on a shadowy wind.

Tell me to stay behind, nio. *I dare you.*

She swung her leg and jumped down from Kodie's back, landing softly in the grass in front of him, refusing to break from his punishing stare.

"Don't get in my way." Her voice was cold and foreign.

"Wouldn't dream of it, princess."

Mariah ignored him as she turned back to Drystan and Quentin, who'd also dismounted. The pair moved to flank her, Andrian standing at her back. As she walked past Sebastian, he tried a final plea to get her to stay, to send

Drystan and Quentin alone, that she didn't need to go herself.

She ignored him with a final, icy glare.

She wouldn't stand idly by when her life was threatened. When the lives of those around her, those who'd become a second family to her, were also threatened.

Red, the color of Cedoric's and Trefor's blood, flooded her vision again.

"Let's go."

They hurtled up the stairs of the building where Mariah had spotted the assassin, swinging around banisters and hauling themselves over railings.

Mariah would've been thankful for all those mornings spent training if that otherworldly power hadn't been thrumming through her veins, a power that whispered of how this was barely scraping the surface of what she could do.

They slowed only slightly as they reached the top of the stairs, a solid wood door before them leading to the rooftop beyond. The building was silent, strangely deserted, its occupants—if there were any—all out on the streets below, part of the disorganized chaos that reigned in the city. It had created the perfect opportunity for the assassin to steal up to that roof uninhibited, free to carry out this mission against her life.

Her vision again flashed red.

This assassin would not live another day on this earth.

She halted just outside the door, drawing her grandfather's dagger smoothly from its new sheath on her hip. She reached a hand behind her, a silent command, and felt Drystan press one of his favored shortswords—of which he always carried at least three—into her waiting palm. It was only then, with her teeth bared back in a silent snarl, unearthly wildness filling her veins, that she kicked the door open and stepped onto the rooftop beyond.

It was silent. Empty.

Mariah turned in a slow circle, her eyes readjusting from the dim stairwell to the brightness of the clear winter day. Wind bit fiercely at her face, her long hair whipping and snapping like a caged beast.

He was still here. He had to still be here, there was nowhere for him to go ...

A flash of black out of the corner of her eye had her leaping forward, Drystan's sharp hiss behind her the only sound of his surprise. The assassin was at the very edge of the roof, running, about to make a flying leap off the flat edge and onto the tiled surface of the neighboring roof—

Darkness arched out through the cold air and wrapped itself around the assassin's neck, grabbing him mid-jump and slamming him back with a violent yank. The assassin landed hard on the rooftop, his breath heaving in audible chokes and gasps of pain.

Mariah didn't bother glancing at Andrian to offer him thanks. She only stalked forward, her eyes glued and narrowed on the writhing figure in front of her.

She knew Andrian didn't expect any gratitude, and with what she was about to do, she would not give it to him.

The assassin, clothed in all black, still lay sprawled on the ground, desperately trying to catch the breath that was choked and slammed out of him. Mariah had suspected he was male, and as she approached, her suspicion was confirmed. He was tall and lean, his body obviously honed for stealth and shadows rather than hand to hand combat.

It was the body of a *coward*.

His gray eyes met Mariah's and widened slightly as she neared, flipping himself onto his stomach in a flash of movement. He was about to push himself up and reach for his own blades, his gaze hardening as he watched Mariah's approach.

There was a sudden glint of silver, a rustle in the air, and before the assassin could even touch the hilt of his own dagger, a dragon-winged blade was burrowed deep in his stomach, Mariah's now-empty hand still outstretched.

The assassin went back down with a gurgle, the sound so much like the one Cedoric had made. He lay there, his lifeblood draining from the wound, his breath rattling in choking gasps.

Mariah kept walking until she stood beside his prone body, her eyes darting once to Drystan and Quentin in silent command before dropping into a crouch beside the dying man, dropping Drystan's blade onto the rough rooftop with a clatter. Her Armature settled around her, Quentin's blade touching the hollow of the man's throat as Drystan made quick work of disarming him. Andrian lingered at Mariah's back, watching with an abject curiosity that tickled her scalp.

She ignored him, focusing her attention on the assassin. When she spoke, her voice was a silent, deadly murmur laced with the raw power commanding her body and flowing through her veins, her fingernails sparking with silver and gold.

"Who sent you."

Not a question.

A command from a queen.

The assassin coughed and gagged. "Your Grace ... I'm sorry ... It w-was ... nothing personal," he choked out, spitting up blood the color of garnets. "I didn't realize you were my target ... did not-not realize what you looked like. I was only given ... your description."

Mariah flashed out a hand to grab the hilt of her grandfather's dagger, still buried in the man's gut.

And she twisted.

The assassin's scream of pain cut through the air, just as Ryenne's had moments before as she'd held her dying Armature in her arms.

"*Who sent you.*"

The assassin's gray eyes met Mariah's with a look of pure, undiluted terror. Mariah saw and smelled the stain that crept across the front of his dark leathers. Whatever he saw staring back at him behind her forest green eyes had him soiling himself, and she couldn't find it in herself to be bothered by it.

In fact, it made her almost gleeful.

His choking words started again.

"I ... never knew. They were ... a-always anonymous. P-paid in advance, used different messengers each time. I-I'm sorry, Your Grace, I didn't know, didn't know ..." his voice trailed off as desperate, pained sobs wracked his body.

"Today, you killed a member of Queen Ryenne's Armature and injured a member of mine. And that doesn't include your admission that I, your queen apparent, was your true target. Those are crimes punishable by death." She paused, and watched as terror continued to seep out of the assassin's pores and into the air around her, the smell of his fear whispering to a deep, primal instinct buried deep in her bones.

It was an instinct that called to the darkness she'd let in. An instinct that craved—*thirsted*—for blood.

"I shall exact your punishment now. I would ask Qhohena to take mercy upon your soul, but you don't deserve that peace. Instead, I call upon Zadione, the Mistress of Death, to carry you into the depths of Enfara for the rest of eternity."

In one smooth movement, Mariah ripped the dragon-winged dagger from the assassin's stomach and sliced it across his throat, his final cries and pleas dying on his tongue and fading into the crisp afternoon air.

And with that one, simple move, Mariah felt a piece of her soul stain a touch darker forever.

Without darkness, we can never experience the light ...

CHAPTER 51

Blood still clung to Mariah's skin, the coppery taste taking up residence in her mouth, her nose, the very essence of her being.

No matter how many times she scrubbed at her skin or tried to chase away the taste and smell and feel of it with wine or whiskey, the blood was still there, clawing at her insides and making her skin crawl like there were insects in her veins.

She'd utterly lost herself. Given herself completely to the dark call of the magic in her veins. And in her rage, she'd let it take control, consuming her until it drove her to slit a dying man's throat, bathing her hands in his sticky, warm blood.

It had felt so unlike the time she'd lost control with the Royals, at the incident that killed old Lord Beauchamp. That had been unintentional, only meant to be a warning, the fatality that day the result of an already failing heart. This ... this was something completely different.

It wasn't that it had been hard to do; no, that wasn't what made her feel sick and haunted.

It was that it had been far too *easy*.

The threaded magic in her veins had sung a song of death, thrumming a symphony of power when she'd felt the life of the nameless assassin drain out over her hands, pooling beneath her feet in dark crimson mirrors. Then there'd been the feeling of the dark, hidden, primal part of her answering the tune of her magic, stirring at the scent of blood in the air as if that was just what it needed to awaken from a long slumber.

Those feelings ... they'd terrified her to her core. Enough to wrench herself back from the grip of her magic, pushing it down into that place where it dwelt in her soul, enough for her to see her reflection in the bloody pools on that roof and *run*, her grandfather's dagger dropping to the ground with a clatter she didn't hear. She'd run down the stairs, run towards where Kodie still stood, reins held firm in Sebastian's grasp. She didn't speak to Sebastian, didn't demand to know why he hadn't returned to the palace with Ryenne and the rest. She'd only ripped Kodie's reins from his grip, swung herself into her worn black saddle, and spurred her horse down the streets of Verith, some inner compass guiding her towards the familiarity of the palace even though it was far from a place she could call home.

After all, it wasn't as if she had anywhere else to go. Not anymore.

Not with the power of a death goddess flooding her veins and threatening to override every piece of who she was.

Or ... who she *thought* she was.

Andrian had found her an hour later, sitting on the floor of her massive shower, scalding hot water raining down from the faucet and the air filled with thick, billowing steam. He'd set her grandfather's dagger, now cleaned and polished and completely spotless of the crime it had just committed, on the counter of her vanity before slowly making his way to the shower. He'd stepped through the glass doors, still fully clothed, and knelt beside her, not bothering to even take off his boots. They'd sat like that for a long moment, Mariah refusing to meet his heavy stare even though she felt it burning her skin as much as the water falling from above, until eventually she felt calloused fingers grip her chin. Andrian lifted her head to meet his gaze, blue eyes molten and glowing in the thick air. When he spoke, his voice was low and soft, just loud enough to be heard over the patter of the water falling around them.

"Vengeance is not a sin, *nio*. Allow yourself this one moment to adjust yourself to the person you are now, the person you had to become to protect those you care for. But don't wish you hadn't done it. Never wish to change an evolution that was always destined to occur."

With those words, he stood, his black clothes and hair dripping, and backed out of the shower the same way he'd walked in. He left her with her thoughts, and to do exactly what he'd just instructed her to do.

She remained there on the tiled floor as she adjusted to her now-shattered soul, weaving those rips and tears in the fiber of her being back together, letting them heal and callous over until she couldn't remember what it had felt like to be soft.

Mariah slept fitfully that night, but she did sleep.

For a few hours, at least.

She awoke bleary-eyed with the weak dawn light, the *pitter-patter* outside her window of an early winter rain threatened to lull her back to sleep. Despite the rain, the air was cold—not cold enough to freeze, but cold enough in her room to see her breath puff in soft clouds in front of her. Mariah peeled back the heavy comforter of her bed, shivering, making a mental note as she padded into her bathroom to ask for firewood to be brought up so fires could be started in the hearths in the living room and her bedroom. She twisted the faucets to her massive, ridiculous bath, leaning against her vanity and staring at her reflection as the giant basin began to fill.

Her eyes looked ... empty. And Mariah hardly recognized the face that stared back at her. She'd never felt more like a stranger in her own flesh.

Soon, her bath was ready, and she gratefully sank into the hot water, the steam sticky and clammy against her skin.

She wasn't sure how long she stayed there, but it was long enough for the water to go lukewarm and the chill to begin to seep back into the hollows of her soul.

Soon, far too soon, Ciana came barging into her bathroom, followed closely by the girl with mouse brown hair who'd dressed Mariah for the *Porofirat*.

Brie. Her name was Brie.

Ciana stomped up to the bath, clucking like a mother hen as she stared down at Mariah.

"Good Goddess, Mariah. How long have you been in there?"

Mariah closed her eyes, pretending to settle herself back further against the headrest of the bath. "Not nearly long enough. Go away."

Ciana snorted. "You're literally a prune. Seriously, get out." There was rustling, and Mariah cracked her eyes to see Ciana pulling out a thick, plush, warm-looking towel from a cabinet. Turning back to Mariah, Ciana held the towel out invitingly, peering around it with a stern look on her brow. Mariah rolled her eyes but stood, stepping into the warmth Ciana offered her. She toweled the moisture from her skin as Ciana watched her, that *look* still on her face.

"What? Stop looking at me like that."

Ciana humphed. "You know, Andrian told me that you were in here doing your own version of sulking—you two are *perfect* for each other, by the way—but enough is enough. It's time to put your grown-ass queen panties on. As you know, shit hit the fan yesterday, and you're needed in the temple at once."

Mariah turned and stared at her friend, blinking slowly. "... Put my 'grown-ass queen panties on?' Seriously, are you ten?"

"Twelve, actually. Now seriously, you need to get dressed."

Mariah tried to laugh—she really did—but all she could manage was a weak smile. However, Ciana took that as a victory and pushed her down in the chair at the vanity as Brie stepped forward with a brush, running it through Mariah's dark, damp hair.

"I'm not sulking, by the way."

Ciana, who'd moved into Mariah's closet, turned back around, her amber eyes flashing to meet Mariah's in the mirror. "Oh, yeah?"

Mariah scowled before looking away. "Yeah."

There was a slight pause, the rhythm of Brie's brush through her hair and the rustle of Ciana yanking out clothes weaving a soothing melody. Ciana reappeared, several articles of clothing in her hands, and once again met Mariah's gaze with a look far gentler than before.

"You want to talk about it?"

Mariah couldn't look her friend in the eye when she answered, the lie heavy on her tongue.

"No."

It hadn't taken Ciana and Brie long to get Mariah ready and pushed out the doors of her suite, sending her down the hallway towards Qhohena's temple.

Mariah was now dressed in soft, black leather leggings, the

insides lined in fur to fight off the chill that had moved in with the rain, winter arriving in Verith like a dark companion. She wore a soft, form-fitting turtleneck sweater, dyed the same black as her leggings, and across her chest was strapped a harness of supple, black leather.

A harness that now secured the scabbards of the two shortswords sheathed across her back, the blades criss-crossed just below her shoulder blades. Her grandfather's dagger, that same dagger that had taken a life less than a day ago, was in its new burgundy garter sheath on her right thigh. Her long, dark hair hung loose down her back, curling around those two shortswords, and she knew her eyes were too bright and gleaming.

After two attempts on her life in a place that was supposed to be her home, she no longer felt safe walking these halls. She now trusted only those who'd sworn oaths to her before the Goddess and the two women she'd welcomed into her court.

Quentin and Drystan, the same two who'd flanked her yesterday, were in the same positions today as she neared the shining golden doors of Qhohena's temple. She turned her head slightly to the side, to Drystan, and spoke quietly.

"How's Trefor?"

His brown eyes darted to hers and held her stare. "He's fine. He'll make a full recovery. The arrow, while it struck deep, hit nothing important, and your quick actions yesterday prevented him from losing too much blood."

"*Our* quick actions, Drystan." She refused to take credit for what she'd done. For what the darkness inside of her had done.

Drystan only smiled softly back at her. "Whatever you say, Mariah."

Mariah's chest tightened. "I ... I plan to see him today. As soon as I'm done with ... whatever this will be." Neither male behind her responded, but she felt the gentle brushes of their consciousnesses down those bridges between their minds, quiet reminders that no matter what she did, they would understand. That there was nothing to feel guilty for, that everyone was just happy she was safe and Trefor would recover.

If only she felt the same.

Drystan and Quentin lingered outside the temple doors, their expressions watchful, as she pushed on the plated gold and slipped quietly inside the room.

It seemed every time she entered the temple it looked slightly different. That first time, for the Selection, the whole space had been so dark, so mysterious and cast in shadow she wasn't able to fully observe the room. This time, however, the temple was lit, the cold sunlight streaming through windows Mariah hadn't known existed. The atrium was open, the dais and altar at the front of the room illuminated brightly by thousands of candles. The wax began to drip down and onto the floor, indicating that they'd been burning for quite some time.

That steady *drip, drip, drip* of the candle wax on the marble floor sounded too much like blood to Mariah's ears. Her hands tightened into fists, the wild magic in her veins roaring back to life.

Until she saw a figure dressed in pale gold robes standing beside the altar of candles, graying brown hair twisted into a wreath around her head as she watched Mariah through narrowed, pale gold eyes. Despite the fire magic that Mariah knew flowed in the figure's veins, she felt as if she'd been doused with a bucket of water.

"Quite the appearance you've chosen for yourself, Mariah. Tell me, is this you making your statement to the kingdom that you intend to always punish its criminals with instant death?"

Mariah froze, no more than a dozen paces from the High Priestess. "No, Ksee. This is me making the *statement* that after the second attempt on my life since being Chosen, I no longer feel safe in my own home."

"Ah." The High Priestess let out a soft, cold laugh. "Taking matters into your own hands, then." She folded her hands in front of her before walking one, two, three steps toward Mariah. Ksee now stood close enough to look down at Mariah from the dais steps, but not quite close enough to be within striking distance of the short swords strapped to Mariah's back.

The fact she appeared to perceive Mariah as that much of an unhinged threat made a part of her want to puff out her chest with pride. At least *one* good thing had come of her actions yesterday.

Those hateful brown eyes bore down on Mariah, an obvious attempt to get Mariah to cave.

"You have forgotten your place, once again, Queen Apparent. This is not a lawless country; those who break our laws shall be punished for it, yes, but we do not mete out such judgment or exact our revenge in the streets like *animals*. The way of Onita is one of peace, and as a representative of our gentle mother Goddess in this palace, it is my *duty* to make sure our queen does not stray from the path of purity and goodness." Her last words came out as a hiss, her eyes narrowing even further. "Should you ever perform a stunt like the one you pulled yesterday again, Queen Apparent, I will ensure that you know *exactly* who truly holds the power in this kingdom."

"And who might that be, High Priestess?" Mariah's magic was raging like a vicious hurricane at Ksee's words. *Animal, lawless, revenge, purity* ... everything Ksee said grated against Mariah's newly awakened instincts. "As much as you and the Royals seem to not want to admit it, I was Chosen by the Goddess. I carry her power in my veins. You may think me wild and like an animal, debasing your pretty little temple with my swords and blades still stained with the blood of those who tried to hurt me, who tried to hurt those closest to me, but I'm here to challenge you, Priestess." Mariah bared her teeth at the older woman as she stalked closer, gliding up the dais steps until she stood no more than a few inches from Ksee.

The priestess, to her credit, did not cower away, even though fear began to flicker in her flat tarnished eyes.

"I *will* be the one to hold the power here, Ksee. I admire Ryenne, but I will not be used as a tool and a figurehead for those who were never meant to have the power they seek. I've read the earliest histories of this kingdom. I know how wild the early queens were. I know how weak they began to grow, as more Royals rose in station and more priestesses realized the only semblance of power they would ever recapture for themselves would be by controlling queens who never truly understood what they carried. Even *I* don't understand that power yet, but let me promise you, High Priestess: *I am learning*. So, get out of my way."

Ksee's face paled, the blood draining from her features. She took one step away, slowly, her eyes darting down to Mariah's right side.

To where Mariah now realized she gripped the dragon-winged hilt of her grandfather's dagger.

Ksee raised her eyes back to Mariah, and as the priestess dipped her head, Mariah felt something alter forever in the air between them.

"My apologies, Your Highness. Queen Ryenne is in the right antechamber. She is expecting you."

And as the priestess bowed stiffly and turned on her heel, stepping down from the dais steps and toward a hallway that must lead to the private chambers of the palace priestesses, Mariah couldn't help but realize the dark gleam she'd seen in

Ksee's eyes meant the palace was now filled with one more enemy than it had been yesterday.

Mariah found Ryenne in an antechamber down the hallway to the right of the altar, just as Ksee said.

The room was magnificent and beautiful, but very different from the rest of the palace. Instead of the familiar white marble, it was black: dark, light-consuming black marble on the floors, the pillars, the walls. All of it was veined through with fine streaks of gold, a perfect refraction to the rest of the palace, subtle but no less beautiful. Above, just like in the throne room and the library, the roof was made of solid glass. Mariah noticed that the rain had stopped, the weak winter sun from behind the lingering clouds setting a chill in the air.

Mariah had a sudden urge to return to this room on a clear, cloudless night. She had a feeling that's when it was at its most magnificent.

"This is the Antechamber of Priam. The palace builders designed it specifically to honor him, so that from the moment you walk in, you feel as if you are in his presence, his watchfulness a comfort to whatever plagues you."

Mariah whipped her head in the direction of Ryenne's voice. The queen stood in the center of the antechamber beside a raised slab of stone, a body laid carefully atop it. A body now draped in a shroud of shimmering gold.

Cedoric.

Mariah was silent as she dropped her gaze back to the black marble beneath her feet. She was familiar with Priam; all Onitans were. The Consort God, Qhohena's partner, and the God of the Northern Star.

He was also the Keeper of Souls, the bridge between life

and whatever awaited beyond. Ceremonies of mourning were his temples, tears and whispers to lost loved ones his prayers.

With soft, silent steps, Mariah moved from the antechamber entrance to the stone slab in the center, coming to a halt beside the queen. Ryenne's hair was now more gray than gold and her face bore even more lines of age, the youthful exuberance she'd had when Mariah first stepped into the palace vanished like a whisper on the wind.

It was no mystery that each time Mariah bonded with another of her Armature, she took years off Ryenne's life. But losing Cedoric ... it was as if the spark had left the queen completely.

Mariah stood in silence beside Ryenne, not knowing what to say, and deciding it was better to say nothing at all than to say something that could open still-bleeding wounds.

Thankfully, Ryenne spoke again.

"He was the second of my Armature to take the bond." Her voice was soft, distant, the emotion hidden behind walls of stone Mariah knew all too well.

"I bonded with Kalen first, of course. I had been drawn to him instantly, as is typical for a true consort. And that first bond ... it left me reeling. I had been raised my whole life for the possibility of the throne; the queen before me abdicated her power around the time I was born, and my family was the most prolific Royal family in the kingdom. Three queens hailed from my line, and with the timing of my birth, it seemed obvious to everyone that I would be the fourth queen born to House Shawth.

"So, I spent the first twenty-one years of my life preparing for the Choosing and the steps that would follow it. I knew exactly what the Selection and bondings would entail. I thought I was prepared. But then I bonded with Kalen, and ... I had never been so overwhelmed with emotion in my life. I had never felt ... never been *allowed* to feel ... so much. It felt like a sin." She took a deep inhale. "And because of that, I never wanted to do it again. Even though I knew I had to.

"When it came time to pick my next Armature to make the bond, I panicked. I almost got onto my horse and rode right into the mountains, fully prepared to abandon my throne and my family and everything I'd ever known." Ryenne chuckled softly at that, lost in her memories.

"But then Cedoric caught me in the stables."

Mariah loosened an exhale that stung her chest.

"He grabbed me and looked me right in the eyes, and I had never been looked at like that. *Ever.* He was so calm, so steady, so full of this patient understanding as I broke down, right there in the stables, in front of a man I barely knew. But he took it all with such grace and never once offered me anything other than a steadfast assurance that who I was, *what* I was, wasn't something to fear or run from.

"I bonded with him that same night. And I never broke down that way again, not when I knew he was there to ground me. Kalen is my fire, my heart, but Cedoric ..." her voice caught. She cleared it once, wiping away an errant tear streaking down her face. "He was my rock. My anchor. And I feel ... lost without him."

Mariah's own emotions were still frozen in her chest, and she had no tears to offer the queen. She wanted to say, "*I'm sorry*," wanted to offer a condolence, a sob, *anything*, but she also knew better than anyone that no words or actions would ever be enough to make up for what had been lost. The thought of losing an Armature, and losing them like that ... she thought of Sebastian, how he was so much like what Ryenne had described Cedoric to be. If it had been Sebastian to take that arrow today, if the solid ground beneath her feet had been ripped away so violently, she didn't think she would've been able to stand. So, she remained quiet, and simply slipped her hand into Ryenne's, gripping the older woman's fingers tightly.

She felt Ryenne tense slightly at the contact, but after a few heartbeats she relaxed, and squeezed back.

"Please ... just ..." Ryenne choked on her words again, tears again welling in her blue eyes. She took another deep breath before continuing. "Just tell me one thing."

Mariah kept her gaze fixed on Cedoric's golden shroud, the outline of his body on the black marble pedestal, as she answered. "Anything, My Queen."

Several more heartbeats filled the quiet space before Ryenne continued.

"Tell me he is dead. Tell me you killed him." Mariah knew exactly who Ryenne meant, could feel the fury and anger and loss spiraling out of the queen from where their skin touched.

"I buried my dagger in his stomach before I slit his throat." How strange, to speak those words in a place reserved for the presence of the gods. But if Mariah opened her senses, let the whispers of the universe filter around her, let her magic inch out just a bit from her skin, she could almost feel a subtle hum of approval reverberating through her.

Perhaps the gods were more vengeful and bloodthirsty than the priestesses wanted the world to believe.

Ryenne's exhale was audible against those silent whispers. "Good."

Mariah squeezed the queen's hand one more time before dropping it and turning away, leaving the queen to her vigil.

She did not turn back, even when she heard Ryenne's final words chase her from the room.

"Thank you ... Your Majesty."

CHAPTER 52

Mariah went straight from the temple to the hospital wing.

She'd put off seeing Trefor for long enough. While she knew he was well cared for, and had been assured by Quentin he would make a full recovery, the guilt had still eaten away at her since she'd stepped out of the shower the day before.

She couldn't stop thinking about the arrow he'd taken, the one meant for her.

Just like the one that had ended Cedoric's life. Had severed him from Ryenne as one might sever a limb from a body. Mariah imagined it must feel about the same.

She shoved it all down, the ever-fracturing pieces of herself she was still desperately trying to hold together. If yesterday had shown her anything, it was that she had to stay strong, had to stay alert and vigilant and watchful for the threats she now knew were very, *very* real.

When she entered the hospital wing, she was greeted not only by Trefor, but by her entire court: all seven of her Armature, plus Ciana and Delaynie. Even Brie was there, lingering to the side behind Ciana, her sharp eyes quiet and watchful. At the sound of the door swinging open in front of Mariah, all ten sets of eyes snapped to her, their attention settling instantly on their queen.

That was what she'd realized on the walk here, as she'd pondered Ryenne's parting words.

"Your Majesty" was not a title given to a mere queen apparent.

It was a title reserved for a queen.

For Ryenne, with the death of Cedoric, so too her time as monarch had ended. She'd lost a member of her Armature, a piece of her soul vanishing along with him, and was no longer fit to lead a kingdom. Especially with most of her magic gone and the immortality it had brought her failing.

With those words, the burden of leadership had fallen heavily onto Mariah's shoulders, whether she was ready for it or not.

And with all those cracking pieces of herself, Mariah didn't think she was. But the gods had left her with no other option than to bear it.

"My Queen!"

A bright male voice cut through the dark tenor of her thoughts.

Trefor. Alive. Well. Speaking.

For the first time since the attack—since *both* attacks—Mariah's face broke out into an uninhibited smile, the kind she'd almost forgotten how to make.

"Trefor." She moved through the large, open hospital wing, her court parting like the tide, until she reached the side of Trefor's cot. Carefully, she unslung the shortswords from her back and unbuckled the dagger from her thigh, Drystan stepping forward and taking the weapons without a word. She sat carefully, just on the edge, and clasped Trefor's hand in hers.

He looked well; there was color in his cheeks, and his skin felt warm and healthy to the touch. The only sign of his injury was the massive bandage wrapped tightly across his chest and left shoulder, the thick gauze fresh and stiff.

Mariah surveyed him closely before meeting his stare and raising an eyebrow. "You aren't left-handed, are you?"

Trefor's answer carried a hint of confusion. "No ...?"

Mariah grinned mischievously. "Good. I would hate for you to lose your sword arm and make it even easier for me to kick your ass."

The entire room erupted into a too-loud roar of laughter, pounds of tension lifting with a single sentence.

Trefor answered her with a grin of his own. "Mariah, the loss of my sword arm should be the least of your concerns—"

A growl rumbled from behind the rest of the gathered court at Trefor's flirtatiousness, followed by booted footsteps. Mariah spotted a flash of dark hair as a figure stalked down the length of the hospital wing and pushed through a set of doors at the far end of the room.

It took every ounce of her control to not roll her eyes into the back of her skull.

Trefor returned his wide, sea-green gaze to Mariah. "I was only kidding—"

"I know," she said, cutting him off. She smiled softly at him again before rising from the cot, looking back over her shoulder in the direction Andrian had disappeared. "I guess I need to go deal with that." Glancing back down at Trefor, Mariah soaked in the joy of being here, with her court, the first real happiness and relief she'd felt in too long. "I am ... so *beyond* happy that you're okay. I don't know what I would do without you." She turned her attention to the rest of those gathered around her, the second family she'd both chosen and been gifted with. "Without *all* of you."

It was Ciana who answered her. "I know what you would do. You would continue on. You would be sad, but you would keep your head high, just as it is now, and you would *conquer*. We all believe in that—in *you*." There were nods and murmurs of agreement. Tears pricked at the backs of Mariah's eyes, and she felt those broken shards of herself weave themselves a little tighter together. She met Ciana's amber gaze to find her friend smiling at her fiercely.

"Now, go." Ciana gestured with her head towards the far end of the wing, at the exit that lay beyond. "The grumpy one needs to calm down, and you're the only one he seems to listen to."

Mariah snorted. "I hardly think he listens to me."

Ciana glared at her. Mariah sighed. "Fine." She looked around to her court again, her heart swelling with gratitude that they were all safe and well and *here*. "Thank you." Her words were barely more than a whisper, but she knew they heard her.

With another breath, Mariah stepped away from her court and towards the rear exit of the hospital wing, pushing through the doors and into a quiet, deserted hallway.

Mariah found Andrian on a balcony off the furthest, darkest section of that hallway. *Typical*.

The heavy glass-paneled doors shut closed behind her as she stepped out into the crisp, afternoon winter chill. Andrian, clothed in his typical black, leaned against the white marble railing, gazing out at the view of the game park below and the Attlehon mountains beyond.

It was curious, Mariah thought, how every balcony or view in the palace seemed to face the great mountain range. She'd yet to step foot onto a balcony that faced the city and the Bay of Nria beyond it. She thought she remembered seeing some from the exterior of the palace, but ... she couldn't quite remember.

Shaking her head slightly to clear her lingering musings, she stepped forward once. Twice. Three times. She kept taking single steps forward until she stood no more than a few feet from Andrian's broad back, close enough to see the steady movement of his ribs as he inhaled and exhaled. She opened her mouth to speak, drawing in a breath.

But he beat her to it.

"You shouldn't be here. You should be with Trefor."

She snapped her mouth shut, bunching her eyebrows together, before taking the last few steps to stand beside him at the railing. This man was so hot and cold that it drove her fucking *mad*.

"He has more than enough support. If anything, I'm sure he would appreciate a little space. I'm just happy he's going to be alright."

Andrian huffed darkly. "Yes. Thank the *Goddess* he's going to be fine."

Mariah's gaze whipped to his face. She noticed for the first time the darkness that had settled in his eyes, the purple of his skin muting the brilliance of the tanzanite.

"When was the last time you slept?"

His eyes flashed to hers and then drifted back away. They stood in silence for several heartbeats, and Mariah wondered for a moment if he was going to refuse to answer her.

But then he spoke.

"It's been ... a while."

Mariah turned her body to face him more fully, leaning her left side against the balcony and crossing her arms across her chest.

"You're not going to give me more than that?"

His blue stare met hers again, just for a second, before hardening and looking back out at the Attlehons.

She sighed and turned back to face the mountains as well.

"I spoke with Ryenne today."

He didn't move a muscle, but she could feel his attention on her, nonetheless.

"She told me of when she'd first been Chosen. When she was going through the bondings with her Armature. She told me Cedoric was the second one she'd bonded with." She paused for just a moment, steeling herself for her next words, the other piece she'd been dwelling on since her conversation with the queen. "She told me she'd needed his steadiness to ground her, after … after her bonding with Kalen. With her consort."

Andrian was still utterly motionless beside her.

Mariah continued. "She told me of the draw that had existed between herself and Kalen from the moment he'd been Selected. How no matter what, they'd craved each other, that they couldn't get the other out of their heads. She told me—"

"What are you getting at here, princess?" Andrian's voice was almost pained as it cut through her speech. She froze, slowly turning her head to face him again.

His eyes were blazing, no longer dark, but returned to their wild and startling blue. The shadows in his blood were slowly beginning to unfurl around his shoulders, winding down his forearms as he gripped the railing.

"Are you trying to convince me of something, *nio*? That I am your *consort*? Is this an attempt to try to get me to take the bond, to do the *one* thing that I swore upon everything I value in this world I wouldn't do? Even knowing the risks to yourself, is this still something that you're asking of me?"

And once again, Mariah was left speechless, her stomach dropping from her body and falling to the game park far below.

She could only hold his gaze, hold her body still to keep from trembling, as she nodded to him once, slowly. She'd just been curious, had wondered if his possessive words in the game park had meant anything real. But in a way, she supposed she *was* attempting to convince him. Convince him of her, of what they were to each other.

For him to take the bond.

Goddess damn this man for knowing exactly how to steal every ounce of strength from her bones with just a few biting words.

Andrian's eyes flashed again at her nod, and his next movements were a blur.

Before she could pull herself together enough to react, he had whirled away from the balcony, an arm sliding around her torso, twisting her until her back was pressed against the railing and he was pressed against her. His shadows unfurled further around his body, tendrils sliding off his skin and onto her arms, wrapping around her legs, twisting into her hair. Her breath caught in her throat: from surprise, from fear, from the warmth suddenly pooling low in her belly, she wasn't sure which.

And then his voice was at her ear.

"Do you long for your own death, *nio*? Is that it? Do you wish to be free of all those duties the world has shoved onto your shoulders, to return to a simpler existence, one without crowns or bonds or threads of magic?" He pressed into her further, and Mariah felt him, hard and demanding against her stomach.

Yeah. It definitely wasn't fear that had her breath hitching higher. Her blood was now heated and thrumming in her veins as he continued.

"There are other, easier ways to die, princess. Maybe I can

show you one. See how much it satisfies that suicidal streak you just can't seem to scratch."

Finally, she found her voice, and the darkness inside her thrummed at the game he dangled before her like a carrot.

"I have no wish to die, asshole," she growled, her breaths coming in whispery pants. She tried to pull her arms up, to shove his chest away from where it pressed against hers, but found that her wrists were bound to the balcony railing by soft ropes of darkness. She turned her lips into a snarl, the beast in her now giddy, as Mariah lifted her gaze back up to meet the matching fire burning in Andrian's expression.

This dance they played was so toxic, so addicting, but every fiber of her being craved it beyond measure.

"And besides," she continued, the snarl on her lips curving her voice into a purr, her own magic unwinding and dancing in her veins. "I know your threats are empty. You would never put my life in danger. Your refusal to take the bond proves that." Her snarl turned into a cruel, wicked smirk.

An answering smirk, a mirror to her own, spread across his impossibly handsome face, twisting it into something brutal and feral that had her magic writhing and practically singing in answer. He leaned in even closer, the bands of darkness around her wrists and ankles pulled even tighter across her skin.

"You underestimate me, princess. You always seem to do that."

"Prove it." The taunt slipped past her lips before she could stop it. Andrian pulled back slightly, the only hint of his surprise, before cold flames licked behind his eyes.

Shit.

"As you wish, *My Queen.*"

That was the last warning Mariah got before Andrian crashed his lips into hers.

Her world went black, everything reduced to the bruising

feeling of his body against hers. Somewhere, distantly, she was aware of shadowy whispers gliding across her skin, unlacing the ties of her boots, slipping them off her feet. Those same shadows hooked into the waistband of her leggings, tugging them surprisingly gently down her hips, lower, until they, too, were discarded beside her boots. Warm hands grabbed the firm flesh of her ass, lifting her and setting her atop something smooth and cold against her skin. Ropes of shadows continued to wrap, gently and securely, across her wrists, her ankles, her upper thighs, her stomach. Andrian's mouth moved from hers, traveling down her neck, peeling her sweater from her body, her tight elastic bra going with it, and she relished the bite of the cold air against her skin. Now bare before him, he returned to his assault. His mouth closed around her breast, his teeth biting at her nipple just as his tongue flicked the sensitive flesh. His right hand wrapped around her throat, pushing her head back, back, *back* until she felt her hair brush against the small of her back, whispering across her hands where they gripped the railing.

The railing.

Her eyes snapped open, the cloudy winter sky overhead doing little to distract her from the deadly drop now far too close for comfort.

"*Andrian*," she hissed through clenched teeth, shaking her head to rid her chin of his hand as she dropped it back to her chest. He was still trailing kisses down her chest and the planes of her stomach, the gleam in his eyes as his gaze met hers one of pure wicked darkness.

"*Princess*," he answered in a growl of his own. "Not so willing to taste death now, *nio*? You seemed so bold before, so sure."

She knew she shouldn't let his taunting get to her.

But, *fuck*, the way he said that nickname, that word she still didn't understand ... she couldn't back down from this, not now.

So, she leaned in, straining against the shadowy ropes around her wrists as far as they would let her. Andrian raised himself back up, letting her crowd into him, until they were eye to eye, panting against each other's mouths.

That was when she let that darkness, the same one she'd given herself to completely the day before, in just a little more, allowing it to spread a manic grin across her face, her expression now one of feral delight.

"Show me how good death can feel, Andrian."

That darkness purred at his answering grin, the shadows squeezed her even tighter.

His mouth crushed back to hers, his hand suddenly at her center, two fingers plunging into her with little warning. Her soft gasp was swallowed by his mouth, and when he curled his fingers, when he hit that *spot*, she bit down on his lower lip. *Hard*.

She almost came undone the second the taste of his blood touched her tongue.

He leaned back from her, panting, the red staining his mouth in stark contrast to the blue of his eyes. His fingers continued to slowly fuck her, *too* slowly, and his eyes dipped to watch as he flicked out his tongue, licking the blood from his lips. Mariah couldn't hold back the soft groan as she watched him, and he met her gaze again, a dark expression with an unreadable emotion written across his face.

"So fucking wet for me, *nio*. Maybe your body truly does crave death."

She bared her teeth. "Or maybe I'm just not afraid of heights."

His laugh was soft and wicked, his fingers absolutely tortuous. "You may not be afraid of heights, but I know you're terrified of falling." He withdrew his fingers from her then, his hands deftly unbuttoning and unzipping his pants as he drew out his cock, gripping his length tightly before pressing his body back to hers. She felt him nudge at her entrance, hissing slowly between her teeth. His next words were whispered against the shell of her ear.

"I say it's time to put that fear to the test, don't you think?"

Before she could process his words, the shadowy ropes binding her wrists, waist, and ankles all loosened just enough so the sense of safety and security they'd been offering fell away. She suddenly felt delicate, sitting there on that balcony, the safety net she hadn't even been aware of vanishing like the smoke that it was.

"Andrian—" Her voice, tinged with panic, was cut off as he fully sheathed himself in her in one smooth, punishing stroke.

The force of his movement slid her hips a few more centimeters toward the edge of the balcony railing. A soft cry left her lips, and his left hand gripped her behind her neck, his forehead resting against hers, a snarl on his face.

"Fear me, *nio*. I am not a place of refuge or safety for you."

She could only close her eyes, an embarrassing whimper escaping her throat, just as he began to stroke into her.

Each press of his hips into hers had her moving closer and closer to the ledge.

Closer to death.

And yet ...

She forced her eyes open and met his brilliant blue stare. He was gazing at her with such intensity, it would rival the sun on the Summer Solstice.

And that was when she felt it.

The same ringing she'd felt so many weeks ago, when she'd spotted him in the palace courtyard on the day of the Choosing, hiding amongst his own shadows. It consumed her, pulled her, wrapped itself around her until there was nothing else in her universe by her, and Andrian, and that *feeling*.

His eyes went wide, and she knew he felt it, too.

The hardness in his gaze, in his whole body, softened, but the punishing pace he'd set did not slow.

And Mariah let herself fall into it, into *him*, headfirst.

She felt her orgasm begin to rise, the wave of pleasure driven further by the breath she shared with Andrian and the look in his eyes that spoke more to her than she would ever let herself even think.

"Andrian ..." His name was a whispered prayer on her lips.

"I've got you," was all he whispered back. With those words, the bindings around her hands and ankles fell away completely, and without a thought her fingers flew up from where they gripped the railing, sinking into the thick waves of his hair, pulling his face into the hollow of her throat. The feel of his teeth as they scraped the skin of her neck sent a shiver racing up her spine and a groan escaping from her lips, her eyelids fluttering closed again.

He moved his own hands, one still holding her securely by the neck, the other traveling from the balcony to her waist. Further in, to her stomach, to where his thumb was able to reach right into the space where they were joined. He pressed the digit against her clit, and light exploded from her skin.

His thumb started to swipe steady circles there, in perfect rhythm with his strokes into her, and as he built her higher and higher, he raised his head and murmured against her lips.

"Come for me, *nio*. Show me your light. Let it *blind* me."

Gasping, Mariah turned her head to allow him deeper access to her neck, deeper access to *her*, and let her eyes open.

Far below her, the valley of the game park yawned open, waiting for one wrong move to swallow her whole.

But instead of fear, all she felt was pure, undiluted

wildness, coaxed higher by the soft brush of a shadow against her back, tangled in the heavy sheet of her dark hair.

Her release barrelled through her like a tornado, her eyes flashing with images of skies and stars and of leaping off that balcony and *falling*, knowing she would be caught.

"*Fuck* ... Mariah ..." Andrian chased her over that edge, falling with her into oblivion and so much more.

They remained there, panting, for several long moments, the silver-gold light emanating off Mariah melting like liquid over the balcony railing. Eventually, she was able to somewhat compose herself, drawing that light back into the confines of her skin. Andrian lifted his forehead from where it rested against hers, staring at her for several heartbeats before stepping back, releasing her from her seat on the ledge. He tucked himself back inside his pants, and then watched her in silence as she made quick work of slipping back into her clothes, brushing her fingers through her wild hair. When she finally returned her gaze to his, took in his guarded, unreadable expression, she knew what awaited her.

"You still won't, will you?"

She didn't know why she asked it; she knew the answer. Despite whatever it was that had happened between them just a few minutes ago, it still hadn't been enough to change his mind.

Still hadn't been enough to get him to put her life at risk. A risk she was more than willing to make, a risk she now wanted more than anything else.

It was *her* life, after all. Not his.

And just as she knew the answer to her question, he didn't respond to it. Instead, he watched her, that odd look still in his eyes, before turning back to look out at the white-capped Attlehon Mountains.

She watched him for a moment longer, sadness filling in the spaces of her still-broken soul. And she knew it then.

Knew that she'd lost him. That he would never allow himself this weakness again.

But, Mariah realized unfeelingly, she couldn't lose something she'd never truly had.

Cold and numb, she moved back to the balcony doors. Placing a hand on the handle, she paused, twisting slightly to speak over her shoulder one last time.

"I wasn't scared, because ... I knew. I knew you would've caught me. That you never would've let me fall."

Mariah stepped through the doors into the darkness of the hallway, back towards the medical wing, before he could respond.

She bonded with Feran later that night.

CHAPTER 53

Mariah gazed up at the glass domed central roof of the library, barely there sunlight filtering through the gathering snowdrifts atop the panels.

She'd wondered a few weeks ago if it would snow in Verith or if the coastal winds would prevent the rains from freezing. It had always snowed in the winters in Andburgh; not as much as it did farther north, but enough for the ground to sometimes look like it was dusted with powdered sugar or the thick trees like they were lightly sprinkled with twinkling starlight.

That weather must've followed her all the way to the coast. Ryenne had told her earlier that day this sort of snowfall was unprecedented, especially in the early winter before the Winter Solstice. Despite the looming Attlehon Mountains, the cold never ventured far into the city itself.

Mariah tried not to think about whether it was some omen foretelling a winter colder than she'd ever known in her lifetime.

Of course, Ryenne hadn't stopped with her small talk of the weather.

Mariah looked down at her hands where they pressed, palms down, into the smooth mahogany of the library table as she ran the Queen's words through her mind for the thousandth time.

"*I'm sure it is obvious to you, but ... I am no longer in any condition to rule a kingdom. Most days, I can barely get myself out of bed. The people ... they cannot see me like this. And I know you are not yet ready to be crowned, and there is still so much left I wish I could teach you, but I fear the burden of leadership must now fall to you.*" Her sad smile had been weak and soulless, emptiness and despair pooling in her ocean blue stare.

"*You are queen now, in every way that counts. And with the Solstice fast approaching, it is now your responsibility to lead it.*" Ryenne had stood, then turned, floating from the room like a wraith.

"*I am sorry,*" were her last words before she'd quietly slipped out, leaning heavily on Kalen for support.

Mariah's heart broke for the queen. Ryenne had certainly made decisions Mariah wouldn't—*couldn't*—understand, and probably never would, but she was the only living person who understood what it felt like to bear the magic of a Goddess. Even if Mariah now knew her magic came with an added layer, an unaccounted source, the same golden threads weaving through her veins had once been a stream flowing through Ryenne's.

But there were ... unintended benefits to Ryenne's concession of power to Mariah. Specifically, how it related to the Winter Solstice.

Mariah suddenly found herself faced with the very real possibility that one of the promises she'd made to Ciana after the *Porofirat* would be coming true far sooner than any of them had anticipated.

"Fucking Enfara *damn* this. Why did these queens all have

to have absolutely *terrible* handwriting? I swear on the Goddess that I'm going to go blind."

Speaking of Ciana ...

"It isn't so bad," chimed in Delaynie's soft, bell-like voice. "Look, this one has a drawing of the *lunestair* pillars in the throne room!"

"Yeah, but what good is a picture if you can't read the words beneath it? We already knew those pillars stored *allume*; that isn't new—"

Mariah groaned, cutting off Ciana's tirade. "Please, for the love of everything the Goddess touches, can we stop complaining about these journals? Yes, they're terrible, but they're literally all we have."

Ciana grumbled but dropped her gaze back towards the worn leather book open in front her. The three of them—Mariah, Ciana, and Delaynie—had sequestered themselves into the library, raiding the deepest stacks, venturing as far into the dark tunnels beneath the mountains as they dared in search of as many journals, diaries, notes, *anything* that looked to have some connection to the past queens or priestesses. Mariah wasn't too fond of searching sources from the latter, but even she knew that at some point, there had to have been at least *one* decent acolyte of Qhohena. She was a pessimist, but she wasn't a cynic.

They were, admittedly, a bit desperate. Her time spent learning from Ryenne had taught her that the *allume* collected on the Solstice had dropped off dramatically in recent years; that much they knew, by Ryenne's own admission. What they didn't know was why—why the current ritual wasn't working, why the *allume* wasn't being harvested, why the Solstice had lost so much of its luster.

And so, there they'd been for nearly three hours, pouring over ancient manuscripts and handwritten journals that, as

Ciana had correctly pointed out, were all written in a nearly unintelligible script, some of the words in ancient Onitan and others in languages Mariah couldn't even begin to speculate on.

That's what the passage of time gets you, she supposed. Lost languages and the knowledge they might've carried.

Mariah rubbed at her eyes, desperate to relieve the pressure building behind them as the hours had passed.

"Mariah?" She cracked a lid back open at the sound of her name, meeting Delaynie's blue gaze. "Are you alright?"

"Yeah," she assured her friend. "Just ... tired. And Ciana is right. But I have no idea where else we should be looking," Mariah paused, closing her eyes again. "Or what we're even looking *for*."

She reopened her gaze in time to see Ciana and Delaynie shoot confused glances at each other. "Aren't we looking for any mentions of the Solstice?"

"I mean, of course, that's what we're reading these journals for," Mariah said, her voice flat with exasperation. "But what we're *really* looking for is how the Solstice used to be. If there is anything that has been forgotten over time regarding the ritual and how we generate *allume* to fill the pillars. And truthfully ... I'm not even sure that kind of information *exists*." She met her friends' stares, understanding beginning to creep into their expressions. "What if there *isn't* more? What if the ritual we currently do truly is the way it was always done? What if ... what if the *allume* system was always destined to fail?"

"Enough." Delaynie slammed her journal closed and stood from the table, her sudden bluntness shocking Mariah. The Lady's normally soft expression had hardened, her blue eyes turning to ice chips as they bore into Mariah.

"So what if the information we're looking for doesn't exist? You have a feeling that there is more to the Solstice than what we have done in the past. That feeling is enough for me to search for answers." Delaynie gestured around them at the journals and scrolls scattered around the table. "If these ancient scraps of paper won't help us, and if there is nothing in your mother's diary that's helpful either, maybe we need to look at other sources." That gaze pierced Mariah. "Starting with *you*."

Mariah blinked her surprise—both at the words, and the fact it was soft-spoken Delaynie who'd voiced them. "*Me?* Trust me, if I knew anything, I would've already shared it—"

Delaynie snorted—actually *snorted*. "No, I don't care about what you know. I want to know what you *feel*. What you've felt on the Solstice, in the past. You've carried Goddess magic in you from the day you were born, even if you hadn't known it. Not only Qhohena's power, but Zadione's as well. We know that *allume* comes from the gods, that it's constantly cycled through us and the earth before returning to its source in the gods' realm. We know that twice a year, on the Solstice, the veil between our realm and the realm of the gods is at its most thin, and we know the magic in your veins allows you to open a window so all the *allume* that has returned to the gods can be pulled back. It stands to reason, therefore, that on every Solstice you have felt *more*. More connected, more awakened, more powerful. Those feelings—those *instincts*—are also those of a goddess and could lead us to discovering how to strengthen the *allume* brought back into the world."

Mariah and Ciana's mouths were both hanging open as Delaynie came to the end of her speech.

Delaynie had never—*never*—spoken so much at once. She was always the quiet one, so controlled and perfectly poised, brilliant and steady as the ground beneath their feet.

Now, she was an earthquake, her frustration and exasperation rolling through the room in waves.

And also like an earthquake, her mood vanished as quickly

as it had struck. She fixed her expression back to its usual one of pleasant courtliness, straightened her spine, and sat back down primly in her chair, smoothing the skirts of her gown.

"Forgive me. I should not have snapped like that."

Ciana was the first to crack, her boisterous laugh ringing out around them.

"By the Goddess, Del! I always *knew* you were hiding a mountain stormcat beneath those fancy clothes."

Mariah could only watch on in stunned silence as Delaynie blushed, her pale cheeks turning rosy. The comparison by Ciana to the mysterious and fierce creatures that were said to roam the Attlehon Mountains was an astute one, but all that wildness vanished from Delaynie in a flash.

Mariah wondered how easily it might be in the future to pull it back out.

"Not quite the comparison a Lady desires for herself, but ... thank you, I suppose." Delaynie took a deep breath before meeting Mariah's gaze. "I was just ... frustrated you had not realized that yet. That we are sitting here, searching for answers, when you yourself may already carry everything we need."

Mariah finally found her voice, her surprise falling away as her mind began to turn. "I ... I never really bothered to think about it. My life before here was so different. Sometimes I forget that me and the girl from Andburgh are the same person —" Mariah's voice cut short, adrenaline flooding her veins, her head whipping around to face the darkness of the stacks and tunnels behind her.

Someone was there. She'd heard it; a light footfall on stone floors.

She'd sent the librarians home that morning. *No one* should be in this library. Silver-gold ropes of magic uncoiled through her veins, pushing out of her skin and wrapping around her left

496

forearm like a whip as her right hand went to the hilt of her grandfather's dagger at her thigh.

"Is someone there? This library is closed." Her voice was strong, aided by the magic flowing through her. She pushed back from her seat, Ciana and Delaynie rising with her, moving around the table to stand on either side of Mariah. They all stood, tense, staring hard into the shadows, searching for any sign of movement.

And saw ... nothing.

Mariah almost started to worry that she'd imagined the sound when she heard it again.

But this time, it was closer. Just out of sight in the darkness.

"*Show yourself*," she hissed, the rope of light slipping into her grip. With a flick of her wrist, she sent her magic out from her hand and into the darkness, illuminating the stacks until it found someone, pressed against the shelves. Something in her core, in the root of that power, suddenly flickered to life as her magic split into two thin chords ...

... and *wrapped themselves* around the hands of the intruder, binding their wrists together and yanking them forward into the light.

Mariah's control stuttered and almost slipped.

This magic ... it wasn't supposed to do that. That'd been one of Ryenne's first lessons to her; that the Goddess's magic, while powerful, was not corporeal. It couldn't touch or grab or harm, no matter how much Mariah might will it.

And yet, there she was, the feeling of someone's skin racing back to her through those threads of light as if they were gripped in her own hands.

Mariah shoved down her surprise, her elation, her *terror* at whatever it was she'd just unlocked, composing herself right before her captor came into view.

The spy was short and slim, and wore a long, dirty, and tattered black cloak that entirely concealed their features from view. Peeking through the ragged hem of the cloak were smaller, slippered feet, the material that had likely once been a soft gray now stained and worn.

A ... woman?

"I apologize for surprising you, but there is no need for this, Your Majesty," the figure spoke in a curious, melodic voice.

Mariah knew that voice.

The silver-gold bindings holding the woman's wrists fell away, and Mariah snapped one up to the hood of her cloak, flicking the material back to reveal the features underneath.

The strange silver shroud she'd been wearing at the ball was gone, but she still wore the same odd gown, the material now dirty and wrinkled. Her face matched her voice perfectly: not young, but not old, her tan skin and raven hair framing a pair of stunning, dark violet eyes.

She was Leuxrithian.

"How ...? What are you doing here? Who in the Goddess's name *are* you?"

The woman only smiled, somewhat mischievously, at Mariah. "Who I am is not important. As for how I am here, the soldiers of those idiot Royals have been chasing me around the palace grounds ever since they caught wind of my presence at the ball." Her violet eyes twinkled. "But I could hardly call myself a Priestess of Callamus, God of the Night Sky and Hidden Things, if I were to have let them capture or find me."

For the second time in only a few short minutes, Mariah was once again gaping.

Impossible. Everything about this woman being here, in the library, right now, was impossible.

And who the fuck *was Callamus?*

"I saw you in the game park. They were about to capture you."

The woman waved a gloved hand dismissively. "They were never even close. I sent them on a three-day trek into the Attlehon Mountains while I circled back to the palace."

"But how did you even get into the palace? And why didn't you tell me who you were at the ball?" So many questions spun through Mariah's head, she could barely pick which ones to ask, the words simply rolling from her tongue unchecked. The thought she'd had moments before slipped out next, something about the name both unknown and familiar to her at the same time.

"Also ... who in the Goddess's name is Callamus?"

The woman answered her with a knowing smile. "This palace has many hidden and forgotten secrets, Your Majesty. I simply rediscovered what was lost. As for who I am, as I said, it was—and still is—not important." Her expression then turned serious, something urgent filling her gaze. "I only revealed the identity of the god I serve because that is absolutely crucial to your success. And listen to me, Your Majesty: you *must* succeed."

Icy fear filled Mariah's veins. "Must succeed at *what*?"

"At the Solstice. At claiming your throne and your power. All of it." The woman took a single step closer, her palms upraised. Mariah's hand was still on her grandfather's dagger, but she didn't tighten her grip.

She always trusted her instincts. And at this moment, her instincts were whispering to her to *trust*, to *listen*.

So, she did.

"I read the *Ginnelevé* journal. As you suggested. I know whose magic I carry. And now that you're back, I'm assuming there is more you want me to know. So, tell it."

The woman's smile was full of white teeth flashing against her dark complexion.

"You are right, Your Majesty, that there is much I want for you to know. However, most of it must be discovered on your own," she paused, shifting on her feet. "But time is of the essence, so I will offer you what you need to know for the Solstice. That is, after all, the entire reason I have traveled all this way."

Mariah kept her expression guarded, her thoughts and emotions locked away, as she met the woman's eyes expectantly. She was aware of Ciana and Delaynie still beside her, shock and confusion radiating from them.

She would fill them in later.

The woman inhaled once, shooting her gaze once around the abandoned library, before returning her violet eyes to Mariah and beginning to speak.

"Much has been forgotten since the time of the First War. When the nations fractured apart and the borders were drawn, so much knowledge was taken and lost by each country. Not just knowledge, but the gods themselves. Here, in Onita, Xara laid claim over three: Qhohena of the Golden Moon; Priam of the Northern Star, Qhohena's consort; and Qhohena's sister, Zadione of the Silver Moon. But those are not the only gods of this world; in fact, there are eight.

"The southern jungles of Vatha, and later Idrix, worship Ydros of the Earth. The voyagers who docked in the Kizar Islands claim Krilene of the Seas, whose consort is Ydros. The settlers of the Kreah desert honor Rulene of the Day Sky, and my people, in our dark northern Luexrithian mountains, follow her Consort, Callamus of the Night Sky. And, of course, we cannot forget *Flétrir*, the Scourge who calls the pit of Enfara home.

"As time passed, so too did the flow of knowledge

between the peoples of our continent. Distrust of those different from us grew, as it does, but for some reason it festered more here in Onita than it did anywhere else. It worsened after Zadione fell from grace, the blame people assigned to her for the deadly losses of the First War making her a figure of hate and evil, a scapegoat for the tragedies of war. If not for the silver moon that still hangs in the sky, I'm sure she would have been forgotten, just as the other gods were. The only vestiges of the gods that persist in Onita now are the number of warriors tied to you, the group of men you call your 'Armature.'"

Mariah's eyes widened. "Seven. Not including Scourge, there are seven gods. And the queen has seven members of her Armature."

The woman nodded to her solemnly.

Mariah looked down at her hands, curling them into fists and then relaxing them as she thought. This was ... so much, but she still had that feeling it was the truth. She was far more calm than she would've expected, as if she'd always known about the truth of her world and was just now remembering.

She supposed, in a way, a part of her *had* always known. The coils of her magic wriggled slightly in response.

"While that explains who Callamus is, I still don't understand how this helps me with the Solstice."

The woman's lips tipped up in a grin. "Ah, yes. Well, I was just getting to that. As I said, Onita once claimed not one, but *two* patron goddesses. But for so many centuries, only one has been called to by the Queen when invoking the Solstice. So, of course, the *allume* captured has only been half of what is returned to the gods each year."

Those words washed over Mariah, settled under her skin, soaked into her bones.

"You're saying that if we want to change the Solstice—to

increase the *allume* produced—we'll need to open the window to Zadione, as well as to Qhohena."

The woman nodded, still grinning.

It was Ciana who spoke up next, her voice wavering slightly, the only sign of her shock.

"But ... *how*? We could never get away with openly worshiping Zadione at the damn Solstice ..." Her voice trailed off as she glanced at Mariah out of the corner of her eye. "Could we?"

Mariah just watched the woman, reading the wicked expression still settling itself across her face.

And she knew. She knew then what she needed to do, what had to happen, how to change the Solstice.

"I read in my mother's diary that Zadione wasn't only the Goddess of Death, but the Goddess of Passion and Wild Things." Another nod from the woman. "That's what it will take, isn't it? Order for Qhohena ... and passion for Zadione."

The woman's violet eyes were almost feverish. "And you know just how to achieve that, don't you, Your Majesty?"

Mariah's mind flashed with memories of past Solstices. It was common for those over eighteen to participate in the celebrations across the kingdom. For most, it was a night of quiet closeness, a time to spill a few drops of blood into the earth and celebrate the renewed flow of *allume* into the land with the magic of companionship.

For Mariah, it had always been something ... different.

She'd tried to forget how intense those nights always were for her, but the memories came flooding back. With them came the additional recollection that whatever it was that consumed her on those nights had appeared to extend to those around her.

She'd never thought much about it. Blamed it on her desire to be different, to be as unappealing to her society as possible so she could one day escape without being missed. She'd never thought it had been a sign of something so, so much more.

Something that could shift the future of Onita forever.

She gave the woman a nod of her own.

"There is one more thing, Your Majesty." The woman took a step back, beginning to retreat into the darkness of the library tunnels. She pulled her hood back over her head, her features once again concealed. Just before she disappeared, she turned her head back over her shoulder, and Mariah swore she saw a flash of violet.

"The pillars are the focus. Do not forget them."

And with that, the woman whisked around, vanishing from the room without so much as a trace.

CHAPTER 54

It had been two weeks since the attack during the parade. Two weeks since Trefor had been shot. Two weeks since Cedoric had died.

Two weeks since Mariah had given herself to the darkness in her soul and claimed a life with a smile on her face.

Two weeks since Andrian had again refused her in all the ways that really mattered there on that balcony.

But with her new resolve and revelations about the upcoming Solstice, she felt somewhat grounded again. Not whole or anywhere close to the way she'd been before, but a spark was lit in her soul, giving her purpose beyond just dragging her body out of bed each day.

Now, though, sitting again at one of the many conference tables she could never seem to escape from, she wished for nothing else than to disappear back into some sort of solitude. Anything was better than fading off into boredom to the sound of the endless droning of the men who joined her at that table.

Lord Hareth was harmless enough. Despite the wary glances he repeatedly shot her way, he hadn't done anything specific to make her hackles raise. *Yet.*

Lord Shawth, seated to his left, was another story entirely. Mariah watched him closely and swore his watery blue-gray eyes hid some sort of secret. She was particularly unnerved by the smirk he kept plastered on his face; but, then again, his thin mouth was never not twisted in some sort of jilting expression.

She refused to meet the gaze of the third Royal sitting at the table. Lord Laurent set her the most on edge, had her constantly brushing her fingers over the hilt of her grandfather's dagger.

A death threat would be enough to make anyone a bit paranoid.

Thankfully, none of the Royals paid her much attention as they prattled on about some trouble with the trade routes along the coast, likely caused by more issues with the pirates who roosted in the Kizar Islands. Mariah's presence was more a formality, something she was expected to attend with Ryenne now indisposed, and she was happy to let her mind wander to the legends she'd grown up hearing from her father about those bloodthirsty sea-faring people who called the chain of islands in the Mirrored Sea home.

Somehow, someway, she would find a way to go there. To see those islands from the stories of her youth with her own eyes.

She knew she should be paying more attention to the Royals' conversation as it swirled around her. That she needed to be more involved. As she'd promised Ciana, she had no intentions of being a mere figurehead to these weaselly men.

But, by the Goddess, only these three men could make discussions about pirates *boring*.

Maybe politics just wasn't for her.

About to offer her opinion on the pirate situation—*why not just use Onita's far superior naval power and sink the Kizar ships to the bottom of the Mirrored Sea*—Mariah held her tongue when Hareth decided to change the course of the conversation.

"It would be an entirely moot issue, of course, if the wards around the city were at full strength. Then, we could strike at the few key pirate vessels we have identified as fleet leaders without fear of retribution from the other pirate lords," he paused, pushing his wired spectacles on his face farther up the bridge of his nose. "The Solstice may be coming soon, thankfully, but we've never truly been able to generate enough to fully charge the pillars. Without the extra *allume*, we simply will never be able to power the wards without risking the light and warmth of our citizens."

"I may be able to offer a solution on that front, Lord Hareth." The sound of Mariah's voice startled even her. The faces of the three Royals swung in her direction, as if they were finally acknowledging her presence there at the table. She held Hareth's gaze, however, and refused to look at the other two.

It wasn't how Mariah had intended to show her hand, but ... she supposed she had no other choice now.

"This Solstice will be unlike those of the past. I've been researching with the Ladies of my court, and we intend to make some ... modifications to the ritual. If our plans render the results we expect, then I anticipate the pillars being as close to full as they've been in centuries—in a millennium, even. That extra *allume* should be enough to power not only every source of light and warmth in Onita, but to fully power the wards around Verith. Finally."

The room fell into an aggressive silence, the stares of the three Royals boring into her like three little termites into a piece of wood. Hareth's gaze was one of surprise, fascination, and a little bit of fear. Shawth was as gleeful and guarded as ever.

She still refused to meet Laurent's stare.

Naturally, it was Shawth who broke the still, tense quiet.

"Would you care to elaborate on these modifications, Your Highness?"

Mariah forced herself to take a deep breath. Another one. Forced her mind to slow and contemplate how best to answer him rather than giving into her instincts and running him over like a charging horse.

Your Highness.

That was how one addressed a queen apparent. Not a queen. And she knew it was no mistake.

"When I sit in this chair, in Ryenne's stead, you shall address me as 'Your Majesty,' Lord Shawth." Her voice was so icy her words nearly froze in her throat. She tried to hold her composure, but magic and power thrummed through her veins, exuberant at the opportunity to yank out this particular thorn in her side. "And, no, I don't care to elaborate. As queen, the Solstice is my sole jurisdiction, no matter how much you may strive to control every aspect of what occurs in this kingdom."

Her blood hummed in her veins as she held Shawth's stare, her head held high. His expression was still one of twisted excitement, not an inkling of fear written on his face.

She would be lying to herself if she said wasn't worried by it.

"I know what you plan." The voice was soft, but familiar, and instantly froze the world around her. Mariah slowly turned her head to finally meet the golden stare of Lord Laurent.

"You do, Lord Laurent?" She poured every bit of bravado into those words, her voice dripping with veiled contempt.

His answering expression was filled with metallic disdain. "Yes, indeed, I do. And truthfully, it does not surprise me. All of us should have known that given the opportunity, a *slut* such as yourself would pounce on the opportunity to defile our most sacred ritual for some form of personal pleasure." The coldness in his voice, his face, his entire demeanor was one of pure wickedness.

And this time, Andrian was not there.

Not that she believed he would dare move against his father on her behalf. Instead, Sebastian and Matheo stood at her back, and she felt the brothers take a single step closer, a soft growl emanating from Matheo's throat. The ground beneath her rolled and shook, but somehow, she kept her grip on her chair firm, her knuckles white under her skin.

"You forget yourself, My Lord," she began, her anger pulling the threads of her magic from her veins. It filtered off her skin, haloing her in their glow.

Mariah wondered if she would ever make it through one of these meetings without putting on some sort of glowing display.

She doubted it.

"I don't know, exactly, what it is I did to earn your disdain, but let me say this. I don't care how powerful or how rich you are or how many daughters of your house have sat where I now sit. I'm the bearer of Qhohena's magic. However I decide to rule shall not be faced with criticism from anyone, *especially* you. The time of weak men leading Onita is over. If you cannot treat me with the respect your queen demands, I will have your tongue removed from your mouth, and then I will have you removed from my city."

"'*Your city*,'" Laurent sneered. "Do you think your fierce words or your little light show scare me? You're nothing more than a petulant child who's been given power without the proper training to carry it. Run the kingdom into ruin if you want; see if I care. When you fall, we will be here to pick up the pieces, but you will be left broken in the streets. And I cannot *wait* to see it."

Mariah bared her teeth at him in a snarl, just as she felt the threads of magic flowing off her shoulders wind themselves into ropes of light, twisting and knotting in the air.

For a moment, she remembered what they'd felt like in the library with the Leuxrithian priestess. How they'd turned corporeal, able to touch and hold and *squeeze* ...

Not now. With Ryenne indisposed, she was now a queen. She'd made promises she *would* see through.

And harming a powerful lord probably wouldn't help her accomplish much of anything.

Laurent continued, taking her momentary silence as she'd lapsed into her thoughts as an opportunity to forge ahead.

"You asked me what it is you did to earn my disdain. Here it is: *you stole my heir from me*. There is nothing I can do to change that now, but I'll make you one final promise. If you dare to use my son in whatever foul scheme you have planned, *Your Majesty*, you will regret it."

"Is that a threat against your queen, Lord Laurent?" Mariah bit out her reply through clenched teeth.

The golden-haired Royal only smiled at her, his white teeth gleamed like a predator setting its sights on a kill. "No, *My Queen*. Of course not."

And with that, he rose from the table, the sound of his chair scraping across the marble floor abrasive in the otherwise silent air, and stalked from the room.

The sudden departure was one final, intentional, pointed insult.

Mariah felt her anger roil, hot and viscous, in her gut. She pulled her magic back under her skin, those threads still bound together in cords as they settled in her belly. The weight of it pulled her down, almost grounded, the silver-gold power curling around her rage and holding it tight. Hareth had gone deathly pale, his eyes darting between Mariah and the door through which Laurent had exited, obviously torn between following Laurent and remaining at the table with Mariah and Shawth.

Shawth who, the bastard, wore a heart-eating grin on his face, his expression filled with something close to mocking glee.

Mariah would've hated him, too, if she hadn't felt both so full of rage and weakly empty at the same time.

After the meeting with the Royals, Mariah didn't think the day could get any worse.

She should've considered that when a day went to shit, it tended to go there all the way.

Which is why she shouldn't have been surprised to find herself ambushed by Ksee in the quiet, secluded courtyard she'd sought out for a moment of peace to clear her head. Today, it would seem, she would have no such luck. She might carry the Goddess's power, but obviously none of her blessings.

At least, none today.

And of course, the priestess was *pissed*. Her face was twisted into an ugly expression of vehement anger, her lips pulled back from her mouth in a snarl.

"How *dare* you," was all she said to Mariah by way of greeting.

Mariah only dropped her gaze from where she'd been staring at the sky above, unable to see Ksee at first as her eyes adjusted to the shadows of the courtyard. She huffed a sigh and forced herself to sit up a bit straighter on the gold-plated bench.

So much fucking gold, everywhere.

"How dare I do what, exactly, Ksee?"

Flames danced in Ksee's tawny gaze. "How dare you choose to defile one of Qhohena's most sacred nights with your sordid behavior? You have no right to spit on the tradition of our people, to—"

Mariah instantly shot to her feet, leveling her gaze at Ksee. She wasn't sure how Ksee had found out, but she figured it must've been one of Ryenne's Ladies. They were assisting Ciana and Delaynie with readying the palace for the ceremony and sending invitations, and had certainly been more privy than most to Mariah's plans. Not *all* her plans, of course— only Ciana and Delaynie knew every detail, but certainly enough to ruffle feathers.

Distantly, she thought that whoever had told Ksee must've told the Royals as well.

It was troubling, but something to investigate later. It was too late to do anything about it now.

"What do you know about tradition, Ksee? Just because you have magic and are titled High Priestess? You don't have the long life of an Onitan Queen. The only queen you've ever known has been Ryenne, and even then just at the sunset of her reign. You may have power in this palace, but you don't carry the Goddess's own light in your veins. And that power calls for something more than what was done in the past, and I'm *obligated* to adhere to it. I've heard the rumors of the threat from the Kizar Islands. I *know* what I'm planning will finally power the pillars, something Onita *desperately* needs. Unless you're now such a traitor that you would rather see our people stay weak and timid, knowing I can offer them more?"

"You are spitting in the face of tradition—"

"Good. Tradition is fucking *useless*."

Ksee reeled back as if she'd been slapped, her muddy eyes wide. If Mariah weren't so distinctly aware of the powerful enemies she was only further creating today, she would've laughed at the look of pure shock spreading across Ksee's face. The priestess took a step back, and then another, slowly regaining control of her emotions, pasting a mask of cold disdain across her features. Her lips pressed into a thin line, and her hands fisted themselves into the golden material of her robes as she regarded Mariah.

Mariah spoke before Ksee could decide on her rebuttal.

"With Ryenne indisposed, the responsibility of overseeing the Winter Solstice has fallen to me. And while I may despise your traditions, no one can deny the Goddess's magic in my veins. I'm the *only* person in the kingdom capable of completing the ritual, regardless of its form. Therefore, the Solstice is under my sole jurisdiction. And if you don't like how I intend to run it, then you can get the *fuck* out of my palace." Her last words came out on a growl, low and grating and animalistic as her pulse thudded in her ears.

Ksee only regarded her with that same icy expression. "Gladly," she said. "I will not have my priestess's faith polluted by whatever sacrilege you intend. I pray Qhohena takes mercy on you." She turned on her heel and strode out of the courtyard, her head held high, back rigid, golden robes billowing around her.

The next day, Delaynie informed Mariah and her court that Ksee and most of her priestesses and acolytes were seen leaving not just the palace, but Verith, their golden procession stopping traffic in the streets as they'd filed out of the city gates and down Xara's Road, their destination unknown. The room had fallen silent at the news, faces lifting into hesitating smiles before falling again as the information settled like a heavy blanket of ash and dust. The Winter Solstice was now solely in Mariah's control, just as she'd thought she wanted.

Mariah wasn't sure whether she should feel elated at that knowledge ... or terrified.

What have I done?

CHAPTER 55

The Winter Solstice was in one week, and preparations were well underway.

The throne room was cleaned, the white and gold marble floors sparkling, the *lunestair* pillars beautiful despite their dullness. This close to the Solstice, the *allume* reserves were nearly depleted, and those pillars held almost none of the telltale magical glow. Furnishings were being brought in, benches and daybeds and loveseats arranged around the massive space. The winter chill from outdoors filtered through the glass roof, but *allume* heat lamps placed around the throne room chased away the cold.

At least there was no fear of rain or snow blocking the views of the moons. It was always, *always* clear on the night of a Solstice.

Mariah had all but thrown herself into the preparations. She kept herself busy, both by coordinating her plans with her court and by physically helping with the cleaning and set up. The busyness, the constant movement, was the only way she knew to keep herself distracted, to keep the fear of the problems she'd likely created for herself at bay. She was so exhausted each night that when she fell into bed, her mind instantly shut off, tumbling her body into a deadened sleep.

For a few hours, at least. Until she found herself jerking awake in the early hours of the morning drenched in cold sweat, chased from sleep by dark memories she chose to not remember. The process would then repeat; working herself to the bone just to get her mind to stop screaming its panic at her.

The work and exhaustion it brought also kept her mind off a certain dark-haired asshole who'd done nothing but make her life miserable since she'd arrived in this Goddess-damned palace.

Mariah hadn't seen Andrian in over a week. The rest of her Armature were constantly with her, either guarding her back or helping her with her duties, and his absence was far too notable.

There would be no surprise if she were to one day wake up to a message informing her that he'd left the city, slipping out of the gates in the dead of night just as the priestesses had.

The Royals had also made themselves scarce, but Mariah wasn't naïve enough to be thankful for that. She knew it was driven by their disdain for both her and for what she planned for the Solstice, not by any semblance of respect. They'd all moved out of the palace and into their city residences in the mountain district, and while the move was expected, Mariah recognized it as the slight it was.

Things had gotten so bad, she couldn't even find it in herself to be thankful the palace was free from those who might meddle or intervene with her Solstice.

It was also not lost on her that within the cacophony of distraction, her magic had fallen dormant. It was quiet, barely a whisper in her gut, only stirring in those early morning hours when the beast of her fear wrestled free from its cage of distraction.

The soft knock behind her on the door to her balcony would have startled her if she weren't expecting it. She didn't bother setting down her tumbler of whiskey or turning around in her seat, even when she heard the door open and click closed. Soft steps moved across the white tile to the empty chair beside her. Sebastian settled himself into it, following her gaze out towards the view of the sun setting behind the white-capped Attlehon Mountains.

"You asked to see me tonight?" His voice was soft, tentative.

"Yes. Thank you for coming." In contrast, her voice sounded foreign to her own ears. She'd been directing and ordering and focusing so much recently she'd forgotten what it was to just ... speak. Mariah turned away from the sunset to Sebastian, meeting his hazel gaze. His expression was filled with so much concern, the same concern that drew her to him in the beginning, when everything was so new and foreign and she'd craved something solid and stable just to hold herself together.

She was no longer that same girl.

Drawing in a deep breath, she continued.

"I wanted to ask you to be my partner—my consort—for the Solstice."

Sebastian's eyes widened in shock, his mouth parting.

"I—Mariah, I'm honored, of course. But ... are you sure? There isn't ... someone *else* you want to ask?"

Mariah blinked at him, slowly. "Yes. I'm sure." Her voice was still quiet, but steady. She turned her head to look back out at the sunset over the mountains.

"I know we've drifted apart over the last few weeks. I know that some things have caused ... tension between us. But it was no mistake that I chose you to bond with first. From that very first day, at the Selection, when even Qhohena's magic picked you first, you've been there for me, without hesitation. Always by my side. Never wavering, no matter how much ... how much *I* wavered. What happened at our bonding wasn't a mistake, either. I think a part of me always knew I would need you, later, and that's why what happened ... happened. So, no, there isn't anyone else I would choose. I want it to be you."

Sebastian was silent for a moment, her words floating into the air between them and drifting over the edge of the balcony, caught up by the winds and wilds beyond.

"I understand, Mariah. Truly, I do. But ... I just have to ask. About Andrian —"

"No. You really don't." Mariah's voice was icy as she interrupted him. She forced herself to draw another deep inhale before continuing. "He made his choice. Multiple times, in fact. And because of that choice, this isn't something I can— or *will*—ask of him. It has to be you."

Sebastian's stare turned quizzical at her words. "It *has* to be me? Are you saying ..."

"Yes, Seb. I'm telling you that you're the only other member of my Armature I've been with in ... *that* way. I know that may come as a shock to you, given my reputation. But I'm not choosing someone I haven't already slept with to stand in as my consort at a Solstice that very well may blow up in my face."

His eyes widened slightly. "Okay, first off, fuck your 'reputation.'" He reached a hand out and gripped hers tightly. "That wasn't what I was saying. I just know how intense the bond was for us, and I was surprised, is all. I have a hard time believing some of the others wouldn't have given in."

Mariah smiled weakly at that. "Oh, trust me, if I'd let them give in, quite a few of them would have. But I know after I bonded with you I could control that particular urge, if I wanted to. And ... I *wanted* to. I didn't want to have that be the foundation of every single relationship with my Armature. The Royals and other lords may whisper things behind my back, or even say them to my face, but they're all wrong. I'm not out of control; everything I do is a choice. And I'm very conscious of every single one of those decisions." She hesitated, and her smile turned into a grimace. "Well ... every decision except the ones made with a particular individual, but I have no desire to get into that right now." She peered back at Sebastian's face and found him grinning.

"You're incredible. You know that, right?"

Mariah's let her first genuine smile in weeks spread across her face. "I have been told that, yes."

He chuckled. "So ... it's just been Andrian and me? Not even Quentin?"

"Goddess, no." She snorted, then giggled. "Quentin wishes. He did get further than any of the others, excluding you. But ... no. Not even him."

Their laughter faded into silence as they watched the sun sink further below the mountain horizon. It was then Mariah asked a question she didn't want to but needed to know the answer.

"Has he left the palace?"

Sebastian whipped his head to look at her, his shock written on his face. "What? Why would you think that?"

Mariah kept her face still, not letting any emotions push their way out. "I haven't seen him anywhere in a week. I just figured, with how he left me last time, that he wouldn't want to be anywhere near me."

Sebastian's stare hardened. "No, Mariah. He hasn't left the palace. He's been keeping to himself, but I promise you, he's been closer to you than you might think. For whatever fucked up reason, he doesn't want you to know it, but he would never leave you. He *could* never leave you."

Mariah wasn't sure that made her feel any better.

It was silent for a few more minutes, and when the sun finally disappeared past the mountains, casting the sky in a soft gray winter glow, Sebastian spoke again.

"I will do anything you ask of me, Mariah. You know that. But I just need you to ask yourself something for me."

Mariah turned to meet his gaze. "What's that?"

"I need you to ask yourself if this is what you truly want."

She only nodded to him, once.

They sat together for a bit longer until the sky faded into night and the stars twinkled into existence. The two moons emerged, their silver and gold light casting shadows across the balcony and against the mountains. It was only when Sebastian finally left her, placing a soft kiss atop her head, and she'd tucked herself into her bed, that she finally let herself answer the question Sebastian had posed to her.

This was *not* what she truly wanted. Not even a little bit.

But she didn't have any other choice.

CHAPTER 56

Andrian hadn't slept.
Not in over a week.
More than that, if he was being honest. He hadn't truly been able to rest since he'd driven the wedge between himself and *her*, had let his fear and his anger and the hate he carried for himself settle in deep and shred apart the only source of light he'd ever found in his dark, cold existence.

He knew something changed there on that balcony. He'd tried to scare her, to convince her he wasn't good for her, that he would ultimately end up ruining her. But instead, he'd felt *it*, that thing charging between their souls. It had only magnified when she'd placed her whole, precious life in his hands, trusting even the darkness of his magic—the part of him always shunned and feared by those in his life—with all of herself.

He'd called her by her name, her *real* name, even after swearing to himself all those weeks ago he never would.

The magnitude of that moment had nearly brought him to his knees.

But instead of dropping to them there, instead of finally breaking only for her, he'd shoved everything he knew she feared and distrusted about him back down her throat. And she'd walked away, the pain and hurt in her eyes shredding his already mutilated soul into further, fractured pieces.

Since that moment, Andrian had decided to give her space. He knew she still rose with the sun and trained with the other Armature in the game park. He followed her there each morning, close enough to bask in the light filtering off her but far enough for his shadows to obscure him from view.

Somehow, she hadn't appeared to notice his presence. Or his absence, for that matter.

It was as if she'd given up. Given up on looking for him. Given up going after him.

Given up on *him*.

And the worst part was he deserved it. All of it.

As the week passed, he'd stepped further and further away, no longer tailing her around the palace like a lost pet. He put more distance between them, deciding instead to seek out his father at the Laurent residence in the mountain district. He figured if he couldn't be by her side, protecting her, then at the very least he could focus his attention on keeping his father distracted, his gaze turned away from her and her Solstice.

If that was the only action in service to his queen he could take without risking her life, then by the Goddess, he would do it. The knowledge of who he was truly serving helped make the painful meals and awkward drinks shared with his father just bearable enough. Lord Laurent was certainly coldly curious about his son's sudden interest in him, but he didn't question Andrian about it, either. Instead, their conversations remained on the most mundane of topics: the state of things in Antoris, where Andrian's younger brother Gabriel currently ruled in his father's absence, that year's crop yields, the gossip amongst the Royal families.

Every once in a while, the conversation Andrian had overheard between his father and Lord Shawth would slip into his mind. He came close, quite a few times, to revealing what he'd heard to his father and asking him to explain. But each time, the words would die on his tongue, and he would choke down more burning whiskey and return the cold smile that was perhaps the only feature he shared with Julian Laurent.

Andrian couldn't recall when, exactly, it struck him that everything inside of him was quiet. And not in a good way.

It must've happened some point after he'd given up on following Mariah. Some point after it became clear she'd given up on him, as well.

His magic had retreated deep inside the darkest parts of his soul, probably the very same part it'd once crawled out of. Where he normally would've felt it whispering and slithering through his veins, he only felt eerie silence, all the darkness instead coiled and burrowed so deep he could hardly scratch it. Just once he tried to summon those shadows out, those shadows he normally had to work to quell and keep hidden beneath his skin.

They'd responded with barely a whisper. A lick of darkness around his index finger. A subtle dimming of the bright sunlight of his room. But the rest of it, the beast he could feel curled up and slumbering, refused to answer his call.

Utterly useless. That was all he let himself think. This magic he had ... it'd always been such a waste.

Just like him.

Perhaps you're no longer worthy of it.

That was what the small, quiet voice of a ten-year-old boy with brilliant blue eyes whispered to him at night. It was those whispers that sent him shooting from his bed, kept sleep an elusive thing he feared he'd never truly know again.

Andrian's shoulders slumped as he walked down the long hallway to the queen's wing and his own quarters. He wasn't worried about seeing her; he knew she was still away, somewhere else in the palace, preparing for the Solstice. He wouldn't have let himself be seen so brazenly in this hallway if he wasn't sure.

His mind was still wandering, adrift in the black sea of his thoughts. He pulled out the one long shadowy tendril that still obeyed his command and absently watched it wind over and under and over the fingers of his left hand. Andrian rounded the corner that would take him to the last few rooms in the queen's corridor when a sound spilled out from the air in front of him.

Not just a sound.

A *voice*.

A voice he would know *anywhere*, even in death.

For the first time in days, his magic leaped in his soul, and his eyes shot up from his hands and collided with those of brilliant, resplendent, glowing forest green.

She was so beautiful. He didn't think he would ever not have the wind knocked clean out of him at the sight of her, all sun-kissed skin and dark hair and fierceness etched across the planes of her face.

Before he could yank back his control, before he could wrap all those feelings back into himself, pull it all in and let himself suffer the slow, agonizing death he knew he deserved, a single word slipped from his mouth. A word that was like a prayer, a call to home, a desperate plea for forgiveness and hope and salvation.

And he realized then he wasn't strong enough to do what was best for her. Would never be strong enough. He couldn't fight it, fight *this*, anymore. There would be another way to protect her; he would make sure of it.

So, he let that word fall from his lips, and didn't pull it back.

"*Mariah.*"

CHAPTER 57

"Mariah." Andrian stood at the end of the hallway, looking nothing like himself. His shoulders were stooped, his presence diminished, the cocky and arrogant male who'd tormented her since she arrived at the palace nowhere to be seen.

But that wasn't what froze her in place, what caused the threads of light in her veins to leap for the first time in a week, for her heart to start hammering in her chest at an uncontrollable rhythm.

It was the sound of his voice.

So broken, so filled with pain and emotion and reverence she felt her knees begin to shake.

It sounded like a prayer.

She felt Feran go instantly alert beside her as the energy shifted in the air, his curiosity poking at her senses down the still-new bond they shared. While he was learning how this new link between their minds worked, she'd grown fairly comfortable with it, and was able to compose herself enough to send feelings of assurance back to him. He turned his head to look at her, staring for a few more seconds than necessary, before brushing past her. Feran strode past where Andrian stood frozen in the hallway, shooting him a hard look before disappearing past the bend.

And then it was just her. And him. Alone.

"Mariah," he repeated, his voice hoarse from disuse or emotion; she couldn't be sure which.

Especially since she hadn't seen him since that day on the balcony when he'd left her, shattered and broken and alone.

"I thought you'd left me." It was all she could think to say, the only words her mind would give her.

Hurt was always the first emotion to manifest itself when challenged, much like a desperate animal cornered by a pack of hungry wolves.

His answer was so quiet, she almost missed it.

"I thought I had, too."

Mariah felt her hands begin to shake.

The movement must've caught his attention, because his intense gaze finally broke from hers and dropped to where her hands were now firmly clenched into fists by her side. Her whole body trembled, but she wasn't sure from what: from fear, anger, hate, joy, or … something else entirely.

Something she couldn't think about. Not yet.

It was a weakness she knew she could never allow, but was worming its way in, regardless.

Andrian lifted his gaze to meet hers once more. He took a tentative step forward, and then another, as if she were an animal in risk of fleeing if he moved too fast.

In a way, she supposed she was.

"Mariah." Her name again, along with another step. "I need to talk to you." A step. "I *have* to talk to you." Step. "There are things I … I have to tell you."

That last step brought him within an arm's length of her.

She could see the purple rings beneath his glowing blue eyes, the shadow of stubble on his chin so unlike his usual, clean-shaven appearance. It made him even more impossibly attractive.

Even in the turmoil of her emotions, annoyance poked up its spiked head at the observation. He'd *hurt* her. Devastated her. It didn't matter how beautiful he was.

Not anymore.

She met his gaze, clenching her jaw with renewed resolve. It was then she saw something in his eyes that she'd never seen before.

Desperation.

"Please, let me talk to you." His final plea was no more than a whisper, his voice raw and aching and just enough to fully wrench Mariah's heart from her chest.

"Okay," was all she could muster in response.

Relief washed over Andrian's face like a tidal wave. He reached out a hand and gripped hers, unfurling her clenched fingers and clasping them in his. He began to draw her forward, toward the double doors of her suite.

And ... she let him.

She let him push open the gilded wood and shoulder his way into the foyer, gently pulling her behind him. Let him close the doors, never once loosening his grip on her hands. Let him guide her further into the open living space, into the kitchen, up to the white and gold marble of the island. Let him turn and grip her firmly around the waist and lift her, as if she weighed nothing, setting her gently atop the counter.

Distantly, she remembered the first time they'd been like this: her sitting on the countertop, him standing between her thighs, words exchanged like daggers thrown through the air.

A promise of a sole distraction.

A promise they should've known could never be kept.

Now, she sat there, silent and trembling, as Andrian rested his hands on the counter on either side of her hips before he hung his head. He was so close to her that the black wisps of his hair brushed against the soft cashmere of her cream sweater, so close she could smell his rain and sandalwood scent.

He smelled like the Ivory Forest, like those trees at the heart of Onita where she'd spent her childhood wandering and learning and growing.

He smelled like *home*.

And then he began to speak.

"I was wrong," he said, his voice barely a whisper, so filled with regret and pain and suffering and everything Mariah suddenly wished she could wipe from him.

But she wasn't sure he was ready for that. Wasn't sure that *she* was ready for that. Not yet, not until she heard what he had to say.

"What do you mean?" Her words were soft and hesitant.

Andrian lifted his head slightly, still not meeting her gaze. He looked instead at the skin of her arm, as if reassuring himself that she was there and real. That he was also those things.

"I was *wrong*, *nio*. So, so, *so* very wrong."

Her voice caught in her throat as she tried to push out her next words.

"How were you wrong?"

"I thought—I *believed*—that what was best for you, was … not me. I thought with every threat, every danger I carried just by being near you, that it would be best for you to be far, far away from me. I figured I would get through the Selection, wouldn't be named to your Armature, and would be sent off as a general to lead a legion somewhere. I would become a war hero, just as my father wanted, and you would be safe, forever.

"But then … you showed up and slashed all of those plans

to bits. And I *hated* you for it. Not only that—I hated *myself* even more. To make it all worse, I couldn't seem to stay away from you. You fascinated me. You got under my skin and made my blood sting and crawl and fucking *hurt*. It made me feel alive, for the first time in my miserable life. So, I found loopholes around my father's ... command. I figured I could fuck you, just once, just enough to sate this obsession, and then I would be able to move on. I didn't expect what you would do to me next."

He finally raised his head further, meeting her gaze, and Mariah's heart nearly stopped.

There were tears—actual *tears*—gleaming in his wild, tanzanite eyes.

"Every single inch of me craved—*craves*—you. I didn't just want to know your body. I wanted to know your brilliant mind, your wild soul, the deepest parts of yourself you would never dare share with anyone. I wanted it all. And I couldn't fucking handle it. It didn't matter that my father re-issued his threat. I couldn't stand that there might actually be someone in this world who would complete me so fully that every fucked up thought I'd ever had would suddenly make sense."

Mariah wasn't sure she was breathing. She also wasn't sure when the tears had begun to roll freely down her cheeks, not until she felt Andrian's large, warm hand there, wiping them from her face before he continued speaking.

"So, I pushed you away. Again. And this time, I thought it was for good." That moment on the balcony. When he'd sworn once again he would never make that final commitment to her, despite the magic singing between their souls.

His other hand moved to cup the other side of her face, and his fingers curled into the thick hair at the nape of her neck. And in that moment, she'd never felt so safe, so ... home.

"But when I did, I fucking *died*. Everything was so

painfully, atrociously quiet. I couldn't sleep, I could hardly eat. I didn't feel *anything* without you in my life. I wanted to avoid you, to prove to myself I could eventually live without you. That I could forge a path as the un-bonded Armature I was always cursed to be.

"Then I saw you in the hallway. Just now. And it was like my heart started beating again. I feel like I've finally woken up, and I realize now I was mostly just a selfish bastard who could never do what he needed to do to truly protect you from the biggest threat in your life: me."

A sob choked from Mariah's throat.

"You brought me back to life, Mariah. And I don't care if this means our very existence is now damned, or if this makes me the weakest man in the entire kingdom. But I love you. And I will love you until the stars blink out of existence and the moons drop from the sky. I love you with everything I am, and everything I will ever be."

Shuddering sobs wracked Mariah's chest as tears flowed freely down her face. Some caught in the pads of Andrian's thumb still resting gently against her cheeks, but most now spotted the cream of her sweater, the tangles of her dark hair, the softness of her leggings. She gripped Andrian's hand against her face, clenching his fingers in hers, and he in turn tightened his hold. He stepped in closer to her until his forehead rested against hers, his body alighting every nerve in her own that had fallen dormant over the last week.

"You brought me back to life too, Andrian." Her voice was a shuddering whisper, but so filled with that new, foreign emotion she couldn't hold it back. That same one she'd been told all her life was a weakness.

A wave of doubt suddenly spread through her stomach, a warning against defying the voice she'd always blindly followed.

But ... maybe that's all it was. A voice in her head. A

projection of her deepest fears, born from a time when being trapped in a miserable crossroad town was the worst thing that could happen to her.

She was no longer in that town, and she was no longer that girl.

None of this made her feel weak. In fact, what she felt right now was a surge of strength, more powerful than any she'd felt in her entire life.

No more fighting.

"A-and ... I love you, too."

Andrian froze against her, his breath catching in his throat. He shifted, and her entire field of vision was filled with tanzanite hidden behind a watery haze, his breath warm and delicious on her lips.

"You ... love me?" He sounded so young; he'd been alive for a decade longer than her, but in that moment, he was just a child, filled with wonder and hope and none of the darkness and pain that shrouded his prior thirty-one years of existence.

She only smiled back at him, let it touch her eyes, hiccupping once as more tears slipped free.

"I do. More than the moons in the sky."

That was when he kissed her.

They'd kissed each other countless times, but this one ... this one felt like the first to really matter. There was that same desperation, that same urgency and feeling that they were living on borrowed time, but there was also hope. Like a caged bird finally set free, the truth of what had long resided in their hearts and souls was out, and it filled Mariah with a weightlessness she couldn't hope to describe.

Andrian's hands and lips and skin were warm against hers. Her magic—those beautiful, silver-gold threads she'd missed so much this past week—danced along her skin, coyly twining themselves with the shadows peeling off his own, a perfect match to each other. Her soft gasps filled the air as he lifted her from the counter, whispering words of adoration against her skin she never could've imagined coming from his lips as he carried her into the bedroom.

And as they shared something neither of them had ever imagined they would have, Mariah questioned what force could ever call this a weakness.

CHAPTER 58

Early morning light woke Andrian from a deep sleep, and he knew he'd never in his life felt so at peace.

It was more than just a feeling of relaxation. It was one of absolute contentment, a quiet, grounded sensation. Something that felt almost like ... *happiness*.

It was all entirely foreign to him. He'd spent so much of his life fighting this feeling, refusing to believe it was ever something he could have. And then *she* had stepped out of that carriage and into his life, and right then, deep down, he'd known. He'd fought it, resisted it with every fiber of his being, but he knew she could bring him the soul-deep joy he'd always so desperately craved.

And there, in her massive, soft bed, the feeling of her sleeping form pressed against his side was fucking *everything*.

It only took a few soft strokes through her hair, down her body, over the rise and fall of her curves for Andrian to slowly wake her. The soft noises she'd made, still heavy and languid from sleep, had nearly driven him mad. Eventually, when his hands dipped lower, stroking the sensitive skin between her thighs and finding her already drenched, his instincts had taken over completely. He'd pushed into her, gently but still claiming, and had lazily fucked her as the sun continued to rise over the horizon. Her breathless gasps hissed against the silk sheets, and in that perfect slice of heaven he'd coaxed her body into release, following her quickly into perfect oblivion.

They now stood in her bright kitchen, the white marble blinding in the weak winter sun, the space warmed by the furnace blazing in the living room. Andrian, now dressed in his favorite black cotton pants, had sent Mikael scurrying from the kitchen with a pointed stare just as Mariah emerged from her room, wearing nothing but his black button-down shirt. It was large on her, but she was tall, with the hem hitting just below the curve of her ass, the long lengths of her legs on full display.

The sight of her, sleepy and mussed and wearing his clothes, filled him with a ridiculous sort of feral, male satisfaction.

It was a sight he had no interest in sharing with anyone that morning, not even the friendly, jovial chef who he was *sure* wasn't interested.

She'd taken a seat on one of the barstools at the island, the hem of that tunic rising dangerously higher. He didn't even bother hiding his heated stare, his cock twitching even as he started gathering the ingredients for breakfast. Out of the corner of his eye, he watched that incredible flush creep across her olive skin, smirking softly as he cracked eggs into a bowl with one hand before adding milk, melted butter, and a dash of vanilla. He then mixed some baking flour and sugar together in a separate bowl before adding it all together, the batter thick and bubbling. Mikael had thankfully already set up a pour-over carafe of freshly ground Vathan coffee on the counter and a kettle on the range, and it started to whistle just when he finished whisking together the batter. Andrian stepped away from the mixing bowl and poured the boiling water over the grounds, the instant aroma intoxicating as coffee began to drip into the carafe. Once full, he pulled two mugs from a cabinet and filled them before handing one to Mariah. She took a ginger sip, the liquid still hot, before eyeing him and speaking.

"What are you making?"

Andrian glanced at her once, schooling his features to hide his thoughts before reaching up to where he'd seen Mikael hide the contraption he sought. His fingers brushed the cast iron, and with a soft grunt he hauled it out from the cabinet and set it onto the counter, connecting the *lunestair* chain to the adapter on the wall. Only then did he finally turn back around to face Mariah, his amusement slipping through his mask at her astonished expression.

"*Waffles*? You're making me waffles? From scratch?" Her eyes shone with an emotion still so foreign to Andrian—to both of them—it nearly dropped him to his knees once again.

Love. That's what filled her expression and those incredible forest green eyes. No point in denying it now.

Andrian smiled softly back at her, trying to put everything he wanted to say, everything that'd taken his entire soul to voice last night, into his gaze before he turned back to his task. He added butter to the now-hot iron and poured the batter into the crevices. He closed it shut, flipped it, and clicked a switch on the side of the device.

"I have a question for you," he said, turning back around and leaning against the counter, his arms crossing over his chest. He knew he didn't want to ask what was on his mind, but he also realized he had to or else he would combust.

Mariah perked up instantly. "What is it?"

He heaved a breath. "Is Sebastian still going to stand in as your consort tonight?"

There it was. The question lingering in the darkest recesses of his mind since he'd awoken that morning. Because, of course, while she'd admitted to things that made his own heart stop ... surely, none of it would change anything for her when it came to this, her very first public appearance as the Queen of Onita. Or, at least, the queen in every way that mattered.

Surely, she wouldn't ruin her perfectly laid plans just for him.

But ... he still had to know.

Andrian was lost in his thoughts for some time, staring at the floor, preparing for the worst before his shadows twisted in his gut and pulled his attention back up to meet her gaze.

Her jaw was hanging open, a look of pure shock and astonishment in her eyes.

"Andrian ... how *little* do you still think of me?"

The waffle iron chose that moment to *ding* loudly behind him.

"You know I don't think little of you at all, Mariah," he growled, turning back to the device. He flipped it over and used a pair of tongs to gently pull the cooked pastry from the cast iron. He set it on a plate to cool before adding more butter and filing the iron again, turning it over and resetting the timer.

He kept his eyes downcast, unsure of what else to say and waiting for her to continue, worried that with that one question, he'd just fucked everything up again.

As usual.

"Andrian."

The tenor of her voice snapped his eyes up, and he whipped around to meet her gaze filled with ...

Amusement?

"Do you honestly believe I would tell you that I *love* you—

something I've never told *anyone* before—then go take another man to be my consort at the Solstice the very next night?"

He was frozen in place.

Every time she said that word—*love*—it made him feel like his entire world collapsed around him and then was simultaneously being built right back up.

Her voice was thick as she continued.

"I want it to be you. No one else. *You*."

His knees buckled slightly. He gripped the counter behind him tightly to keep himself from slipping to the floor.

The waffle iron dinged again, and Andrian quickly straightened and turned, flipping the device and plucking out the pastry. Setting it on a plate next to the other, he picked up both servings and strode to the island, depositing them both in front of Mariah before moving to stand beside her. She turned her body as he approached until, once again, he stood between her thighs.

Andrian slid a hand into her thick, near-black hair, staring down into those bewitching eyes.

He'd never seen anything more beautiful than her.

Would he ever stop thinking that?

"I don't want you to be with anyone else, either. I want it to be me."

She exhaled sharply, her surprise written across her features before it morphed into something slightly darker and incredibly more sexy.

Fucking Enfara.

She spoke again. "So ... we're really doing this, aren't we?" Wickedness gleamed in her eyes.

The shadows in his blood thrummed and leaped in his veins.

It seemed that wildness, no matter if it was born in the light or in the dark, was cut from the same cloth.

"Yeah. We're really doing this." He leaned in and pressed a kiss to her lips, the energy between them sparking in the air and zapping against their skin. The contact was quick, and he pulled back just a moment later, whispering his next words against her cheek.

"Let's go show them what moonlight really looks like, *nio*."

CHAPTER 59

Mariah knew she *should* be nervous as she stood before the mighty golden oak doors leading to the palace throne room. The same doors she'd walked through, no more than a few months ago, completely unaware of what the room beyond had waiting for her.

She knew if she were sane, she would feel scared for what this night could bring, for the enemies she would only be further creating. The kingdom hung balanced on the edge of a knife, hinged on whether this would all actually work.

By the Goddess, she hoped it worked. And not just because Mariah wanted to prove Ksee and the Royals wrong.

But because the girls like Ciana, who were desperate for a notion that the way things were wasn't the way they always had to be. Those lives could be better, *had* to be better, and this was the first step to taking back just a morsel of their power.

Her blood heated as she thought of what she needed to do tonight. And as her blood heated, her magic sang.

Oh, this would work, alright.

She glanced back over her right shoulder at Ciana, who

stood looking every bit the golden right-hand Lady of the Queen of Onita. She was resplendent in a sheer, gossamer gown, the corset ribbed with gold, strappy gold sandals snaking up her calves. Ciana caught Mariah's gaze and cracked a half-grin before darting her eyes quickly to the left, an unmistakably heated look in her gaze.

Mariah turned her head to look at the target of Ciana's stare, the same figure who stood on her left, a tall, dark, quiet shape, always steady and present.

Sebastian. *Interesting.*

He'd taken the news of his substitution like a saint. He'd simply wrapped Mariah into a tight embrace, squeezing her once before releasing her and leveling Andrian with a meaningful look.

She couldn't even begin to speculate everything behind that look.

Tonight, Sebastian was dressed like a dark knight: soft, black leathers, a black tunic that opened at the collar, his hair unruffled and his face clean-shaven. His eyes, though, were also locked on Ciana, but once he felt Mariah's stare he whipped his gaze away to meet hers. He smiled softly at her, his expression almost ... sheepish?

Even more interesting.

Mariah curled her lips slightly at the corners before she broke Sebastian's stare, turning back to face the door just as she snuck a quick, final glance down at her own appearance.

Her gown—if it could be called that—was almost entirely sheer, the paneling tight and opaque across only her most intimate parts. Her olive skin was bare beneath swaths of fine lace, patterned in intricate swirls mirroring the golden snowdrop blossom tiara she wore upon her brow, a gift from Ryenne she'd received earlier that day. Her skirt was tied around her waist, and a length of black satin hung around her legs and brushed against the floor. The material of the skirt didn't wrap all the way around her body, instead leaving a two-inch swatch of her upper thigh and leg bared, a more dramatic version of a slit in the skirt. On her feet were simple, black and gold heeled sandals, and her hair fell in waves around her shoulders, loose and unstructured and wild.

Mariah felt just like that painting she'd found that day in the abandoned gallery. The one depicting the dragons, in full color, so wild and fierce and feral. Something about that thought had the darkest part of herself roaring awake, setting her magic twisting through her veins. Those threads seeped to the surface of her skin, washing her skin in a subtle golden glow, the only light or color adorning her outfit. Setting her face into a wicked grin, she pushed open the throne room doors and strode through, Ciana and Sebastian on her heels.

The second Mariah walked through those doors, her attention instantly fixed on what awaited her at the other end of the hall.

She ignored the gathered crowds seated on the couches she'd spent the past two weeks arranging in the cavernous room, all of them residents of the city who were invited to attend the Solstice at the special request of their queen. She ignored the hush that washed over them as she stepped forward, a goddess of the night sent down to the earth beneath the light of the burning moons hanging low in the sky above.

She ignored all of it.

Mariah's entire being was focused on the dark prince lounging in the golden throne of Onita as if he owned it.

That hadn't been part of her plan. But by the Goddess, she fucking loved it.

A smirk played across her lips as she continued her walk

down the long pathway through the throne room. The closer she moved, the more details came into her vision: the too casual posture, the leg propped out straight in front of him, the elbow on the armrest with his chin in his hand, the indifferent expression. She could make out the details of his clothing, the same ensemble Sebastian wore—that all her Armature wore. The only difference was the circlet atop his black hair, the masculine, silver twin to her own.

He looked like a conquering king, content upon his captured throne.

And she'd never in her life been more attracted to him.

Mariah reached the foot of the dais and paused for just a moment, staring up at Andrian. Sebastian and Ciana shifted away from where they'd followed behind her, moving to join the other members of her court already gathered to the right of the dais. Her attention prickled slightly, a temptation to turn and observe the group of people who'd become like family to her, to see who each had chosen to pair with for the night.

But she clamped down on that urge. *Not now.*

First, she had to confront her usurper.

Then, she had to take her first step down the long path of saving her kingdom.

Mariah gathered her black satin skirts in her hands and took a single step up the dais, her leg baring even further. Andrian remained still as stone, but she didn't miss how his pupils dilated and his nostrils flared.

She cocked her head to the side and spoke.

"I believe you sit in my throne, Consort. I should like it back."

He lifted his head from where it rested against his closed fist. He watched her for a moment before he lifted an eyebrow, an insolent and impertinent movement. Mariah heard some shocked inhales from those in the gathered crowd, but she only suppressed a grin.

She fucking *loved* this game.

"*Your* throne? What is your claim to it, *princess*?"

The only sound in the shocked silence of the room was a choking laugh—*Quentin*—followed by a grunt as someone—*Feran*—elbowed him in the gut.

Mariah finally let the grin she'd fought fill her face. She took the final few steps up the dais until she stood before Andrian, positioning herself between his spread, muscular thighs. She gazed down at him, directly into the heated, brilliant blue of his eyes, and saw the only part of his facade he wasn't trying to hide.

The look she caught there in those vibrant depths, one of absolute reverence, adoration, and love, had her breath catching in her throat.

All of this was ... still so new, so foreign. Her own mask slipped for just a moment, just enough to blink away her tears with a soft smile before composing herself.

She wondered, briefly, if she would ever get used to it. This feeling that kept threatening to knock her off her feet.

Mariah let go of her skirts still clenched in her right hand, the satin falling around her body and brushing his breeches with a *swish*. She reached up with the same hand and ran her index finger down the side of his face, slowly following the sharp cut of his jaw before hooking it under his chin. Her magic bubbled up out of her, pushing from her skin as those silvery-gold threads twined together, down her arm and finger until they brushed the skin of his face. It sang in the moonlight, so much more brilliant tonight than on any other, its power strummed in the air like the strings of a harp.

Focusing her power into the thread now gripping Andrian's chin beside her finger, she pushed up.

In a smooth movement, a movement balanced on the end of her index finger and the single coil of magic extending from it, Andrian rose from the throne. Mariah stepped back to allow him room to stand, her grin widening as his mask slipped, shock and awe flashed across his face as he stared at her.

She hadn't told him about the interaction with the Leuxrithian priestess in the library. What she'd discovered her magic could do. She'd thought it would be more fun to show him.

And, by the Goddess, she'd been right.

Her grin was wicked as she wordlessly answered the question written in his eyes.

Yes, that's right. My magic can bind and hold, just as yours can.

"I lay claim to this throne by the magic in my veins, the magic of the first queen, the blessing of the Golden Goddess that carries with it the lifeblood of our world. It chose me, and I choose it, and as long as it sings its song in my soul my seat upon this throne shall never be denied."

Andrian's face went wicked as he listened to her practiced speech. Her back was still facing the crowd, but she knew every single person gathered in that cavernous hall heard her words. This was her statement, her claiming of the birthright she hadn't even known existed until mere months ago. A birthright she was now sure, more than anything, she *wanted*.

She released his chin, and with a quirk of his lips Andrian stepped to the side, gesturing to the throne and inclining his head, the closest he would ever get to a bow.

"Then, by all means, My Queen."

Her lips quirked, just once more, before she stepped forward to stand in front of the throne. She turned on her heel, the satin brushing against the cold metal behind her, and faced the crowd awaiting her.

But she did not sit.

"Honored guests," she began, her voice carrying through the room on nearly invisible strings of light. "We all know the Solstice as a night when the barrier between our world and the realm of the gods is at its most thin, when our Goddess stands closer to us than she does on any other night. Over the past six months, *allume* has flowed through our kingdom, filtering through the earth and back into the gods' plane. The only way to recapture it, to pull it back through that veil, is for the Goddess's magic, *my* magic, to serve as the tether, and for the magic in all our blood to be the anchor.

"We all know this. It's a cycle that has long fueled our people, advancing our kingdom to technological heights and ensuring comfort for all Onitan citizens. But the method used in this solstice cycle ... it has become flawed. Imperfect. We've forgotten the true nature of *allume*, of magic, of the gods themselves. We've grown stagnant, formal, simple in our way of bridging the gap between our world and that of the gods."

Mariah looked out over the crowd, the attention of hundreds of eyes locked on her.

And then she smiled as she let her next words flow through her.

"Qhohena is not just a Goddess of Light and Life. She is a Goddess of *Power*. And tonight, we will open new doorways and celebrate her in a new way. A *better* way."

Her words hung in the air, sank into the ground, and then washed back up as a wave of applause rolled through the throne room.

Mariah turned her head to meet Andrian's gaze, her movements slow under the weight of those cheers. He nodded to her, just once, darkness glinting in his eyes, and her grin turned feral.

She hadn't shared all the truth with those gathered. They weren't ready for it; not yet.

They weren't ready to hear that Onita had the favor of not just one goddess, but two. Just as there were two moons in the sky. They weren't ready to hear that tonight, they would be worshiping the power of not just Qhohena, but of the Unspoken One, the Silver Death, the Goddess of Wild Things and the Untamed.

After all, Zadione was also a Goddess of Tricks. At least those old journals and diaries had taught Mariah *something* useful.

Andrian, still beside her, extended a hand, and she took it.

The din of the crowd around her rose to an even higher clamor as she moved with him around the throne, glancing down once at the *lunestair* panel that lay behind it. She stared at it for a heartbeat before lifting her head and training her attention on one of the massive, dull *lunestair* pillars on the side of the dais, the milky opaque stone beautiful even without the shine of *allume* to brighten its depths.

Mariah prayed desperately to anyone who listened that by the end of the night, those pillars would be filled with the light of freshly harvested *allume*. More than the kingdom had seen since its first era. She moved to a pillar, bringing Andrian with her, until they both stood directly before it, close enough to touch.

The crowd quieted at her movement, confusion sweeping across the room. She saw Andrian shift beside her, and then heard shocked murmurs race as they saw what he'd withdrawn from his belt.

Her grandfather's dragon-winged dagger.

Of course, knives were a part of any Solstice. The shedding of blood by the people of the kingdom into the earth was how the magic bound itself to the land.

But no one *ever* stood this close to the pillars. And with that dagger now in Andrian's hand, she knew the crowd had figured out what, exactly, she planned to do.

Don't forget the pillars.

To touch the pillars was considered sacrilegious, an abomination of every blessing Qhohena had ever bestowed upon Onita.

And Mariah planned to do more than simply touch them.

It was what had driven the priestesses and the Royals from the palace. But if this worked, if she could show the kingdom that so much was wrong, that so much could be improved, then she would be one step closer to a better world.

A world where girls like her could have a place to belong, and girls like Ciana could have hope.

The murmurs of the crowd died into a hushed, stunned silence as Mariah inhaled once, turned to gaze up at Andrian, and extended her left palm to him and the knife he wielded.

The slice across her palm was quick and stinging, but she barely felt it.

The second blood welled to the surface of her skin, she moved her hand forward, palm open, still holding Andrian's stare, and pressed it against the dull gray of the *lunestair* pillar.

Light erupted into the room, a flash so bright and vibrant it likely could be seen all the way across the Mirrored Sea.

That light lingered in the air for a moment, a blinding blaze, before it sank, coiling back into itself. As it condensed and receded to its point of origin, it formed a rope of power, a rope funneling not into Mariah but into the pillar itself. She withdrew her still-bleeding palm from the stone, and a single, silver-gold thread of light followed her, a flexible tether to that pillar.

Murmurs began in the crowd again, but this time, they

weren't horrified or shocked. Instead, they were excited and curious; the tenor shifting to something warm and vibrant.

Mariah smiled.

The wildness of the magic swirled around her. The *allume* she was bringing into this world, tethered by not just Qhohena's magic, but Zadione's as well, also brought with it heat and energy and passion, and it was hard to resist its pull.

She'd felt that pull, too, on every other Solstice before this one. Hadn't known why she and those around her ... *reacted* so much differently on that night.

But now she knew, and it all made perfect sense. And she was grateful, then, that she'd felt this energy before, had known what to expect so she could resist its urges and complete her task.

It only took one glance at Andrian, though, for her resolve to waver. His burning intensity had taken root in his stare, his gaze ravenous at the sight of the blood on her hand and the magic spilling through the air.

Mariah forced her eyes away from his, pushing her legs to take a step towards the second pillar on the other side of the throne. Her movement was slow, though, and with a quick flash, Andrian shot out a hand and pulled the ties of her satin skirts. Unbound, they fell to the ground around her in a billow of fabric, leaving her clothed only in the lace bodysuit she wore beneath the skirts and the black heels on her feet.

She froze, glancing down at her now-bare legs before slowly turning to meet his gaze once again. His tanzanite eyes were on fire, his expression hungry as he surveyed her, razed her, devoured her.

Holy *fuck*.

She lifted her left hand, the same hand that was still bleeding, that thread of light still bound to her, and gripped his chin. Blood stained his skin and dripped onto his black shirt and the skin of his chest, the feral marking making her already heated blood go molten.

"Not yet, *Rhoi*." The name slipped from her mouth and shocked even her. His eyes flashed, first with confusion, then with something ... else.

It was an old Onitan word, a word every child in the kingdom grew up learning, just as they grew up learning about the line of queens. It had first been a word given by Qhohena to Priam, her Consort God, and had appeared several other times throughout history.

She hadn't known exactly what caused her to say it now, to say it to him.

All she knew was that it meant "*king*."

Andrian watched her as the word hung in the air between them, her hand still gripping his chin. She slowly dropped it, releasing her hold on him, but his own hand shot out, wrapping around the skin of her wrist and pulling her closer, his lips meeting hers with a spark of light and shadow and blood and magic.

The murmurs of the room grew louder, accompanied by the sound of steel being unsheathed, then of blood beginning to drop to the floor. Small cuts in the palm, a simple offering of blood by the people to amplify the power she was tethering to herself, to those pillars, feeding the land with life so its people may prosper in the months to come.

But that magic ... it was also hers, in a way. Bound to her and her emotions, her feelings. The more she felt, the more it would be amplified around this room, the city, the entire kingdom.

And right now, she felt *so much*. Too much. Unbearably much.

She pressed herself further against Andrian, molding herself to the hot feel of his mouth on hers, the clash of his teeth against her tongue. He was hot and hard against her stomach, and her thighs clenched, blood dropping instantly to her core.

Not yet.

She groaned but pushed back from him, breaking their kiss, panting against his mouth as they shared breath. His gaze was still ravenous, but she only stepped back and turned away, facing the second pillar beside the throne.

They weren't yet done with the ritual. And despite her spinning emotions, she was determined to see this through.

She stepped over her discarded skirts, her heels clicking against the marble until she stood before the second pillar. It was so much like the first, the *lunestair* dull and gray. Andrian stepped up behind her, his body hot and familiar. She froze at the feel of him, hard against her back, all thoughts in her mind stuttering out.

She felt him chuckle, then heard his voice whispering in her ear. "Not yet, *nio*."

It wasn't lost on her that she'd thought those same words to herself no more than a few moments before.

Goddess, what a brilliant, perfect asshole.

She lifted her right, unmarred hand up before her, and turned her palm to face her—to face *them*. Andrian shifted and withdrew the dragon-winged dagger, reaching around her to take her hand in his. With careful precision, he again sliced her palm with the blade, blood welling to the surface along with the stinging pain. He released her, and she didn't hesitate before turning her hand and pressing it to the pillar.

This time, the eruption of light and the wave of power that washed through the room nearly knocked her off her feet. She sagged against Andrian, his arms instantly encircling her, her right palm still glued to the now-glowing pillar.

This time, as the wave gradually resided, it left a heavy layer of wild and feral magic in the room, like a gossamer curtain pulled over eyes. The edges of the world were all tinged and blurred with the colors of silver and gold.

This magic was a drug, and Mariah ... Mariah was high on it.

She was now leaning fully on Andrian, wanting nothing more than to bathe in the magic floating around them, to stay there forever beneath that beautiful shroud. It took her a few heartbeats to realize he was whispering something in her ear, and focused her attention on that, on his words.

"The ritual, *nio*. We're not done yet. Finish it, and then you'll have me all to yourself."

Her eyes snapped open, some of the fog lifting slightly from her magic-addled brain. She glanced down at her still-bleeding hands, at the threads of magic now flowing from both palms, connecting her to both pillars and the *allume* flooding into the world.

There was one final step she needed to take. One final step to connect her tether to the earth beneath their feet, so every drop of blood contributed tonight could be used to capture *allume* and bring it to dwell within the *lunestair* pillars.

She stood, her legs shaky, before moving finally to the *lunestair* panel behind the throne.

Before, this panel had been the only component to the Solstice, the only place deemed acceptable for the queen to touch. Ryenne would tie herself to the earth, and hope the magic in her veins was enough to summon sufficient *allume* to power the pillars for another six months.

It never would've been enough. Eventually, the magic would've run out, and Onita would've been vulnerable to anyone who wished her harm.

Her palms still bleeding, those two threads flowing from her blood and binding her to either pillar, she knelt before the *lunestair* tile. Andrian didn't touch her, but she felt his presence at her side, ready to catch her when this was done. With a deep inhale, she pulled as much of the magic washing through the room to her, closed her eyes, and pressed both palms to the tile.

The threads from the pillars leaped from her to the panel, tunneling themselves down into the ground, spindling throughout the entire kingdom. A shudder of power wracked through the earth, a tremor strong enough to wake the dragons of the world that had long since gone to sleep.

Mariah sat, kneeling and panting, on the floor behind the throne for several long heartbeats, her palms still bloody, as the waves of power subsided.

When she could finally think again, she had only one thing to say.

"Holy *shit*."

A chuckle tickled her ear. Andrian's deep voice whispered against her skin.

"You are ... magnificent, *nio*. You did it. You fucking *did it*."

She twisted around to meet his gaze, hyper-aware of his closeness and the wild power still coursing through her veins.

She felt positively feral.

Before Mariah could lunge for him, take him right there on that dais, he leaned back and chuckled again. "We still have an audience, *nio*. End the ritual, let your guests enjoy the rest of their night," he paused before leaning close again, nipping gently at the soft skin of her ear. "Just as I intend to enjoy *you*."

She shivered.

With every shred of self-control she still possessed, Mariah pushed herself to her feet, rising to stand behind the throne. She moved to the side, to the crowd waiting for her there. Most now sat in pairs, either on the ground or on the couches, their eyes dazed with the weight of the magic in the air as they clutched still-bleeding palms. The white and gold marble was speckled with red, but as Mariah watched, those droplets of blood began to form themselves into rivulets, flowing directly over the gold veins in the floor, traveling to the panel behind the throne. Her eyes followed the ruby red river, and when the first of that blood touched the panel it sank into the glowing *lunestair*, just as hers had, joining the magic of the earth.

The pillars pulsed brighter.

It was *working*.

"The magic is bound." Despite her unsteadiness, her voice was strong. Hundreds of eyes turned to her expectantly. "The ritual is done. Celebrate the blessings of our Goddess; revel in her magic. This power is for you, the people, and tonight we've taken it back."

Soft cheers and murmurs of wonder grew louder as the crowd bowed as one before falling silent and filing from the room, the shroud of magic leaving most in a distant daze.

Mariah doubted any of them, even if they'd attended a Solstice in the capital before, had ever felt magic quite like that.

Within minutes, the throne room was empty. Even her court had slipped out, and her curiosity pricked as she wondered where they'd all gone.

Or who they'd gone *with*.

But then, a familiar, firm warmth was against her back. Arms banded around her as Andrian's hot breath tickled her cheek.

"Come, my queen. Let me fuck you on your throne."

With a wicked smirk on her lips, she let him do just that.

CHAPTER 60

The *lunestair* pillars on either side of the golden throne gleamed with an incandescent light that hadn't been seen in a thousand years.

The opaque stone, once dull gray guardians beside the throne, now shone with so much light it spilled out through the golden veins spindling through the marble floors. The same golden veins that had drawn upon the freely gifted blood of the Solstice attendees, anchoring the *allume* flooding into their world.

The Solstice was ... everything she'd hoped it would be. Just that morning, Sebastian had returned from a meeting with the captains of the city guard, the look of giddy pride upon his face causing her own expression to break out into one of uncharacteristic glee. The *allume* levels of the wards were measured, he'd told her. And they were burning at a strength that was ... *impossible*. A strength not seen in generations.

She'd leaped into his embrace, and they'd toasted with a glass of the finest wine she could find in the study. Even Ryenne had stopped by Mariah's suite upon hearing the news.

Her demeanor was still so muted and broken, her aging now pronounced by slower steps and a posture beginning to stoop and hunch, but she'd grasped Mariah's hand tightly and softly whispered her congratulations. She'd been accompanied by a now gray-haired Kalen, leaning heavily on his arm as she retreated back from the rooms, her blue eyes again hollow and distant. It had broken Mariah a little, to see her like that, not knowing when that final piece of magic would leave her and set her free to join Cedoric in the afterlife.

Of all the things they'd discussed, she and Andrian still hadn't broached *that* subject.

The sound of soft footfalls behind her pulled a piece of her attention away from her thoughts and those shimmering pillars. She didn't turn from her vigil, though, not even as warmth enveloped her back, or when a muscled arm looped itself around her waist, slender tendrils of shadow snaking around her head and caressing her cheek. Mariah let Andrian pull her close, let him tuck her body into his, let herself revel in the feeling of solid strength he offered her.

It was a foreign feeling, letting herself be touched by him as an expression of love, and not just lust or a need for distraction.

Foreign, but welcome, nonetheless.

Mariah's lips tilted up slightly at the corners as she closed her eyes, leaning her head back against Andrian's shoulder, losing herself for a moment in her happiness. There was still so much to worry about, but this moment … in this moment, nothing could go wrong.

"We did it." Her voice was soft and content.

"No," he said, the sound rumbling deliciously through his chest as his grip on her waist tightened slightly. "*You* did it."

Her mouth widened into a full grin before she twisted in his grip, tilting her head up just enough to meet his mouth with hers. She melded herself to him, sinking into the feel, the touch, the taste of him. Mariah loosened the threads in her soul, and light sparked on her tongue, across her skin, twining into the air to dance with his shadows.

Slowly, begrudgingly, she broke off the kiss and pulled away from him. Mariah drew her magic back under her skin, the soft silver-gold light fading from the air. She met his tanzanite gaze, the wild blue hazy and filled with that emotion she was still coming to know, still trying to not let shock her every time she saw it. She smiled at him again, softly, before pressing one final kiss to his lips and stepping fully from his embrace. Turning on her heel, Mariah strode up the dais steps until she stood before the left pillar, watching the silver-gold *allume* twist and dance in its depths.

"This was only the first step towards a better future. The *allume* is back, yes, but ... Andrian, you know as well as I do that it isn't—won't be—enough. Not with all the different players in this world."

It was something she'd been thinking about for the past week. That once this task was done, she would have to step fully into leading a kingdom.

And as much as she hated to admit it, she still had some work to do before she would be able to accomplish it on her own.

Even though he now stood a few paces from her, Mariah still felt Andrian tense, his entire demeanor shifted into one far more on edge than it was mere moments before. "You cannot *possibly* be suggesting what I think you are."

"I wish I wasn't. But ... we need them, Andrian."

Before he could respond, she lifted up a hand, her palms bound to cover her healing wounds from the Solstice, and pressed it against the *lunestair* pillar. Now that she'd already done it and proven it was certainly far from sacrilegious, she barely hesitated to touch the shimmering stone.

Waves of silver and gold magic washed over her the second her skin met the cool smoothness, power swirling around her body and soul. The essence of that magic mingled with her own, the threads of power in her soul unraveling and thrumming with the *allume* dwelling within the pillar.

After all, like would always call to like.

But then ... she felt something. Something deep within the brilliant light of the *allume*. Something that felt ... dark, and sinister, and *wrong*. Unlike the *allume*, it wasn't born from trust and joy and pleasure, but instead cried out to her with feelings of pain and fear.

A wave of cold washed through Mariah, drenching her in sudden panic, her magic recoiling on instinct. She wrenched her hand away from the pillar, cutting off the vile feelings before they could sink into her. The instant her skin left the stone those feelings fell away from her like cobwebs, the sickly blackness at her fingertips a few moments before lifting like a cloud. The threads of her magic even appeared to shake it off, as if shaking off the remnants of a bad dream.

A dream, she thought. A figment of her imagination, that was all. A remnant from her inability to truly believe she had actually accomplished what she'd set out to do. Mariah was Goddess-blessed; no darkness would dare infiltrate that which she'd helped create with the blood in her veins and the power in her soul.

Setting her shoulders, she turned away from the pillar, again facing Andrian. His face revealed nothing to indicate whether he'd noticed whatever had coursed through her a moment before, and ... she didn't ask him.

Better to forget. It wasn't real, after all.

She met his gaze with her own and set her face into her familiar proud mask, a wicked smile playing across her mouth.

"Let's go speak with our Royals, shall we?"

The great manor house was made of brick the color of ash.

At Mariah and Andrian's back was a massive, wrought-iron gate, the paved and manicured street beyond silent in the late morning air. Deep in the mountain district, this street lined with other, similar manors, each one resplendent with the ancient wealth and grandeur of the generations of power they housed. This was where the Royal families and other high-ranking lords kept their Verithian residences—whenever they weren't staying in their suites in the palace itself, of course.

This particular manor, the largest and most beautiful on the street despite it appearing to be leached of all color, belonged to none other than Lord Shawth, relative of Queen Ryenne, the Lord of Khento and the head of the most influential of those Royal families.

Mariah still struggled to understand why the mere fact that four past queens had been born to House Shawth meant its Lord deserved such kingdom-wide respect. It was the women of his house who were blessed with real power; she could see no blessings upon the men besides their name.

Notice of their visit was sent that morning, preceding them by hours. Their carriage pulled in through those gates, swinging open and shut behind them on near-silent hinges. Feran had also come with them, driving the carriage himself, and Mariah thanked the Goddess once more for bringing him to her, not only for his way with the horses but for his steady watchfulness behind them as they now stood at the bottom of the manor steps. She inhaled once, a deep breath, and glanced down at her dress before meeting Andrian's gaze.

She'd known the importance of this meeting. And for the first time since arriving in Verith, perhaps in her life, she'd tried to dress accordingly.

Her gown was an elegant cream, the full skirts as close to traditional Onitan fashion she was willing to go. The modest sleeves and scooped neckline covered most of her skin, and the bodice was detailed with golden threads which she prayed to Qhohena would give her all the strength and patience she'd need to survive this meeting. She wasn't known for her skills at diplomacy; this much she knew. But for the future of her crown and fate of her kingdom, she'd do her best to quiet the dark rage dwelling within her soul.

Andrian shifted closer beside her, his arm brushing hers as his fingers twined around her hand and gripped her palm, pressing against the bandage there. Her eyes shot down to their joined hands, a contemplative look on her face, when Andrian spoke.

"I want you to know ... I don't regret anything."

She lifted her gaze back to his as he continued.

"I thought a part of me would regret giving in to you, would regret the danger I've now put you in. But I don't. I know you, Mariah. There's no danger that could challenge you. Someone has tried—and *failed*—twice. There's nothing you can't face." He paused, leaning even further into her until their foreheads touched. As he closed his eyes, she felt him inhale deeply.

"Show them that."

"*Well*, isn't this a lovely sight?" The snide voice crawled over Mariah's skin, grating against her nerves. Her jaw instantly clenched, and she leaned away from Andrian just enough to turn to face the manor's double doors. Those doors were now open, and within them stood a familiar middle-aged male, his fine doublet carrying the black sun sigil of his house.

Lord Shawth wore a sneer upon his face, his eyes locked on Mariah and Andrian's joined hands before they lifted to meet Mariah's stare.

"Come inside," he said, his voice still dripping with sweet poison. "Lord Laurent is already here. We've been waiting."

Mariah choked down her retort, swallowing her anger at his less than respectful greeting. Releasing Andrian's hand, she gathered her full skirts and stepped up the manor steps, following Shawth through the double oak doors.

The resplendent foyer greeting them mirrored the wealth of the estate's exterior. A massive portrait of Lord Shawth hung on the right wall, and while he'd perhaps been younger when it was painted, Mariah was certain the artist had taken certain ... *liberties*. Especially with the thickness of his hair, the pallor of his skin, the fullness of his chest.

Mariah had to choke back to a snort at the man's narcissism. How typical of a man made great by the power of women.

Averting her gaze from the portrait, Mariah continued after Shawth, Andrian steady at her side. Shawth led them down the foyer hallway before turning right, pushing through yet another set of double doors of rich mahogany, the handles cast in gold and polished to perfection.

The room beyond was a parlor room, obviously decorated with a man's taste: two fine, brown leather chairs, a great oak desk, and a gray suede couch. All dark and masculine—it was a room clearly meant to either intimidate those who didn't belong or bring comfort to those who did. Against a wall was a bar made of wrought, plated gold, well stocked with the finest wines, whiskeys, and smokes.

Mariah doubted these men were worthy of the vices they consumed in this room.

Her eyes wandered away from the decor to the room's

other occupant. Already seated in one of those fine leather chairs was Shawth, and she forced herself to dismiss the disrespect at seating himself before her. She needed to keep her pride in check, to choke down the indignation and fury already twisting the magic in her gut. So much had gone right at the Solstice, but there was still so much to do, so much to fix before there could be real change.

But when Mariah turned her attention to the man seated next to Shawth, she wondered how far her resolve would take her.

Lord Julian Laurent was sprawled in the second leather chair, not bothering to rise when she entered the room, his gaze brazen and impertinent as it perused her and the man beside her. Andrian tensed, the air around him quickly beginning to darken and thrum with icy wrath. Without breaking Laurent's stare, Mariah reached out her hand and rested it lightly on Andrian's forearm, the muscles there taut beneath the sleeves of his dark jacket. She knew it was more than just rage coursing through him, the brush of a tendril of shadow against her cheek whispering to her the truth.

He was *terrified*. Of his father, of being here, with her. Of the threat made against her life by the man now seated mere feet from them. Terrified that here, in this parlor room, Julian would somehow make true on the oath he'd sworn to his son.

Mariah would have none of it.

She squeezed Andrian's arm gently, just once, hoping to convey all her conviction through that single touch. Chosen and blessed by not one, but *two* goddesses, she carried more power in her veins than seen in written memory. These small men before her would not—*could* not—hurt them.

Mariah released Andrian before stepping forward, moving towards the gray suede couch opposite from where the two lords sprawled. Andrian followed her, his shadows still tickling at her back, not receding into his skin until they'd taken a seat on the couch.

And there they all sat, watching each other for several heartbeats, no one wishing to break the tense silence settling over the stifling room. Finally, Mariah steeled herself, swallowing down her rage and her pride and every instinct screaming at her to do anything *but* what she was doing, and spoke first.

"I thank you both, My Lords, for agreeing to meet with me."

Both men regarded her with unreadable expressions.

"Your note was curious," Shawth said first. "I decided perhaps it would be in all our interests to at least hear you out. Especially considering the last time we spoke ended on ... less than pleasant terms."

"Yes," Laurent spoke next. "We were *intrigued* by your sudden change of heart. And we did agree to meet. With *you*." His baleful golden stare cut to his son. "I was not aware we would be bringing along *companions* to this meeting."

Mariah knew he was only trying to goad her, to tempt her into saying something she knew, deep down, she shouldn't. Not yet.

But being level-headed ... it wasn't her strongest trait.

"I believe the word you are looking for, My Lord, is Armature. Or perhaps Consort. That is one I have only very recently come to enjoy. *Greatly.*"

So much for subtlety.

The tension in the room became so palpable, Mariah could've sliced it with her grandfather's dagger strapped to her thigh beneath those full, ridiculous skirts.

"Careful, Queen Apparent." Laurent's voice was deadly quiet. "For the sake of Onita, I am willing to put aside our *differences* and listen to what you have to say, but my patience will only extend so far."

"Alright, that's enough." Shawth shifted in his seat as she spoke, yet Mariah caught amusement dancing in his watery blue eyes. "While I must admit it is entertaining to sit here and watch you taunt our dear Lord Laurent with your exploits with his son, that is not why we are here. You said you had a proposition for us; let's hear it."

Mariah snapped her attention to Shawth, internally grappling with the molten rage threatening to flood her control. She forced herself to calm, taking a single inhale, and then started to speak, the practiced words flowing from her tongue.

"My Lords. We all know how valuable unity between the Crown and the Royals is to the continued prosperity of Onita. Such a partnership has existed for thousands of years, and is, without a doubt, one of the sole reasons why our kingdom is the most powerful on the continent." She paused, directly meeting the stares of both lords, letting them see the sincerity of her words before continuing.

"As Lord Laurent has said, we've certainly had our disagreements in the past. I know I'm young, and proud, and to you I must appear naïve to ruling. However, I know I cannot do this alone. The queen rules from her seat in Verith, but Onita is vast. The continued cooperation of the lords and Royals is imperative to ensure our borders are protected and our people are fed.

"My request to you both is this: join my court. If you do, *both* of you, the other lords will follow. Help me continue to maintain Onita's prosperity in the centuries that are to come. I intend to rule in a way honoring Qhohena and Priam, and I hope to bring back the ancient glory Onita enjoyed in its earliest days, before, during, and after Xara's rule. Already, my improvement of the Solstice has proven to be a massive success: the pillars have never been more full, our kingdom now flowing with more *allume* than it has seen in a thousand years, the wards finally at a strength to quell whatever threat is brewing in the Kizar Islands. Our people will prosper—"

"Yes. Let's talk about the Solstice, shall we?" Shawth's voice was cold, his gaze ... *excited*.

Mariah's blood turned to ice as the realization struck her like a blow.

This was why they'd agreed to meet with her. Not because they had any intention of listening, of ever working with her.

This had all been a trap. One into which Mariah had walked all too willingly.

Her heart hammered in her chest as Shawth continued.

"You, a common-born, disgraceful *whore* from the outskirts of the Crossroad City actually did it, didn't you? You managed to take control of our most sacred night, to convince so many in this city you are *blessed*, that the meaningless magic in your veins somehow makes you chosen for something more than what you are: a figurehead for greater men. You perverted something pure and used it to revel in your sins, to disgrace your station, your title, and the very throne you somehow think is *yours*. No magic will ever make you a queen, Mariah; only blood can do that. You can fuck as many lord's sons upon that ancient and glorious seat as you like, but you will *never* be my queen."

As Shawth spoke, Laurent's face slowly turned into a vile, twisted grin. Mariah held her face in a vacant expression, all her thoughts and focus trained on staying utterly still. But beside her, she could feel Andrian thrumming with rage, his shadows again dancing in the air around him.

All while she kept herself blank. Unfeeling. Numb.

"Did you really think we would not know about your

sacrilegious cavorting with my son? What was it he said to you? '*Let me fuck you on your throne*'?" Laurent snorted. "Pathetic. As if that throne will ever belong to you. Although, I must say, if you've acquired a taste for men of Royal blood, I am sure I can service you better than my son ever could." Laurent was all burning, undiluted rage, the embodiment of the flames dancing in his veins. "After all, his blood is tainted by that cold Leuxrithian *bitch* I was forced to marry and bed. Maybe one day I can show you what it is like to fuck a true Onitan Royal—"

Laurent's head snapped back against his leather chair as shadows wrapped and twisted around his neck, his arms, his legs, even sliding around his mouth, gagging those vile words and trapping them in his mouth. Mariah simply watched him struggle, his eyes bulging as he grappled for breath, his son's magic squeezing tighter and tighter. Giving herself to the cold numbness curling through her veins, she rose from the couch, holding the gazes of the lords before her.

"Release him, Andrian."

And despite the uncontrollable anger rolling from him, he obeyed.

The shadows vanished from Laurent immediately, and he doubled over in a wracking cough, his hands going instantly to his throat, the skin around his wrists and ankles already turning an angry red.

"I will only say this once." Her voice was flat and cold and dark. Both lords watched her, looks of pure loathing in their eyes.

"I tried to make peace, but it seems I've failed. Despite your treasonous words, I'm Qhohena's chosen, and I carry the power of the Goddess in my veins. I don't need you. If this is a burden the Goddess wishes me to shoulder on my own, then I will." Finally, something flickered deep within her, a tendril of light that brought with it a fury so potent, so chilling, it almost felt foreign.

It was all those threads of silver, separated again from the gold. Zadione's magic leaped up, fueled by that spark of rage, and wound itself into her veins until it was all she could see, all she could feel. It seeped to the surface of her skin until she was ringed in an unholy silver light, wrathful and avenging like the goddess of death who'd bestowed that power upon her. A tremor of fear stole into the eyes of those two Royals, and she let herself bathe in the sick joy it brought her.

"You will both leave Verith. *Immediately.* You're no longer welcome at my court or in my city. You may return to your family strongholds, where you will live out the remainder of your miserable existences. If I ever see either of you again, I will not hesitate to cut your tongues from your mouths and feed you your own testicles before I roast you over a spit."

Without another word, Mariah strode for the parlor room doors, stepping into the foyer and the manor exit beyond, Andrian following closely at her heels.

Before she left that manor built of stones the color of hate, she threw a final command over her shoulder.

"You have until sundown to be out of this city. Should you fail, I will not hesitate to chase you both from Verith like the rats you are."

And with that, Mariah left the two lords. The carriage ride back to the palace was as silent as death. Andrian, by her side the entire time, was frozen in his anger, his rage so potent she could taste it. She could offer him no words of comfort that would be true.

So, Mariah only held his hand, and steeled herself for the future that had found her.

CHAPTER 61

Andrian had never felt a rage quite like the one burning through him now.

While in the carriage back to the palace, when Mariah had felt so cold and numb seated at his side, he'd felt only unadulterated fury. An anger so intense it stole his breath, hammered his heart, pulsed his magic through his veins.

His rage still hadn't subsided, even as they pulled through the palace gates. In fact, the more time passed, the more his fury burned hotter, growing more intense and focused with each passing second.

That monster had called her a *whore*. Had called his mother—his gentle, timid mother with her stories of her wild northern homeland—nothing more than a *Leuxrithian bitch*. Andrian had always known there was no love lost between his mother and father: it was an arranged union, forged to broker peace and keep the Onitan border secure.

Andrian let his mind wander back to the day he'd received word of his mother's demise. How all the warmth in his world was sucked out by his father's words, telling the tale of how she'd "slipped and fallen" in the kitchens of their keep, her skull cracking on the hard cobblestone flooring.

"A tragic accident," his father had called it.

But after today, and those hateful words ... Andrian no longer believed that to be true. He'd always had his suspicions, but it was if all the puzzle pieces were finally clicking together in his head.

His rage only grew hotter, consuming him like a dying star.

He could feel Mariah's eyes on him, watching him as they strode through the palace hallways towards her chambers. Andrian wasn't sure if she could sense his rage was fueled by so much more than the vile words exchanged by the lords, and truthfully, he wasn't in the mood to explain it to her.

A quiet, softer part of him, the same part still desperately craving the happiness she could give him, gently urged him to *tell her*, to *talk to her*, to let Mariah wrap him up in her beautiful light and wash away the dark rage devouring him.

The shadowy beast in his veins won, though. The gentle side of him snuffed out until all that was left was anger and hatred and darkness.

He followed Mariah through the doors to her suite and saw Sebastian and Ciana rise from where they were seated on the couches in the living room. Ciana's face blanched as she took in Mariah's still-numb expression. There was no need for them to ask how the meeting had gone; it was likely written clearly across Mariah and Andrian's faces.

Andrian hung back in the archway between the foyer and living room as Mariah moved to her friend, his hands clenched and his jaw tight. He watched Sebastian run a close, inspecting gaze over Mariah, his face flickering with concern. Turning his hazel eyes to Andrian, his stare hardened as he took in the lines of tension and fury woven into every angle of Andrian's being.

The second their gazes locked, Andrian made a decision.

His queen was home and safe, and there was something he had to do.

"I'm going back out," Andrian said, the sound of his voice grating against what remained of his control. Mariah whipped around, her unfeeling mask slipping just enough to let her shock permeate through.

He didn't meet her gaze.

Instead, Andrian leveled his raging stare at Sebastian, letting his thoughts flow through his gaze to the male who'd been raised with him, the male who likely knew him better than anyone else.

She's in your care, brother. Whether I return or not.

Somehow, by the grace of the gods or goddesses or whoever the *fuck* was in control of their miserable existences, Sebastian understood him. He dipped his head in the faintest whisper of a nod. Andrian steeled himself one more time before moving his stare to Mariah, letting himself fall into those forest green depths one last time.

The dam she must've had on her emotions was clearly burst, a line of tears now streaming down her face. She looked so ... broken, so lost, so desperate for an answer he could sense she was about to come to him for.

An answer he didn't have, and even if he did, couldn't give her.

But ... he could give her this.

"I love you, *nio*. No matter what happens, that will always be true."

Before his resolve could shake, he turned on his heel and strode from her suite. Her choking sobs behind him were a sound that would haunt his nightmares for an eternity.

The hooves of Andrian's horse pounded down that pristine paved street, the estates lining it flying by in a blur of frost-covered trees and iron fences.

It wasn't long before Andrian wheeled up his stallion, turning off the street and through a set of polished, bronze gates. He pulled up on the horse and came to a stop before a proud, gleaming manor house made of ancient golden brick. Servants were milling about the courtyard, loading carriages with various household goods, and many of them turned to look at him with shock written on their faces. He paid them no heed as he swung himself from his horse, the beast's sides drenched in sweat from their furious ride from the palace, and fixed his gaze on the pale oak doors leading into the Verithian residence of House Laurent.

He strode up the front steps. Kicked in the doors. Anger drove every move he made. More servants inside greeted him, scrambling frantically out of his way as he stalked into the house of a family that had never felt like his.

He'd once thought being Marked was his greatest curse. Now, he realized it was his greatest blessing. It had saved him from spending a lifetime in this gods-damned place, with people who'd barely seen him as anything more than a disappointment.

He may have lost a title that day, but he'd gained a family.

Andrian came to a halt at the end of the foyer, a grand double staircase rising before him.

"*I wish to speak with Lord Laurent!*" Andrian's roar echoed throughout the manor. His hands moved to the blade at his hip, palming the hilt as his heart pounded in his chest.

He waited. One, two, three heartbeats, servants scurrying away from the entryway the only acknowledgement of his arrival. A growl was low in his throat before he moved for the right arch of the stairway. If his father wouldn't face him himself, he would track him down.

But the second his right boot touched the first, gleaming step, a low, drawling voice sounded behind him.

"Now, there is no need to yell, Andrian. After all, I do believe this was once your home. Unless all the time these past years spent with those savages who now call themselves *Armature* has caused you to forget even the most basic of decencies."

Andrian froze, his blood ringing in his ears. He turned, slowly, until he met the gaze of his father. Julian Laurent stood in the hallway to the foyer, his stance too casual, his shoulders loose and his hands in his pockets.

Andrian's answering voice was one of deep, glinting steel.

"Don't you *dare* speak to me of decency," he said. "I ... *I know what you did.*"

"You're going to have to be a little more specific, *boy*," Laurent said, his voice airy and bored. He tilted his head, the nonchalance of the movement driving Andrian further into rage-fueled madness. "I have done many things, and I suspect I will do many more before I die."

"*Mother.*" Andrian's answer was soft, a deadly whisper. His father's tawny gaze flashed to meet his. "I *know*. I know it wasn't an accident." He took a step forward, off the stairs. "I didn't realize it until I heard the way you spoke of her to Mariah." Step. "You despised the fact you had to marry her, someone who was not *pure* Onitan, someone who would *taint* the blood of your line." Step. "So, the second she gave you an appropriate number of heirs, you had her murdered. Or maybe, you grew the balls and did it yourself. Either way, her death was *your fault*. Wasn't it?"

Andrian now stood no more than a few feet from his

father, his chest heaving. Julian Laurent watched him thoughtfully before huffing his breath out in a chuckle.

Andrian flinched.

"By the gods, you have developed quite an imagination during your time away from my household, haven't you?"

"Do you deny it?"

Laurent's gaze turned cold, colder than the ice often freezing the ground of Antoris, the same cold Andrian had grown up in and had just recently learned could be melted.

"No. No, I do not."

Andrian's vision flooded with darkness as his grip tightened around the hilt of his dagger, ready to draw it, to spill blood there on the smooth tile of his cursed family's home.

But his father wasn't done talking.

"I don't deny that I killed your mother. I did it myself, in fact. You are right; I always despised her, and after the birth of your brother ... well, she had outgrown her usefulness to me. So, I slammed her head into the kitchen counter and left her there to bleed out, alone. I think I may have even spat on her savage Leuxrithian face after I watched the light fade from those disgusting purple eyes."

Andrian's voice, when he was able to find it, whispered of a slow, painful death.

"You will *die* for that."

Julian regarded his son with a contemplative look that had Andrian's shadows snapping and twisting in the air around him.

"No, I don't think I will."

Then, before Andrian could react, Laurent's gaze darted behind his son. In a too-fast movement, multiple sets of arms banded around Andrian, wrestling his wrists behind his back. He whipped his head around to see the faces of the men who held him, their expressions blank and empty. Andrian let loose another roar, his shadows coiling up like vipers ready to strike ...

... Until shackles clamped down over his wrists, and that magic snuffed out, the familiar movement in his veins he'd finally come to accept as a part of him vanishing in a breath.

Deistair. Sunstone. Beyond illegal to possess, and the only substance that could nullify the magic of one so gifted.

Andrian went limp at the loss, at the severed connection to the soul he'd forgotten he had.

"It is time you were brought back into the fold, my son. You've spent too much time away, but that doesn't matter. You will just need a"—he paused—"change of attitude, so to speak, and all will be well."

Something blunt struck the back of Andrian's skull, and the world faded into blackness.

Distantly, just before the terror and darkness took him, he heard his father's voice, one last time.

"You should have remembered my promise, Andrian. I *always* keep my word."

CHAPTER 62

Mariah ate her dinner alone that night.

She wasn't in the mood for company, even from those closest to her. Sebastian and Ciana tried to convince her to let them stay, but she'd refused.

And Andrian was entirely the one to blame.

That look she'd seen written on his face before he'd left ... it had haunted her all day. She'd needed him after the meeting with the Royals had gone so poorly. She'd held herself together just long enough to make it back to her room, had prepared to release those floodgates as soon as they were safe and alone. But then ... he'd just *left* her. She knew he could see the need in her eyes ... but he'd left, regardless.

She'd wanted him to be the one she could always rely on. The one who would always be there to steady her when she stumbled or hold her strong when the burdens of the world threatened to bury her. But at this first true test, this first moment when no one else would've been able to catch her, he'd vanished and left her to fall.

So, Mariah had let her sobs break free and had let Sebastian and Ciana comfort her the best they could. But they both knew that while she deeply appreciated them both ... it wasn't them she needed.

When Mikael arrived a few hours later to ready her dinner, he'd worked in silence as Mariah had sat in one of the chairs facing the Attlehon Mountains. She felt nothing, not even when he'd set food down before her, asking her if she wished to dine alone.

She'd answered with a quiet, "yes," and he'd left her with sadness on his kind face but no further words.

Mariah still sat there, an hour later, her food untouched. She'd watched the sun set, the rays refracting off the mountains. Dusk was fast approaching, and with it came the fear of what the night and her future would bring.

Whatever was next for her, she would have to face it on her own.

And ... she wasn't sure she'd be able to withstand it.

A loud bang from behind sent her shooting to her feet, her hand instantly wrapping around her grandfather's dagger on her thigh. There were low footsteps moving through her foyer, and then the last person she'd expected to see in her chambers that night emerged from the entryway.

Andrian, his onyx hair windswept and tanzanite eyes blazing, stood beneath the arch, and lightning lanced through the air.

He'd come back. She knew she should be furious with him for leaving, should snarl and scream for abandoning her to go do Goddess-knows what. But in that moment, seeing him again ... she forgot her anger. All she could think was that it was Andrian, and she was Mariah, and she needed him so desperately she could hardly breathe.

It was a fact that would never change, no matter the trials they would face in their futures.

Mariah felt her face crumple just as Andrian surged across the room, gripping her in his arms. He held her so tightly, so frantically, his heart beating wildly in his chest against her ear.

If she hadn't already shed so many tears that day, she would've wept. As it were, all Mariah could do was loose a few shuddering breaths and inhale his scent, trying desperately to mesh it with the very fibers of her own being. Finally, after what could've been a few seconds or a few hours, she pulled back from him, lifting her head so it rested against his strong, solid shoulder.

"Where did you go?"

He exhaled heavily. "I had to get out. Clear my head. I should've stayed with you; I'm sorry. But ... I was too worked up and just needed to let off some steam."

Mariah drew her eyebrows together. "The guards told me they saw you riding into the city like you were being chased by an army of demons."

"Yeah. That's what I did to clear my head. I took a ride."

Mariah didn't pester him further. She understood that feeling better than anyone else, that driving need to just escape on horseback at a pace where no one could catch you.

"I'm glad you're back."

Instead of responding to her, he leaned back, tilting her chin up so he could meet her gaze. Mariah stared into those tanzanite depths and thought she caught a glimpse of something almost *manic* gleaming back at her. She studied him closely, her magic prickling beneath her skin as she held his stare.

"Mariah, we need to talk." His fingers gripped her chin as his eyes burned even brighter. Warning bells began to clamor in her head, her power threading through her veins—

"I'm tired of waiting," he said, interrupting her thoughts. "There's no point to it anymore. The lords won't help us, and you need to assume your full power in their absence. Let's bond. *Tonight.*"

Mariah could only blink at him in shock, the warnings in her head suddenly silenced. Her magic guttered out in her veins.

No wonder he appeared manic, if this was the question he'd wanted to ask.

"Are you drunk?"

He cracked a smirk. "Only on you."

She grinned back at him, huffing a soft laugh. "Funny. But … Andrian—"

"Don't overthink it, Mariah. It's time. We both know it. Right?" He blinked down at her, urgency in his eyes.

Her smile turned dazed, and she nodded. *Is this really happening?*

His answering expression was one of pure delight. "Good. Meet me at the starlight hour, just before dawn, in the western courtyard by the stables. I'll be waiting for you." He bent down and met her lips in a gentle kiss, his hand still holding her chin. Hunger stirred in her core, but he pulled back before she could wind her hands into his hair and hold him close. He was grinning down at her again.

"Soon, Mariah. Try to get some sleep; tonight, you truly become a queen."

He turned to go, but Mariah grabbed his arm before he could leave.

"Andrian, wait," she said, her voice breathless. "Before you go, can you tell me one thing?"

"Of course. Anything."

She stared into those tanzanite eyes she'd come to love so much it hurt. "What does *nio* mean?"

Andrian's features froze for a moment before they melted into yet another dazzling smile. He reached up and took the hand gripping his bicep, bringing her knuckles to his lips. He whispered a kiss across the back of her hand before dropping it and answering.

"I'll tell you tonight."

And then Andrian was gone, and Mariah was left in a daze, her stomach twisting and turning in knots of excitement and another feeling she couldn't quite place. She finally forced herself to scarf down the now-cold plate of food, step quickly into the shower to rinse herself of the stress of the day, and then curl herself into bed, anxious to sleep off the last few hours before she finally ascended to her birthright.

CHAPTER 63

The dream began in darkness. Deep, swirling eddies of darkness twinkling with the barest presence of light in its depths.

Slowly, Mariah began to see that twinkling light form into stars, the thick fog swimming through her mind and her dream parting to reveal ... something.

She wasn't sure when she'd fallen asleep—or, given her nerves and excitement, *how* she'd even managed it. But yet, there she was, caught in the webs of a dream ... or at least something akin to one.

She'd dreamed before, usually in abstract images and mere feelings she would hardly ever remember the next day. But there was something different about this dream. She felt a heightened level of consciousness here, a distinct knowledge that while her body might be slumbering, her mind was very much awake.

Slowly, that thing she'd seen deep in the parting shadows began to move, growing larger and larger as it approached her.

It glowed with a brilliant silver light, like a star given form, and morphed into a shape the closer it came.

Not a shape.

A person.

A *woman*.

She was veiled in silver light, a radiance hiding most of her form from view, but Mariah could just barely make out her feminine shape. That near-blinding light started to recede with each heartbeat, and her features were slowly revealed.

The woman had dark skin, a rich ebony contrasting with the silver-white of her hair, the strands crafted from spun starlight. She wore a stunning, flowing gown of silver gossamer, the material floating around her and weaving with the silver light shrouding her like a halo. Small animal bones on her shoulders pinned the material of her gown together, and more bones were woven into the silver curls of her hair. She was beautiful, ethereal, and very clearly *not* human.

Mariah knew in an instant who she was.

"Zadione," Mariah breathed, her voice a mere whisper into the dark void surrounding them.

Yet the Goddess of Death heard her all the same. Her face, filled with otherworldly power, gave way to ... a *smile*, warm and vibrant.

"It is a pleasure to finally meet you, Mariah Salis. Although, perhaps it is just you meeting me, as I certainly know you." Something glimmered in the Goddess's silver eyes, something youthful and wild and so very familiar to Mariah it felt like coming home.

And she knew why. Her mother had told her, in that hidden note in the journal. And she'd come to accept it, to embrace it, those silver threads in her soul now as much a part of her as her own heartbeat.

"I have your magic." She didn't know why she said it; she

already knew the answer. But being here, in the presence of that immortal being ... it made her feel so young, so insignificant, so *curious*.

Zadione froze, her silver gaze still leveled at Mariah, and simply nodded once.

She offered no other explanation. But Mariah needed *more*.

"But ... how? Why? Why *me*? And why are you here, now? What is *happening*?" The questions flowed from Mariah's mouth like a rushing river bursting through a broken dam.

The Goddess's expression melted into something that spoke of compassion...and sorrow. "I am sorry, Mariah. But there is not enough time right now to answer your questions. If you survive this war, then I promise you, all your questions shall be answered. And, Mariah," Zadione's tone shifted, her stare turning hard and burning, the ancient power of death she embodied blazing in her eyes. "You *must* survive this war."

Cold dread and confusion swirled through Mariah, a whirlpool threatening to pull her down into the depths of the void around her. "What war? There's no war in Onita ... is there?"

At her question, the temperature of the void plummeted, any warmth from the silver light around them winking out. The youthful wildness that had permeated through Zadione vanished, and the figure before her shifted into the ancient, grotesque embodiment of death that made her so feared. The bones on her gown grew and melted into her skin, her hair fading from silver starlight to the color of bleached bones. Her eyes sunk back into her skull, and her fingers lengthened into talons, claws that could scrape out a soul from a body and leave behind only a lifeless husk.

Even with the magic of that very being in her soul, Mariah felt herself shrink away.

No human, no matter how far they thought they'd fallen,

could comfortably look upon the face of death and not feel fear.

Then the Goddess of Death spoke, her once-brilliant white teeth now cracked and pointed, her voice like the final wheeze of breath leaving the lungs of a dying man.

"There has always been but one war, and it threatens more than just Onita. The One Who Fell, the Scourge of all worlds, has awoken. And he *will* come for you." Death pinned Mariah with a stare, peeling back all her layers and walls and shriveling her from within.

"I have warned you, all your life, that love is a weakness. You are a threat to everyone who serves him, the only one who can stop him. He wants you *gone*. And if you do not forgo all weaknesses, he will get what he wants. Now—*wake up*."

CHAPTER 64

Mariah's consciousness slammed back into her body as she shot from her dream, panic drenching her skin in a cold sweat. Her chest heaved as she fought to catch her breath. She sat up, pulling her knees up to her chest and dropping her face between them, her hands pushing the sweat-damp strands of her hair back from her face.

After several moments, when she was confident her heart wouldn't burst from her chest, she finally pushed herself from her bed. With still-trembling hands, she grabbed a discarded robe from the floor and wrapped it tightly around her body. She strode into the living room, to the balcony door, unlatching the lock and pushing open the hinges, the cold air of the winter night filtering in as she pulled in deep breaths and stared at the sky.

The night was clear, the stars above brilliant as they twinkled in the vastness of the inky black. The waning twin moons were still high in the sky, casting their silver and gold light upon the world below. Just near the horizon, she could see the faint violet glow beginning to creep its way into the void of the night sky.

The starlight hour. The hour just before dawn, when those who danced in the night beneath the glow of the moons enjoyed one final moment of joy before the rise of the sun. A time when magic was at its most unpredictable, most unstable.

A thrill stole through Mariah at the sight, chasing away the lingering heaviness of her dream. She remembered what—or, rather, *who* waited for her right now in that western courtyard, an area where the trees were cut back so the moons above could be enjoyed in full.

A perfect place.

Mariah moved away from the window and back into her bedroom, quickly dressing herself in warm, fleece-lined breeches and a soft sweater to ward off the chill of the winter night. She pulled on her boots and shrugged on a thick wool cloak before walking past her bed once more, heading towards the doors to the living space. The dragon-winged dagger taunted her from where it sat on her nightstand, still sheathed in its new garter of fine red leather. She shook her head once and left it there, stepping quickly into the living room of her suite.

She would have Andrian with her tonight. There would be no need to carry that dagger. Not here, in the safety of her home, even with the threats she'd faced before. She could hardly remember that night with the Uroboros, not with her mind filled with love and burning tanzanite.

Those threats had passed, and she would no longer live in fear.

She strode quickly through her suites and towards the double doors leading to the hallway beyond. Right before her hand touched the gold-plated handle, she hesitated, her dream suddenly rushing back to the front of her thoughts. The

Goddess's voice pounded in her head, as if it were more than just a mere memory.

"*Love is a weakness. Wake up.*"

Mariah stood still for seven heartbeats, warring with herself over the dream, and whether that's all it was—*just* a dream. Ultimately, she steeled herself against the waves of unease, shoving it down deep inside and turning the key, locking it away.

This was Andrian. Her final Armature. Her consort. Yes, she loved him; that was no longer a secret. But, if her dream was real, this couldn't be what Zadione meant. She needed his bond, his strength, if she were to weather whatever this coming war might bring.

Maybe Zadione's warning about a conflict was tied to whatever brewed in the Kizar Islands. That would make the most sense. She would begin her investigations into it tomorrow.

With that, Mariah steeled her resolve and twisted the handle, the door swinging open on those silent hinges, closing it behind her with a soft *click*. She hurried off into the dark, quiet hallway, ignoring the whispers chasing her into the shadows.

Mariah stepped into the moonlit courtyard and spotted Andrian immediately.

His back was to her, but he was gilded in silver-gold moonlight, his fine black clothing outlined in the dimness and his raven black hair glinting in the soft luminescence. A prince of darkness, reveling in the last hours of the night, waiting for his queen to join him after far too long. He stared at the far wall, the alcoves within veiled in thick shadows, and stood utterly still except for the soft breeze rustling his perpetually tousled hair.

"Andrian?" His name was a whisper, but he still heard, turning with a jolting movement to face her. Even from the distance between them, Mariah could see his tanzanite eyes sparkling in the subtle starlight. He smiled, but didn't speak a word in greeting or take a step towards her.

She rolled her eyes. Of course, even now, he couldn't make this easy. Couldn't stop finding a way to challenge her.

It made her smile.

She started forward, slowly, and his eyes tracked every step she took. His intense attention on her warmed her blood, and when she stood before him, close enough to touch, he finally moved. He drew his left hand from his pocket and wrapped his fingers around her right wrist, pulling her hand up and away from her body. He met her stare before dropping a pointed gaze at her left hand, and when she raised it, he looped that wrist in his left hand too, until both her hands were held in a loose grip between his long fingers. His right hand remained in his pocket, and while he appeared as calm as ever, she could feel his pulse hammering beneath where her fingertips rested on his forearm, could feel the feverish heat emanating from his skin. Her smile pushed higher, touching her eyes. She loved that he could no longer hide; not from her.

Finally, he spoke.

"Are you ready?" His voice was quiet and unreadable.

She held his gaze. "Yes. Without a shadow of a doubt."

"Good. I have no doubts either." He smiled at her again, but it didn't quite touch his eyes, didn't quite fill the devastatingly beautiful planes of his face. Suddenly, with her hands gripped in his, she was hit by a prickle of unease that started low in her chest and washed out towards her skin. She broke his stare and glanced more carefully around the courtyard.

And ... that was when she noticed it. Alarm clamored through her soul, her magic instantly unspooling and writhing as she surveyed the courtyard.

There was no circle of candles, no chalk etched on the ground, no wickedly sharp knife to draw the blood needed to bind their souls. The space around them was utterly bare, nothing that was needed to complete the bonding ceremony present.

"Are ... are we going somewhere else? I don't see the candles or the knife—" She stopped herself when she looked back at him, her words frozen with confusion and shock on her tongue.

His smile had devolved into a smirk, the coldness on his face morphing him into a stranger. Her confusion melted further as the heavy weight of terror pressed against her skin, her magic surging just as Andrian's grip on her wrists tightened to the point of pain. Before her magic could force its way out, his right hand, the one that had remained in his pocket, flashed, his movements impossibly, *inhumanly* fast. Cold stone replaced the heat of his grip, and with a quiet *click* that beat against her skull like the fall of a hammer, her magic snuffed from her veins, those threads vanishing like a whisper across the stars.

Vanished, along with the six mental ties, those bridges of magic connecting her to her Armature. The familiar presence of those consciousnesses against hers were extinguished, as if they'd never existed in the first place.

In an instant, she was so suddenly, coldly, horribly *alone*.

She looked down at her wrists, slowly, taking in the cuffs of tawny gold stone streaked with black now encircling her skin. She didn't know what it was, had never once seen or read about anything like it, but it felt vile and dark and *wrong*, as if it were *lunestair* but twisted and corrupted into something evil.

And Andrian had just shackled her wrists in it.

That thought had her heart shattering into a million pieces, fracturing along with her already damaged soul.

Mariah turned her gaze back up to his, her disbelief, shock, horror, humiliation, and brokenness writing themselves across her face. Her focus solely on him, she barely noticed the movement behind him—six men emerged from that dark alcove he'd stared into so intently when she'd arrived. She ignored them as they moved around him to stand behind her, their quiet steps those of trained assassins.

"Andrian?" Her voice dripped with the blood of her broken heart.

His smirk didn't falter.

"You made this all far too easy, *My Queen*." She flinched back from his sneer, as if he'd physically struck her. "So pathetically trusting, so desperate for love and attention that you've always sought from the wrong people. You believed every word I fed you, gobbled it down like you were facing a death sentence and it was your last meal." Andrian leaned in close, his breath whispering against the shell of her air, something that used to bring her such pleasure.

Now, it only made her want to slump to the ground in horror and pain.

"As if anyone could ever love a *whore* like you."

That was when she broke fully. Her soul fragmented, pieces of gold and silver and black shards falling around her, picked up by the early morning breeze and carried far, far away from that brilliant castle on the coast.

Tears streamed down her face as he withdrew and turned on his heel, putting his back to her. The men behind her moved, and the rustle of a burlap sack pulled at her fractured attention. She opened her mouth, one last time.

"How ... *how could you?*"

Andrian froze, twisting just enough to look back over his shoulder, hate glimmering in his cold blue eyes.

"My father sends his regards."

And with that, the sack was thrown over her head, smelling of sour tears and the worst kinds of pain.

Hooded, bound, and broken, Mariah was hauled away by the men who'd come into her home, let in by one she'd foolishly thought she could trust. She was thrown into the back of a carriage, rolled away from the palace, out of Verith. Farther. She didn't try to keep track of where she was, where they were headed, who was with her.

She was utterly broken, betrayed, and alone. And there was no one coming to save her.

Not even herself.

To be continued...

ACKNOWLEDGMENTS

Just the fact that I'm sitting here, writing these, is perhaps one of the most surreal things I've ever done.

Okay, maybe that's a lie, but looking back on the crazy journey that led to the creation of Threaded, I honestly cannot believe it all came together. This story, these characters, would not exist without my people. When they say writing a book takes a village ... they really aren't kidding.

First, to my family, who have never done anything other than encourage me—even when they STILL find my random childhood word ramblings laying around the house. Mom and Dad, while I hope you never read Threaded (specifically Chapters 35, 39, and 53) (and if you do, please don't tell me), your support is everything to me. This has been a tough year for us. Writing this book has helped me cope. Not once did you tell me it wasn't a good time, and instead lifted me up with pride and encouragement. I love y'all—more than the moons in the sky.

To my book besties, Lauren and Anna-Marie: the internet is a weird place, but it brought you both into my life, and by the Goddess am I so happy it did. You both have been with me since the very beginning of Threaded's creation, when I had only drafted maybe twenty chapters and was still figuring out where this story was going to go. Threaded literally wouldn't even have a TITLE without y'all. All that credit goes to both of you. You guys are the best internet friends a girl could ever ask for.

To my work wives, Abby, Christie, and Haley: similarly, you guys all put up with my insanity of trying to write and publish a book while working beyond full-time (y'all know what I mean). Your daily excitement and toleration of me sending unedited snippets or art or cover designs or god-knows-what-else made this whole process so much more enjoyable.

To my editor, Brit: I know I've said it a million times, but Threaded wouldn't be half of what it is without you. Your passion and love for this story helped me fight back the imposter syndrome that so often reared its ugly head. Thank you, thank you, thank you.

To my alpha/beta readers, Jess, Vanessa, and Les: your excitement for this story and these characters, along with your critiques and tough love, contributed in more ways than y'all will ever know. THANK YOU.

To everyone on Bookstagram who has been following along with this process for no joke a year and a half: the best parts of my day are when I get to chat and hang out with you guys online. Our community is, without a doubt, unbeatable.

And finally, to you, the reader. I'm tearing up just thinking about how much I owe to you and how much I appreciate you. You took a chance on a chaotic little indie author like me, and for that I am eternally grateful. Thank you for making all my wildest dreams come true.

ABOUT THE AUTHOR

Tay has been a fanatic of stories, especially those with epic love and a dash of magic (and dragons?) for as long as she can remember. After a few decades of inhaling every book she could get her hands on, she decided to sit down and write the stories that had kept her up at night for just as long.

When not reading or writing, Tay still often finds herself daydreaming, but hopefully it's now vastly more productive. A walk through the woods, a day by the water, a glass of smooth bourbon whiskey, or snuggles with her pup also make her unreasonably, ridiculously happy.

instagram.com/tayrosebooks

Printed in Great Britain
by Amazon